"ARE YOU HURT?"

"Just my pride that your old Toby has more sense than the three of us put together." Noah grinned.

"Are you all right?"

"Fine. I thought the boards looked rotten."

"So you tested them by trying to kill yourself?"

He laughed as he looked up at Emma. "That was not my intention."

"You scared me near to death," Emma scolded. "I thought you would be drowned. Both you and Sean." Her bottom lip trembled, and she held it still with her teeth until they began to chatter. When Noah put his arms around her, she leaned her face against his chest.

"It's all right," he murmured against her bonnet. "Sean and I are both safe—but maybe not sound. I'm not sure I can say we are of sound mind."

Emma laughed. She could not help herself, even when she still shook with fear. "Do you always do such stupid things?"

"Not always," Noah murmured. "Sometimes I do smart things." And he clasped her face between his strong hands and captured her mouth.

Dear Romance Reader,

In July of 1999, we launched the Ballad line with four new series, and each month we present both new and continuing stories set everywhere from medieval England to the American West—the kind of passionate, romantic stories you love best, written by the most gifted authors. At the back of each book, we tell you when you can find subsequent books in the series that have captured your heart.

Premiering this month is **Light a Single Candle,** the first in the dramatic new trilogy *The MacInness Legacy*. Written by sisters Julie and Sandy Moffett, the series is about three long-separated sisters who discover their heritage includes witchcraft. Talented newcomer Pat Pritchard is next, with the first in a pair of books about two men whose lives are changed by a game of poker. Meet the first of the delectable *Gamblers* in **Luck of the Draw.**

Reader favorite Kathryn Fox returns with another of her *Men of Honor* in **The Seduction** in which an intrepid young reporter looking for scandal in gold-rush territory finds passion instead. Finally, beloved Jo Ann Ferguson introduces a heartwarming new series called *Haven*. In **Twice Blessed,** when an orphan train stops in this small Indiana town, a shopkeeper becomes an instant "mother"—but when she meets a widowed father new to town, she dreams of becoming a wife.

There's romance, passion, adventure to spare. Why not read them all? Enjoy!

Kate Duffy
Editorial Director

HAVEN

TWICE BLESSED

JO ANN FERGUSON

ZEBRA BOOKS
KENSINGTON PUBLISHING CORP.

http://www.kensingtonbooks.com

ZEBRA BOOKS are published by

Kensington Publishing Corp.
850 Third Avenue
New York, NY 10022

All Kensington titles, imprints and distributed lines are available at special quantity discounts for bulk purchases for
sales promotion, premiums, fund-raising, educational or
institutional use.

Special book excerpts or customized printings can also be
created to fit specific needs. For details, write or phone the
office of the Kensington Special Sales Manager: Kensington
Publishing Corp., 850 Third Avenue, New York, NY 10022.
Attn. Special Sales Department. Phone: 1-800-221-2647.

Zebra and the Z logo Reg. U.S. Pat. & TM Off.

First Printing: March 2002
10 9 8 7 6 5 4 3 2 1

Printed in the United States of America

To Pat and Tom Weimer,
dear friends who know there are many
ways to make a family.
Here's an Indiana story for you!

Also look for these Zebra romances by Jo Ann Ferguson

CHAPTER ONE

Haven, Indiana 1876

"Stop! Stop, thief!"

The pencil froze in Emma Delancy's hand as she looked up from the counter of her busy store. A thief? Here in Haven? Here in this village on the Ohio River where everyone knew everyone else and everyone else's business? Here where even those with locks on their doors never bothered to bolt them?

She stared around the store. Although cans and boxes covered every counter and filled the shelves reaching to the ceiling, she knew exactly where everything should be. Mrs. Chandler was looking at the bolt of pink cotton that would be perfect for a gown once warmer weather settled in along the river, and Mr. Richards carried two cans of tobacco toward the counter. Everything else was in order.

Then why was someone calling, "Stop, thief"?

Another shout spurred her out of her shock. Flinging herself around the counter that held a scale at one end and glass canisters filled with candy at the other, she pushed past her paralyzed patrons. A small form burst out of the shadows by the barrels of flour halfway to the door, almost plowing her down.

"Stop, thief!"

Emma did not pause to see the man who was shouting. She had to keep her eyes on the slender shadow, or she would lose it. The thief was silhouetted in the sunlight before vanishing out onto the store's front porch. Hearing the thud of running steps, she raced after the thief. Thief? If her eyes had not fooled her, she was chasing a lad. Brown hair and skinny . . . oh, heaven help her, she hoped it was not Jesse Faulkner, who had been endless trouble since he arrived in Haven to live with his uncle, Reverend Faulkner.

Blinking in the sunshine that still was not strong enough to warm air that held a lingering taint of winter, she looked both ways along the usually quiet street. She heard another shout and saw three men standing on the other side of the road in front of two houses that were separated by the livery. They were looking to her left. The kid must have gone in that direction.

More shouts came from behind her, but she gathered her black skirt and lacy petticoats higher as she sped around the corner of the store. The narrow alley between her store and the bank next door was almost lost in the shadows and smelled of things better left unexplored.

Her breath strained against her corset, and her steps faltered. Was she crazy? Did she think she could, encumbered by her heavy skirts, catch a lad? Lurching forward, she cursed under her breath when her hairpins gave up the battle and her hair fell down her back. Broken pins skittered against the bank's brick wall. She pushed her hair out of her eyes.

She had to get to Jesse—if it was the minister's nephew—before anyone else did. Someone had to give the kid a chance to explain what was going on. Someone who knew what he was going through.

She faltered at the thought. She had been foolish to think she had put what had happened in Kansas behind her. Yet just the thought of a boy being falsely accused of some petty larceny brought out all the instincts to protect him as she had protected herself.

So far.

"There! There he goes!"

She recognized that voice. Reverend Faulkner must have heard the commotion from the church on the far side of Haven's village green. This was getting far too complicated. She had hoped to catch the lad, find out what the ruckus was about, and end this quietly. Now . . .

Emma pressed back against the weathered boards of the store. From the barn behind the store came the sound of Toby's whinny. The old horse, which pulled the store's delivery wagon, only got upset when someone he did not recognize entered the barn and wandered too close to the bucket of oats he watched over from his field. Someone must be in the barn even though the door was shut.

She patted the back door into the store's storage room. The door was closed, but she knew it was not locked. If she could persuade the boy to slow down and admit what he had done, she would let him wait in the storage room until the furor simmered down. Lewis Parker, the town's sheriff, might not agree with her, but she did not want to see a good boy get in trouble because of one mistake.

Everyone deserved a second chance, a chance to explain what and why something had happened. She believed that

even more fervently than she had seven years ago. Then she
had not been given the chance to explain that she had no
idea her husband intended to rob the bank where he worked.
Everyone had assumed she knew every detail about Miles
Cooper's plans, and that she was guilty, too. Her one attempt
to explain she knew nothing of Miles's schemes had led to
her arrest. But the sheriff had had no place to put a woman
in his jail, so he had left her, under guard, in her house.
That had given her the chance to flee in the middle of the
night and escape from joining her husband on the gallows.

She had come here to the so aptly named Haven, where
no one guessed she was the widow of the infamous Clerk
Cooper, who had emptied the safes of other banks throughout
Kansas before he persuaded her to marry him to give him
a cloak of respectability in her small town.

She had made her own second chance. Now all she had
to do was convince the boy to let her help him do the same.

Her eyes widened as a shadow prowled past one of the
barn's broad windows. The motions were furtive and cautious. Did the boy realize he was cornered in there? The
only other way out was through Toby's field and over the
tall fence that daunted even the nimblest boys in the village,
or through her backyard. Pressing her fingertips under one
of the clapboards, she smiled. She might still be able to put
an end to this without more uproar.

The shadow vanished within the barn. Did he think she
was no longer after him? He might think he could hide in
there until everyone got tired of looking for him. If she was
sure he would be cunning enough to do that, she would turn
around and tell everyone he had eluded her.

Simple and over and done with. Forgiven and forgotten.

The shadow moved in front of the window again. Blast
it! The boy did not have the sense to stay hidden. She must
talk to him straightaway.

Emma ran to the barn, ignoring the stitch under her ribs. Throwing open the door, she darted in and took a deep breath that was flavored with the scents of hay and manure. Toby neighed softly, but she did not go to calm him. She scanned the barn. Where was the kid? If he thought she would—she screeched as arms seized her, dragging her back against a hard chest.

"Got you!"

The voice was too deep and the chest too wide to belong to a lad. Who was it? She wanted to draw in her breath to scream, but the arm was an iron band around her stomach. When she was shoved up against the barn wall's uneven boards, her breath gushed from her in a gasp.

She stared at a man whose face was hidden by the shadows within the barn. She did not care who he was. Trying to slip out of his strong grip, she cried, "Release me this instant."

"You aren't going to get away this time. If you think—damn! Who are you?"

Emma wanted to fire that same question back at him. Her eyes were adjusting to the dim light. She would have said that she knew everyone in Haven, but she had never seen this tall man before. The fine line of a day's growth of whiskers edging his chin could not ease its stubborn line. His lips were straight. His eyes were wide with shock. Then they narrowed, revealing furious sparks. His broad hands could span her waist, she discovered when he tugged her away from the wall not much more gently than he had thrust her against it.

"Will you get out of my way?" he demanded.

"*Your* way?" She rushed to the door and threw back over her shoulder, "Let me handle this."

She was horrified when her arm was seized again. Spun back to face the man, she tried to peel his fingers off her. His other hand caught hers.

Bending closer so his eyes were even with hers, he growled, "Lady, stay out of this. It's none of your business."

Emma opened her mouth to retort, but he bolted from the barn and back down the alley. What an unmannered cad! Who did he think he was to order her about like that? Who was he?

Her breath caught. Maybe Jesse Faulkner was not the boy everyone was chasing. She had heard rumors about bands of thieves who went up and down the Ohio, sneaking ashore and helping themselves to whatever they wished. As much as the idea curdled in her stomach, getting the sheriff's help might be necessary.

She closed the barn door behind her. Glancing around the alley, she fought back a shiver of fear. Robberies and trouble were the last things they needed in Haven. They were the last things *she* needed. An investigation could create all kinds of questions she knew might lead to other, much more difficult questions.

Anxious voices came from the street. The search must still be on. Her eyes widened when she saw the door to the storage room was ajar. Maybe the lad had been hiding in there all the time.

Emma inched the door open. The storage room was a quarter of the size of the store. Dust clung to every board. The air was close, thickened by the sunshine that filtered through cobwebs creating lace across the single window.

"Is someone in here?" she called, trying to sound cheerful. "I won't turn you in. We can work this out ourselves."

Shouts from the street oozed through the uncaulked boards. She eased around the crate containing the new plow Mr. Jennings had ordered. The sewing machine ordered by that strange bunch out in the peculiar community just down the river had arrived on the train last week and was waiting for someone to come in to get it. Neatly stacked by the

window were the medicines that were ready whenever anyone had an ailing animal.

Nothing seemed out of place. Maybe the lad had already
left. That rude man might have run past the boy. Served the
man right.

A thump was as soft as distant thunder. She whirled. The
sound had come from the other side of the storage room.
But from where?

Emma smiled. The lad must be hiding behind the crates.
This could still be ended quickly if she could persuade him
to show himself.

When she came around the back of the crates, she saw
no one. Had she been mistaken? Maybe the thud had come
from outside. Hearing more shouts, she wondered how many
people had joined the search.

Leaning her hand on a barrel of cornmeal, she glanced
around the room again. If the lad had come in here, he must
be gone.

The door swung open. "Are you in here, Emma?"

"Back here, Reverend Faulkner," she called. Why hadn't
she gone for him immediately to help her? The squat man
was the gentlest person she had ever met, and she could not
imagine him not finding a way to forgive even the most
heinous criminal. She started to turn, then discovered her
skirt had somehow become wedged between two barrels.
Tugging on it, she asked, "Did you catch the thief?"

"Sheriff's heading out toward the mill. Someone saw the
lad fleeing that way."

She yanked at her skirt, but paused when she heard threads
snap. She did not want to rip it. She hated mending. Standing
on tiptoe to peer over the top of the stacks, she said, "Thanks,
Reverend."

"Are you all right, Emma?"

"Fine, fine," she hurried to say when he took a step

toward her. It was easier to lie when she did not stand face-to-face with the minister. "Maybe the lad was scared enough so he won't come back. Just let me know when they catch him."

"You'll hear the cheers back here." He paused, then asked, "Do you need some help?"

"No, thank you. I'm just getting a couple of things."

She sighed as the door closed behind Reverend Faulkner. Folding her arms on the edge of a crate, she leaned her head against it. Blast! The whole village was acting as if the kid had robbed a bank.

With a shudder, she straightened. She had to keep tight rein on her thoughts before they betrayed her. Even though she had hoped the past was the past, forgotten and done with, her fingers trembled as she loosened her skirt from a splinter on the barrel.

Emma froze as a shrill creak assaulted her ears. What was happening? Only she and the delivery man from the railroad station ever came back here. The train was just in. She had heard its arrival minutes before the shout of "Thief!" went up, so the drayer would not be arriving for another hour or so. She stared in disbelief as the top of the fancy coffin Mrs. Lambert had requested for her husband shifted.

She pressed her hand over her breast, where her heart was struggling to beat. Behind her, she heard a choked curse, but she could not drag her gaze from the coffin. Slowly, slowly, as if a dead body within were fighting its way back to life, the top rose.

"What the—" muttered a deep voice behind her.

She moaned as the top struck a barrel. The fancy coffin would be ruined. Someone leaped from it and raced past her. She tried to grab the lad, but her fingers caught only air.

Emma turned to run, but hit someone behind her. She bounced back and stared at the man who had treated her so crudely out in Toby's barn. "You! What are you doing here?"

"Trying to catch a thief," he shouted before racing out of the storage room.

Emma ran after him. As she stepped back out onto the street, her name was shouted. She waved to Reverend Faulkner, who was standing on the store's porch.

Reverend Faulkner grinned and pointed toward the green. A crowd had gathered near the retired cannon sitting in front of the Grange Hall. More stood on the porch of the Haven Hotel, which was, in truth, little more than a boarding house. The minister called, "They've caught him."

Emma was torn between satisfaction and regret. If the boy had not been so scared, he might have heeded her. She took a deep breath. Maybe she still could help him.

"Excuse me, Reverend Faulkner," she said.

She walked toward the crowd. Twisting her hair at her nape, she sought through it for some vagrant hairpins. In vain, she realized, and let her hair fall back along her white blouse.

She elbowed aside two men who were laughing together, not bothering to apologize. She paused as if the spring air had solidified into a wall as she stared at Lewis Parker, who had his back to her.

Although no taller than the minister, the light-haired sheriff was as slim as the cannon's barrel. No one in Haven was fooled by his size, because every fall for the past three years at the county fair he had won the title of champion boxer. He held the wiggling boy with ease.

Lewis smiled. "Miss Delancy! I was just about to send for you. Look what I've got here." He did not loosen his grip on the lad's ear, and the boy grimaced with a half-swallowed moan.

Emma walked closer, wishing the boy would look up. With his head hanging so the brown thatch of hair drooped over his face, he could have been one of more than a dozen boys in town. Seeing him up close, she realized he could not be more than eight or nine years old. All of this excitement over such a young child?

Lewis held up a hammer and a bag. "And here's what he took, Miss Delancy."

She glanced at him. He used such formality only when he was in the midst of his official work. The rest of the time, he addressed her by her given name, like everyone else in town. Her brow ruffled as she examined the items. The hammer showed signs of heavy use.

"Did he take these things from the store?" Lewis asked.

"No. I don't sell this kind of hammer." She hefted the bag of nails. "And this isn't a full pound of nails. Less than half, I'd say." She turned the small burlap bag over and looked at the faint red lettering. "These didn't come from my store. I think there's been a mistake."

"But I heard someone yell there was a thief."

"I did, too. Maybe it's just someone's idea of a joke."

"It's not a joke." A man stepped out of the crowd.

Emma locked eyes with the irritating man who had twice kept her from catching the lad. In the sunlight, she could see that, beneath the battered brim of a felt hat, his hair was a reddish brown, a shade lighter than his eyes. The air was chill, but sweat darkened his collar and lathered his shirt and suspenders to his chest, which had been so hard against her. His shirttail hung out of his trousers, drawing her gaze to the well-worn denims that followed his muscular legs. His boots might once have had a shine, but now were dull with dust. This was a man who was toughened by strenuous work and proud of it.

As she looked back to his face, she swallowed her gasp when he gave her an unexpectedly roguish smile. It seemed to suggest he knew far more about her than any living man should. With a slow, sensual perusal, his gaze slipped along her, appraising her as she foolishly had him. Heat swelled each place his eyes touched.

He put his fingers to the brim of his hat. "Ma'am."

"Who are you?" Lewis asked. "This your boy?"

"Hardly." The man's lips became straight again.

Emma said quietly, "Sheriff, why don't you ask the boy his name?"

"What's your name, boy?"

The youngster's shoe traced a pattern in the dust as he mumbled, "Sean O'Dell."

"O'Dell? There aren't any O'Dells around here," the sheriff retorted. He gave the boy a shake. "Tell the truth, lad."

Reverend Faulkner stepped forward and put his hand on the sheriff's arm. "He's telling the truth, Sheriff. I recognize him. He's one of the young'uns who just arrived on the train."

Lewis's voice grew hard. "On the orphan train from back east? Is that true, lad?"

"Yes, sir," the boy murmured, an Irish brogue lilting through his words.

"You're not making a good new start, lad." He turned to the man who was still frowning. "And who are you, mister? Are you with these kids?"

"I am Noah Sawyer, and I want you to punish this boy for theft."

His brows arched. "Strong charge, Mr. Sawyer."

"Only the truth. That boy stole the hammer and nails

from my wagon over there." He pointed to a dilapidated buckboard in front of the store.

The sheriff looked at the boy. "Is that true?"

"I didn't really steal them." He shuffled his toe again in the dusty road. "I was just looking 'round. I wanted to see what this place was like. We went through lots of towns on the train, and I wanted to see one up close. So I was looking 'round. Then he came up and I got scared and I ran and he chased me and—"

"I think I've got a good idea of what happened." Lewis smiled when he turned back to Mr. Sawyer. That smile wavered when Mr. Sawyer continued to scowl. "Sounds like it was just a boy's curiosity, sir."

"Sounds like he was poking his fingers into things that don't belong to him," Mr. Sawyer fired back. "There's a big difference between looking and helping yourself."

"True, and I'm sure the boy knows the difference." He gave Sean another small shake. "Tell the man you do, son."

"Do know that, sir," he said, not looking up.

"Now that you've been caught?" Mr. Sawyer asked.

Emma suspected she would regret getting more involved in this, but this commotion had gone on long enough. "May I speak with you a moment, Mr. Sawyer?"

"Sure." He spit out the word as if it were strained by clenched teeth.

She glanced around at the crowd. "Privately?"

"I haven't got anything to say that I'm ashamed to have everyone hear."

Fire coursed across her cheeks, and she knew she was blushing. His answer suggested she had a reason to guard her words. Another shudder ached in her stiff shoulders as she hoped no one guessed how right he was. This was going all wrong.

With what dignity she still had, she said quietly, "Mr. Sawyer, he's just a boy."

"A boy who is old enough to know better than to try to help himself to tools that don't belong to him."

She took his sleeve and drew him to the edge of the road. Paying no attention to the shocked expressions around them, she found it more difficult to ignore Noah Sawyer's frown. His gaze led hers down his arm to her fingers. Abruptly, she was aware of the firm muscles beneath that cotton sleeve. When his hand covered hers, she could not silence her gasp. Something twinkled in his eyes, but vanished as he lifted her fingers away.

"Miss Delancy, isn't it?" he asked coolly.

"Yes."

"Miss Delancy, I trust you'll resist using your feminine wiles to persuade me to change my mind. I assure you you'll be wasting your time and mine."

"Mr. Sawyer," she said as she clasped her hands tightly and hoped that the fire again burning her cheeks was not coloring them bright red, "I'm asking you to reconsider. Every child makes mistakes now and then."

"He made a mistake *now*. Some of those tools could be very dangerous for a young boy who doesn't know how to use them properly. That he ran carrying that bag of nails and a hammer warned me he didn't have respect for the tools. If he'd fallen, he could have injured himself horribly."

She faltered on the retort she had been about to snarl back at him. Because he had spoken only of his determination to see the boy punished for daring to steal his tools, she had not guessed he was worried young Sean would get hurt. Maybe Noah Sawyer was not the icy-hearted beast she had labeled him.

"You should have told me before that you were concerned about the child's safety," she said.

"I didn't think explaining myself to you was as crucial as stopping the boy before he was hurt, Miss Delancy." He paused and glanced at the storefront across the street. "Delancy? Like the name on the store?"

She nodded. "Yes, I own the store."

Surprise flashed through his mercurial eyes, and she could not keep from raising her chin. During the past seven years, folks in Haven had gotten accustomed to having a woman running the village's store. Mr. Sawyer would just have to get used to it, too.

"Then," he said calmly, "you must be well aware it's vitally important that a young thief learns his lesson so he won't repeat it."

"I think the boy has learned his lesson. Heavens above, Mr. Sawyer, he's a stranger here and just a boy. He was curious, that is all."

He opened his mouth to reply, but she did not give him the chance.

"Mr. Sawyer, you must be new in Haven, too."

"How do you know?"

She laughed, then wished she had not when his scowl drew his lips tighter. "If you're planning to stay around here, you need to learn the folks in Haven trust each other." She motioned toward the store's front door. "I haven't locked up since the first week I came here."

"You could be robbed blind."

"I could, but I haven't. The Andersons live right across the road, and they would be certain to send for me if they heard anything amiss."

His brown eyes narrowed as he combed his fingers through his russet hair. "You don't live above the store?"

"No. Mr. Baker lives up there. That was part of the deal when I bought the store from him. I got it lock, stock, and Mr. Baker. He claims to be half deaf, but he doesn't, I assure you, miss a thing that happens in the store. No one could sneak in without him hearing.''

''That protects you—''

''It protects all of us.'' She folded her arms over her blouse, which was probably as dusty as his shirt. ''Let me give you some advice, Mr. Sawyer, whether you want it or not. You're new in town, and this isn't the best way to make a good impression on your neighbors.''

''So you think I should just let the kid go without punishment? Is that how you do things here?''

''He's far from home, whatever it was, and in trouble. Isn't that punishment enough?''

''If someone does something criminal, he should have to pay for it.''

''Here in Haven, we help each other instead of trying to make trouble for each other.'' She faltered, then hurried to say, ''Mr. Sawyer, trust me on this.''

When his eyes widened, she knew her request had startled him. He jammed his fists into the pockets of his denims and nodded with reluctance as he looked back to where Lewis was talking quietly to the boy.

''It seems,'' Mr. Sawyer said, ''I'm in the minority on this. All right. I'll give the kid this one mistake this one time.''

''That's all I ask. Simple justice.''

He laughed tersely. ''You've got a strange idea of justice, Miss Delancy. A real strange idea. I'd be right interested in knowing why a shopkeeper is so generous with a thief.''

She knew she should say something, anything, but every word vanished from her head. A single wrong word might reveal what had happened before she fled Kansas.

When she did not reply, he tipped his hat to her. ''If you'll excuse me, Miss Delancy, I think I'll retrieve my hammer and nails and be on my way.''

As he walked back to the sheriff, Emma wrapped her arms around herself, suddenly as cold as if a blizzard were sweeping along the street. A panicked laugh tickled her throat. Once she had shared Noah Sawyer's opinion about those who broke the law. Punishment should be as heinous as the crime.

That had been before she learned how many victims a crime could truly have.

CHAPTER TWO

Emma was not sure why she agreed to walk with Lewis over to the Grange Hall to return the lad to the chaperones who had brought these orphans on the train from the east. Maybe it was as simple as wanting to avoid speaking with Mr. Sawyer again.

She could understand his irritation at having young Sean O'Dell poking through his tools in the back of his buckboard. That his anger had come first from his fear for the child's well-being, rather than the theft of his tools, had unsettled her. It had been easy at first to be aggravated at him. When his concern for the boy had proven he was not a cad, she had not had her anger to keep her from realizing how his eyes suggested he was thinking of things far different from a mischievous lad.

"Hope he won't be trouble," grumbled Lewis.

"I'm sure he has learned to be more careful," Emma said, giving Sean a smile.

The lad looked away, glowering. She had never guessed such a young child could wear such an aged expression.

"Not the lad. Sawyer."

"Why do you think he'll be trouble?" She wondered what the sheriff had noticed that she might have missed. Had she let Mr. Sawyer's concern about Sean dupe her as she had vowed never to be duped by a man . . . again?

Lewis shrugged. "Just a feeling. He shouldn't come into town and give orders as if he owns the place."

Emma hid her smile as she twisted her hair into a single braid so it did not fly about her face. She should have guessed that Lewis would be annoyed by Mr. Sawyer's demands. The folks in town closely heeded the sheriff's counsel and trusted him to keep the peace in any way he deemed necessary. Now Mr. Sawyer had come along and questioned the sheriff's authority.

"He was upset," she said.

"Why are you defending him? He was angriest at you." He frowned. "It's not like you to have your head turned by fancy talk."

She laughed as they reached the steps of the Grange building. The clapboards had been recently whitewashed.

"What's so funny?" the sheriff asked.

"Men! You accuse me of letting him wheedle his way around me, and he accused me of trying to wheedle my way around him." She shook her head. "You're both completely wrong."

"Miss—Emma, I didn't mean . . ."

She patted his arm. "I know." She paused at the bottom of the quartet of steps that led up to the front door of the Grange. "If you've said what you wanted to say, I need to get back to the store. I had customers when I ran out, and the wagon from the station should be delivering supplies soon.''

''Reverend Faulkner said he wanted to speak with you before you went back to work.''

''About what?''

The sheriff shrugged again. ''He didn't say.''

Emma climbed the steps and went into the Grange. Everyone was acting a bit strange today. Maybe it was spring fever. She hoped so. Spring seemed late this year, for snow had fallen earlier in the week.

The Grange Hall was extraordinarily warm, so she guessed the stoves had been lit at dawn. She had forgotten the talk about orphans coming to Haven from . . . where? New York City, someone had told her. That would explain Sean O'Dell's Irish name and accent.

Walking across wood floors that Mrs. Parker, the sheriff's mother, kept brightly polished, Emma guessed every resident of Haven and the outlying farms must be crowded into the room. Most of these people were members of the Grange, but work and the distance into town kept some folks from attending every meeting. She nodded to the people she passed, but looked for Reverend Faulkner.

Her steps faltered when she saw almost a score of children clumped together at one end of the hall. They stood on the stage. It was a section of the floor that was raised a single step and served as the podium for the Grange leaders during the meeting. Some of the children were staring about in curiosity while others stood with their arms around each other as if they feared they were about to face a hungry lion. Their clothes were obviously new, and she guessed they had been given these outfits when they left New York to wear when they reached the end of their journey. No luggage was to be seen, and she wondered if the children had anything other than the clothes on their backs.

"Poor dears." Alice Underhill, the schoolmistress, shook her head in regret. "Abandoned on the streets in New York City, left by parents too drunk to care about them."

"Or maybe too sick," Emma replied. "Those buildings in the city are said to be so close that no air or light can reach the inner rooms."

"What is *she* doing here?" Alice's tone became venomous, surprising Emma, because her friend usually was pleasant to everyone she met.

"She who?"

Alice pointed to a woman who was speaking to a little girl at one edge of the platform. "She is one of *those* folks."

Emma understand instantly. Most of the residents of Haven avoided anyone who called River's Haven home. The strange community had been forming around the time Emma had arrived here. They had bought a handful of farms on several of the hills overlooking the river and now lived there in a community. Occasionally they came into Haven, and Emma had done business with them, ordering supplies from Chicago or Louisville or Cincinnati. She found them to be quiet and courteous, and they always paid cash for what they ordered.

She had no problems with them, but she knew others in Haven did. It was whispered throughout the village that the people in River's Haven had peculiar rules about marriage and raising their children. So many stories flitted about that Emma had stopped listening to them.

She had to admit the woman talking to the child looked as prim as a puritan with her gown of the same unremitting black as her hair. The two men accompanying her made no motions that suggested the three of them were more than neighbors.

When she saw a woman she did not know speaking to the trio, she asked, "Who's that?"

"Mrs. Barrett from the Children's Aid Society in New York City," Alice Underhill replied. "She and her husband oversaw the care of the children during the train ride here. You don't think she's considering giving one of these children to *those* people. Someone should set her to rights right away."

Emma pretended not to see the glance the schoolmistress gave her that suggested Alice thought Emma was the perfect one to do that. "Have you seen Reverend Faulkner?" she asked.

"The reverend! Just the person to speak to Mrs. Barrett to let her know how wrong it would be to place out a child with *those* people." Alice scanned the room. "Oh, dear! I know he's here, but I don't see him."

"He was talking with Judge Purchase when I came in," Mrs. Parker said as she poked her way into the conversation.

"Good afternoon, Mrs. Parker," Emma said, smiling.

"I didn't expect to see you here, Emma."

"I walked over here with Lewis," she replied, noticing how Mrs. Parker's eyes lit up. The sheriff's mother had been trying to persuade her son to call on Emma for more than a year. Lewis had once, but they quickly decided it was worthless to try to be more than good friends, especially when he was sweet on Reverend Faulkner's oldest daughter. "Lewis told me I'd find Reverend Faulkner here."

Alice gasped, "What's the sheriff doing here?"

"One of the children decided to look around Haven, and Lewis found him before he could get lost." That was almost the truth. Mrs. Parker was the most prodigious gossip between Cincinnati and Louisville, so the less she knew of Sean O'Dell's escapades, the easier it would be for the boy to settle here.

"Dear me. I do hope these orphans aren't going to upset Haven." Mrs. Parker rubbed her hands together.

"I suppose all the ones old enough will be coming to school." Alice smiled. "That will keep them out of trouble."

"They probably won't be in school until after the planting is done," Emma replied.

Alice nodded. "That's true. They're here to learn to work hard instead of wasting their lives drinking cheap whiskey. Look, there's Samuel Jennings. Well, well, I hadn't thought an orphan train would bring him into town."

Emma looked to where a tall man stood off to one side. He was wearing a grim expression that could not detract from his classic features. His clothes, like many people's in the Grange, shone where hard work had worn them thin.

"Do you think," continued Alice, "that he'll say anything to anyone or just stand there?"

"He's shy."

"Too shy," Mrs. Parker said. "I don't know if I've ever heard him speak. I swear he wouldn't shout fire in a burning building. I wonder what he wants."

"Probably someone to help him on his farm," she replied as she watched Mr. Jennings walk over to where two children held the hands of a younger child between them.

Mrs. Parker rolled her eyes. "Don't wish that on any poor child. It must be as quiet as the grave out there."

Emma excused herself. She did not want to listen to more gossip about the people who were generous enough to open their homes to these children who had nothing and nobody. Like the people in the River's Haven Community, Mr. Jennings was a good customer at the store. She found the man who had a farm just down river from Haven to be quiet and unassuming and always polite.

Quite the opposite of Noah Sawyer.

Bother! Why was she even thinking of that boorish man? Yes, he was handsome, but there were other handsome men in Haven, and they had not cluttered her thoughts like this.

"Emma!"

She had to fight the yearning to throw her arms around
Reverend Faulkner, who had rescued her from her own
uneasy thoughts. Hurrying to where he stood at the opposite
side of the room from the River's Haven residents, she said,
"Lewis Parker told me you wanted to speak to me."

"I most certainly do, but first . . ." He turned to the
tall man standing beside him. It was not, she realized with
astonishment, Judge Purchase. This man was much younger
than the white-haired judge who presided over any cases
heard at the county courthouse since he had taken over from
the late Judge McShane. With a smile, Reverend Faulkner
introduced the man as Mr. Barrett.

"It's a pleasure, Miss Delancy," said Mr. Barrett, who
resembled a cadaver with his gray, sunken cheeks.

She wondered if he avoided the sunshine. Maybe he lived
in one of those horrible tenements in New York City.
Affixing a smile of her own, she answered, "The pleasure
is mine, sir. I am delighted to meet someone who cares so
much for these poor children's welfare that you have traveled
all this way with them."

"Reverend Faulkner was telling me how you jumped to
the defense of young Sean O'Dell."

"He did no harm other than adding a bit of excitement
to the afternoon."

Mr. Barrett chuckled, the sound dry and rasping to match
his appearance. "You have a generous heart, Miss Delancy.
Very few people would be willing to have one of these
children come into town and create a hullabaloo."

"Emma does have a kind heart," Reverend Faulkner
hurried to say. "However, I believe we're embarrassing her,
Mr. Barrett. Her face is becoming quite red."

"I don't expect praise," she said, wishing she could find
a way to change the subject to why the minister had wanted

to speak with her, "for something I believe many people would have done."

Reverend Faulkner exchanged a glance with Mr. Barrett. She could not guess what it was meant to convey until the minister cleared his throat and said, "As you came to the lad's defense with such speed, Emma, Mr. Barrett and I thought you might be able to find work for young Sean in your store."

"What would I do with a lad of his age? He can't be more than nine years old."

"A year older than that, according to the lad, but many of these children have no idea of when or where they were truly born." The minister sighed. "I learned that from speaking with Mr. and Mrs. Barrett. These poor youngsters have suffered more than any child should."

"I understand that. What I don't understand is why you would think I should take Sean into my home."

He smiled. "Emma, the lad is obviously not afraid to learn about new things, and he seems eager to know more about Haven."

"Or get himself into trouble."

"But with the right guidance to put all that childish energy into the proper direction, he could be of great help to you in the store." Again he looked at Mr. Barrett before saying, "I've heard you say on many occasions you'd dearly love to have help at the store."

"Help, yes, but you're asking me to be a mother to that child."

Mr. Barrett shook his head. "That isn't necessary if you don't feel comfortable with making the boy a part of your family, Miss Delancy. These children are brought west in hopes of getting them the education and training for the future that they would never have the opportunity to get in New York City. Shopkeeping would be an excellent trade for the boy, for, as you have seen, he's eager to know more about the world around him. Unlike the other children, he hasn't shown interest in the farms we passed on the train. I believe he would be much happier living in Haven than on a farm."

"Maybe Mr. Anderson at the livery—"

Reverend Faulkner intruded to say, "He stopped me on the street during the chase and let me know that I need not ask him to take in the boy."

"Your store would be the perfect place for Sean, Miss Delancy," continued Mr. Barrett as if neither of them had spoken. "Rather than as a member of your family, you could consider him an apprentice."

Emma guessed he had repeated these words with slight variations many times over. "You're very persuasive, Mr. Barrett."

"My job requires me to be so."

"I *could* use help at the store. That is true, but it's also true that I know nothing about raising boys. I have only a sister." She looked hastily away from Reverend Faulkner's kind eyes, not wanting him to guess she was not being honest.

The minister put his hand on her shoulder. "I knew we could count on you, Emma. Why don't you go back to the store while we talk to the boy?"

"So he might not wish to be at the store?" She could not keep the hope out of her voice.

Mr. Barrett shook his head. "We at the Children's Aid Society serve in a parental role, Miss Delancy, and it's a parent's place to make such decisions. Not the child's, for no child, especially one as young as Sean, can possibly make such a choice alone.''

"Go on back to the store," Reverend Faulkner said. "We'll be there shortly with the necessary paperwork to have Sean O'Dell stay with you."

Emma nodded, then backed away as the two men continued talking. She turned and almost stumbled, although the floor was smooth and even. When someone asked if she was all right, she murmured an answer that she was.

Another lie. Letting Reverend Faulkner and Mr. Barrett talk her into taking this child had been among the most foolish things she had ever done. Almost as foolish as letting Miles Cooper woo her into becoming his wife to give himself a legitimate place in her hometown.

She shivered as she stepped back out of the Grange, not from the cold, but from the memories that poured forth to taunt her. No, nothing had been as stupid as marrying Miles Cooper.

Hurrying across the green, where the grass was still brown from winter, Emma sought the sanctuary that always helped her force scenes of the past from her head. She had found a home here in Haven, and, within her store, she could focus on the present and leave behind her the events of seven years ago. She even could walk past the brick courthouse where Lewis Parker had his office without wanting to flee in fear.

Her steps slowed when she saw the weathered buckboard was still in front of the store's porch. When Mr. Sawyer came out of the store carrying a large bag of seed, he swung the sack into the back of his buckboard as effortlessly as if it were a feather pillow. Bending to lift another that was on the porch, he paused. He stood and leaned one elbow on

the wagon's side. Again he tipped his hat to her with a grace
that suggested he would be as comfortable in an eastern
ballroom as here on the streets of Haven.

"Miss Delancy, I think I owe you an apology."

She shook her head, hoping someone or something would
delay Reverend Faulkner and Sean in the Grange Hall. Having them show up now might infuriate Mr. Sawyer again.
Now he was very much at ease, wiping sweat from the back
of his neck with his shirtsleeve. She noted tiny, perfect
stitches where the sleeve had been recently mended. Her
stomach cramped with sorrow, and she had to swallow her
gasp. That the man obviously had a wife should not disturb
her so much.

"You don't owe me an apology," she replied, struggling
to make her voice have its normal cheerfulness. "You were
angry, and rightfully so."

"Rightfully so? That's a change of heart for you." He
smiled at her.

She wished he had not, for he had one of those smiles
that could be described only as devastatingly charming.
Miles had had a smile like that, too. She had promised
herself she never would be suckered into believing a man's
disarming smile again. And she had not . . . until now.

"Mr. Sawyer, I assure you it isn't a change of heart."
She did not add that she had refused to let her heart change
in any way during the past seven years. It was set on the
course she had chosen when she fled Kansas in the middle
of the night. "The boy was wrong to be poking about in
your wagon, but curiosity isn't a crime in Indiana."

"I thought Hoosiers were known for minding their own
business."

"Haven is like every small town. Gossip brightens many
lives around here."

"But not yours?"

She needed to put an end to this conversation straightaway. All she had to do was excuse herself and go into the store to do any of a dozen tasks waiting for her. Yet she lingered, intrigued by his easy strength and his warm eyes.

"I find," she said, "it is simpler not to listen and trouble oneself about things that may not be true."

"A good credo."

"Credo?" she repeated, in spite of herself.

"A credo is—"

"I know what it is. I just haven't heard anyone use the word around here in everyday conversation."

His face closed up as if she had accused him of stealing that seed from her store. Hefting the other bag into the buckboard, he motioned toward the door and said in the cool tone he had used before, "If you don't mind, Miss Delancy, I'd like to settle up for this so I can get back to my farm in time to do the evening chores."

"Yes . . . yes, of course." Emma edged around the wagon to step up onto the porch. Noah Sawyer had to be the oddest man she had ever met. She had no idea why he was getting all testy over a comment she had meant as a compliment.

His hands grasped her waist and swung her up to stand on the porch. Those wide hands sent heat through her blouse and corset to sear her skin and weaken her knees. She teetered, then grabbed one of the supports holding up the roof. The hands on either side of her waist kept her from tumbling back to the ground.

"Are you all right?" asked Mr. Sawyer, with what sounded like muffled amusement.

Emma looked down at him from the porch and frowned when she saw the mirth in his eyes. "Mr. Sawyer, I don't know how things are done where you come from, but around here, women aren't manhandled."

"Without their permission?"

"Yes."

"I shall remember that the next time I halt a lady from walking blindly into a puddle."

"A puddle?"

He pointed to what she knew was not water, because she saw the horse droppings beside it.

"Thank you," she murmured.

"My pleasure."

"You can release me now. I'm not in danger of falling off the porch." She put her hands over his at her waist.

The humor vanished from his eyes, and they burned with a far stronger emotion. His gaze cut into her, threatening to tear away the façade she had built with such care. Jumping up onto the porch beside her, he moved so they stood facing each other. His hands slid around her waist in a questing caress, and her breathing came fast and uneven in her ears.

Then he drew his hands away so quickly she would have guessed he had sensed the sudden burst of warmth within her. His eyes shifted away, and she bit her lower lip. She had not wanted him touching her. Yet now she was bereft, a feeling that frightened her. Behind her safe web of half-truths, she had been able to keep herself separate from the strong, dangerous emotions she could not trust. In less than an hour, Noah Sawyer had unbalanced the precious equilibrium she had created for herself in Haven.

"I'll get that invoice for you now," she said as she went to the door. Walking ahead of him was a mistake, she realized. His gaze drilled into her back. She did not turn to ask him to explain himself and the peculiar behavior she seemed to have too few defenses against.

A door inside the store opened, and she jumped back before it could strike her. Arms surrounded her in a far too intimate embrace, for she was pulled back against Mr.

Sawyer's chest so tightly that the buttons on his shirt cut into her.

"You may release me," she said quietly as she had on the porch.

"Do you always get yourself into endless mishaps?" His breath curled around her braid to caress her nape.

"I have yet to get into a mishap." She tried to escape his hold.

"You shall if you keep squirming."

Emma clenched her hands in front of her. "So shall you if you don't release me immediately."

He drew away his arm and surprised her again by chuckling. "You speak your mind, I see."

"I've never found it wise to refrain from doing so." She walked over to where a man hobbled down the steps, and she offered him her arm. "Why don't you sit on the bench here, Mr. Baker?"

Noah Sawyer frowned as he took off his hat and knocked dust out of it. From her words, he would have guessed Mr. Baker was an elderly gentleman. This man must be on the young side of forty. His left leg had been amputated just above the knee, and Noah wondered if Baker had served in the War Between the States or had suffered an accident around here. Probably the former, because Miss Delancy had said the man was half deaf, which could have been caused by the concussion of cannon fire.

A smile tugged at one corner of his lips as he looked at Miss Delancy. He had not guessed the owner of Delancy's General Store would be such a pretty blonde. That soft gold had fallen over his hands when he had held her in the barn, trying to keep her from getting mixed up in chasing the kid.

He let his gaze edge along her splendid curves as she

made sure Baker was comfortable on the bench. Her practical white blouse and dark skirt emphasized her slender waist, and his arm recalled how it had held her twice now. He would not mind holding her again, longer and when she was not trying to escape. Knowing he should look away, he cursed silently when she looked up and her amazing green eyes narrowed.

"How much?" he asked, his irritation at himself sharpening his voice. "How much is it for the two bags of seed?"

"Let me check what the latest price is." She gestured toward the man on the bench. "Mr. Baker, this is Mr. Sawyer. Mr. Sawyer is new in Haven." Without another word, she walked toward the counter at the other side of the store.

"New, eh?" asked Baker.

"Recently bought a farm outside of town." He made sure he spoke his answer as loud as Baker had asked his question.

"So you're the one Collis sold his place to."

"Yes."

"Heard you got taken on the price." Baker grinned. "Said he sold it for twice what it was worth."

"Odd, for I've been told I got a real bargain to get the land and the woodlot, too."

"He sold you the woodlot for that price?" Baker's smile vanished as he cursed, not lowering his voice.

Noah glanced at where Miss Delancy was taking down a stack of papers held together by a string. She did not react to Baker's language, so Noah guessed she had heard it before. A woman who did not chide a fellow for speaking his mind was a pleasant change from those who threatened to swoon if rough words were spoken in their hearing.

"The liar!" grumbled Baker. "Collis let everyone think he'd gotten the better end of the deal with some gent from Chicago. Bragged about it, he did."

"Then he was telling you some great tale. I got a good deal, and I'm from Cincinnati." He kept his curses unspoken.

Not once had he mentioned Chicago to Jeb Collis. He would not have been so careless. Cincinnati. Chicago. Both cities were a long ride from Haven, so Collis could have confused them easily, but Noah wanted to make sure no one connected Chicago with him. Maybe he should have gone to a bigger place than Haven, a place where he would have been anonymous among the crowds.

That would have created other problems, because Haven had so many of the things he had been looking for. The people here seldom traveled far beyond the borders of their town, and even though they enjoyed gossip, they were so busy with their farms they had little time to snoop into anyone else's concerns.

"Did you catch the lad?" asked Baker, changing the subject.

Glad to talk about something else, he answered, "The sheriff did."

"One of them orphans off the train, was he?"

Miss Delancy was right. Baker did not miss anything that happened on the street in front of the store. Although Noah was tempted to accuse the man of faking his deafness, he knew seeing the sheriff take the boy back to the Grange Hall on the other side of the village green must have revealed the truth to Baker.

"Yes, he is," he replied.

Baker spat toward a bucket beside a stack of cracker boxes. "Those kids are bound to be trouble. Lazy troublemakers. I've never met a Mick who wasn't."

"Is that so?" Noah asked, surprised that Baker was upset because the children were Irish. This was a prejudice he had not expected to find here in southern Indiana. He had encountered such intolerance in New York and in Boston

and even in Chicago . . . dammit, he had to put Chicago out
of his mind, as he had put almost everything to do with it
out of his life.

He had thought Haven would be different, not bigoted like
the big cities. He chuckled. Haven? Had he really believed it
would be one simply because of its name? He must have,
because he was here.

"What is so funny, Sawyer?" Shifting on the bench,
Baker scowled at him. "Are you laughing at me?"

"No, at me."

He walked across the store and leaned his hands on the
counter only inches from where Miss Delancy was flipping
through a sheaf of papers. He recognized the railroad's name
on the top of each of them. She looked up, and he found
himself wanting to get lost in those soft green eyes again.

"I told you I would let you know the price as soon as I
found it, Mr. Sawyer," she said quietly.

He noticed her fingers shook as she turned the pages. Was
he unnerving her that much? He would not flatter himself
into believing that. Something—or someone else—must
have upset her, because she kept glancing past him toward
the door. She must be waiting for someone.

That was no surprise. A fine-looking woman like Miss
Delancy would have callers. *Miss Delancy?* He wondered
what her given name might be.

"Here it is." She pushed the invoice toward him. "The
price includes the shipping, Mr. Sawyer."

Now she was all business. He could be the same. Pulling
out his wallet, he handed her enough coins to pay for the
seed.

"Thanks," he said, putting his wallet into the back pocket
of his denims.

"Let me know if there's anything else you need." Color
flashed up her face at her unfortunate choice of words.

Noah did not listen to the voice tempting him to tease her. They had gotten off to a bad start, and as he planned to stay around Haven for as long as possible, he would be wise not to alienate everyone in town. He suspected Miss Delancy's opinions carried a lot of weight in this small village, where everyone would come into her store eventually.

He set his hat back on his head and tipped it toward her. "I sure will, Miss Delancy. Thank you for your help."

"Getting supplies for my customers is my job."

"I wasn't talking about that."

Again pink washed along her cheeks, but this time it was not embarrassment. She was pleased. When she smiled, he did, too.

"You're very welcome, Mr. Sawyer."

He took the page she held out to him. For a moment, it was a bridge between them, joining them in some nebulous way. Then she released her side and began to tie the other papers back together in a neat stack.

He folded the invoice and stuck it in his pocket along with his wallet. As he walked out of the store, he heard her cry, "Botheration!"

He turned to see her standing on tiptoe to put the pages back on the upper shelf. All around her other papers tumbled to the floor.

Mr. Baker was trying to get to his feet, calling, "Let me help you."

"No, let me," Noah said. "It's my fault."

"It's no one's fault." Miss Delancy tried to capture some of the papers, but even more fell.

Noah strode back to the counter as she disappeared behind it. He saw her on her knees as she gathered the papers into a single pile. Over her head, the shelf trembled. He catapulted over the counter, ignoring the scale that rang like a bell when his boot struck it. Then he steadied the shelf and shoved back the heavy books before they could fall.

"What are you doing?" she cried. "Are you—"

"Trying to keep you from getting some sense knocked into your head." He drew his hands back slightly, but the shelf tilted again. He used his hands as bookends to lift the books down to the counter. Dropping them there with a thump that drew a grin from Mr. Baker, he said, "These were ready to knock the spots off you."

She looked up, brushed her hair back out of her face, and gave him an uneven smile. "Thank you, Mr.—"

"Noah. My name's Noah. And yours?"

"Emma."

He smiled. That name fit her perfectly. Short and to the point, a very no-nonsense name. "Let me help you pick these up."

"No need," she said, stacking the pages again.

"It's no trouble." He squatted beside her in the narrow space between the shelves and the counter. When he noticed she was being selective about which ones she took, he asked, "Do you need these in any particular order?"

"I keep them by date of the order, but you don't need to bother."

"It's no bother."

She raised her eyes again, and he smiled as emotions sped through them like a runaway train. Hastily, she went back to work. "Thank you, Noah." She picked up one page, then dropped it back to the floor and reached for another. She tossed that one aside again.

"What date are you looking for?"

"Anything from January."

Noah looked around himself and chuckled when he leaned against the counter so he could hoist one foot and pull out a page beneath his boot. "This one says January." He brushed dirt from the page with the date written in big letters across the top. "Sorry."

"You don't have to apologize. 'Tis my fault for trying to shove everything up on that high shelf."

"Did you ever think of getting a step stool? I suspect the owner of Delancy's General Store would be glad to order one for you."

She laughed, and he wondered if she had any idea what crazy things that lilting sound could do to a man's gut. She must not, because she said only, "I'll have to speak to the store's owner and see about ordering one. Do you see any others with January on them?"

"No . . . wait!" He stretched past her to pick up a page that had slid away from the others.

His fingers remained above the page as he stared into her face. She was so near he could taste her sweet breath as it burst from her in soft gasp. All he had to do was close his arm around her and press his lips over hers to discover if her kiss would be as luscious as he suspected. He watched her eyelashes lower to curve along her cheeks as he leaned toward her. Was she trying to shut him out or inviting him to kiss her?

Footsteps sounded hollowly from the front porch. Noah grasped the page behind her and shoved it into her hands. He gathered up more of the papers and placed them on the counter as he stood. Recognizing both the minister and the boy who had stolen his hammer, he stepped back as Emma peeked over the counter. Who had persuaded Reverend Faulkner to take that troublesome boy?

"Reverend Faulkner!" she cried, firing a guilty glance at Noah that suggested they had been doing something far more illicit than picking up scattered papers.

Coming around the counter, Noah chuckled under his breath. That glance told him her thoughts had not been so different from his. As he bid her good day and went back out the door, he smiled. Maybe coming to Haven had not been such a bad idea, after all.

CHAPTER THREE

"Disgraceful! Completely disgraceful!" Mrs. Randolph dropped the newspaper back onto the worn counter.

Leaning one elbow on the glass jars where she kept candy for the children, Emma smiled. "Mrs. Randolph, you should not read about what is going on in Washington, DC. It always upsets you."

The elderly woman, whose hair was still the color of the mourning she wore for her husband, who had died a dozen years ago, tapped her finger on the front page of the Indianapolis newspaper that was only a few days old. "They are thieves! I say it's time we told them that. With the surpluses they have in the federal treasury, they should be sending some of that money back to us here in Haven. Miss Underhill could use new primers at the school, and the sheriff . . ."

Emma let Mrs. Randolph continue to vent her spleen, but paid no attention to the specifics of her complaints today.

Mrs. Randolph did not care if anyone listened to her, for she would gladly talk to herself if no one else was about. Or maybe she thought everyone listened so intently they were speechless. She even sat and talked with Mr. Baker for hours on end, refusing to admit the man could not hear her soft voice.

"Here you go," Emma interjected when Mrs. Randolph halted her tirade to take a breath. Handing the small package wrapped in brown paper to the old lady, she added, "See you tomorrow, Mrs. Randolph."

"Young fools! Not one of them has the brain of an earthworm. Twice as slimy."

Emma came around the counter and gently steered Mrs. Randolph toward the door. The old woman was still outlining each shortcoming of the federal legislature as she walked down Main Street. Leaning her head against the open door, Emma watched, wanting to be certain Mrs. Randolph did not walk right past her small house on the corner of Maple Street. More than once, lost in her outrage, Mrs. Randolph had wandered halfway to the bottomland down by the river before she had turned about to come home.

Smiling, Emma straightened and stretched her tired shoulders as Mrs. Randolph opened the gate in the recently painted picket fence surrounding her house. Haven had more than its share of eccentric characters, which might be the very reason Emma liked living here. The townsfolk accepted everyone's idiosyncrasies, even hers.

She turned the sign in the door to let any stragglers know Delancy's General Store was closed for the day. The sun had not yet set, but it was Saturday evening, and she always closed early on Saturdays. Few customers came in after mid-afternoon. Saturdays were for baths and courting. She would enjoy the former tonight, but not the latter. Thank goodness Harvey Schultz had finally gotten it through his sweet head

the last time he had walked her home from practice for
the village chorus that she was not interested in more than
friendship.

"Sean?" she called.

The boy peeked out from the storage room. The apron
she had given him hung past his knees and was spotted with
dust and flour and something she could not identify from
where she stood. In the past two days, the boy had treated
each hour as a special adventure. He was fascinated with
everything in the store, and she wondered if he had ever
been inside a mercantile before his arrival in Haven.

"I'm here, Miss Delancy."

Lifting her own apron over her head, she looped it onto
the peg beside the door. "Sean, I told you you may call me
Emma, if you'd like."

"My ma always said a man calls a lady 'miss.' "

"Whatever is comfortable for you." She held out her
hand for his apron.

He untied it, then grasped at his waist. Several things hit
the floor and bounced. His face blanched as she bent and
picked up one of the pieces of candy.

"Did you take this?" she asked.

He nodded, grinding his toe into a space between the
floorboards as he had dug it into the dirt when he stood with
the sheriff in the street.

"Why, Sean?"

"I like candy."

"You could have asked for some rather than trying to
sneak it out of the store."

"It costs a whole penny for the bag!"

She set the hard candy on the shelf next to a bolt of lace.
"You've been working hard, Sean. If you keep helping
around the store as you have, I believe you deserve a bag
of candy each week."

"Really?"

"Yes." She fought the tears that wanted to fill her eyes. If he saw them, he was certain to be upset. "Why don't you pick up the candy? Don't eat any before supper."

"Miss Delancy! Not even one?"

She smiled and ruffled his hair. "Maybe one, as long as you promise to eat all your supper."

"Yes, ma'am!" He hung up his apron next to hers. In quick order, he had gathered up the candy. He wrapped it in a page of the newspaper Mrs. Randolph had left behind and stuck it in his pocket.

Emma tied on her straw bonnet and settled her knitted shawl over her shoulders. The night was going to be chilly again. She needed to speak with Reverend Faulkner to see if there was another coat in the used clothing box at the church. The one Reverend Faulkner had brought to the store was too small for Sean, whose arms hung out of the sleeves above his wrists.

She blew out the lantern in the storage room and locked the back door. In her mind, she heard Noah Sawyer's laugh. She could not fault him for laughing at her when she had been so silly to announce in front of half the village that the store was always unlocked. Lewis had warned her later that she should have been more reticent. She might trust the residents of Haven, but trains and the steamboats on the Ohio often stopped in town.

"Who knows who might have been listening when you said you didn't lock up?" he had asked her. Since that afternoon, she had locked the store, although she knew there probably was no need.

"But you never know what people will do," she whispered as she turned the key in the front door. She pushed thoughts of the past out of her head. She tried to smile as she added, "If you keep talking to yourself, people will think you're as batty as Mrs. Randolph."

"What did you say, Miss Delancy?" asked Sean around the candy he had popped into his mouth.

"Check that the barrels on the porch are shut, please."

He rushed to obey, and she sighed. Sean was a great deal of help. If she could convince him to stop sneaking food from the store, it would be a sign he was beginning to trust her. He was polite and helpful and watched every motion she made as if he were seeking a way to flee at the first opportunity. She hoped she was wrong, but he resisted every overture she offered to help him feel at home in Haven.

It has only been a few days.

She needed to remember that, for it felt as if it had been a year since she agreed to take him to help at the store and welcomed him into her house. Maybe because she had not been able to relax a moment since Reverend Faulkner had made his suggestion about placing out Sean with her.

Emma walked along the street with the boy. There were no walkways in Haven. Folks here were used to dust on their shoes, because most of her customers came from the farms surrounding the small village. Even the people who lived in town, as she did, liked soft earth under their feet. Otherwise, they could go and live in Chicago or New York.

The aroma of mud from the river filled every breath. Lights glowed from lamps in the windows they passed, and shouts resounded along the street, then cheers. The village's children savored the brief hours they had when schoolwork and chores were completed. Games of hide and seek lasted until darkness and bedtime called for an end.

She looked at Sean, about to ask if he wanted to join the other children. He was staring at his feet instead of watching the games on the green. Raising her arm to put it around his shoulders, she stiffened when he cowered away.

"I won't hurt you," she said.

He hunched his shoulders and kept on walking.

With a sigh, she followed him around the corner to the cozy house on the other side of the barn behind the store. The red paint glowed dully in the fading light. Waving to Alice, who lived across the street, she climbed the five steps to the porch.

Emma opened the front door and smiled when she heard Cleo's soft purr. Bending, she picked up the calico cat. Another cat was asleep in the biggest window behind the sofa. By the potbellied stove, a nondescript shaggy dog wagged its tail before coming to its feet and stretching.

"I see you all missed us." She laughed as she put Cleo on the sofa. Patting Butch on the head, she asked, "Have you been sleeping the whole day?"

The dog's tail wagged faster.

"You have a horrible life, don't you?" Going out into the cramped kitchen, she swung open the screen door. "Out with you, Butch."

Emma could not help laughing again as the dog ran out the door with Cleo in pursuit. The two, which she had raised from abandoned waifs, had no idea they were supposed to be enemies. She was not sure if Cleo thought she was a dog or if Butch believed he was a cat. Either way, they treated each other like littermates. Queenie, who seldom deigned to leave her sunny spot on the windowsill, ignored both of them.

"Why don't you wash up before supper, Sean?" she asked.

He did not reply, but she heard the door open and close again.

Taking off her bonnet, she went back into the parlor. She sat beside Queenie and rested her elbow on the back of the sofa. She stroked the black cat as she gazed out the window at the barn.

She never had thought sanctuary would be so serene . . . and so boring.

They were coming. She could hear their voices— shouting, angry, lusting for vengeance. The familiar voices with such an unfamiliar fury.

She whirled. Escape. She must escape, or they would make her pay for the crime that was not hers. She had to leave.

Now . . . before it was too late.

The shooting at the bank was over, but the questions would now begin. And she had no answers. At least, none anyone would believe.

How could she have been so stupid? That question had been on everyone's lips as soon as last week's grim events became known. No one would listen to her. Even if a few people did, no one else would believe them. After all, how could she have been so stupid?

She had believed Miles when he said work was going well, that all their dreams would come true, that soon he would have enough money to take her on that honeymoon to St. Louis she had dreamed of when she found she loved him.

And she had believed he loved her.

Everything had been lies. There had been no work, and she had nothing left but nightmares.

Tears burned in the back of her throat, but she refused to let them fall. Had Miles ever loved her, or had that been just another lie?

She had been a fool. Never again would she be such a fool.

Picking up the small carpetbag she had packed

clandestinely, she looked around. Only the fire on the hearth lit the room. Yet she could see the quilt lying across the back of the battered settee, the tarnished candlesticks on the mantel, and the rag rug covering the uneven floor. She would never see any of these things again.

A fist struck the front door followed by a shout of, "Open the door!"

She took one step toward the back door, then another, hoping no shadow would reveal where she stood. Her breath snagged on the fear halting her heart.

"This is the sheriff. Open up, or we'll take down the door."

Time and hope and all her dreams had run out. She turned and pulled the quilt off the settee. Throwing its dark side over her shoulders, she fled through the kitchen and out into the night, far from the men milling around the front porch.

She had to leave.

Now . . . because it was too late.

Behind her, she heard, "She has to know."

"How could she not know?" another voice asked.

"Only a fool wouldn't have known."

"Maybe she knew before he—"

"No!" Emma sat up and clutched the bed covers to her breast. "No, I didn't know! I didn't know! I . . ."

She silenced herself before she could wake Sean, who should be asleep in the other bedroom. She cradled her face in her hands as icy waves crashed over her, drowning her in the fear she could not escape. Cold sweat oozed along her back.

It was over!

It was over, except in her dreams. No, this was no dream. It was the nightmare that crept out of her memories to haunt her. Could the authorities still be looking for her with the intention of hanging her?

She should not have fled Kansas. That labeled her as guilty, but she could not stay and let them paint her with Miles's wickedness. She had been a fool. A fool to believe him and his tales of the wondrous life they would share. Now every night, as the past tormented her, she was paying the price of his crimes.

Slipping her feet over the edge of her bed, she drew a bright blue coverlet around her shoulders. She went down the stairs and into the parlor. Rain struck the windows. Usually she liked that homey sound, but not tonight. She lit the lamp and sat on the rocking chair at the base of the stairs. With her feet drawn up beneath her, she huddled against the cushions.

She feared she would never find an escape from what she could not forget. Even though she had done nothing wrong . . . no, she would not think of it any longer.

It was over.

It was over. She did not need to look over her shoulder every moment. She did not have to avoid people, knowing what they were thinking when they would not meet her eyes. She did not have to start at every noise as if—

A fist pounded on the front door once, then twice. Some-one shouted her name.

Emma leaped to her feet. A yowl exploded through her head, and sharp claws struck her bare foot. Queenie raced out of the room, every hair on her back raised, looking like a furious porcupine. She heard Sean jump out of bed upstairs.

Ignoring the blood oozing across her left foot, Emma started for the door, then paused. Who was calling at this hour? It must be—as if on cue, the short case clock by the stairs chimed twice. Two in the morning! Who was knocking on her door at this hour?

She took a step toward the kitchen and the back door, then stopped. Taking a deep breath, she struggled to calm herself. This was Haven. The past was miles and another life away.

"Emma!" The man's shout sounded desperate. "Please open up! We need your help!"

Muffled weeping ripped Emma from her terror. Someone was sobbing with heart-wrenching grief. A child! Sean? She glanced up the stairs, then realized the sound came from the front porch.

She ran to the door and threw it open. Lifting the lamp, she looked out into the night. "Noah!"

"We need your help."

"We?" She pulled her gaze from him to see a dark-haired child next to him, clinging to his trousers and crying. Both of them were drenched from the rain. He carried something wrapped in a blanket in his arms. Another child?

Throwing the door open as far as it would go, she called, "Come in, come in."

"Thank you." His voice rumbled oddly about her parlor.

She was shocked to realize that, except for Reverend Faulkner, she could not recall the last time a man had come to her house. Shaking that irrelevant thought from her head, she drew the child—a little girl, she noted—in and closed the door. On the stairs, Sean was gripping the banister, his mouth as wide as his eyes.

"Is here all right?" Noah asked, pointing to the bare floor in front of the parlor stove.

"All right for what?" Emma set the lamp back on the table and blinked as its glare shimmered on his black silk vest and white shirt, which were newer than what he had worn when she saw him at the store.

"For you to check him over and see if you can help."
He squatted, putting the blanket and what was wrapped in
it on the floor. Water pooled around him.

The little girl tugged on Emma's coverlet and whispered,
"He's hurt. He's hurt bad. Can you make him all better?"
Luminous tears filled her brown eyes.

Emma was not sure which one to respond to first. She
flinched when she heard a yip and a low growl. A dog?
Butch was sleeping in the barn. She stared at the blanket.
Noah Sawyer was carrying a dog into her house in the middle
of the night? What was this all about? She wanted to ask,
but silenced her curiosity. Her questions might lead him to
ask some of his own.

"Emma, please!" He grasped her arm and pulled her
closer to the dog. "I've been told you have a way with
animals. Can you help Fuzzball?"

"Fuzzball?" She knelt beside him.

He did not look at her. "I know it's a foolish name for
a dog, but Belinda chose it." He lowered his voice beneath
the little girl's weeping. "Can you help him?"

Emma reached toward the small, brown dog. It could not
be more than a pup. "Shh," she said. "Good Fuzzball."

The dog snapped at her and growled weakly.

Noah bent forward to calm the dog. "She's going to help
you, Fuzzball." He cleared his throat, looking abashed to
be caught talking to a dog as if it were a child. "Sorry,
Emma. He doesn't understand."

"Of course not. It's all right. I get cranky when I'm not
feeling my best, too, as you know."

"I guess I do." He met her eyes and gave her a swift
smile.

She looked away from the naked honesty on his face. It
made her uncomfortable. When he pushed a strand of hair
back behind her ear, she gasped. Surprise burst into his eyes,

and he jerked back. He stared at his hand, clearly unable to believe he had done something so familiar.

"Just hold Fuzzball while I check him," she said, hating that her voice quivered. She did not want her breath to grow frayed at the touch of this man, who was still very much a stranger. She gritted her teeth to keep her question steady. "What's wrong?"

"He's been shot."

Her fingers froze on the rough blanket as she stared down at the blood soaking through it from the dog's right hind leg. Slowly she raised her gaze to meet Noah's eyes, which were as brown as the pup's, but now were filled with a fury that warned he would be a fierce enemy.

"Shot?" she asked. "Who shot him?"

His mouth worked before he asked, "Will you help him before we go into all that? If he dies—" He glanced over his shoulder. "If something happens to him, Belinda will be heartbroken."

Emma nodded. "Hold him while I check him." Without looking up, she asked, "Sean, will you get some towels so they can dry off?"

"Yes, Miss Delancy." He ran back up the stairs.

"Sean?" repeated Noah, grasping her hand as she reached past him to push Cleo's nose away from the dog before the cat created more problems. "What's *that* lad doing here?"

"Noah, can't everything else wait until I've had a chance to tend to your dog?" She twisted her hand out of his loose grip.

He nodded with reluctance, but his mouth remained in a tight frown.

Emma bent to look at the dog so she would not remind Noah that he should not come to her house begging a favor and then sound irritated because she had opened her home to someone else in need. Nor should he touch her so frequently. It unsettled her far too much.

When he cradled the dog's head in his hands, she could not help noticing how gentle they were. His fingers were long and tapered, like an artist's, but possessed that gentle strength. Something had stained them, outlining every thread etched into his palm.

Emma told herself to concentrate on the dog, not Noah's hands. She quickly discovered the bullet had only nicked the dog's leg.

"Keep him still, Noah." She stood.

"Where are you going? If you need something from the store, I can get it for you."

"No need to go to the store. I've got some medicine and bandaging in the kitchen."

She gathered what she needed and came back into the parlor. She cooed soothing sounds as she knelt again. Fuzzball relaxed beneath her touch. It was true. She did have a way with animals, for she had learned to tend them at her father's side on their farm in Missouri before they moved to Kansas. He had supplemented his storekeeping income by taking care of his neighbors' beasts when they ailed.

Hearing sobs behind her, she said, "Noah, I can tend to Fuzzball alone. You might want to see to your young companion."

"Companion? Oh, Belinda." He came to his feet and crossed the room to where the little girl was sitting in the rocker by the stairs.

As he comforted the little girl who must be his daughter, Emma washed the dog's wound and bandaged it. She doubted if the wrapping would stay on long, for Fuzzball would want to tend to it himself as soon as he was able. And that was the best kind of healing, her father had taught.

People should let their beasts do what they could to heal themselves.

But a touch of laudanum would keep Fuzzball from chewing off the bandage tonight. She watched as the dog licked the diluted medicine eagerly. When he rested his head on his front paws and began to snore lightly, she washed her hands.

Tending to the dog had been the simple part, she knew when she stood again. Noah was scowling at Sean, who was coming down the stairs. The boy glared back at him, his rounded chin jutting out like a foolish prizefighter's.

It was scant comfort that she probably would not have to worry about the nightmare returning tonight. She doubted if she would get any more sleep during what was sure to be a long night.

CHAPTER FOUR

Emma smiled at the little girl, who was still wiping tears off her pudgy cheeks. The child was sitting on the sofa, her short legs in damp stockings sticking straight out past the cushions. Emma guessed the little girl was no more than five years old. One black braid flowed down her back, and she twisted the other in her fingers.

Gently Emma took her hands and bent so her eyes were level with the child's. "Your name is Belinda, right?"

"Yes, ma'am," she whispered. "How is Fuzzball? Is he going to die?"

"Fuzzball is going to be fine, but you'll have to let him rest a lot in the next two or three weeks. He has to get better slowly."

"He isn't going to die then, is he?"

She smiled her thanks to Sean as he held out two towels.

Handing one to Noah, she dropped the other one on Belinda's head. The little girl abruptly giggled.

Noah's stern face eased, and Emma could not mistake the love he had for this child. Was that the reason he had come all the way from his farm in the middle of a rainy night to find help for the dog? His gaze turned toward her. His eyes narrowed. She wanted to ask him if he was distressed because she had witnessed his feelings for his child. That would only start another argument, and she was too tired for that tonight.

"No, Belinda, he isn't going to die," she said as she rubbed the child's wet hair gently. "He shall be right as rain in no time."

"Good, because I don't want Papa to have to shoot that mean old Mr. Murray."

"Belinda!" Noah said, embarrassment filling his voice. "She's just distressed, Emma. She doesn't mean what she's saying."

Emma straightened and smiled. Handing the damp towel to Sean, she thanked him before saying, "I understand. If . . ."

Her smile fell away before Noah's candid stare. It reminded her that she was wearing nothing but her nightdress. Its muslin did more to emphasize her curves than to hide them. A grin edged along his lips, and his eyes began to twinkle as they had when he had leaned toward her behind the counter in the store. A flush swept over her, warming her and making her aware of every inch of herself . . . and him. She had thought he was about to kiss her then. And now?

When he took a step toward her, she edged back. She did not know this man well, but surely he would not do anything inappropriate in front of his own child. Would he? She knew how poor a judge of character she was. Her kind heart had betrayed her before.

He reached out, and she struggled not to scream. She was not sure who, other than the children, would hear her in the middle of the night.

"Allow me, Emma," he said with a chuckle.

Heat slapped her face as he settled the coverlet on her shoulders as if it were a fine silk cloak. As his fingers smoothed the layers of fabric along her shoulders, his breath coursed through her hair, grazing her cheek in an invitation she doubted he intended.

She had not realized he was so tall until they stood here in her cozy house. His chin could rest on the top of her head, but as he bent toward her, she could see nothing but those earth-brown eyes.

"Thank you, Noah." She looked at the little girl, who was staring down at her dog. There had been much talk at the store about a widower and his child who had moved onto the farm a few weeks ago. She wondered why no one had mentioned how good looking Noah was. Maybe because he had infuriated all his neighbors already.

He glanced at the dog. "I appreciate your taking care of this emergency for us in the middle of the night. When Fuzzball came home all bloody, I wasn't sure who could help. I remembered someone talking about your tending to one of their animals."

"How did Fuzzball—" She smiled, as he did, when she spoke the silly name. "How did he get shot? Belinda said something about Mr. Murray. Do you—"

"Can we talk somewhere without little ears listening to every word?"

As he waited for Emma's answer, Noah glanced at Belinda, who was perched on the sofa, a three-colored calico cat curled up against her. Her head was bobbing as she fought to stay awake. He did not want to chance her hearing what he had to say, even when she was half asleep.

Beside her, Sean O'Dell was curled up, asleep. Noah sighed. Apparently Emma had tamed the wild youngster already. He hoped so. Belinda did not need to be learning anything from one of those kids who had been placed out around the village.

Looking back at Belinda, he resisted the temptation to take one of the embroidered pillows and set it behind her. It was not easy being both mother and father to this child, because she kept him on his toes with her many questions and her delightful insights into the commonplace. Although she had been in his life so few years, he could not imagine what his days would be like without her in them to fill each one with joy.

"Alone?" Emma asked.

At the edge to her question, he turned back to Emma. He could not blame her for getting the wrong impression. Their last meeting had not been under the best of circumstances. He had to admit he had not gotten the wrong impression about her. He smiled as he noted how tightly she held the blanket closed around her. Too late, he wanted to tell her, for the image of her in that light pink nightdress that matched the color in her cheeks was seared into his mind. With her tawny hair curling around her neck and cascading in a golden river down her back, she looked like an angel, even as she put the most devilish thoughts into his mind. He wanted to reassure her he had not used a wounded dog and a heartsick child as a way to get into a lady's house so he could ravish her.

But damn, she was ravishing!

"Noah?"

The impatience in her voice freed him from the fantasy that, if she had guessed what he was thinking, would have gained him a well-deserved slap. "Yes, Emma." He cleared his throat. "May we speak privately?"

"I have coffee left over from supper in the kitchen. It should still be hot. If not, I'll put some more water on."

As well as every light, he thought as he nodded and followed her out into the small room beyond where the dog slept in front of the stove. She was showing good sense. Something he should have as well, although it would be so much easier to be sensible if she were not still draped in that blanket which brought out the green in her eyes and the warm flush of her lips.

"Please sit down," she said as she took the pot off the warming shelf on the large black stove. It nearly filled the small room.

Open shelves overflowing with boxes and dishes were set on all the walls except by the stove and where the window over a dry sink offered a view of the rain. He noticed no two plates on the shelves were the same color and wondered how she had amassed such an odd collection. A door was almost hidden in the shadows. He noticed it only because the wind rattled it. With the lantern overhead cascading light down upon the bright yellow oilcloth on the table, it was a cozy room.

Noah pulled out one of the chairs and frowned as it wobbled. "Is it the floor or the chair that's uneven?"

She smiled. "I suspect both are." Her smile vanished when he tipped up the chair to examine it. "What are you doing?"

"This chair has a loose rung. A bit of glue and a couple of small nails will make it steady again."

"You sound as if you know quite a bit about chairs."

Turning the chair upright, he sat on it cautiously. It would hold him . . . for now. "I need to know more than a bit about chairs and tables and bedsteads. I make furniture."

"But you bought the Collis farm."

He took the cup she held out to him. "It has a good

woodlot. The maple and birch will be enough to keep me in wood for several years. I'm hoping there's still plenty of cedar left in there." Taking a sip of the coffee as she sat across from him, he smiled. "You brew a strong cup."

"It wasn't so strong earlier. If you'd like me to make a fresh pot—"

When he put his hand on her arm to keep her from jumping to her feet, he was astonished at the flash in her eyes. He had seen it before, but not on her face. Fear. He pulled his hand back.

"The coffee is fine," he said, although a dozen questions battered at his lips. His motion had been nothing more than polite, but her fingers quivered as she lifted her cup. Putting his own on the table, he added, "I want to thank you again for opening your door to us at this hour and for taking care of Fuzzball, Emma."

"I'm glad I could help." Emma drew in a deep, steadying breath. She was acting as frightened as a child and with just as little reason. "In Haven, we try to be friendly neighbors."

"So you've told me." He swirled the coffee about in his cup. His expression became hard again. "Too bad I haven't seen much sign of that."

She dampened her lips. "What did you want to tell me privately?"

"Do you know Leo Murray who has the farm next to mine?"

"Of course."

"What do you know about him?"

She laughed without humor. "A lot."

"What can you tell me?"

"I don't like to speak ill of people—"

"But there isn't much good you can say about that crotchety old man."

She rested her elbows on the table and let the steam from

her cup billow into her face. Nightmares and night callers. She was going to be useless tomorrow. Fortunately it was Sunday, so she needed to worry only about not falling asleep at church. Reverend Faulkner might understand, but others would not. She tried to concentrate on what her unexpected guest was saying, but it was difficult when she wanted so desperately to yawn.

"You believe Mr. Murray shot your dog?" she asked, clenching her teeth so the yawn could not escape.

"I *know* he shot Fuzzball."

"But why?" She gripped her cup and frowned. "Mr. Murray is very protective of his animals. Did you let your dog get into his sheep?"

"That's what he says."

"Then he had a right to scare your dog away."

"By shooting it?" He stood and drained his cup. Setting it in the dry sink, he shook his head. "There are other ways to keep a dog from chasing sheep."

Emma sighed. "Look, Noah, you're new here, and I suspect you're new to farming."

"How did you know that?"

"Just a guess, from your reaction to Mr. Murray's warnings. Did you used to live in a city?"

He hesitated, then said, "Yes."

She frowned, unable to guess why he would be so reluctant to answer such a harmless question. She was tempted to tell him she was probably the only one in Haven who would not pry into someone else's secrets. Nobody else would be as circumspect. Small town folks loved gossip.

"Are there lots of rules out here in the country I should know about?" he asked, leaning back on the dry sink.

She wished he had remained sitting. With the table between them, she could pretend not to notice the brawny muscles his wet shirt was unable to hide. He was as roughly hewn as the wood he worked with. Again she found herself staring at his hands. Only a man who loved his work would work hard enough to raise those calluses.

Taking a sip of coffee to keep herself from staring more, Emma said, "There are plenty of rules out here in the country. Not like the rules in the city, where you need to know when and where to cross the street. Our rules have to do with making and keeping good neighbors."

"And one of the first is not to let your dog chase your neighbor's sheep?"

"One of the first," she said, meeting his gaze evenly, "is that a farmer has a right to do whatever he must to protect his livestock from marauders."

"Marauders?" His brows rose, but no mirth eased his rigid lips. "Fuzzball is just a rambunctious pup. He wouldn't have caused any damage."

"You can't know that. Neither could Mr. Murray, because other dogs have chased his sheep, leaving him with miscarrying ewes and dead lambs. He saw your dog in his field and assumed the worst." She curved her fingers around her cup as she met his gaze evenly. "Next time he'll shoot to kill."

"How do you know he wasn't trying to kill the pup this time and missed?"

"Mr. Murray is a crack shot. He has to be, or else he might hit one of his herd. You may not believe it, but he did you and Belinda a favor tonight. He's given you fair warning, and now it's up to you to keep Fuzzball away from his sheep. Next time, he won't be so generous."

Noah frowned and sighed. "I hadn't thought of it that way. He was generous to me, like you convinced me to be generous to the O'Dell kid?"

"Exactly."

"And like you're now being generous again to the boy. How did you get him dumped on you?"

"I didn't get him dumped on me. I agreed to take him because the representatives from the Children's Aid Society believed he'd be happier in town than out on a farm. He has been very helpful around the store."

"So you haven't had any problems with him?"

She shrugged, hoping he did not take note of how stiff her shoulders were. The small issue of Sean stealing candy was nothing she needed to share with anyone. "Nothing but for Sean and me to get accustomed to each other. He's going to start school on Monday, and that will help him learn more about the rest of the children here in town. They'll help him become even more comfortable here."

"Another way neighbors help each other around here?"

"Yes."

Pushing himself away from the sink, he said, "I guess I've got a lot to learn."

"I guess you do."

"And you've been too generous to me, too, Emma. I wish I could repay you for—"

"That isn't necessary," she replied as her mind taunted her with ways she would like him to express his thanks. Those strong hands had been so gentle when they had been around her waist. Although she had told him to recall himself on the street, that did not mean she had not been delighted in his touch then . . . and would be now.

"I could fix your chair," Noah replied.

Smiling, she said, "If you want to fix something, please fix the coffin Mrs. Lambert ordered for her husband. The top was scratched when Sean jumped out of it in the storage room. I don't want to deliver it to her like that."

"The coffin is still in your back room? After a week? When's the funeral?"

"Mr. Lambert isn't dead." She laughed. "He isn't even sick."

"So why did his wife buy him a coffin?"

"Who knows? I sell folks what they want. I learned long ago not to ask why. I might get answers that start to make sense."

He chuckled. "What would make sense right now is to say thank you again and be on our way."

"Keep an eye on Fuzzball's leg for a couple of days." She started to stand, then gasped as pain seared her left foot.

"What is it?"

She drew back the coverlet, which had seared liquid fire across her instep when she moved it. Four red welts were outlined in blood.

"You're hurt!" he gasped. "Why didn't you say something before this?"

He knelt and cupped her bare foot in his broad hand. She watched as he tilted her foot so he could see the trails of blood. Against her skin, his fingers were rough as a woodworker's should be, but gentle. She could imagine him stroking a piece of wood as he decided how he would turn it into something beautiful and useful.

Her heart thudded against her chest when his hair brushed her leg. Her fingers tingled with the craving to sift through those dark strands. Would it be as coarse as his fingers or as silken as his water-stained vest?

He looked up at her, and, for a moment, his gaze held hers. Or was it more than a moment? She could not tell.

She must have hidden her thoughts, because he asked only, "Is your foot terribly sore?"

"Not as sore as Queenie's tail, I fear." Emma drew her foot out of his hand and brushed the coverlet over her ankle, which had been too boldly displayed. "Queenie is my cantankerous cat. Her tail, unfortunately, was right under my foot when you startled me with your knock on the door.''

"You should tend to this foot before it gets infected.''

"I shall.'' She smiled. "I shall retrieve the powders I used to tend to your dog and take care of my careless foot.''

He stood as she did, and she again took a step back to put more than a hand's breadth between them. She bumped into the table and clutched its edge. In silence, she gazed up at him.

For the length of a pair of heartbeats, he did not move. Neither did she, for she was not certain she could when his gaze held her in a warm embrace.

His hand came up to cup her cheek. She could not silence her gasp as he lowered his face toward hers as he had in the store. Reverend Faulkner and Sean would not be coming in to intrude this time. Every inch of her waited in eager anticipation for his kiss. This was foolish, but she suddenly wanted to do something utterly foolish. Letting him kiss her was the most foolish thing she could imagine now. It was the *only* thing she could imagine now.

His gaze swept her face as his thumb brushed her jaw. Her knees trembled, and she reached out to steady herself. When her fingers settled on his chest, he became motionless again. She wanted to yell at him to kiss her. She wanted to chide him and tell him to unhand her this very moment. As his other hand curved along her cheek, she feared she could not endure a second more of this exquisite suspense.

Then he kissed her . . . on the cheek as he said, "Thank you again, Emma, for keeping Belinda's heart from breaking.'' He stepped away and motioned for her to precede him into the parlor.

Emma turned stiffly and fought to calm her pounding heart. She should be grateful that Noah was showing more good judgment than she was. This longing for him to kiss her was not at all like her. The horrible dream and her exhaustion must have banished her common sense.

Keeping her steps slow, she walked into the front room. Fuzzball was snoring by the stove, and Belinda was curled into a ball almost as tight as Cleo as they slept together on the sofa. On the far side of the stove, Sean was now rolled in the blanket he must have gotten from his bed.

Noah looked from the dog to his daughter and smiled. "This is going to be a challenge," he whispered.

"Wait here." She rushed up the stairs and collected the two quilts from the bottom of the trunk at the foot of her bed. She brought them downstairs and handed one to him. "These will keep the two of them dry. I'm sorry. These are the last two I have."

"I shouldn't take them."

"It's still raining hard."

He grimaced as he looked out the window. "The creek was already high from the snowmelt farther north. I hope this rain doesn't continue too long. We should hurry. My buckboard is out front. They'll be dry once they're under the oilcloth in the back."

"If you can carry Fuzzball, Noah, I'll get your daughter." She did not want to speak Belinda's name, for that chanced waking the little girl.

"She's heavier. I should—"

"If she wakes up while I'm carrying her, she won't bite me." She smiled. "I'm not so sure we can say the same about your dog."

"That's true, but she is heavy."

"So are the barrels at the store." Emma did not give him another chance to argue.

Going to the couch, she slipped her arms beneath the little girl. Belinda murmured in her sleep, but did not wake as she was lifted. The scent of perfumed soap surprised Emma.

Such soaps were a costly luxury. When she turned, she could not mistake the love on Noah's face as he looked at his daughter. Maybe he could deny his daughter nothing.

She bent her head as she stepped off the porch. Rain pelted her, and the wet grass soaked her feet and the bottom of the coverlet. She picked her way carefully to the wagon. She waited while Noah settled the senseless dog in the back, then handed him Belinda.

His fingers caressed hers as chastely as his hands had touched her face in the kitchen. Again the pulse of longing throbbed through her, and she hoped he could not see her eyes widen.

"Thank you again, Emma," he said as he drew the oilcloth over the sleeping girl and the puppy. Then he untied the reins from the post by the road.

"I'm glad I could help."

He climbed into the front seat of the buckboard with ease. "I hope your foot—and your cat's tail—heal as quickly as Fuzzball's leg."

"I hope so, too." She stepped back onto the grass as he clucked an order to the horse.

As the buckboard rattled into shadows and was swallowed by the night, she did not move, even as the rain streamed down through her hair. Yes, her foot would heal quickly, but she had the uneasy suspicion Queenie's claws were not the only thing that had gotten under her skin tonight.

CHAPTER FIVE

Noah wiped the back of his neck with a dirty kerchief. Sawdust clung to the creases of his shirt and itched on his bare forearms as he stuffed the kerchief in the pocket of his brown denim trousers. He counted the handful of stars already poking through the twilight where clouds had not claimed the sky. A cow lowed in the distance, but the sound could barely be heard over the rush of water from the Ohio River at the bottom of the hill.

The creek met the Ohio only a few hundred feet from here. He scowled as he realized the frantic rush of water had come from the creek as well as the river below. If the water kept rising at this rate, it would flow over its banks and down here into his woodlot. Then he would have to wait for the wood to dry before he could begin working on it. The hour was too late to drag even one of these logs back to the barn beside his house.

It would be a long night while he made sure everything in the barn was secure and watched the rising water. He swung his ax over his shoulder with the ease he had gained from many hours of practice. Humming a tuneless song under his breath, he climbed back over the pile of logs he had cleaned of branches and twigs. A good day's work. Tomorrow, if the creek did not jump its banks, he would hitch up old Patches and get these logs to where he could start stripping off the bark.

He settled his suspenders over his shoulders and reached for the branch where he had left his coat so it would not get filthy. Gladys would be furious if he showed up on the porch "half dressed," as she called it. The housekeeper had a way of keeping him and Belinda in line. He tried to imagine what he would have done if Gladys had not been willing to come to Indiana with them.

When he ran his hand through his hair, leaves and dust billowed out. He drew the kerchief from his pocket again and wiped the debris from his nape so it would not itch. He might not get a chance to bathe tonight. He chuckled. Being too busy worrying about the cold water in the creek could keep him from enjoying some hot water in the tub.

Mud caught at his boots as he climbed up onto the road. His smile faded. The morning's rainfall would raise the creek even higher, and he had heard the Ohio roaring all day. If the Ohio's waters rose above the bottomlands, his whole farm could be washed away.

As he turned toward the low, rambling house that was now his home, a motion in the opposite direction caught his eye. He peered through the twilight to see an earthbound star twinkling. Not a star, but a lantern. Something was near the bridge leading back toward Haven. In the light that bounced as if hooked onto a child's ball, he saw a wagon and a horse facing the bridge over the creek. The wagon was not moving.

He hoped it was not Murray coming to complain again about the pup getting into his sheep. Three times during this past week, Noah had had more than an hour wasted while he had endured listening to the old man's lectures.

The horse by the bridge whinnied nervously, then rose with a shrill neigh onto its hind feet. The lantern fell to the ground, sending light up on the frightened horse.

Noah threw his ax to the road and raced to the black wagon that was larger than his buckboard. The stupid horse could fling the wagon and itself into the creek. He rounded the front of the wagon and halted.

A woman, her face hidden by the gingham ruffles on her bonnet, was trying to grasp the horse's bridle as a child shouted in the back of the wagon. Her soft, calm words were smothered by the horse's panicked neighs. As the horse's flailing hoofs came close to her, she leaped back, but did not flee.

From the other side, Noah tried to catch the horse's head. Leather burned his palm as the horse jerked away from him.

"Damnation!" he growled.

"There's no need for such language."

Amazement filled Noah as he met eyes that snapped with frustration through the thickening twilight. The gingham bonnet was sitting on Emma Delancy's tawny curls that, as they had every time he had seen her, were escaping her hair pins. Glancing at the wagon, he saw Sean O'Dell peeking over the seat. It was almost dark, but he could read the large white letters on the side.

Delancy's General Store, Haven, Indiana.

"Emma!" he shouted. "What's going on here? What's wrong with your horse?"

"Later!" She grabbed for the horse's head again and

cheered when she captured the bridle. Instead of snarling at the horse, she bent her own head close to it and whispered something, her voice as soft as sawdust. She ran her hand lightly along the horse's mane. It quivered, but did not try to pull away again.

Noah was silent while she continued to soothe the horse, whose sides strained with each breath. The horse's eyes no longer rolled back in fear, and its ears rose from where they had been pinned to its skull. Only when the beast lowered its head and rubbed against her shoulder did she relax.

He went to the wagon and lifted out the boy in case the horse got another notion in its head. Putting his hand on Sean's shaking shoulder, he asked, "Are you all right, boy?"

"Yes, sir." He grinned, revealing a missing tooth that had been there last week. "That horse is plum crazy."

"I agree."

Sean's grin widened, and Noah found himself smiling back at the lad. Clapping him gently on the shoulder, Noah turned to where Emma was still stroking the horse.

"Did something spook him?" Noah asked as he picked up the lantern and set it back on the seat. The glass had cracked, but the flame still flickered.

"I'm not sure. Toby should be all right."

"Toby? The horse?"

"Yes."

"I'm not worried about your horse. What about you? Are you hurt?"

"No, I'm fine. Sean?"

"Right here," he replied, but stayed on the edge of the road.

Noah smiled. The boy was showing good sense to keep some distance between him and that crazed horse.

She wiped her hands on the stained apron over her dark

skirt and simple white blouse. "Toby just gets ideas into his head sometimes, and nothing will get them out."

"What got into his head this time?"

Emma shrugged in answer to Noah's question, then wished she had not. She winced as pain ricocheted through her shoulders.

"Are you all right?" he asked.

"I told you. I'm fine. Just a bit sore. When Toby tried to pull the reins out of my hands, he almost took my arms with them." She forced a smile as she met the concern in Noah's gaze.

Her aching shoulder was forgotten when she found herself becoming lost in his dark eyes. Only the low whoosh of the horse's breath reminded her that anything existed beyond the scarcely restrained fires in those eyes. When Noah came around the horse, putting his hands on the reins near her fingers, she shivered, hoping and yet fearing he would touch her.

Since he had called at her house with his daughter and their dog, she had tried to put him out of her mind and concentrate on getting Sean settled into Haven's school. She had prided herself on believing she had her thoughts of Noah Sawyer under control and would not succumb to the spell of his warm gaze the next time they met. She had been deceiving herself.

He bent toward her, and her breath shattered over the swift beat of her heart. Could he hear its thumping? Could he guess how the scent of freshly cut wood drifted from him like the most beguiling cologne?

Emma swallowed roughly and closed her eyes as she released that breath when he knelt and lifted Toby's front hoof. He examined it before checking the others. Rising, he wiped his hands on his denims, which were lathered to his legs with the sweat left by hard work.

"Looks to be all right," Noah said. "He didn't step on anything to scare him."

"I knew that." She refused to lower her gaze when he regarded her with astonishment. She had not intended her answer to be so sharp, but it was irritating that he seemed completely unaware of the tenuous sensation that had joined them together for a single heartbeat.

"You did?" He rested his arm on the horse's back. She wondered if his cool pose was a pretense. Maybe so, or maybe his skin tingled in anticipation of a caress as hers did. His hooded eyes and the growing dark masked all emotion. "Then what do you think caused a horse of his considerable years to act like an unbroken yearling?"

"I told you. He sometimes gets—"

"Ideas." His mouth twisted into a wry grin. "So you said. What upset him?"

"I'm not sure." She looked at Sean, who was inching toward the wagon. "We were heading back into town after finishing our deliveries out to the River's Haven Community. We got here, and Toby refused to go any farther."

"The creek is high. Maybe he's afraid of fast water." He chuckled. "There's a reason folks use the term horse sense, you know."

"The water has been high before, almost every spring. It's never bothered him before."

"Something sure has spooked him tonight."

Emma watched, baffled, when Noah went to the bridge that was barely wide enough for her wagon. He squatted to peer at it.

"What are you looking for?" she asked, taking the lantern and holding it up so he could see better.

"Not sure." Standing, he walked out onto the wooden bridge. When he bounced on each plank, she almost laughed. He had to be the oddest man she had ever met.

Sean gave a whoop and raced out onto the bridge, jumping about as Noah was.

She shook her head. Maybe Toby was simply mad, and that madness had infected both Noah and Sean. Yet she had to smile to see Sean acting like a child. Too often, he was as somber as a judge.

Suddenly she heard a crack like a cannon firing. Sean shrieked as the board broke beneath him. He vanished, and she screamed in terror. In those wild waters, he could be swept away and drowned.

"Sean!" she cried, stepping onto the bridge. "Sean!"

"Get back!" Noah shouted. "Get back off the bridge. You may fall through, too." He dropped to his knees. As he reached into the black hole with one hand, he motioned her back with the other. "Stay where you are!"

"But Sean—"

"I see him. Hold on, boy."

Emma sank to sit on the damp grass near the road and watched, one hand pressed to her mouth while she held up the lantern with the other, as Noah's calm voice drifted to her. The words were lost in the rush of the water, but that did not matter. Sean must be able to hear them.

She jumped to her feet again when Sean's head appeared through the hole. Noah yanked him up and tossed him onto the shore. She caught Sean, who clung to her, his face wet with his tears. In amazement, she realized that was the only part of him that was wet.

"How . . ." she whispered.

"I caught onto the boards." He gulped back a sob. "Just like we used to catch onto the trolley back home."

She smoothed his hair as she had Toby's mane. Looking over his head, she raised the lantern again and called, "Noah, get off the bridge!"

"I'm trying to do that."

Trying? Her breath caught again in horror. "What's wrong?" she cried. "Do you need help?"

"Stay back!" He tested the board next to the one that had broken. When it screeched like a beast in pain, he ran.

The board crumbled into splinters that raced away on the torrent. He jumped to his left. That board wobbled, and he leaped away just before it dropped into the water, dragging down the railing, which was consumed by the maw of a raging whirlpool. He flung himself toward the shore. Within seconds, the bridge had disappeared, leaving only the naked supports jutting out from the bank.

"Stay here," Emma whispered to Sean, handing him the lantern. "Make sure Toby doesn't take it into his head to go now."

"Yes, ma'am." His voice shook.

She squeezed his shoulders once more, then ran to where Noah was rolling over. She knelt beside him and put her hands on his shoulders to help him sit. "Take it slowly. Are you hurt?"

"Just my pride that your old Toby has more sense than the three of us put together."

"Are you all right?"

"Fine. I thought the boards looked rotten."

"So you tested them by trying to kill yourself?"

He laughed as he looked up at her. "That wasn't my intention."

"You scared me near to death! I thought you would be drowned. Both you and Sean." Her bottom lip trembled, and she held it still with her teeth. Then her teeth began to chatter. When Noah put his arms around her, she leaned her face against his chest.

"It's all right," he murmured against her bonnet. "Sean and I are both safe—although maybe not sound. I'm not sure I can say we are of sound mind just now."

She laughed. She could not halt herself, even when she still shook with fear. "Do you always do such stupid things?"

"Not always. Sometimes I do smart things." He clasped her face between his strong hands and captured her mouth.

The tender persuasion of his lips swept away her protest at his untoward behavior more swiftly than the water in the creek. As her arms curved around his shoulders, he deepened the kiss until her breath grew rough. Her fingers clenched on his shirt when his tongue slipped between her lips to caress each responsive spot in her mouth. He allowed no mysteries to hide within her mouth, setting each slick shadow alight with his tongue, until she moaned against his lips.

Raising his mouth from hers, he held her gaze as he reached for the ribbon on her bonnet. He untied it and pushed it aside as her fingers combed up into his hair, which was as coarse as raw silk. She closed her eyes when he bent forward to tease her neck with fervid flicks. She drew his mouth back to hers so they could share each breath in this glorious storm of sensation.

"Miss Delancy, it's beginning to rain," said Sean from behind her. "Can we go?"

Emma pulled away from Noah, hoping her face was not a brilliant crimson in the light from the lantern the boy held. Groping for her bonnet as she forced a smile for Sean, she flinched when her fingers settled on Noah's thigh. His hand clamped over hers, holding it in place.

She looked at him, desperation tightening her voice. "It's raining. We should get going."

His other hand cupped her cheek. "I thought we were."

"Noah!"

With a laugh, he stood and drew her to her feet. He turned to Sean and said, "Lead on, my man."

"Where?" Sean rocked from one foot to the other, clearly uneasy.

"Back to Toby and the wagon. Miss Delancy and I will be right behind you."

Sean nodded and rushed to clamber into the back of the wagon. As he leaned forward to hook the lantern in its place on the side, he waved for them to follow.

Emma took a single step, but Noah's hand holding hers kept her from hurrying to the wagon. The rain was thickening into a mist. She wanted to find some shelter before the fall became heavier.

"Will you release me?" she demanded.

"That's no way to talk to your host."

She frowned. "Host?"

"You can't drive into Haven tonight. I doubt that bridge can be fixed until the water goes down. Even then, it'll take me and several other men a few days to repair it. The only other way back to Haven will take you hours." He smiled and doffed an imaginary hat. "So I guess you'll be staying the night out here on this side of the creek. If you don't want to bunk in with Mr. Murray, you can stay at my house."

"I—I—"

"Don't get all bashful on me. In addition to Belinda and Fuzzball and Sean, my housekeeper will be at the house. We'll be properly chaperoned."

Emma smiled and nodded. "Thank you."

"You're very welcome." He tipped her chin and gave her a quick, fiery kiss.

"Noah, we aren't very well chaperoned here."

As if Sean heard her, he called, "Are you going to stand there all night being lovey-dovey while we get drenched?"

"Lovey-dovey?" Noah laughed. "The boy has quite the vocabulary."

"So I'm learning. Some words he uses I've never heard before, but he assures me that they're all the rage on the streets of New York City."

"It seems we both have a lot to learn."

Emma was glad the lantern's light did not reach this far. She knew she was blushing, for his tone made it obvious what lessons he would like them to study together. The very thought sent a pulse rushing through her, as unstoppable as her yearning to be in his arms again. She saw his amazement when she threw her arms around him and kissed him before turning to hurry to the wagon.

Hearing Noah's laugh, she smiled as she climbed up onto the seat at the front of the wagon. He walked out of the darkness, and the raindrops glistened on him as if he were bathed in stars. But even those were not as dazzling as his eyes, which revealed he would not be satisfied with these few kisses.

He took Toby's head and guided the horse as she began the slow process of turning the wagon. From the back, Sean shouted out a warning each time it came too close to where the road fell into the creek. She steadied the wagon so it would not roll too far.

Once its rear wheels were closest to the ruined bridge, Noah went to get the ax he had left back along the road. He leaned it against the dash as he swung up to sit beside her.

"I should thank you for your hospitality."

"It's no more than I should do after you opened your house to us last week."

"How's the pup?" Thank goodness, she could speak of something mundane. Maybe now her mind would stop conjuring up images of Noah's face in the moment before her eyes closed as his lips found hers.

"Why don't you come and see for yourself?"

Emma nodded. Everything would be back the way it should be once they reached his house. It must be the white one she had passed less than a mile up the road. A quiver glided along her as she wondered what she would do or say during the ride to his farm. She never had been bashful before, and she enjoyed jesting with her customers at the store. So why was she abruptly acting like a schoolgirl who was flustered by a good-looking man's kiss? It was time she acted like the woman she was . . . a woman who would be a fool to let passion endanger her.

Again.

CHAPTER SIX

"All set?" Noah called, his voice seeming even more stygian in the dark.

"Yes." Emma decided simple answers were best. That way, she might be able to keep her mind on the importance of not getting involved with this handsome man. She could not risk ruining his life as Miles had ruined hers.

"All right. Let's go, then. Gladys gets crotchety when I'm late for dinner."

"Gladys?"

Stepping up to sit beside her, he leered like a stage villain at both her and Sean. He added as the boy giggled, "You need not look so discomfited. Gladys is my housekeeper." He whispered against where her hair was now falling onto her shoulders. "In spite of any gossip you may have heard, I'm not keeping a mistress hidden away out on the farm."

"No one has said . . . I didn't mean to suggest—"

His laugh prevented her from stumbling through her inadequate excuse. "Of course you didn't. I was just teasing you because you looked very serious all the sudden."

She slapped the reins on Toby's back and tried to see through the darkness. When Sean held up the lantern, she said, "Blow out the light. I can trust Toby."

"And me?" asked Noah.

"Trust you? I don't know you that well." She did not add that several well-meaning busybodies had shared with her throughout the week every word of gossip about the widowed Mr. Sawyer, who would be, according to many in Haven, a perfect match for the unmarried Miss Delancy.

When Sean laughed, she guessed Noah had made a silly face at the boy. She relaxed against the slats of the seat. Noah rested his elbow on the back of the seat and leaned his chin on his fist. She glanced at him and quickly away, because, when she turned her head, his lips were so close.

"Don't you recall, Emma, how I saved you and yon Toby from what might have been mortal danger?" Noah asked.

"Are you trying to be a knight in shining armor?"

"*Your* knight, lady fair. Here to protect you from rotten boards and a dunking in that creek."

Emma laughed, then yelped as the wagon dropped into a chuckhole. "Sean, are you still with us?"

"Yes, Miss Delancy!"

Noah's voice became serious. "If you wish, I can drive."

"I know the road better than you do." She steered Toby around a corner and into the blacker shadows woven beneath the trees. "I've been delivering to my customers along these roads for over seven years."

Emma was relieved when the trees thinned and lights from a house pierced the night. The rain was becoming steadier. When Noah offered to steer the wagon along the road to his barn, she was grateful. She doubted if she could find an unfamiliar road in the dark. When his fingers touched hers as she passed him the reins, she quivered.

"Something wrong?" he asked.

"Why do you ask?" She was proud how her calm voice concealed the turmoil inside her.

"You seem as jumpy as a cat in a doghouse."

"I saw you and Sean nearly get washed away. Doesn't that give me a reason to be on edge?"

"I thought I might be the one unsettling you." Even in the sparse light from the house, his smile was bright.

She kept her hands folded in her lap. "Did you?"

When he chuckled, she could envision how his brows had shot up at her answer. Another shiver coursed through her. She was amazed how easily she could reconstruct the strong lines of his face out of her memory.

"Here we are," he said as he drew back on the reins and stopped the wagon under a thick maple. Its budded branches offered no refuge from the rain.

"You were lucky to get such a well-proven farm." She turned on the seat and lifted three of the quilted pads she used to protect her deliveries. Handing one to Sean and another to Noah, she drew the third one over her bonnet. It would offer only temporary protection from the rain.

"You always seem to have the very thing I need," Noah said as he tied the reins around the metal strip atop the dashboard before draping the quilt over his head.

She was unsure if his words had a double meaning. She decided to act as if she had noticed nothing brazen about them. "That's part of running a store, I suppose. I have to keep current with anything that my customers might need."

"I didn't know you were so interested in farming."

"My customers, for the most part, are farmers. If I wanted to be ready to sell them what they need, I had to learn about their jobs as well as mine."

"So you didn't grow up on a farm?"

"No." She turned quickly to check Sean again. After her probing of Noah's past, she should not be surprised that he was asking questions. That his kisses had been mind-numbing was no excuse for not considering the consequences of trying to learn more about him.

His chuckle had little warmth. "I guess that terse answer is a warning to mind my own business."

"I didn't mean . . ." She was not sure what to add, because she had meant exactly that. Anyone prying, however innocently, into her past made her nervous. A single wrong word could expose the truth she had hidden since her arrival in Haven. If anyone had any idea of what had happened in Kansas, she might not be able to escape hanging this time as she had seven years ago.

Noah cleared his throat, and she started with a gasp. He stepped down from the wagon. When she started to move, too, he motioned for her to stay where she was. She looked down and saw rain falling into a puddle.

"Sorry," he said. "Didn't mean to startle you."

"I'm just a little nervous." That much was the truth. Talking here in this dusky bower with a man as handsome and enigmatic as Noah Sawyer, even with Sean watching, would have been enough to unnerve her under any circumstances.

He lifted Sean out and then said, "Slide over here, Emma. I'll help you down so you don't ruin your pretty shoes."

She laughed. She was wearing shoes that were as scuffed as his boots. Doing as he asked, she put her hands on his shoulders while he assisted her down. He released her as soon as her feet touched the ground. She was amazed how disappointed she was that his fingers had not lingered . . . for just a second.

"Why don't you go up to the house?" he asked. "I'll put Toby here in the barn for the night."

"I can do that. Sean, run to the house." She glanced toward where the Ohio was an ebony ribbon wider than it customarily was. "You've already got a lot of work ahead of you here, Noah. If the river rises much more . . ."

"Don't even say it."

"It'll ruin your fields." She frowned as she went to unhook Toby on one side from the wagon while Noah did the same on the far side. "You're behind on your planting."

"If I till the fields."

"You aren't going to farm here?"

"I haven't decided yet." When he glanced across the open meadows that were washed of color by the thin veil of rain, the firm lines of his silhouette teased her finger to run along his aquiline nose and the firm line of his lips.

"But you bought all that seed from me."

He chuckled as he led Toby away from the wagon. Tossing the quilt back onto the wagon, because the rain was letting up, he said, "Just in case. I can resell it if I decide not to use it. Jim Moore stopped by a few days ago and asked about renting some of the fields to graze his stock."

"I'm glad to hear that."

"Really? Why?"

"Jim and his wife have an even dozen children, with one more on the way. Renting out more land will help him increase his herd."

"You're speaking of cows, not children, I assume."

Emma smiled. "You assume correctly, although it seems the Moore family grows as fast in the house as the number of head they raise in the fields."

"Supper!" came a shout from the house.

"I told you Gladys gets crotchety if I'm late." He took

the horse into the barn. When she followed, he asked, "Don't you trust me to look after him?"

"Old Toby can be pretty persnickety about what he eats. No oats at night, or he'll get sick."

He opened a stall door and slapped Toby on the rump. The horse went in, but gave him a glare that suggested Noah would be sorry for doing that. "Does hay agree with him?"

"Yes, and plenty of water."

"There's hay in the stall, and I don't think we need to worry about water." He laughed again when a drop of water fell on the very end of her nose. "The roof could use some work."

"I hope this is all the rain we get."

"I do, too." He held out his hand. "Let's go."

She hoped he did not notice how her fingers trembled when she put her hand in his. He gave no hint of what he was thinking, and the darkness hid his face as he led her out of the barn. Pausing at the wagon to collect her lantern, he handed it to her, then edged closer. Did he plan to kiss her again? Here in his front dooryard?

The step of the wagon pressed the back of her skirt, giving her no escape when he did not release her hand. But did she want to escape? As she gazed up into the shadows which concealed his eyes, she wanted to become lost once more within them. His fingers slid up her wrist, setting her skin to tingling as if she had grasped a telegraph wire.

He folded his arm, drawing hers up against him. The odor of pine pitch from his woodlot struck her on each breath, but she could think only of the warmth of his fingers against her wrist and the firm muscles woven across his chest. She breathed in tempo with him, aware of how the tips of her breasts would graze that hard wall if the quilts were not between them. Could he tell how her heart beat like thunder rolling across the fields?

"Miss Delancy!"

She started to turn at the young voice, but Noah continued to hold her hand. "Belinda and Sean are waiting for us on the porch," she whispered.

"I know." He brushed a strand of hair back under her bonnet, and she closed her eyes to savor the rough texture of his work-toughened skin against her cheek. His finger trailed along her jaw, curving beneath her chin to tilt it toward him. "How about, if it stops raining, I give you a tour of the farm after dinner?"

"It's dark," she murmured, opening her eyes to discover his dangerously close to hers.

"I know." He gave a hushed chuckle.

Emma was uncertain what she should say and was spared from having to decide when a whirlwind pushed its way between her and Noah.

Belinda flung one arm around her father and the other around Emma. "It *is* you, Miss Delancy. I told Gladys it was your wagon coming into the yard. Then that boy came up to knock on the door."

"His name is Sean."

The little girl nodded as her father took off the quilt and wrapped it around her. "I remember now. What did you bring us?"

Noah squatted so his eyes were even with his daughter's. "She brought us her company along with Sean's for dinner."

"No candy?"

Emma held out her hand to the little girl while they walked up the hill to the house. "Why don't you ride into town with me tomorrow, and we shall see what is in the candy jar at the store?"

"Can we, Papa?"

"Maybe not tomorrow." He looked up at Emma, his

expression now grim. "We shall have to wait and see in the morning. Right now—"

Belinda's excitement raised her voice. "Right now, come and see Fuzzball, Miss Delancy. He'll want to see you, too." She grabbed Emma's hand and pulled her toward the house.

Emma looked back over her shoulder to see Noah following as he laughed indulgently. No one could doubt who possessed Noah's heart. He adored his daughter, and that love was returned by Belinda.

A twinge ached within Emma. This was no time to think of how some nights, when she sat with her cats and Butch, she listened for footfalls that would never come. She was not alone. Sean lived with her now, but the child, no matter how hard he was trying to fit in, did not have the steps she longed to hear coming up the walk. She had missed hearing the assertive sound of a man's boots, even though the last man who had walked home to her in the evening had caught her up in his tangled web of treachery and crime.

She had not needed to be alone . . . if she did not want to be. She could let Noah take her on that tour later. And Noah Sawyer was not the only man around Haven who would be glad to keep the unmarried Emma Delancy from being lonely. She shoved those thoughts out of her head as she swung clasped hands with Belinda and hurried up the four steps to the front porch.

Noah watched as Belinda led Emma and Sean into the house after pointing out the swing on the far side of the porch. The two children giggled eagerly about the idea of using it later.

He should be glad Belinda had intruded when she did. Things were getting out of hand. He could not blame Emma. She had only come to his side to make sure he was not injured. *He* had tugged her into his arms and let the temptation of her soft lips overwhelm his good sense. He could not rid himself of the luscious sensation of Emma against him. She had not stiffened as he had half expected, proving she was not as prudish as she pretended to be. She could not hide the passions that roused more than his curiosity about this lovely woman.

Light glittered from the windows where lace curtains soon would be fluttering out on a spring breeze. As he walked along the porch, the unmistakable scent of chocolate coaxed him to put Emma out of his mind as he lingered over images of rich, dark cake with white sugar frosting.

Even that was impossible.

"Good day in the woodlot?" asked a raspy voice as the screen door slammed close. A woman nearly as tall as he came out onto the porch.

He smiled. "Are you keeping an eye on me, Gladys?"

"Someone has to." As she rubbed her hands into her stained apron, her smile transformed her plain face beneath her graying hair. "Miss Delancy is paying a sick call on the pup at Belinda's insistence. The boy is sitting in the kitchen, staring at the cake."

"I should have warned Emma what she was about to endure."

"Nonsense! They're having a grand time." She did not move from in front of the door, warning she had more to talk to him about before he went inside. That amazed him, for he had not thought Gladys would let dinner wait even if the world were coming to an end.

"How is Fuzzball doing?" he asked.

"Much better."

"I'm very glad to hear that." He leaned one hand against the clapboards that needed painting, like all the buildings on this farm. "Did Belinda stir from his side all day?"

"Not an inch. After a week, she needs to spend a day or two out in the sunshine."

"First we have to have some sunshine." He glanced uneasily toward the river again.

Gladys jabbed a stray hair back into her conservative bun. "That Miss Delancy did a fine job bandaging up the pup."

Noah frowned. "Is that jealousy I hear?"

"You could have gotten me, Mr. Sawyer. I would have tended to Fuzzball."

He patted her meaty shoulder. "You almost swooned when Belinda scraped her knee. This was worse."

"Belinda is a child. The pup is a beast."

"True." He gave her an apologetic smile. Was this all Gladys had to speak with him about? He wanted to get inside and return to Emma's company. "I didn't want to bother you at that hour, Gladys."

"So you bothered Miss Delancy?" Her eyes narrowed as she gave him a calculating smile. "I can guess why now that I've seen that pretty young thing. I should have known you'd be the first to heed all the talk about how she needs a gentleman calling on her."

"I heeded that she was good with animals." He folded his arms in front of him. *This* was what Gladys wanted to discuss. He should have guessed. Gladys watched over him as if he were a virginal miss who must guard her virtue. "And she was very good with Fuzzball."

"So you didn't go to get her help because she has hair as golden as ripe wheat?" Her smile wavered as she glanced back at the door.

"No." *Or not totally*, he added silently.

"But now you've brought her and the lad here to spend the night. That's going to cause talk."

"Talk is what folks here seem to like to do best. It doesn't matter if there's any truth in it."

"Some of it is true. Heard how you and she had some private talking right in the middle of the street the last time you went into town.'' She chuckled. ''It doesn't take much time for a man and a woman to figure out they would rather talk 'bout courting than the boy helping himself to an old hammer and half a bag of nails.''

He grinned and wagged a finger at her. ''Gladys, I'm going to need that old hammer and the nails now that the bridge into town is gone.''

''Gone?''

''The creek swept it away.'' He did not see any reason to upset her with a recitation of all that had happened.

''So that's why she's here!''

''Why else?''

''Why else, indeed?'' With a rusty laugh, she stepped aside. ''I thought you might like having a pretty lady here for dinner and whatever.''

''Whatever shouldn't be on your mind.''

''Should be on yours!'' Gladys wafted her apron at him before opening the door. Over her shoulder, she shot, ''And another word of advice.''

''Which is?''

''Next time you go courting, Mr. Sawyer, take the young gal something other than a wounded pup.''

The door slammed in her wake, and Noah laughed. Gladys was as plainspoken as he used to be. His smile drifted away on the twilight breeze. There were a lot of things he *used* to be, but he needed to think about what he was now.

Gazing around the yard and down toward the barn, which was an ebony block as the clouds lowered in the sky, he rested his head against the pole holding up the porch roof. He had been damned lucky to find this place. It was close enough to a village to make it easy to get what they needed, and it was far enough away to give him privacy. Off the main road that followed the creek, the farm looked no different from dozens of others amid the lazily rolling hills.

This place *was* perfect. Especially now that inside the house was a lovely lass who . . . Dammit! He had spent all day today trying to concentrate on work. Instead of figuring out which tree would give him the right boards, he had let Emma Delancy's face trespass into his mind, so easily he could recreate it and spend hours admiring each quirk of her lips and the bright fire in her eyes.

Now she was inside, and even Gladys, who preached propriety to him, seemed to think he would be a fool not to take advantage of the situation.

He smiled wryly. He was no lad suffering puppy love for the girl next door. He had Belinda and this farm to think about. Maybe some other time. Maybe when things settled down and he could feel really comfortable here, he might enjoy asking Emma again about taking that tour of the farm alone. His laugh was sad. By that time, she probably would be wooed and wed and have a child of her own. Her husband would not appreciate her answering the door in the middle of the night to a strange man, a child, and a wounded pup.

His smile became a frown as he stared up at the clouds again. It was odd, now that he had a chance to think about it. Emma had not asked him how the dog had gotten home or who had spoken to him about her. That lack of curiosity disturbed him for some reason he could not name.

Maybe because he was trying to learn to act the same way, not asking unnecessary questions that might start a dangerous conversation. Could it be she had something to hide, too?

As he reached for the door, he murmured, "Everyone has something to hide."

He held out his hands to Belinda, who ran along the narrow hall toward him. Some people had things that were important enough to give up everything for. He swung her up in his arms, hugging her, but his gaze was caught by Emma's as she came out of the parlor, smiling.

He looked hastily away, burying his face in Belinda's soft hair. Yes, some people had things that were important enough to give up everything for. That had always seemed so easy to remember, but now he could not keep from meeting Emma's eyes, which glowed almost as brightly as Belinda's. As every muscle responded to that sweet fire, he tried to remind himself of the reason he was here, the reason he had given up everything to protect the child in his arms, the reason he should not think of holding Emma instead.

It had always been so easy to remember . . . until now.

CHAPTER SEVEN

Emma thanked Gladys for passing her the plate with the roast chicken on it. Taking a piece, she handed the plate to Belinda. When the little girl had trouble balancing it, Emma held one side while Belinda selected what she wanted.

"Thank you," Noah said as he took the plate.

Emma mumbled something. Looking around the table in the elegant dining room, she tried to hide her amazement. The room had recently had new wallpaper hung. The cabbage roses were the same color as the fancy china on the stylishly modern oak table. She had seen these dishes and the table in a catalog she had received at the store. Not Mr. Montgomery Ward's catalog, which most of her customers used for the things she could not otherwise get for them. This furniture and even the rug on the wide-board floor had all been in that fancy catalog from some company in Chicago. She remembered the picture clearly, because she had admired the claw-footed table and wished she could have something like it for her house.

The furnishings in the parlor were just as new and expensive, and the runner going up the stairs did not appear to have been walked upon for more than a few weeks. She guessed she could find pictures of them as well in that catalog. Upstairs in Belinda's room, the only thing that seemed *not* new was a wonderful dollhouse with a collection of delightful furniture to fill its six rooms.

Yet Noah was a furniture maker. He had told her that, and earlier, on the way toward Haven, she had seen the area in the woodlot where trees had been cut, although she had not seen him then. Belinda had told her Noah had made the dollhouse and all the furnishings. Making such a delightful toy for his daughter was a reasonable thing for a man who worked with wood to do. But if he was a woodworker, why was all the furniture in his house from some factory in Chicago?

A flash of lightning tore through her thoughts. Belinda moaned and hid her face beneath the lacy tablecloth as thunder shook the house.

Noah picked her up out of her chair and set her on his lap. "It'll be all right, pumpkin." Over her head, he said quite unnecessarily, "Thunderstorms frighten her." He pulled her chair closer to his and said, "Sit and have something to eat, Belinda. I'm right here."

"Can I stay on your lap? Please!"

He ruffled her hair and smiled. "If you eat everything on your plate."

"Including the vegetables?"

"Yes."

Belinda's nose wrinkled and her lip twisted with disgust, but she reached for her fork. When lightning flashed again, she pressed her face to Noah's shirt. He kept his arm around her.

The expression on his face made Emma uncomfortable, because it was private between the little girl and her doting father. She looked away and smiled swiftly at Gladys, who was taking a bowl of peas from Sean. He let go of it too quickly, but Gladys caught it before it could fall to the floor, scattering the peas across the rug.

Emma was about to chide Sean for being so careless, then saw *his* expression. He was staring at Noah and Belinda with both disbelief and envy. Wanting to reach across the table to take the boy's hand and say how sorry she was that he was so far from any family he might have still alive, she folded her hands in her lap. Saying that would embarrass everyone at the table.

Turning away so Sean would not see her dismay, she was astonished to see Noah staring at *her*. What did he hope to see—or was it nothing more than that he had seen Sean's dismay and was trying to avoid looking at the boy, too? No, for his gaze edged along her face like a caress. Her fingers curled against her palm before she could give in to the yearning to touch his whisker-scored cheeks as she had by the creek.

Gladys began to talk about the weather. A safe topic, Emma decided, though if this storm became a cloudburst, both the creek and the Ohio would threaten a rampage through the low-lying areas.

She ate, but barely tasted the food. The way Sean swallowed his chicken with gusto, she guessed it was delicious. She tried not to think of how Noah had kissed her with the same fervor, forcing her thoughts to focus on her store. Although the village was high enough above the river to be safe, she needed to bring out the supplies she kept ready in the storage room for those who might get flooded out.

Emma did not realize she had finished until Gladys went into the kitchen and came back into the dining room with a chocolate cake. Putting it on the table, she sliced through the dark frosting. Crumbs fell across the plate that she held out to Sean.

"For me?" he asked, not taking it.

"Yes." Gladys looked at Emma, clearly confused.

"It's your dessert, Sean," Emma said in a hushed voice. "Take it and thank Gladys."

"Thank you," he said in the most insincere tone she had ever heard. His nose turned up. "Miss Delancy, you can't want me to eat *this*. It looks disgusting!"

"Sean!" she gasped. "Remember your manners."

"*My* manners? I'm not trying to serve someone dirt."

Gladys chuckled. "Dirt, do you say, my boy? Is that any way to talk about my fine cake? You certainly liked the looks of it when it was in the kitchen."

"Then it was all fine and covered with smooth candy."

"There's no candy on the cake."

"Saw it myself. Sure, that I did." His brogue thickened as he argued with the housekeeper. "Thick brown candy melted all over it."

Emma said quietly, "I believe he's describing the icing on the cake."

"Icing?" Sean regarded her with a scowl. "Miss Delancy, it's too warm for ice. If it'd been cold enough, the creek wouldn't be racing like a copper after a pickpocket."

"If he isn't going to try it," Gladys said, "I shall. I never let a good dessert go to waste." She patted her side. "Just to *my* waist. The mark of every cook."

As the others laughed, Sean scowled. Belinda slid off her father's lap and walked over to him. Handing Sean a fork, she said, "Try it. It's good."

"It looks like dirt."

"It isn't dirt. It's cake. Try it."

Sean hesitated, then dug his fork into the cake, taking mostly frosting and only a few crumbs of cake. That he was willing to trust Belinda and not either Emma or Gladys was yet another reminder of how he had lived in a world where no adult was trustworthy. He might trust Emma enough to work for her and let her offer him a room in her house, but he could not believe she would not sit and watch while he was served dirt on a fine china plate.

Slowly he raised the fork to his mouth. He sucked the piece of cake off from it so quickly that she knew he barely trusted Belinda as well. He gasped and dug his fork into the cake, this time getting less of the icing and more of the cake. He bent over the plate, eating it so quickly that Emma feared he would choke.

Noah laughed and put his hand on the boy's shoulder. "You don't have to wolf it down. There's plenty of cake, because Gladys always makes two. So enjoy it and have another piece if you want."

"What is it?" Sean asked, his eyes wide.

"Chocolate cake." Emma hesitated before asking, "Haven't you had chocolate cake before?"

"No, ma'am. I wouldn't forget something that tasted like this. It may look like dirt, but it tastes like heaven."

Gladys choked back a gasp, but Emma knew this proud boy would not want anyone's sympathy. Reaching for another piece of cake, she put it on a plate and set it in front of where Belinda had been sitting. The little girl rushed around the table to enjoy her own dessert.

In the most off-hand voice she could manage, Emma said, "If you think this is good, Sean, wait until summer comes and we make ice cream."

"Ice cream?" He paused, leaving his fork halfway to his

mouth. His eyes glistened with excitement. "You have ice cream here in Indiana?"

"We will in the summer, when there's nothing better than to sit on the porch and enjoy a big bowl."

"Is it safe?"

"What do you mean, Sean?" Noah asked. "Why wouldn't it be just fine to enjoy some ice cream?"

Sean looked around the table, then put his fork back on his nearly empty plate. "I know you all have been trying to be nice to me, but I do know how to fire a gun."

"Do you now?" Noah glanced at Emma and was not surprised to see her face abruptly pale. No doubt, she was imagining this lad helping himself to someone's Colt and firing it off on Haven's street. She had let her generous heart persuade her to take in this child, but now she was having to deal with the reality of an urchin who had survived the tough streets of New York on his own.

"Sure." He grinned, his thin chest puffing with pride. "I learned from Dickie when I started doing errands for him in Satan's Circus."

Gladys made a choking sound as if she had swallowed a chicken bone.

"Satan's Circus?" Noah asked carefully.

"That's the name some preacher gave to the area where I lived around Fifth Avenue and Thirtieth Street." Sean took another bite of cake, oblivious to the sudden silence around the table. "Dickie kept a saloon and a bordello. He sometimes let me sweep up, which was good because then some kind gent would let me finish his dinner while he went off with Gini or Mabel or one of the other gals. Usually I just ran errands for him. Then I got a penny to buy my own supper."

"Sean," Emma began, "this isn't conversation for—"

"Let me." Noah pushed back his chair. "Sean, come with me."

"Where?" asked the boy, again the wary youngster who had tried to flee in Haven.

"Guns aren't a topic for ladies. Let's go in the kitchen and talk man to man."

Sean stood, but brought his plate with him as he went out into the kitchen.

At Emma's soft call of his name, Noah turned to see her on her feet, too. Her eyes looked almost as apprehensive as Sean's. That annoyed him more than he expected. By Jiggs! Did she expect him to take a hickory stick to the lad in his own kitchen? She should understand he wanted to keep Belinda and poor Gladys, who looked about ready to swoon, from hearing the lad's sordid tales.

He did not answer her as he went into the kitchen. As the door closed, he heard Emma asking Gladys if she needed a cool cloth for her forehead. Emma would be able to deal with his housekeeper. He needed to concentrate on finding out how much Sean knew about guns and firing them before the boy did something foolish like trying to show someone his skill.

This room was Gladys's realm, so she must have been very distressed to let him bring the boy in here without following after to be sure they did not jostle any of her cooking dishes or touch the big black stove that was set between two windows that gave a view of the area she planned to turn into a vegetable garden. Lightning flashed through the window and sparked its reflection in the water bucket by the back door. At the square table in the middle of room, Sean sat, finishing up his cake as his feet swung back and forth inches above the rag rug.

As the thunder sounded, closer than before, Noah glanced toward the window again. No rain yet. Maybe it was just a noise show that would pass the river valley by and head north, away from this watershed.

Noah pulled out the bench across from Sean. Sitting, he asked, "What did you mean by it not being safe to eat ice cream on Emma's front porch?"

"Indians, of course."

"What?" He fought not to laugh. All of this was about something so silly?

"This is *Indiana,* right?" Sean asked.

"Yes."

"So there must be Indians here!"

Noah feared he would choke on his laughter, but kept it from bursting forth as he said, "I'm sure there are, and I'm equally sure they're living in farm houses like this now, not tipis."

"Miss Delancy doesn't seem to be scared of them," Sean said as if he had not heard Noah. "She drives around without a gun in her wagon. She opened the door in the middle of the night when you brought the dog to have her take care of it. There could have been wild Indiana Indians on the other side, ready to take her scalp." He grimaced. "Women don't have a lick of sense, sometimes."

"Now who told you that?" This time, he could not keep from chuckling. He doubted if he had ever met a more sensible woman than Emma Delancy, for she ran her business with such good business judgment.

"Dickie."

Noah smiled. "You might be better off not mentioning your friend Dickie around here."

"Do you think some of his enemies will chase me out here and try to get me to tell them all of Dickie's secrets?"

"Maybe." He hated lying to the boy, but Sean needed to live in this small town instead of the foul streets where he had eked out a way to keep from starving until someone must have sent him to the Children's Aid Society. "Nice ladies don't like to hear about those sort of things."

"Oh." Sean's eyes grew round as he nodded. "I should have remembered that."

"Good." Standing, he smiled when he realized Sean's wide eyes were focused on the chocolate cake. "Do you want some more?"

"Yes, sir, Mr. Sawyer. I sure would."

"Help yourself to as much as you'd like."

"Thank you, Mr. Sawyer." He reached for the knife.

"All the knives in this house are for cooking and eating. Do you understand?"

"Yes, sir, Mr. Sawyer."

"And no guns here or in Miss Delancy's house or the store."

"But what if some thief comes in and tries to steal from her?"

Noah shook his head. "Not even then. Sheriff Parker is in Haven to take care of such things. Do you understand?"

"Yes, sir, Mr. Sawyer."

Noah suspected the boy would have agreed to just about anything if Noah would stop talking so Sean could have another piece of cake. He saw the boy set the knife to cut a huge slab. Sean glanced at him and shifted the knife to a more reasonably sized piece.

More than ever, Noah was certain Emma had absolutely no idea of what she had let herself in for with this kid. Had he when Belinda came into his life? But at least he had known her from the day she was born. He wondered how many more secrets Sean held in his past and how Emma would handle them.

Secrets . . .

He pushed through the door and back into the dining room before that thought could take form. This was not the time to let unspoken secrets intrude. He had worked too hard for too long to make a mistake now.

Emma knelt on the floor to tuck the blanket under the pallet where Sean would sleep tonight. On the bed set beneath the window that sliced through the slanted ceiling, Belinda was already asleep. On the bottom of her bed, the puppy was sleeping with its head on its paws. The bandage on its back leg glowed like an angel's wings in the light from the hallway.

In a whisper, she said, "If you need anything, Sean, I'll be in the room right across the hall."

"Miss Delancy?"

"Yes?" She wished he would call her Emma as Belinda already did, but she must wait until he was comfortable enough to believe he could live here in Haven for as long as he wanted.

"If we stay here tonight, Cleo and Queenie and Butch won't have anyone to look after them."

"Alice Underhill always comes over to check on them when she sees that the wagon hasn't returned. Sometimes my deliveries take even longer than today's."

His nose wrinkled. "The schoolteacher?"

"One and the same. She's a good friend."

"Why would anyone have a teacher for a *friend?*"

Emma heard Noah's muted laugh from the doorway. She hoped Sean did not, because he needed to learn to fit in at school and to do his lessons. Alice had told her that, for now, Sean was the only one off the orphan train who was attending the village school. Maybe the situation would be easier when some of the other children from the train came to school.

"Miss Underhill will check on the animals," she replied,

"so you can get some rest. If you need to get up for any reason, don't wake Belinda."

"I know how to be quiet. I could tiptoe in and out of any crib without anyone being the wiser."

"Crib?" she asked.

Noah cleared his throat before saying, "He's speaking of a bordello, Emma."

"Don't worry," Sean went on. "I'll be quiet, and I'll be here to let Belinda know that the thunder won't harm her. Just as I did for Kitty Cat in New York."

"You had a kitten?" she asked.

He grinned. "Kitty Cat is a little girl. Her real name is Katherine Mulligan, and she came here with me on the train. Me and Brendan Rafferty took care of all the little ones on the way here." His smile wavered, and tears rose up into his eyes. "I hope Kitty Cat is all right."

She brushed a stubborn cowlick back from his forehead. "I can ask Reverend Faulkner which family she is with. Then maybe you can go and see her."

"I know where she is. I saw her today."

"At Mr. Hammond's farm?"

He shook his head. "At the last place we stopped."

Emma stiffened, but kept her smile from vanishing. The last place they had stopped was the River's Haven Community. Although she did business with the residents there, she did not approve of their odd ways of having what she had heard described as ever-changing marriages.

"Why don't you go to sleep now?" She came to her feet and slipped out of the room.

Noah left the door open a crack, then turned to her. The hall seemed abruptly too narrow, making her feel as if drawing in a single breath would be dangerous. He did not move, and she did not dare. Would her feet carry her toward the stairs or into his arms? She could not risk finding out.

She was unsure if he sensed her disquiet, but he motioned toward the stairs. When he stepped back so she could pass, she rushed down the steps, her petticoats whispering behind her. She paused at the base of the stairs. This was not her home, so she could not wander about without an invitation.

Again she wondered if he could read her very thoughts, because he said, "Let's go into the parlor where we can sit and talk more comfortably."

"Thank you." She entered the room and faltered. The furnishings were, like the ones in the dining room, an exact copy of a page out of a catalog. Every item was here, just as it should be, from the brass andirons on the hearth to the painting of a snowy winter hill on the opposite wall. The sofa and its matching chair were covered in burgundy fabric that was the perfect complement to the braided rug that reached nearly to each wall.

Only one thing was different. A photograph of a young woman was the sole item set on the mantel. Wanting to ask if that was Noah's late wife, she forced her gaze away from it as she sat on the sofa that was stiff with newness.

"I think the storm has passed," Emma said to keep the silence from becoming overwhelming.

"The one outside? Yes, thank heavens." He sat on the chair to her left, surprising her. She had thought he would sit beside her. Maybe he had his own reasons for being cautious so that what had happened by the creek did not occur again. He let his clasped hands dangle between his knees as he leaned toward her. "What about the one inside you?"

"Inside me?"

"You went as rigid as a tree trunk upstairs when Sean was talking about his friend."

"It wasn't because of his friend. It was because he was speaking of the River's Haven Community."

"Ah. When he told you that the little girl was at River's Haven, you were bothered more than when you heard about Sean's activities in New York."

"His *activities* in New York are a part of his past now. What goes on out there is right here."

He sat straighter. "That statement doesn't sound like you, Emma. You've always seemed to me to be the champion of the misunderstood."

In spite of herself, she laughed. "Is that how you really see me?"

"That was my first impression."

"Noah, I don't care what those who live out at River's Haven do. What I care about is Sean making friends and a home in Haven. If he pays calls out there, even to call on that little girl, he may be ostracized in town."

"You care a lot about this boy, don't you?"

"Someone must. I don't think anyone else ever has. Maybe the folks at the Children's Aid Society, but they ripped him out of the city that has been all he's ever known."

Something struck the window like a dozen small pebbles, and Emma flinched. Turning, she saw water washing down the glass. Pebbles would have been better than rain when the creek was so high.

Noah muttered something under his breath and stood. Going to the window, he put his face close to the glass to peer out into the night.

"Unless you have the eyes of a cat," she said to his back, "you aren't going to see much."

"You're right." Walking back to the middle of the room, he added, "Gladys said she would leave the coffeepot on. Do you want a cup?"

"At this hour? I shan't sleep a wink all night if I drink coffee now."

"Then sit with me while I have a cup." He scowled at

the window, where rain pelted the glass. "It may be a long night."

She looked at the window. The lamp's glow made the night a solid black wall beyond the window. Rising, she went to the front door and opened it. She stepped out onto the porch and listened.

Beneath the patter of the rain that was quickly growing heavy, she heard the unceasing roar of running water. She gripped the back of a rocking chair set to one side of the door next to the porch swing.

Knowing Noah had followed her outside, for she had heard his quiet footsteps, she said, "The creek is probably halfway up the road to here."

"I hope you're wrong. If the water has come that far, then all the wood I cut this week may be floating down into the Ohio. My only hope is that the logs will be caught by the standing trees downstream." He walked toward the steps to the yard.

"I'm right." She put her hand on his arm to stop him. "Don't go. The water is already too high and too fast for you to get back to your woodlot. I'm sorry, Noah, but I can tell by the sound of the water rushing past that it's about a quarter mile past the bridge."

"You can tell that just by the noise?"

She nodded. "I've been in Haven for over seven years now. I've seen the Ohio and the small creeks rise more quickly than you could believe possible. Here, along the river, anyone who doesn't pay attention to nature's signs is going to be in trouble. It would have been better and safer if the snow had melted more slowly."

"The snow was gone here before we moved in."

"But it takes longer to melt up in the hills and mountains east of here. All that water rushes down into the Ohio faster than the river can hold it." She jumped back as wind blew rain onto the porch. "That's why Haven is built up on the hill, not along the shore. It got flooded out when it was first built, and folks were smart enough not to let it happen again."

He stared through the darkness. "Something makes me suspect Collis sold this farm to me because he was tired of the water flowing out of the creek."

"No," she said with a soft sigh. "He left because his wife and baby sickened with measles and died last fall. I don't think he could bear to look at this place, because it was so full of memories. He told me he was moving out west, but I think he was running away."

"Do you blame him?"

"Of course not. Lots of people run away for lots of reasons." She wanted to bite back the words, but it was too late.

Noah turned to face her. In the light that filtered through the dining room curtains, she could see his expression—a mixture of amazement and wariness. Why would *he* be upset by her stupid remark? Unless . . . through the window she could see the obviously new furniture. She searched his face, looking for sorrow. When she found it in the lines threading his forehead, lines she had not taken note of before, her own eyes swam with tears. Were Noah and his sweet little daughter fleeing tragedy, too? Not even a whisper of gossip in Haven hinted at what had happened to his wife. Maybe she had died as devastatingly as Mr. Collis's wife and child.

She wanted to ask, but again halted herself. The simple act of inquiring might convince him to try to open the door to her own reasons for being in Haven. That must stay as closed and locked as the jail cell where Miles had spent his last night before his hanging.

Noah's hands on her shoulders turned her slowly to face him, freeing her from her own memories. Even with darkness enfolding them, her eyes were held by the shadowed intensity in his. His kiss burned into her lips with the power of the lightning. She pressed to him, unable to lie to herself any longer. She was intrigued by this dynamic, enigmatic man.

His hand swept along her back, bringing her closer to his hard muscles, which had been sculpted by long hours of work. The longings awakened beside the creek surged through her. She wanted to touch him, to be touched with the craving that swept all other thoughts from her head.

Yet even as she answered his need with her own, she slowly became aware of a sound. She turned her head, but his fingers against her cheek brought her mouth back to his.

"Noah!"

"Hush, sweetheart," he whispered, his lips brushing hers with a bewitchment that surged through her.

"The water! The barn!" she gasped as he seared her neck with liquid fire, each touch of his tongue an effervescent ecstasy.

"Let the barn float away." His fingers combed through her hair, loosening it to swirl around his hands. Capturing her anew with his compelling eyes, he tilted her lips beneath his.

Exerting all her strength, for she had to fight her own longing to stay in his arms, Emma broke away from his embrace. "Are you mad? Can't you hear the water is getting closer?"

Noah frowned. "It's getting louder. You were right, Emma. Lots of folks have lots of reasons for putting some miles between them and the past. I just hope we don't need to put some miles between us and the creek before daylight." He slapped the railing and cursed as the water pooled there splashed him. "If this rain would stop, the creek would be certain to go down."

"It may not be the creek you need to worry about if the Ohio climbs the hill."

"Don't even say that!"

"You have to keep the bigger disaster in mind."

"I've had enough big disasters to know they never can be out of my mind." He cursed again and reached for the door.

"Noah, what are you talking about?"

"Don't ask tonight. We've got too much trouble on our hands now to worry about anything else."

She was unsure whether to be distressed or grateful that he had put an end to this conversation inching toward dangerous territory that must be left unexplored. What she did know was that this man embodied a greater peril than anyone she had met in Haven, because he was tempting her to lower the walls she had built with such care after she fled Kansas.

CHAPTER EIGHT

Noah stood by the fence. He ignored the rain and the darkness. All he saw was the water flowing through the fallow field.

He glanced toward the sky and muttered, "Fire and flood. What's next? Pestilence?"

Keeping the umbrella Emma had insisted he bring over his head, he walked to the barn. The horses shifted nervously until he reached over the stall door and patted them.

"Don't worry. You aren't going to drown." He grimaced. "Now I'm talking to horses. Maybe you were right, Ron. Maybe I am losing my mind to attempt this." He cursed under his breath, then aloud. His younger brother had not been right when he said Noah's plans were doomed to failure. He had not been right five years ago, and he was not right now.

Opening the barn's back door, Noah shook his head as

he stared at the bloated Ohio River. He swore he could see it rising even as he stood there. It was not far below the lip of the hill. If the water reached the top, it would flood the rest of the fields as well as the barn. The house was set a bit higher, but it would be cut off from everything else on its little island until the water cascaded through its rooms as well.

He sighed as he turned to retrace his steps. The wind grasped at the umbrella, but he did not let it soar away. Walking up to the house, he shook water off the umbrella before he went inside.

Gladys rushed to take his coat out to the kitchen where it could dry by the stove. She clucked like a hen fretting about her chicks.

Noah smiled. Gladys had been with him for longer than Belinda had, and the housekeeper had accepted—without too much grousing—every change they had gone through in the past five years.

His smile faded as he saw Emma standing in the doorway to the dining room. She held out a steaming cup to him, and he found himself imagining her welcoming him home like this night after night. A foolish fantasy. Not only would she usually be busy at the store during the hour when he finished his chores, but his life was too full of complications now. He hoped to stay here on this farm, yet knew that might not be possible. Her feet were planted firmly in Haven. He needed to be ready to go wherever he had to in order to protect Belinda.

"Is it so bad?" she asked, and he knew she believed his unsettled thoughts were focused on the creek.

Where they should be, instead of noting how her blouse had come loose from her black skirt on her right side. His gaze edged up from her slender waist to her breasts, which were outlined by the lace along the front of her blouse. It

was, he noted, rumpled from where he had pulled her into
his arms.

He took the cup of coffee she handed him. Taking her
hand, he laced his fingers through hers. The warmth of her
palm against his invited him to pull her into his arms again.
Instead, he said, "It isn't good, Emma. The creek is already
in the field across the road, and the Ohio is almost to top
of the hill behind the barn."

Emma swallowed hard. She had other questions, but she
doubted if her voice could be as calm as his. When his
fingers squeezed hers, she drew her hand out of his. Clear
thinking was not easy when he touched her. Turning so she
did not have to see his reaction, she asked, "Don't you think
some of this furniture should be moved upstairs?"

"I want to let the children sleep for as long as possible."
He ran his hand along the dining room table. "I doubt if I
could get this up those narrow stairs alone."

"I'd be glad to help."

" 'Tis kind of you to offer, Emma, but I wouldn't ask a
woman to—"

"Balderdash!" She sat, resting her elbows on the table.
When he pulled out his chair and sat, she added, "I tote
about heavy crates and cans all day at the store, so I can
help move some furniture. It'd be a shame for all your new
furniture from Chicago to be ruined."

"Chicago?" His wide hand pinned her wrist to the table
as he slammed down his cup and glowered at her. "What
gave you the idea this furniture came from Chicago?"

She frowned. "Release me."

"Answer my question."

"When you release me and explain why you're acting
like a madman simply because I expressed concern about
your things."

His fingers slowly lifted off her wrist. Picking up his

cup, he took a deep drink. The silence dragged on, and she wondered if he was waiting for her to say something more or change the subject. She would, if she could think of anything other than his angry expression. There had been something else in his eyes, a wild, fearsome glow that frightened her.

Finally he said, "I'm sorry, Emma." He sighed.

"Tell me why my question upset you so much."

"If you tell me how you know this furniture came from Chicago." He smiled abruptly. "Turnabout is fair play, they say, and speaking of that will keep my thoughts off the swelling creek."

She let some of the tension ease off her shoulders and nodded. Caught up in his peculiar response to her comment, she had forgotten—for a moment—the real trouble looming not so far from his front door.

"Fair enough," she replied. "I saw this very room of furniture in a catalog put out by a company in Chicago. They were one of the first to rebuild after the fire." She glanced at the window as another flash of lightning blinded the darkness, making it seem even deeper. "I'm not sure which is worse—fire or flood."

"I would prefer not to have to face either tonight." He stood and went to the window. "I should check on the barn and make sure the horses aren't up to their withers in water."

"You haven't answered my question. What upset you?"

He did not face her. "You."

"Me?" Her voice came out in a squeak.

"Yes, you." He came back around the table and drew her to her feet. "You've upset me more than anyone has in a long time. When I should be thinking of a week's work being lost as it glides away down the Ohio, I think instead of how your golden hair refuses to stay in its bun."

She put her hand up to her hair, but he drew it aside as

his finger teased the soft, sensitive skin directly behind her
ear. An unstoppable thrill soared along every nerve, setting
each one afire with a craving that ached deep within her.
As his lips curved in a smile, she raised her gaze to meet
his eyes. She could no more look away than she could have
willed her heart to stop the frantic pulse echoing through
her in a wild rhythm which somehow matched the beguiling
stroke of his fingertip.

"Can you read my thoughts?" he whispered.

She almost said yes, for she had few doubts what he was
thinking when he spellbound her with a simple caress. In a
voice as low as his, she answered, "Why do you ask that?"

"Because I was thinking in the foyer about how I'd like
to hold you again, and you've given me the very opportunity
I was wishing for."

With his finger beneath her chin, he tilted her face back.
So slowly she nearly cried out her longing for his touch, he
bent to kiss her. The tip of his tongue caressed her lips,
heating them to a flame which burst into wildfire when his
mouth claimed hers. She stroked the hard muscles of his
back as she boldly teased his tongue with her own. Stepping
closer to him, she exulted in the unyielding planes of his
body.

"Mr. Sawyer, I . . . well, well! It's about time." Gladys's
chuckle had a very satisfied sound.

Emma eased out of Noah's arms, but he kept his arm
around her waist. With a laugh as lighthearted as his housekeeper's, he asked, "Time for what?"

Gladys winked at Emma. "I swear, Mr. Sawyer, you
haven't spoken a sentence in the last week that didn't include
Miss Delancy's name in it. 'Tis about time you stopped
talking." Untying her apron, she added, "I'm going to go
to bed now, Mr. Sawyer. Let me know if you need anything."

She chuckled as she reached for the door. "Looks as if you've got all you can handle right now."

As the door closed, Emma laughed. She handed the cup of coffee back to Noah as he regarded her with a smile. "Don't look so amazed," she said. "Haven may look pretty settled now, but it was a bit rougher around the edges when I first got here. I've heard much worse."

"About you?"

"Not in Haven."

"What convinced a young woman to come here to take over the general store?" he asked, toying with a loose strand of her hair.

Something struck the house, and he rushed to the front door. Emma was relieved at the interruption. What had she been thinking to allow the conversation to wander in the direction of her past?

"I need to go and check what that was," Noah said, grabbing another coat from the hook in the hall. "Stay here."

Emma ran to get the umbrella, but he was gone before she reached it. She flinched when she heard something else bang into the house. The wind was rising along with the water. Being outside was more perilous than ever, but she could not quell her curiosity. She reached to open the door to see what might be visible from the porch.

She froze as she heard a sharp cry of, "Help me!" It did not come from outside, but from upstairs. Whirling, she grabbed a handful of skirts and lifted them to an immodest height as she raced up the stairs. She ran along the hall and threw open the partially closed bedroom door. The moaning became louder.

One of the children! She took a single step, and her foot struck something soft. She heard another groan.

Dropping to her knees, she gasped, "Sean! What's wrong?"

"Sick," he whispered. He clawed at the floor, and she realized he was trying to get to the door. He was too sick to stand.

"Your stomach?"

"It's going to explode. I think I'm going to die."

She scooped him up into her arms. She tried to stand, but dropped back to her knees. Pain rushed across them, but she paid it no mind. Again she fought to stand. A hand under her elbow assisted her. She nodded her thanks to Gladys.

"Take him to the parlor. I'll bring a bucket," the housekeeper ordered.

Emma nodded again. Her teeth were clenched too hard to speak. She hoped she could get down the stairs without dropping Sean. The boy was heavier than she had guessed. She hurried along the hallway at the best pace she could manage.

He moaned as she carried him down the stairs. Gladys reached them with a bucket just as Sean threw up. Sitting on the bottommost step, Emma kept her arms around him as his stomach fought to expel everything in it.

When he was done, she carried him into the parlor and placed him on the sofa. She was glad when Gladys followed with the bucket. The housekeeper handed her some damp cloths.

"Thank you," Emma said. "I had no idea he might be sick or I wouldn't have brought him here and chanced Belinda becoming ill, too."

"I don't think that's why he is sick." Gladys lingered by the sofa. "I noticed when I went into the kitchen that the chocolate cake is gone."

Emma shook her head as she dabbed the cloth against boy's forehead. "Sean, you should have known better."

"It was so good." He groaned. "I never tasted anything like it. I was going to take just a little piece more. Then I . . ." His face became an odious shade of gray.

She held the bucket under him while he was sick again. When she leaned him back on the sofa, she heard the door open.

Noah came into the house, water dripping from every inch of him as his wet clothes adhered like a second layer of skin. She looked away. Now, when Sean was so sick, was not the time to admire those strong muscles so temptingly outlined against his soaked shirt and denims.

"Let's go," he said.

"Go?"

"Gladys, get Belinda. We have to leave. Now!" Striding into the parlor, he motioned with his head. "Let's go, Emma. I have your horse hooked to your wagon and mine saddled. You and Gladys and the children can ride in the wagon while I guide your horse."

"Can't we wait for dawn so we can see? We could drive right into the rising water."

"The river is rushing through the barn now. If we stay here another hour, we may be swimming in this room."

"There's a bridge farther up the creek that may be high enough to let us get across and into Haven, which should be safely above the water line." She heard her own uncertainty. If the water rose high enough to enter Haven, her store would be one of the first places underwater.

"Maybe."

"I have to hope so. It should be—" She turned back to Sean as the boy groaned and reached for the bucket again. She held it for him as he retched.

Noah frowned. She hastened to explain why Sean was ill, because she knew all of Noah's thoughts were about his daughter.

With a sigh, Noah said, "I did some stupid things myself when I was a boy. Can he travel?"

"I can," Sean averred, trying to lift his head. He groaned and dropped back onto the sofa.

As he reached to pick up the boy, Emma said, "Just a moment." She gathered her skirts up and ran into the kitchen. Snatching Sean's dry coat from the chair set near the stove, she carried it back into the parlor. "Put this on, so he doesn't get wet and take a chill."

"Hurry. We're all going to be wet if we don't leave," Noah replied.

A squeal of excitement came from the front hall, and she saw Belinda wiggling in Gladys's arms. Behind them, the puppy followed gamely, even though he limped on each step.

"Let's go!" Gladys grabbed an umbrella and hurried out the door.

Emma started to follow them, but paused when Noah called her name. Startled, because he had been so determined for them to leave without delay, she turned.

"Will you bring Martha's photograph with you?" he asked quietly.

She nodded. Going to the fireplace, she lifted down the small frame and slipped it into a pocket in her skirt. "It should be safe here."

"Belinda would be heartbroken if it was lost." He hurried to the door and out onto the porch.

She heard him calling instructions to Gladys and knew she should rush after him. Instead, she looked around the room. It was as perfect as the pictures, but she feared, with the picture now in her pocket, this parlor had as little life as the items in the catalog. Everything was too new, and there was nothing to suggest Noah and his daughter lived here. With a sad sigh, she went to the door.

The wind grasped her in dozens of hands and tried to shove her along the porch. When she wobbled, stronger hands caught her. She gazed up into Noah's taut face, lit by the lantern on the wagon and the lamps in the house.

"I should go back in and blow out the lamps!" she cried.

"Why? If the water rises much more, they'll be doused. If the house escapes the flooding, the lamps will burn themselves out." He held out his hand.

Again she did not have to ask him what he wanted. She pulled the frame out of her pocket and handed it to him. He wrapped it in a piece of oilcloth and stuck it under his coat. Draping another piece of the heavy cloth over her shoulders, he steered her to the wagon and handed her, from the upper step, right onto the front seat.

Emma gasped as the rain struck her face as it was driven by the wind. She looked back to see the others beneath a huge tarpaulin covered with enough pieces of bark for her to know Noah must have taken it from where he had been protecting dried wood from the weather.

"Will you be able to drive?" Noah jumped over the railing and grasped the reins of his horse.

"Yes." She shivered as Gladys put Belinda, who was now wearing the kitchen tablecloth over her head, on the seat beside Emma. The little girl held an umbrella over Emma's head, but it could not protect her from the rain that was nearly vertical. "Sit down, Belinda, and keep the umbrella over your head."

"But, Emma, you'll get all wet."

"I have to be able to see where your father is going."

With a lead that was connected to Toby, Noah asked, "Which way?"

"To the left."

He laughed tightly. "*That* I knew."

Emma smiled in spite of the rain. "I guess you did. We'll

be turning left again onto a road about a half mile from here. It should lead us right to the bridge. If it's out, Samuel Jennings's farm is about another mile past it.''

Noah bowed his head as the storm swirled around them and gave the command to Patches to start. Behind him, he heard Emma echoing his command to her horse. He tried to see through the storm. Just as he was going to call to Emma to darken the lantern, its light vanished.

Water splashed beneath the horse, and he heard the wagon striking the puddles in the deepening pool where his yard had been. He should have gotten them out of here after the previous time he had checked the barn. Instead he had waited, hoping the river would halt its steady progress up the hillside. Looking over his shoulder, he saw the bright windows of the house. There was nothing there that could not be replaced . . . again.

Just where Emma had told him there would be a road to the left, he turned. The road here was thick mud. He could feel Toby straining to pull the wagon through it. If the old horse refused to move forward, they would be reduced to walking. But the old horse kept going.

"Here!" called Emma. "Turn left here to get to the bridge."

Wondering how she could see what he did not, he reminded himself she had been traveling these roads for seven years. He squinted through the rain and saw a narrow road on the left. It looked barely wide enough between two lines of trees to allow the wagon through. He turned onto it and looked back to be certain Emma could steer her wagon between the trees.

"Keep going!" she shouted as she competently guided the horse onto the path. "This bridge isn't too much higher above the creek than the other one."

Wondering if there was anything this woman could not

handle with competence, Noah continued down the road. The roar of the creek became deafening. When he released Toby's head, he drew his horse beneath the trees as he let the wagon pass until he could take the lantern off its side. He saw Emma's grim but resolute expression when she glanced at him.

"I'm going ahead to see if the bridge is still there," he said.

"Good! I'm not sure if I could turn the wagon here, and Toby balks at going backward very far."

Noah bent and kissed her quickly. He saw her smile as he opened the lantern. Taking that sight with him to help battle off the storm, he rode through the trees until he was ahead of the wagon. Back on the road, he followed it toward the creek.

Water was being thrown up onto the shore, but the bridge was still there. He sighed with relief until he noted how narrow and rickety it appeared in the lantern light. Hearing the wagon rattle up behind him, he held the lantern high, so Emma could see him. He went back to where she sat next to Belinda.

Emma's hair was in drenched strands around her shoulders, but she smiled as she said, "It's still here."

"I'm not sure how strong it is, so I'll go first."

"Noah—"

"Don't argue with me about this, Emma. I'm not going to risk all of you."

"Just yourself?"

He took one of her hands off the reins and pressed his mouth to it. He was sure the water must sizzle away, for her skin was lusciously warm, even in the midst of this damp, chilled night. Or was it his own reaction to her loveliness and her concern for him? He could not recall the last time someone had been concerned *for* him, just *about* what he might do.

"Wait here," he said. "I'll call back if it's safe to traverse."

"We could just go on to Samuel Jennings's farm."

"I know you want to check on the store." Seeing her eyes grow wide with astonishment, he did not give her a chance to reply. He rode toward the bridge.

His horse shied, and he guessed Patches was spooked by the sound of the fast water. Patting the horse on the neck, he swung down out of the saddle. He considered leaving Patches here while he crossed the bridge, but the horse's weight would help determine if it was safe for the wagon to cross.

He drew in a deep breath, wiped rain out of his eyes, and grabbed the reins. The bridge creaked even before he stepped onto it, and he knew it was fighting the current that was trying to wash it away. Holding the lantern out so he could watch where he placed his feet, he put his foot on the bridge. It was surprisingly solid. He crossed the boards, wanting to cheer when Patches stepped off on the other side.

He thought of lashing Patches's reins to a bush, but let them fall to the ground. If for some reason he could not get back across, he did not want the horse to be bound here and drown. Patches whinnied lowly, and he patted the horse's haunches.

"Saying thank you or good-bye?" he asked, then laughed. "I'm talking to horses again."

He raced back across the bridge and lifted the children out of the wagon. Lowering the back, he helped Gladys out.

"Go!" he ordered. "Get across while you can."

Gladys grasped both children by the hand and rushed into the darkness.

He reached up to help Emma down from the driver's seat,

but she cried, "What are you doing? Get over to the other side, then call me to let me know you're out of the way."

"Do you think I'm going to let you drive this wagon across that bridge?"

"No, you aren't going to *let* me. I'm going to do it because I'm familiar with both Toby and this wagon. You aren't. That bridge is barely wide enough for the wagon to cross, and you could drive a wheel off the side and send the wagon and Toby and you into the creek."

"Emma, be sensible."

"*You* be sensible." She slanted toward him, her wet palm curving along his cheek. "Go, Noah, please!"

For a moment, Emma thought Noah would argue more. Then he nodded. "But I'm going to go right in front of you so you can see where you are driving."

"All right," she said with reluctance. She did not want him to be on the bridge with her and the wagon. If the bridge collapsed, they would both be killed. Then Sean and Belinda would have no one but Gladys.

He grasped Toby's leading rein again and looked back at her. She slapped the reins lightly to tell Toby to go forward. Steeling herself for the old horse to refuse to go over the bridge, she released the breath burning in her chest when each step of his heavy hoofs echoed on the boards. She could barely hear the sound over the crash of the water against the bridge supports.

She shrieked when the bridge was struck. Debris hit her. Bark and twigs. A tree must have been ripped out of the ground and washed here.

"Let go of Toby!" she cried.

"Emma—"

"Go! Off the bridge! Now!"

The lantern light bounced as he raced toward the other

shore. She slapped the reins on the horse's back. "Get us out of here, Toby!"

The bridge wobbled as it was battered again. She tightened her grip on the reins in case Toby got one of his strange ideas. She quickly realized the only idea he had in his head now was the same one she had. With the speed of a horse half his age, he pulled the wagon across the bridge.

She cried out in terror when one of the wheels bounced off the boards. Toby did not slow. The wagon struck the far shore, sending a concussion of pain through her. She did not release the reins as the wagon bounced up and onto solid ground.

Drawing in the reins, she closed her eyes and let the rain and wind twist around her like an insane whirlpool. She heard a crack and turned in the seat to see Noah standing by the shore. In the light from the lantern, she saw the bridge was now encased in the branches of some huge tree. The branches broke and were forced beneath the bridge even as she watched.

He walked to where she sat. Putting his hand on her knee, he asked, "How are you?"

"Tired and cold and wanting to get out of the rain," she said, setting her hand atop his. "Let's get back to Haven."

He smiled. "That may be the best idea I've heard all night."

"Me, too, Noah." She began to laugh.

"What's so amusing?"

"Noah and the flood."

"We may need to build an ark or two if it keeps raining like this."

She looked up at the sky. "It won't be stopping before morning."

This time, he did not ask her how she knew about the vagaries of weather along the river. He just nodded. When he had helped the children and Gladys back into the wagon, he swung up into his saddle. He handed her the lantern, and she darkened it.

"How far are we from Haven?" he asked.

"If we don't have to bypass any water, we should be there in an hour." Emma looked over the back of the seat. "Are you all set?"

"We're set," Gladys answered.

"How is Sean?"

"Better," the boy replied, his voice still weak.

Following Noah and his horse, she steered the wagon beneath the trees and toward Haven. The name had never seemed more appropriate.

CHAPTER NINE

"I am afraid it will be very crowded," Emma said as she pulled another pillow from the very back of the linen closet. She handed it to Belinda, who carried it into the room that had become Sean's. The little girl and Gladys would be sleeping in his bed tonight. Sean had a pallet in the kitchen, where he was already asleep with Cleo and Queenie curled up against him. The two dogs had been sent to the stable because neither of them would stop barking.

"No more crowded than we would have been at my house," Noah replied. He handed two blankets to Gladys and set two more on the floor.

Until they arrived at her house, Emma had not guessed Noah had put some supplies under the oilcloth along with Gladys and Sean. He had brought the blankets and food into the house while she was checking the store.

Although the furious rush of the river could be heard even

through the downpour and the closed windows, the river's water was not close to reaching the top of the hill where Haven sat. Soaked and tired, Emma had come back to the house, promising herself she would get up early and have the store open for anyone who might need emergency supplies. She had quickly changed into dry clothes and braided her hair like Belinda's so the wet mass did not strike her on every step.

Emma watched with a smile as Belinda gave her father an enthusiastic kiss good night. Gladys steered the little girl into Sean's bedroom.

"Let me help," Noah said as he turned to her and held out his arms.

For a moment, Emma considered throwing herself into those strong arms as she gave in to the panic she had submerged during the trip from his farm. She only handed him the blankets and pillows for the sofa in the parlor. She gathered up more of the wet clothes that had been piled in the hallway. Going downstairs, she tiptoed into the kitchen and hung them to dry by the stove.

She smiled when she smelled freshly brewed tea. Gladys must have made it before she had gone upstairs to bed. Unlike coffee, tea never kept Emma awake, and its warmth would be comforting tonight. She poured two cups, then eased back out of the kitchen, closing the door behind her so they did not disturb Sean.

"Some tea, Noah?" she asked, trying to sound cheerful.

He shook his head. "Not now." He was at the window and staring out at the storm.

She set down both cups. Going to him, she leaned her cheek against the strong sinews of his back. Her arms slipped around him, curving up along his chest as she whispered, "Thank you for getting us all back here safely."

"Me? *You* were our guide. If you hadn't been there, I'd

probably be stuck back on the other side of the creek, bailing out the parlor now." He cursed, then added, "I never expected to be flooded out right after we moved in there."

"I'm so sorry."

"You've got nothing to be sorry for."

"You may have lost your home."

"It's a house. Everything in it can be replaced," he murmured. "I'm just very grateful to you."

"*Just* very grateful?" she whispered.

With a low groan, he faced her and pulled her up against his chest. She wrapped one arm around his shoulder. Her fingertips grazed the rough texture of his cheek before stroking his lips, which could burn into her, revealing the pain and fear she had hidden during their precarious journey back to Haven. His face blurred as tears of commiseration filled her eyes.

He tilted her lips toward his as an odd intensity burned in his eyes. "No, I'm most assuredly not 'just very grateful,' Emma. Don't you think it's about time for me to admit that?"

His husky words seeped through her, washing away her fear into a stronger, infinitely sweeter sensation. Slowly her hand rose to sift through the wisps of his dark auburn hair that was only half dry. At her touch, that odd intensity deepened, and he drew her more tightly to him.

She could feel his heartbeat through his damp shirt. Its pounding matched the pulse roiling through her, faster, sharper, unrestrained. She steered his mouth toward hers.

His lips grazed hers, offering her a tenderness beyond any she could have imagined. Too quickly he raised his mouth away, and she looked look up into the magical, mysterious depths of his eyes. "Noah, please . . ."

"Please?"

"Don't stop with only that kiss."

He put his hands along the side of her face. Their coarse warmth thrilled her.

In a ragged voice, he whispered, "You don't know what you're asking."

"I do. I'm asking you to kiss me."

"Only that?"

"Isn't it enough for now?"

"You're a grown woman. I think you know what the answer to that is, sweetheart."

She looked away. She did know the answer to that, but she could not tell him how she knew it. Then she would have to explain she was really a widow, not a spinster. She shivered as she was caught, anew, in the horrific maw of her memories.

He whispered her name, and she met his eyes again. His finger beneath her chin drew her back toward him. Tingles pulsated from his fingertip, and she did not resist when he tilted her face upward.

"You look exhausted, Emma."

She was not sure whether she wanted to laugh at his jest or cry because he was not kissing her. With a sigh, she said, "You're right. I can't afford to be drowsy in the morning, because the store will be busy. Why don't we go to bed?"

"Now there is an invitation to be truly grateful for."

"Invitation? What invitation? What are you talking about *now?*"

"This."

This kiss was anything but cursory. His lips seemed determined to discover each inch of hers. As his arms tugged her up against him again, his tongue delved into her mouth with a scintillating, teasing caress. She heard her own breath grow uneven, but she gasped with pleasure when his mouth moved along her jaw and then trailed fire down her neck. His thumb gently tilted her chin so he could lave the curve of her ear with his tongue and his unsteady breath.

She quivered and pressed closer, fearing her knees would collapse as the bridge had. Her fingers sought up along his shirt, rumpling the damp fabric beneath them. Boldly, she slipped her hands beneath it and slid them up his back, savoring each firm sinew.

He drew in his breath sharply and combed his fingers through her hair to curve them along the nape of her neck. Tilting her head, he found her lips again. The rough texture of his day's growth of whiskers burnished her with yearning. Effervescent kisses sparkled across her cheeks and along her neck. Their eager breaths, straining to escape, merged and threatened to consume her. Her hands tightened on him. She wanted to hold on to him amid the storm of craving.

Slowly, reluctantly, his lips drew back from hers. Smiling, she twisted a single finger through the thick hair at his temple. He turned to kiss the sensitive skin at her wrist. When she gasped, shocked by the billow of craving that raced to the very tips of her toes, he chuckled.

"That invitation is the one I meant," he whispered. "You look at me with promises in your eyes, even as you send me off to sleep on this sofa alone."

"Sleep is what I need most tonight."

He laughed and kissed her lightly. "You sure know how to tell a man what he wants to hear!"

"I didn't mean—"

"Whatever you meant, you're right. Sleep is what I want most right now, too."

"Should I return the thanks for your gracious compliment?" She stepped back, hoping humor would cover the empty feeling when his arms were no longer around her.

"Sleep well, Emma. We both are going to be busy tomorrow."

"And tonight," she said as the door opened from the kitchen and Sean peeked out, his face a bilious shade of green. "I'll be right there with some ginger tea to ease your tummy, Sean."

He nodded and went back into the kitchen.

"Do you think you should send for the doctor?" Noah asked.

She shook her head. "There's no reason to ask Doc Bamburger to come out on such a stormy night when I can tend to Sean." Turning to Noah, she added, "Why don't you sleep in my room tonight? I should stay here close to Sean. I think he's going to have a rough night." She took a step toward the kitchen.

He halted her by catching her hand. "I don't want to sleep in your bed without you there, Emma."

She stared up into his hungry gaze, unable to speak. She must not say what she was thinking, for she wanted him there with her, too. But this was moving too fast. She had made a mistake once by letting a man sweep her off her feet. She could not do that again.

"Good night," she whispered.

"It could have been." His quick kiss threatened to blister her lips with its delicious fire. "Sleep well, sweetheart." Seizing her shoulders, he relit the flame on her mouth with his fervor. When he released her, he whispered, "Sleep well *tonight*, sweetheart."

She watched him walk up the stairs, but turned to go into the kitchen. It was going to be a very long night, and she needed every minute of it to think about what she was going to do about this longing for Noah Sawyer.

"I'll be with you in just a moment, Mr. Hammond," Emma said as she added another item to the lengthy list in

front of her on the counter. She was keeping a tab for each
of her customers, who would pay her when their crops were
sold in the fall. Also, she needed to know what to order by
telegraph down at the railroad station later today. The trains
were still running on the north-south rail, but she was not
sure how long that would continue. The waters were inching
closer and closer to the town.

The store was a chaotic mess, as she had guessed it would
be. Although she had come to unlock the door before the
clouds lightened with the rising sun, there were four customers waiting for her. All were looking for supplies to keep
them going while they tried to stave off the rising waters.
The rain had slowed from last night's cloudburst, but was
still falling.

"Let me help you with that," came Noah's voice from
the other side of the store.

He lifted a box down to hand to Mrs. Asbury. A box of
self-rising bread mix, she noted. When he handed her a can
of lard as well, Emma guessed Mrs. Asbury was planning
to make bread to send to the families who were refugees
from the flood.

As Emma finished adding up one customer's purchases,
it seemed two more arrived. She smiled as she saw the
children's delight with the candy jars she had set down
where they could reach them. Belinda sat on a wooden
kitchen chair next to the jars and announced to each child
that the candy was free today.

"She'd be a good barker at a circus," Emma said as Noah
came behind the counter to stack cans of beans for Reverend
Faulkner, who had welcomed three families to live in the
parsonage and four more who were sleeping in the meeting
room at the side of the church.

"She's enjoying being the center of attention with all the
older children gathered around her." He chuckled. "Since

she met Sean, she's been asking me to send her to school
here in town so she can see the other children.''

"It would be a good idea.''

"Not until the flood waters go down.''

She could not miss the frustration in his voice and the
regret in his eyes. Early this morning, he had tried to get
back across the creek to check on his house. The bridge was
still there, but the water was flowing over it now. He had
been forced to turn back.

"How much, Emma?'' asked Reverend Faulkner, drawing her attention back to him.

"Take them. No charge.''

"Emma!'' The minister wagged a finger at her. "I've
heard you say that over and over. You'll put yourself out
of business with such generosity.'' He tapped the counter.
"You tell me the fair price for these cans.''

"A dollar.'' She kept her smile in place, guessing that
he knew as well as she did that a dozen cans of beans and
another dozen of deviled meat usually cost at least twice
that amount.

He drew out his wallet and placed a dollar on the counter.
"A down payment only, Emma. I'll pay for the rest when
I can.''

"Reverend, there's no need. It's the very least I can do
for those who are flooded out.''

He looked past her to Noah and smiled. "I'd say you are
doing considerably more than the very least, Emma.'' He
tipped his somber hat to her. "Pray that the rain will stop
soon.''

"I have been!''

With a laugh, the minister edged out of the way so the
next customer could reach the counter.

Emma was kept so busy the rest of the morning she did
not realize it was past the time for lunch until her stomach

gave an embarrassingly loud growl. Before she could say anything to Mrs. Pelletier, who was staring at her in amazement, a sandwich was held out to her. She looked over her shoulder to see Gladys holding a very full plate of ham sandwiches.

"Just what I needed," Emma said with a smile.

"What you need is to take a few minutes to sit and eat without working." Noah gently elbowed her aside. "Go and eat. I'll take over here."

She pointed to the list. "Put each item sold on here, and then you should—"

"I think I can handle it." He ran the back of his hand along her cheek. "Trust me, sweetheart."

She heard the buzz of whispered comments from the other side of the counter, but she paid them no mind. Smiling at Noah, she said, "I do trust you."

"Because you'll be just over there watching everything I do?"

She laughed. "Exactly."

Slipping from behind the counter that was almost as bare as the store shelves were becoming, she sat on an empty cracker barrel next to the stove that was valiantly trying to fight back the dampness. Rain splattered in each time the door opened, and the floor had pools left by the water tracked in on boots.

Belinda came over and sat next to her in a rocking chair. The little girl's legs barely hung over the edge of the seat, but she got the chair rocking.

"Are you hungry?" Emma asked, holding out half of her sandwich.

"Nope. I already had two." She giggled, then said, "I mean, no thank you."

"You have very pretty manners, Belinda."

"And I'm pretty."

Emma grinned at the little girl's lack of modesty. "Yes, you are pretty. You have big brown eyes just like Noah."

"No, I look like my mother. Everyone says so."

"Oh." She did not want Belinda to know how amusing her assertion was. Cocking her head, she said, "Now that I look more closely, I think you are right."

"Have you ever seen my mother?"

"Only in the photograph on the mantel at your house."

Her nose wrinkled. "That doesn't look like me. That is an all-grown-up lady."

"Someday you'll be an all-grown-up lady, too."

"Maybe." She jumped down from the rocking chair and squeezed through the patrons to pass out more candy to the children coming into the store.

Emma ate her sandwich quickly. Many of her patrons were shocked to see Noah behind the counter, and she had listened to him repeat over and over that Emma had opened her house to his household. He was repaying her by helping at the store. Knowing looks were flashed in her direction, and she simply smiled back. Let the busybodies and the gossips have fun with this. Nothing anyone did or said could tarnish her delight with the memory of Noah's kiss.

Coming to her feet, she laughed softly. This was the first time since she had come to Haven that she delighted in her memories instead of cowering away from them.

Emma went behind the counter and tapped Noah on the shoulder. He whirled, a strained expression tensing his face. His eyes were wide and brought to mind a treed critter. He released his breath, and his smile returned.

"Are you all right?" she asked.

"You startled me."

"I'd say I did. Are you always so jumpy?"

He picked up the list and shoved it into her hand. "You

have customers, and Gladys has a sandwich or two waiting for me. We'll talk later.''

She nodded as she set the list back onto the counter. A single glance told her he had kept track of the items sold far more neatly and precisely than she. She greeted her next customer, but looked past the man to watch Noah walk out of the store. Her tap on his shoulder had unsettled him more than she ever could have anticipated.

By the time Emma had tended to her final customer, it was dark. The low clouds and the rain had brought an early night. She had to be grateful. Sleep had been sparse last night between Sean's aching tummy and her own ache for Noah's arms around her.

She checked the stove, banking the fire so the store would not be even damper in the morning. While she blew out the lanterns, an odd light caught her eye. She realized it was from her own house. This was the first time she had been in the store at the same time the lamps were lit in her house. The idea of going home to a well-lit house where there were others waiting for her was delicious.

However, she turned away from the soft glow. Going back to the counter, she picked up her list. The shelves, crates, and jars around the store were almost empty. No one wanted to be caught without provisions if the worst happened and the river rose to flow down Haven's main street.

An umbrella waited by the door, and she smiled. It was hers, all dry and ready for her to use. She had lent it to Belinda to go back to the house. Someone must have returned it.

Drawing in the back of her skirt where black ruffles fell below the narrow bustle, she stepped out into the darkness. The rain was easing, no longer frantic. At any other time, she would have welcomed this rain, for it would nourish the flowers that were beginning to sprout in her yard.

She lifted her skirt and petticoats high enough to reveal the tops of her button-up shoes as she picked her way down the street. A light breeze tugged at the list she held in the same hand as the umbrella. She tightened her grip on it, and the umbrella wobbled. She righted it, but not before she got wet.

With relief, Emma threw open the door of the telegraph office, which was in the same building as the railroad offices. Kenny Martin was sitting by the telegraph, just as he seemed to do every day and every night. Even water coming up through the gaps in the wide floorboards would probably not budge him. He was young, not too many years older than Sean. With his dark hair slicked back with some sort of pomade and his shirt immaculately pressed, he never seemed to be tired. She wondered when he left the telegraph office to change shirts. Maybe he had a supply in the cupboard beyond the desk that held all his equipment.

She almost giggled. Turning to put the umbrella by the door so it would not drip water in the small office, she chided herself. Too little sleep and too much tension was making her giddy. She needed to concentrate on her task.

"Howdy, Emma," Kenny called.

"I need an order telegraphed."

Kenny held out his hand and whistled. "That's quite a list."

"I'd like you to send it to Montgomery Ward & Company up in Chicago."

"Telegraph an order to them?" He looked as shocked as if she had told him that she was about to go ice skating on the Ohio. "They take their orders by mail, Emma."

"Tell them this is an emergency. We're low on supplies here, and we aren't sure how much longer the trains will be able to run if the river keeps rising. Sign it with my name and with John Taber's."

"Along with his title of being Master of the Grange Hall here?"

Emma smiled. "If you would, because Montgomery Ward & Company wrote him a nice note last year when the Grange's autumn order went in. Maybe his name will catch their attention and get the order here even more quickly. You know how they want to stay on the good side of all the Grangers and the local Granges."

Kenny bent his head over his telegraph equipment and began to tap out the message that could be heard already in Chicago. She found it difficult to believe, as well as fascinating.

Thanking Kenny, she slipped out of the door of the telegraph office. She raised her umbrella, took a single step, and bounced off someone.

"Oh, forgive me!" she gasped. Tilting back her umbrella, she looked up at a stranger. That surprised her into silence. Very few outsiders, other than the children placed out from the orphan train, came to Haven. What was a stranger doing here in the midst of this crisis?

"My fault, miss." He tipped his hat, then grimaced when water ran off it. "I was hurrying to get in out of the storm, and now I'm causing you to linger in it. Good evening, miss."

She nodded and started back up the street toward the store. When she realized the man was walking behind her, she resisted the yearning to turn around and ask if he was following her. That was silly. She had thought seven years in Haven would have eased her fear of any stranger. Certainly by now the law in Kansas had given up the search for her.

Emma walked into her store without realizing where she was headed. *This* had become her haven, a place where she could help her neighbors and live the life she should have had in Kansas.

Something moved in the shadows, and she shrieked.

Noah stepped out of the shadows. He steered her to the rocking chair and sat her in it. Drawing up the chair Belinda had been using, he said as he sat, "You look as if you came face to face with your own ghost."

"Do I?" She shivered and looked out the front window of the store. Let Noah think she was pale because he had startled her. And he had, but that had not upset her as much as the stranger who had followed her up the street. The man had every right to be in Haven and to go to the Andersons' Livery Stable. She was letting her own memories haunt her. "I was down at the railroad station, and I could hear the river is higher than it has ever been."

"And that frightens you?"

"I wish it would stop raining."

"It will by dawn, I suspect."

Emma took a steadying breath and nodded. "Yes, probably by dawn, but the river won't reach its crest for several days."

"By then everything I own may be sailing down the Mississippi."

Sympathy ached within her. Putting her arms around his shoulders, she leaned her head against his shoulder. She wished there was something she could say, but she could not think of anything.

His fingers swept along her face and tilted her mouth beneath his. Kissing her with the strength of the emotions burning within him, he drew her closer until even the shadows inching across the floor could not come between them. She forgot the Ohio and the rain and everything but his strong arms around her and his firm body caressing her.

With a sigh, Emma drew away. "Noah, I need to—"

"I know. Let me help you." He brushed her hair back

from her face and stood. Offering his hand, he said, "One more time, I need to say thank you."

"You? I couldn't have dealt with the rush today if you hadn't been here." She put her hand on his. "I should be thanking you."

"But keeping me busy helped me not to think of how the river might be running through my parlor now."

"I don't think the water is that high yet."

"I hope you're right." He drew her to her feet and toward him. He did not release her hand when footsteps raced into the store.

"Supper is ready," Belinda announced with every bit of five-year-old self-importance she could muster. "Gladys says you both need a good, hot meal and you shouldn't dawdle."

Noah chuckled and gave a playful tug on her braid. "We wouldn't think of it."

When he offered his other hand to Belinda, his daughter grabbed it and grinned. Emma walked with them to the doorway and knew that, for the first time in seven years, she felt as if she were going home. She treasured that thought, because she knew how fleeting that feeling could be.

CHAPTER TEN

Emma paused in sweeping the store's porch and looked between the livery and Doc Bamburger's office. The afternoon sunshine was so bright off the Ohio that she had to lower her eyes. Smiling, she continued pushing the dried mud off the boards. The rain had stopped almost a week ago, and the river and creeks were sliding back between their banks.

Her smile widened when she saw Noah coming around the corner. He had been gone long enough to reach his farm and come back with news. Waving, she lowered her hand when she saw the set of his jaw. The news, she knew, would not be good.

Without speaking, he took her hand and drew her into the store. The only person inside was Sean, who was putting some cans of meat onto the shelf at the back of the store where they would not get ruined by the heat from the stove. Noah shut the door and turned the "closed" sign face out.

"What are you doing?" Emma asked, shocked.

"We need to talk without other ears listening." He glanced toward Sean.

Raising her voice, she asked, "Sean, will you check the boxes of laundry soap in the storage room? I need a count of how many we received."

"Right away, Miss Delancy." He grinned at them before going into the storage room.

Noah closed that door, too, then walked back to her, dried mud falling from his boots with each step.

Before he could speak, she asked, "How's the farm?"

"It's even worse than I'd guessed from what I heard of others farms along the Ohio." He shook his head. "The barn is gone completely. Not even a stick of wood to suggest it ever stood."

"Noah, I'm so sorry."

He shrugged, the motion as stiff as the river mud on his sleeves. "Between the creek and the river, half of the trees in the woodlot are ripped out of the ground. The ones I'd cut before the rain came are still there, but they've been smashed to pieces by the force of the water."

"And the house?"

"The house got some water on the first floor, but nothing that won't dry."

"That's good news, then. You know you're welcome to stay at my house until your house is dried out."

"I know." He stared at the door to the storage room, his jaw working as if he needed to fight his own words.

She put her hand on his arm, ignoring how the still damp mud there stuck to her fingers. "Noah, something else is wrong."

"Can you read my thoughts so easily?"

"It doesn't take much skill when every word you speak is clipped and you closed my store to talk to me privately. The loss of your barn isn't something that needs to be discussed without others around. What does?"

His gaze caught hers, and she gasped. Fury filled his eyes, a volatile, dangerous fury that seared her, making her wonder if this could be the kind man who had held her with such tenderness. Only when he dropped something into her hand could she escape that glimpse of rage.

Emma frowned at the small wooden box she held. Opening it, she saw an indentation in the velvet inside. The shape was instantly identifiable. As she closed the box, she said, "This holds a pocketwatch."

"*Held*. The watch, which my brother gave to me, is gone."

"How's that possible? No one could have gotten to your house when the water was surrounding it."

He took the box and tossed it onto the closest barrel. "It wasn't stolen during the flood, but before." He glanced at the storage room door again.

Emma whispered, "Are you accusing Sean?"

"He had the opportunity to sneak into my room and steal it while we were outside."

"Maybe you just misplaced it."

"I knew exactly where it was, because it was in the same place it's been since we arrived in Haven. In the top drawer in my bedroom." His frown did not ease. "That wasn't the only drawer that had been pawed through."

"And you believe it was Sean?"

"Don't you?"

She closed her eyes and nodded. "He took candy and other food when he first started working in the store. Even when I gave him permission to take as much as he wanted, I discovered he was hoarding the food beneath his bed."

"Hoarding? Why?"

"I haven't asked, because I wanted him to come to trust me." She rubbed her hands together to wipe the mud from them. "He still calls me 'Miss Delancy,' so I don't think he has come to trust me yet." Motioning for him to wait where he was, she went to the storage room door.

She opened it and saw Sean hard at work counting the boxes of laundry soap. On that, she could not complain. The boy toiled at the store from the hour it opened until it closed, protesting when Emma insisted that he go to school. Her hopes that he would want to play with the other children still went unrealized.

"Sean?" she called.

His head popped up. "Yes, ma'am?"

"Leave that for now. I need you out in the store."

"Coming."

Guilt pricked Emma. Sean was so eager to help her. Had he been equally eager to help himself to Noah's pocket watch?

Waiting by the door, she put her arm around his shoulders. He flinched, but his thin shoulders did not grow rigid as, shortly after his arrival in Haven, they had any time she had touched them.

"Mr. Sawyer, how's the farm?" he asked.

"The barn's gone, but everything in the house is there." He picked up the wooden box. "Everything but what was in this."

Now Sean's shoulders became stiff. Emma steered him forward a single step, then realized she would get nowhere forcing the boy toward Noah like this.

She faced him and said, "Sean, I want you to be honest with me."

"Yes, ma'am." The uneasy glance he fired at Noah added

to the cramp in her stomach, for it revealed the truth before she could ask him a single question.

But she had to ask. Putting her hand on his shoulder again, she said, "Noah is missing the pocket watch his brother gave him. Do you know where it might be?"

"Are you accusing me of lifting it?" Defiance raised his chin.

"I asked you if you know where it might be. Sean, you said you'd be honest with me."

"With *you*."

"You can be honest with Noah, too."

He shook his head. "He was going to have me thrown into the lockup when he accused me of stealing that old hammer and the bag of nails. I didn't mean to take anything out of his wagon, but he wouldn't believe me. Why would he believe me now? He'll send me off to jail and throw the key away."

Emma knelt in front of the boy. Taking his trembling hands, she said, "There's no jail in Haven, and no one is going to send a boy your age to jail."

"In New York—"

"This isn't New York. This is Haven, Indiana, and we don't send children to jail." She paused, then asked, "Sean, do you know where Noah's pocket watch is?"

Sean ground the toe of his shoe against the floor. "Yes, I know where it is."

She looked from Sean's tear-filled eyes to Noah's scowl. In the same quiet voice, she asked, "Will you tell me?"

"He won't whip me, will he?"

"No."

"What 'bout you?"

"Sean, look at me," she said.

For the length of two heartbeats, she thought he would not obey. Then he raised his gaze from the floor.

She wiped a tear off his cheek as she whispered, "Do you think *I* would whip you?"

"No."

"Then tell me where the pocket watch is."

"In my room."

Noah started to speak, but she held up her hand to silence him. There was one more thing she had to know.

"Why did you take it, Sean? Did you think it was pretty?"

"It's made of gold," he answered lowly. "I know gold is worth a lot of money. I thought I might be able to sell it to someone and buy a train ticket."

Emma feared her heart was going to break in her chest. She had not guessed Sean wanted to return to his life in New York. "If you're so unhappy here, you only needed to tell me, and I would have contacted the Children's Aid Society. They would have arranged for you to go back east."

"Me go back?" He shook his head. "I don't want to go back there. I wanted to get money to buy a ticket for my little sister to come here. I miss her. I figured you might let her stay with us for a while." He lowered his eyes again. "Now you probably want to send me packing."

She struggled to speak past the tears clogging her throat. When Noah's hand settled on her shoulder, she glanced up at him again. The anger was gone from his face, replaced by compassion.

"Sean," she said, "I don't want to send you back. Not ever. This is your home, and we're going to be a family, if you wish." She caught another tear before it could roll along his face. "And I can contact the Children's Aid Society to find out about your sister."

"Will you?"

"Yes, but you must not steal again. Not from me or from Noah or from anyone. Not ever. Do you understand?"

"And then you won't make me go back?"

"No matter what you say, no matter what you do, I shall not send you back. Not ever. Do you understand that?"

"Yes . . . Emma." His voice broke on her name.

She pulled him into her arms and held him as he sobbed. Leaning her cheek against the top of his head, she fought her own tears. Noah stroked her hair, and she looked up at him.

It was a beginning. A small one, but a beginning just the same. Maybe Sean—and Noah—would trust her with the truth. She closed her eyes and bent to press her cheek to Sean's head once more. They might trust her, but she could never trust them with the truth of her past.

Not ever.

Belinda bounced into the store, calling Sean's name. He burst out from behind the counter, then paused as he looked back.

"Go and play ball on the green!" Emma waved them both out the door. "I think I can handle the store by myself this afternoon."

Wiping her hands on her apron, she walked out from behind the counter, too. Sean had missed having Belinda around when Noah had moved his family back out to the farm. Knowing the truth now, Emma suspected Sean was letting Belinda replace—temporarily—the little sister who was left behind in New York.

The letter she had written to the Children's Aid Society should have reached New York by now, but she was not sure how long it would take the Society to respond. She had cautioned Sean to have patience. Each time mail was dropped off at the railroad station, he had stood close by as she sorted it and put it in the proper cubbyholes. There were two dozen niches, each one labeled with a name belonging to a family in Haven. Those who lived outside of town could find their mail in the box she kept locked beneath the counter.

There had been no answer from the Society . . . yet.

Going to the door, Emma leaned one shoulder on the frame as she watched the children chase a ball around the green. The open area was finally deserving of its name. Leaves were bursting out on the trees, giving them a soft green fuzz at the end of each branch. Grass was beginning to grow. Later in the spring, the ladies of the Haven Improvement Committee would plant flowers in the concrete boxes on either side of the old cannon.

Steps climbed up onto the porch. She turned, smiling. "Mr. Atherton, how are you on this lovely afternoon?"

The man, whom she had bumped into with her umbrella during the rain, tipped his hat to her. He was dressed, as he had been each time she had seen him, in an impeccable gray coat and trousers. His vest had a narrow white stripe that set off the spats over his polished shoes. With his blond hair smoothed stylishly back, he seemed to belong in a big city like Louisville instead of backwater Haven. She had heard he was a friend of the Smith family who lived out of town about a mile east. That neighborly connection had soothed her disquiet about why he was here.

"It *is* a lovely afternoon, Miss Delancy." He glanced into the shadowed store. "Do you have a moment?"

"Of course." She stepped inside and asked, "How can I help you?"

"I'm looking for tobacco for my pipe."

"There's some on the third shelf to the left. If you don't find the type you like, let me know. The Grangers are planning to finalize their spring order to Montgomery Ward & Company this evening."

He took down a jar of shredded tobacco, opened it, and took a sniff. Setting it back on the shelf, he said, "I'm surprised you sound so pleased about that, Miss Delancy. What they order from that mail order company, they don't buy from you.''

''I buy from Montgomery Ward & Company, too, both for me and for the store. Not everyone can afford to order when the Grange sends in its order and pays cash. At the store, they can buy and pay me when the crops are harvested.''

''I see.'' Opening another jar, he took a sniff and smiled. ''I'd like some of this.''

She took the jar to the counter where she could measure out what he wanted. ''How much?''

''What's left in the jar would be fine.''

Weighing the tobacco, she put it into a bag and handed it to him. He dug a handful of small coins out of his pocket. Setting them on the counter, he said, ''I've heard that you steadied many nervous souls during the recent flooding.''

''There weren't many nervous souls.'' She smiled. ''We've become accustomed to the river's moods.''

''Odd, for I heard you saved several lives. A whole family who was in danger on their farm.''

She laughed. ''Tales get exaggerated. My wagon brought all of us into Haven. We were fortunate that the bridge was still passable. Noah deserves as much credit for getting us here as I do.''

''Noah?''

''Noah Sawyer. It was his family that was nearly trapped out on their farm.''

Mr. Atherton's face lengthened, making him look like the hound whose name he shared. ''That must have been frightening for all of you. How did you all manage to fit in one wagon?''

''Noah had his horse, and I drove the wagon with his housekeeper and the children.''

"His children?"

"His daughter and the boy who is living with me since he arrived on the orphan train." She walked back to the door and laughed as she watched Belinda trying to catch Sean, who stayed just out of her reach. "As you can see, no harm came to them. We were lucky."

"Yes, I'd say you have been very, very lucky." He put the packet in his pocket. "You could have been caught in the high waters and washed away." He tipped his hat to her as he stepped outside. "Thank you, Miss Delancy."

"Mr. Atherton?"

"Yes?" He paused on the steps to the street.

"Will you be staying in Haven long? I can order some more of the tobacco to have here for you if you are going to be visiting for a while."

He smiled. "I'll let you know, Miss Delancy. Right now, I think I shall be leaving shortly. I have some business to tend to north of here. Good afternoon."

Looking once at the children to be certain they were not thinking up some trouble, Emma went back into the store. The train had come in today, so she had some crates to unpack so Sean could break them up for firewood. The boy had proven he knew how to use a hatchet with care, and he had been delighted when she gave him the job of chopping up boxes.

She heard footfalls, but did not have to turn to identify this patron. Her ears sought for the sound of those steps all day long, and the echo played through her dreams at night.

She smiled. "Good afternoon, Noah. I thought you might be in today."

"Why?"

"Grange meeting is tonight."

He regarded her with bafflement. "I'm not a member of the Haven Grange."

"That's a surprise. I thought all the farmers along the river were members."

"I'm not really a farmer, so I never gave it much thought."

"But the Grange gives all of us a sense of community here in Haven." She smiled. "Maybe a lot like what those folks out at River's Haven have. I'm obviously not a farmer either, but I enjoy the meetings and the gatherings. We have dances and singalongs. You should come sometime and bring Belinda and Gladys."

"Maybe one of these days. Right now, I'm busy with Belinda and trying to fix up the buildings on the farm." He gave her a lopsided grin. "What is left of them." He tossed his hat onto the rocking chair and walked to where she stood. Tugging her into his arms, he said, "Good afternoon, sweetheart."

She laughed. "You're supposed to say that when you come into the store, not now."

"But it is a good afternoon." His voice dropped to a rasping whisper. "Do you want to make it a better afternoon?"

"What do you have in mind?"

He laughed. "I don't think you want me to talk about that right here in the middle of your store. Maybe I should just show you."

"All right. You show me, and I'll let you know if it made my afternoon better."

"A challenge? You're going to like this."

"Will I?" She smiled up at him as she locked her fingers together behind his nape.

He put one finger under her chin. Tilting her mouth toward his, he whispered, his breath warming her lips, "I think you're really going to like this."

She thrilled in the eagerness in his kiss. She had dreamed of his tongue grazing her lips, of his strong hands on her.

Waking in the middle of the night, covered with sweat, her body aching for him, she had yearned for this.

But no dream was as splendid as this. As he drew her even closer, her hands glided up his back. She wanted—she needed—to savor his strength.

"So what do you think?" he murmured.

"I like this."

"What about this?"

Her teasing reply became an uneven gasp when his hand rose from her waist to cup her breast. His thumb grazed its very tip, and she melted against him, wanting this and so much more. When his hand curved up along her in a lingering caress, she moaned against his mouth, which claimed hers once more.

He drew back, his breath as frayed as hers. "What do you say, sweetheart?"

"I . . ." She looked past him.

Noah released Emma's hands as she went to wait on Mrs. Randolph. The old woman must not have noticed them, because all her questions were about whether her newspaper had arrived on this morning's train. Opening the stairwell door, Emma retrieved the newspaper and sent her out onto the porch to read it.

"You keep the mail in the stairwell?" Noah asked as he walked over to the counter.

"Now that Mr. Baker has left, I might as well use it for storage."

"Baker left? When?"

"Just as the rivers started rising. He said he'd had enough of these floods, and he wanted to go somewhere else. He has family up in Wisconsin, I think. He was eager to go. I think he had work waiting for him, because he told me to keep the furniture upstairs. He said he'd buy new when he got there." She shook her head. "There may be furniture up there. All I could see when I went up were piles of papers. Newspapers and sheets that were so yellowed I doubt they even could be read any longer.''

Putting his hands on her waist, he picked her up and sat her on the counter. He wanted to fall into the heated warmth of her green eyes and lose himself in her forever. Her voice vanished beneath his mouth as he explored her succulent lips. They softened beneath his, and he stepped closer. When he held her, he yearned to explore every facet of the fire glowing in her eyes.

As her fingers moved in a meandering path up his arms and across his back, the answering response rushed all along him. His own fingers stroked her soft breasts and the curve of her gently rounded hips. When she gasped into his mouth, he was sure her breath would set his very soul on fire. Through her skirt, her legs pressed against him in an invitation to share the pleasure. He drew her to him until he could feel the pounding of her heart, which matched the throb aching through him.

He did not speak the curse stealing his rapture away as he heard someone step up onto the porch. Reverend Faulkner, he knew when he heard the minister talking with Mrs. Randolph. He looked back at Emma and said, ''Your store is too busy.''

''You could help me down,'' she said, her tone sharp, but her eyes still dazed from his touch.

''I could.'' He leaned one hand next to her on the counter as he drawled, ''Or I could tell the shopkeeper I'd like some more of what I just sampled.''

''If you don't help me down, the only way you'll sample more is by placing an order with some out-of-town distributor.''

Grasping her at the waist again, he set her on her feet. He did not move back, so she was still caught between him and the counter. He framed her face with his hands as he murmured, "I prefer what I've found here in Haven to anything from out of town."

"Emma, where are you?" called the minister from the door.

Although he did not want to, Noah stepped aside. He chuckled under his breath as Emma tried to jab her hairpins back in place. Her hair had been delightfully tousled before he drew her into his arms. Knowing that the minister could not see what he was doing, he reached up and loosened a strand to fall down her back. His finger followed its silken stream, and she quivered at his touch.

"Here—" Her voice squeaked, and she shot Noah a glare before saying, "I'm over here, Reverend."

"There you are. Takes longer every year for these eyes to adjust from the sunlight. Who's that? Ah, Noah, just the man I wanted to see." Reverend Faulkner wove his way through the store as if he were being bounced about like the children's ball.

"Whoa, Reverend!" Emma rushed forward to keep a stack of cans from collapsing in his wake. "He'll wait until you get there."

"True. Good news will wait," the minister said.

"As well as bad news," Noah replied with a chuckle.

Reverend Faulkner poured himself a cup of coffee from the pot on the stove. "Fortunately today, all the news I have is good. Good for you, Noah."

"I could use some good news."

The minister smiled, looking back at Emma. "We're going to have a barn raising."

"I'd be glad to help you. I do know something about building."

"Help me?" Reverend Faulkner chuckled. "Noah, the barn raising is going to be at your place."

"Mine?" When he saw Emma's bright smile, he knew the minister had already conferred with her on this.

"As soon as Emma lets me know your supplies are in," Reverend Faulkner said, "we'll gather out at your place and help you rebuild that barn."

"They should be in on the next train," Emma said, coming back to stand beside Noah. He wondered if she could guess that the brush of her sleeve against his was enough to throw every other thought out of his head—even this extraordinary offer. "On Thursday, Reverend Faulkner."

"Excellent." The minister rubbed his hands together in anticipation. "It will take a while for the wood to be delivered out to your farm, Noah, so we will plan next Saturday for the barn raising."

Noah looked again from Emma's twinkling eyes to the minister's beatific smile. "I don't know what to say."

"Say you'll have Gladys make several of her luscious chocolate cakes," Emma said, putting her hand on his arm. "If you provide those and something to drink, folks will be glad to bring along potluck as well as their tools to help get the barn up."

"Was this your idea?" He knew he was treading on dangerous territory when the minister was here to witness this, but he could not keep from putting his hand up to caress her cheek.

She nodded. "Yes, and everyone is eager to help after they saw the work you did here in the store during the flood. Folks here in Haven like to help one another."

"God helps those who help themselves," the reverend intoned, then laughed.

"Good advice," Noah murmured as he put his arm around Emma and drew her back to him. He did not care who was watching as he kissed her with the longing he was finding more and more difficult to govern.

When he released her, she wobbled and smiled. That smile tempted him to toss her back up on the counter and not let anything or anyone halt him from savoring every pleasure she could share with him. He ran his thumb along her jaw and saw the light of desire afire in her eyes.

The minister clapped him on the shoulder and said, "I trust you won't thank *all* of us like that."

"You don't have to worry about that."

As Emma spoke to the minister, making arrangements for the following Saturday, Noah watched, his elbow on the counter. No, the minister did not need to worry about Noah kissing anyone else. Who would have guessed, after five years of traveling, he would find what he was looking for right here in this small town? Now all he needed to do was make sure he did not lose it . . . again.

CHAPTER ELEVEN

Belinda came running into the kitchen. "They're here! They're here! Come and see!"

Noah glanced with regret at his half-finished breakfast. He should have eaten earlier, but he had wanted to have the floor of the barn ready when the others arrived. Reaching for a piece of toast, he kneaded his right shoulder. The hard work on this farm reminded him how many years he had been supervising others instead of doing the work himself.

"I have some liniment ready," Gladys said with a knowing smile. "Miss Delancy was able to provide all the ingredients except the chloroform." Counting off on her fingers, she said, "At the store, she had the alcohol I needed and laudanum and oil of hemlock—"

"Don't tell me all the ingredients. I'd rather not know."

She laughed. "Of course, you could just have that young lady rub your shoulders for you."

"Now there's a good idea." Picking up the piece of toast, he hurried out to where the barn floor was already surrounded by carriages and wagons.

His usually quiet yard was filled with greetings and children tumbling out onto what grass had been able to grow back after the flood. The sentinel trees along the field still stood, but the smaller ones had been washed away. Yet already the grass and weeds were filling in what had been stolen by the Ohio.

Women were taking the baskets that their menfolk lifted out and handed to them. Seeing the number of people parked under the trees and the line of vehicles coming down the road, he wondered if the long planks he had set out on sawhorses on the other side of the house would hold all the food. As the women streamed toward the house, he nodded to each of them until his head spun.

Noah was astounded to see two wagons filled with people in the unrelieved black worn by the folks out at River's Haven. No one had given him any idea that the people who kept so much to themselves in their isolated community would come to help here.

"Don't look so amazed," said Emma, coming down the hill from the house with Sean in tow. "The River's Haven Community has often helped us. They just don't want our help. It's the perfect day for a barn raising."

"Sunny and not too hot." He took her hand. "Although it seems much warmer now that you're here, sweetheart."

She laughed, but her rosy cheeks told him she was pleased with his suggestive words. He hoped she had thought as often as he did about the fiery kisses they had shared at her store.

"Well, well," said Gladys after she had greeted Emma and Sean. "Don't that beat all."

Noah had to agree when he saw Murray's dilapidated

wagon bouncing down the road. His cantankerous neighbor parked it next to the others. Taking out a bag of tools, Murray strode toward the barn.

"You'd best get to work," Emma said, giving Noah a teasing shove. "Let Reverend Faulkner direct the teams and see which one can get their wall up the quickest."

"A contest?"

"A barn raising bee should be fun." She smiled at Gladys. "I hope you have some special dessert for the winning team."

"I will."

Emma turned to Sean as Noah and Gladys walked away in opposite directions. "There's a baseball and a bat in the back of the wagon. Get it out, and take the other children out into the field over there."

"No." His tone was abruptly sullen.

"You don't know the rules? They're quite simple."

"I know how to play baseball. I just don't want to."

"Why not?" she asked softly.

"The kids in Haven don't want anything to do with us kids from the train."

She kept her sigh silent. When Sean had stopped complaining about being ostracized at school, she had thought the situation had gotten better. All that had changed was that he was suffering in silence.

"Take the ball and bat," she said, "and find some of your friends from the train. There are certain to be many of them here today. If the other children want to play, too, they'll join in."

He folded his arms in front of him. "I don't want to play with the Haven kids."

"You play with Belinda."

"She's different. She doesn't look down at me."

Putting her hands on his shoulders, she said, "Sean

O'Dell, no one can look down on you if you keep your own chin high. But if you keep your own nose high in the air, you'll never see the ones who are trying to catch your eye to become a friend.''

"I don't understand."

"Think about what I said, and you may." She gave him a shove as she had Noah. "Go and get the ball and bat, and see what happens."

"All right." His glum answer suggested she had no idea what she was talking about.

Emma wished she could call him back. His steps were heavy, and he was staring at the ground. If he wanted to stay in Haven, and now she knew he did, he needed to find a way to bridge the differences between himself and the other children. She smiled when a redheaded boy ran up to him and greeted him with a big hug. Because she did not recognize the boy, she knew he must be one of the orphans.

Going into the house, she headed for the kitchen. It was as busy as a beehive and buzzed just as loudly. Gladys was keeping order somehow with all the women who had brought food and were looking for a place to put it. The housekeeper waved rather desperately to Emma.

Like someone going down for the third time? Emma laughed at the thought and waded into the cacophony. Greeting her neighbors, she saw one woman standing off by herself. In amazement, she realized it was the woman from River's Haven who had been in the Grange Hall the day the orphan train arrived. No one else was talking to her.

"It's nice of you to come for the barn raising," Emma said with a smile.

"Thank you." The woman's black hair glistened beneath her simple bonnet.

Emma recognized the terse answer as a dismissal, but she

went on, "I saw you at the Haven Grange when the children arrived from back east. My name is Emma Delancy."

"I'm Rachel Browning." Her face lost its cool sternness. "You were at the Grange Hall with Reverend Faulkner, weren't you?"

"Yes. I was talking to him and Mr. Barrett about Sean O'Dell, who's now living with me."

"Sean O'Dell is with you?"

"Yes."

"May I ask you some questions, Miss Delancy?"

"Of course." She gestured toward the door out of the kitchen. "I would like to go outside. Would you like to come, too? We can talk out there while we watch the barn raising and the children at the same time."

Miss Browning hesitated for so long that Emma thought she would say no. Then she nodded. As Emma walked back toward the front porch, she noted how the women coming into the house cut a wide path around Miss Browning.

"You shouldn't let it bother you, Miss Delancy," Miss Browning said as she held the door open for Emma.

"It?"

"The looks I seem to attract wherever I go." She smiled, and Emma was astounded at the transformation. Miss Browning's face came alight with her smile. "The looks everyone from River's Haven attract. Don't let them bother you. I don't . . . anymore."

A dozen questions whirled through Emma's head, but she silenced all of them. She could not use this opportunity to pry into the closed ways of the River's Haven Community. When she delivered items from the store, she was allowed to drive down the main road. There she sat in her wagon while the supplies were unloaded.

"Miss Delancy?"

Emma hoped Miss Browning had not said more than that, because she had not heard anything but her name. "Yes?"

"You said Sean O'Dell is living with you?"

"Yes."

Miss Browning hesitated, then said, "Kitty—I mean—"

Emma laughed. "Sean calls her Kitty Cat whenever he speaks of her, which is often."

"She speaks of him, too. Often."

"They miss each other, it seems." She heard shouts from the direction of the barn. Hammers hit wood, and laughter was unrestrained—both from the barn and from the field where the children were playing baseball. She could not tell if both the Haven and the orphan train children were playing together, but it seemed there were too many in the field to be just the children off the train. "Is Kitty Cat here?"

Miss Browning shook her head. "The children remained at the Community to finish a project they had started in school earlier in the week."

"Sean will be very disappointed." She sat on the railing and let the soft breeze uncurl the strands at her nape.

"I'd like to find a way for the two of them to have some time together."

"You would?" Emma could not have been more surprised if Miss Browning had thrown her black skirt over her head and danced a jig on the porch.

"I'm not sure how yet, but I plan to speak to the Assembly of Elders to find out if there's a way. First, I wanted to be certain you'd welcome her in your home."

"Sean's friends are always welcome."

Miss Browning smiled again. "Thank you, Miss Delancy. I'll be sure to petition the Assembly of Elders as soon as possible."

"Good luck."

Miss Browning started to reply, but someone called to

her from down closer to the barn. Guilt banished her smile.
Not just guilt, Emma realized, but a flash of rebellion. That
amazed Emma, for she had thought everyone in River's
Haven accepted their odd laws. The very fact Miss Browning
had suggested a way for the children to meet again might
be a revelation that she had not completely acceded to those
ways.

As Miss Browning hurried away, Emma went back into
the house. She should be helping Gladys in the kitchen.

She had not gone more than a pair of steps when Belinda
popped out of the parlor. With a laugh, Emma caught the
little girl before they collided.

"What are you doing inside, Belinda? I thought you'd
be out playing with the other children."

"They say I'm too small." She took a bite of the cookie
that had already sprinkled crumbs down the front of her
ruffled, light blue dress.

"You should show them that they are wrong. Tell them
you're able to catch the ball."

"But I can't."

"Then you can always cheer for everyone else." She
squatted down so her eyes were level with Belinda's. "Tell
Sean that I said I thought you'd do very well in the outfield."

"Everyone is out in the field."

"Not out in the field. Outfield."

Belinda's forehead threaded. "Isn't that just the same?"

"Not in baseball."

Straightening, Emma found her gaze caught. Not by living
eyes, but by those in the photograph on the mantel. She
should not be standing here as she stared at Noah's late
wife's portrait. She could not look away. The smile the
woman wore was so happy and hopeful.

"That's Martha," Belinda said and took another bite of
the cookie.

"Who?"

Belinda pointed at the photograph. "That's Martha."

"I thought it was a picture of your mother."

"It's Martha."

"Who is Martha?" She should not be asking these questions, but her curiosity had been piqued. She had assumed that the photograph was of Noah's late wife, which was why it held this place of honor.

"Martha was Mr. Sawyer's sister," Gladys said, shooing Belinda out of the house. "She died a while back."

"I didn't mean to snoop."

Gladys laughed. "Of course you did. Mr. Sawyer should have told you who was in the picture. After all, he had you tote it out of the house for him when the river was trying to run right through here." She waved her hands and apron. "Now you shoo, too. The house during a barn raising is fine for us old folks. You should be out watching the work."

"The other women—"

"Are here with their *husbands!* Now shoo."

Emma grinned. Gladys was proving to be an ceaseless matchmaker, and the match she wanted to see made now was one between Emma and Noah. Her heart fluttered at the thought of becoming his wife. The very sound of Noah's voice thrilled her. And when he drew her close, she could lose herself in the enchantment of his touch.

Hearing Gladys laugh as she wandered out onto the porch again, Emma walked down the steps. She took a deep breath. It was no longer thick with the mud washed up from the river, but filled with the return of everything green. Soon, except for the unweathered wood on the barn, there would be no sign the river had flowed up over its banks here.

"Good morning." Mr. Atherton tipped his hat to her as he walked back toward where the wagons were parked.

She smiled, wondering how she could have been so wrong

when she had been uneasy about this man being in Haven. Her first impressions were usually reliable, but she had been so wrong about him. "Mr. Atherton, I didn't realize you were still in Haven."

"I'm leaving on the next train north, but I wanted to thank you for making a stranger feel welcome."

"Others haven't?"

He laughed. "No, no, I didn't mean to suggest that. The people here have been very friendly and have taken the time to answer all my silly questions."

Emma stiffened in spite of her efforts not to. "What silly questions?"

"Oh, about how this town was settled and the residents, both new and old." His smile remained warm, so she guessed he had not taken note of her reaction. "I haven't had a chance to visit this part of the state before, so I figured I should learn all I could. Your story about fleeing just ahead of the flood is probably the most fascinating one I heard."

"It wasn't fascinating at the time," Noah said, coming to stand by her side.

"Noah," Emma said, hoping her voice did not sound breathless as it did so often when he was near, "this is Mr. Atherton who has been visiting Haven. Mr. Atherton, Noah Sawyer."

Mr. Atherton's smile grew so wide it revealed all his teeth when he shook Noah's hand. "I suspect it wasn't fascinating at the time, but Miss Delancy has given you much of the credit for saving her, your housekeeper, and the children."

"She's too modest." He put his arm around her shoulders, and she could not keep from nestling closer to him. "If it hadn't been for Emma guiding us into Haven, I believe we would have ended up sitting on the house's roof while the water swirled up around us."

Tipping his hat to her again, Mr. Atherton bid them a good day.

Noah smiled as he turned her in his arms and locked his hands together behind her waist. He brought her lips to his. Although the kiss was swift, she could see his longing for more.

And she longed to share it with him.

"Thank you," he whispered.

"For the kiss?" She laughed. "I should say it was my pleasure."

"For all of this, sweetheart." He whispered against her right ear, "My muscles are going to be very weary tonight. Do you think you could rub them for me?"

She quivered as his breath caressed her, enticing her to toss all caution aside. "I would be glad to."

"Good!" He released her and chuckled. "That'll be much better than the concoction Gladys calls liniment."

She took his hand as they went back to where the framing for the walls was already nearly done. Each wall was lying on the ground near the foundation. Even as she paused on the road that once had led to the barn, she heard shouts. One team was ready to raise their section into place.

"Be ready to help all my tired muscles," he murmured as he gave her another swift kiss before running toward one group of men who were calling to him.

Leaning back against one of the trees, Emma smiled as she savored the thought of her fingers stroking his brawny back and shoulders. She closed her eyes as she imagined touching him even more intimately. For more than seven years, she had not wanted to become involved with any man. Friendship, yes. A bit of innocent flirting. That had been all right, too. But nothing more. Then the most outrageously enticing man she could have ever met burst into her life and tempted her to break all her vows to keep everything simple.

More shouts came from the direction of the barn, and she cheered when she saw two sections of the wall slowly rising. The men knew that, even if it was a contest, they must take care with this work so no one was hurt. Most of the members of each team pushed on what would be the outside and lifted the skeleton of the wall. Two men stood on the barn floor ready to nail support boards to the wall to hold it in place until the rafters could connect the roof to the walls.

Although she wanted to see which team was done first, her eyes focused on Noah, who was swinging his hammer with smooth strokes. He was laughing with the others on his team, and she could see how delighted he was to be working with wood and building something. He had not said much about the woodlot, but she knew there had been even more damage than he had led her to believe.

Applause and shouts rang out as the first wall was secured into place. The winning team was congratulated. Then the men continued their work. The guttural rasp of saws cutting through wood matched the rhythm created by the thud of hammers.

Alice Underhill walked up the hill carrying an empty bucket. Two cups rattled inside it, and Emma knew the schoolteacher had taken water to the workers.

"It's coming along well," Alice said with a smile.

"At the rate they're going, the whole barn will be done by tonight. I'd thought we might be dancing tonight under the moonlight."

"The dance will have to be postponed a few weeks. Everyone will dance next at Sally Young and Isaac Smith's wedding."

"That's not until . . ." She laughed. "Time slips away from me when I am busy with the store and with Sean."

Alice smiled. "And Mr. Sawyer?"

"Yes, he does keep me from thinking about other things,"

she said with a laugh. Denying what must be a favorite topic of the town's gossips would be worthless.

Especially when it was true.

The soft radiance from the moon glistened off the new barn as Emma came out of the house to look west, where the lingering sunset was fading. She wiped her hands on the damp towel. At last, all the dishes were done. Belinda and Sean were asleep upstairs, finally settling down after Emma had agreed to tell them a story. It had been about a fairy-tale princess at Belinda's request, and a train engineer—Sean's preference.

She smiled. Tonight Sean should not wake with a sick stomach. Emma had watched him with the desserts, but she had not worried after she saw how he took the smallest piece of chocolate cake.

The peepers were singing their songs from every direction. Frogs provided a deeper undertone to the melody of the twilight song. Looking up, she saw a bat swooping to catch its supper. Even as she watched, the first star pricked through the night sky. She took a deep breath of the air and let it sift back out of her in a sigh.

"That sounds very tired."

She glanced to her left to see Noah's silhouette as he stood from where he had been leaning against the porch railing. Smiling, she said, "Not as tired as you, I'm sure."

"It was a long day." He cupped her chin and tilted her face up toward his. "A most amazing day. I never expected anything like this when I came to Haven."

"Haven is a special town."

"I'd never argue with that." He stepped back, holding his hand out to her. "Do you want to see the work up close?"

Emma nodded. If she spoke, she might blurt out how she had thought he would kiss her. Really kiss her. Not just the brief, teasing kisses of earlier today. Putting her hand in his, she tossed the towel over the porch railing. Dew oozed through her shoes as they walked down the hill to the new barn. A hint of chill came from the direction of the river, but vanished with the breeze.

"Can Belinda and I escort you and Sean to the wedding the week after next?" Noah asked quietly.

"Escort us?" She laughed. "The church is just on the other side of the village green from my house."

He kneaded his shoulder and grimaced. "After the work today, I'm not certain how much farther I'll be able to walk even by then."

"We don't need to go to look at the barn now."

"I'm jesting." He grimaced as he continued to rub his shoulder. "I think."

"I promised I would massage your shoulders for you if you wished."

"I do, but I thought you'd like to see the barn." He ran his curved finger along her cheek. "If I sit down, I'm not sure I'll want to get up again for a long time."

"But if you're that exhausted—"

He laughed and, tugging her hand, led her down the hill at a near run. She almost tripped, but regained her feet and drew her skirts up so she could match his steps. When they reached the bottom of the hill, he twirled her about as if they were both as young as Belinda.

As they slowed, she said, "Now *I* am exhausted! I didn't save any stamina for dancing tonight."

Noah brought Emma's lips to his. When he lifted his mouth away after only the briefest kiss, he heard her soft moan of denial. It tempted him to lean her back in this damp grass. Instead, he led her to where an opening in the barn wall was waiting for the door to be hung.

Their footsteps echoed hollowly on the barn floor, which was littered with sawdust and curls of wood from where the rafters had been planed smooth. He watched as she slowly turned around in the milky light that poured through what would be the hayloft windows once the hayloft was finished and glass was put in place. As the moon's glow accented her face and her beguiling curves, he walked to her.

Drawing her into his arms, he asked, "What do you think?"

"I think you all did a lot of work here today."

"I did doubt this much of the barn would be finished by the time we quit for supper."

"You'll have more faith in the folks of Haven after you have been here for a while." Emma reached up and brushed Noah's hair back from his eyes. "We may argue like family, but that's because, in so many ways, we *are* family."

"Family?"

"In a way."

"I just wanted to make sure you and I wouldn't be considered brother and sister. It'd make things much more difficult when I want to do this." His lips captured hers.

When his fingers combed through her hair, her hairpins clattered to the floor. Emma's hands glided up his back, and she tasted the need in his deepening kiss. She gave herself to this passion, wanting more. She gasped against his mouth when his hand curved down her back, pressing her hips to his hard male muscles.

He put one arm under her knees and lifted her to lean against his chest. Against her hair, he whispered, "I hope you saved a bit of strength, sweetheart."

"Noah, we should—"

"Yes, we should." His mouth slanted across hers as he carried her across the barn.

She opened her eyes when he paused and lowered her toward the floor. They were surrounded by shadows, but this spot was awash with the cool, smooth light from the moon. When she discovered he was placing her on a pallet, she knew what she should have guessed from the moment she saw him on the porch. He had been waiting for her . . . just as she had been hoping to find him waiting for her.

He knelt beside her and ran his fingers through her hair. Then he leaned over her and whispered, "I always seem to be thanking you, sweetheart, with words. Now let me thank you without words."

"Noah, you know this is crazy, don't you?"

"I don't know if it's crazy, but I know it's right."

"Do you always do what you think is right?" She ran her finger along his hard jaw, which was surprisingly smooth. He must have shaven after dinner, for his whiskers had been visible then.

"Always."

"Even—"

He silenced her by reclaiming her lips. Her hands swept up his back. She wanted to touch him, to assure herself that this was really happening, that this loving man wanted her.

Pulling away enough to speak, she protested weakly, "You should rest. You worked hard today."

"That's what you told me the first night I stayed at your house." He laughed. "You also told me you don't need me to feel obligated to you, but debts must be repaid. You did something very nice for me today. Let me do something very nice for you tonight." He pressed his lips against her throat, and a cascade of yearning billowed up from within her.

"Only very nice?" she murmured.

"Much more than very nice." His tongue etched a path of fire along her skin, and she swayed toward him.

He did not resist the invitation. He drew her beneath him, so she could discover the so-very-male texture of him.

Her eager hands slid beneath his shirt to stroke the warm skin along his back. When he gasped and whispered her name against her neck, she wanted to cede herself completely to this pleasure which enfolded her to him.

His tongue teased her ear as he whispered, "I was sure I would go mad before I could persuade you to come here with me, sweetheart. I thought you'd never finish those accursed dishes tonight."

She framed his face so she could see the desire softening his stern features. "Neither did I!"

"Think how much more quickly you'd have finished them if . . ."

"Would you stop talking and kiss me?"

With a laugh, he whispered, "Gladly, sweetheart."

His fingers brushed her breast as he slipped his arm beneath her. At her gasp of excitement at his bold seduction, he pressed his mouth over hers, refusing to be denied what she had dreamed of night after night when he slept on her sofa. Each audacious caress of his tongue elicited a stronger need within her. She had been the proper storekeeper for too long after giving up her dreams to a man who turned them into nightmares. Now she was going to savor this sweet dream coming true.

The buttons on his shirt undid with such ease that she smiled. That smile became a soft whisper of his name when he began to unbutton her blouse. The touch of his fingers on her breast added to the heat deep within her. When each side of her blouse dropped to the pallet, his eyes glowed like the stars overhead.

The quiver focused on that growing warmth as he leaned

over her again. The caress of his skin against hers above
her corset and shift was as fiery as that light in his eyes. He
held her gaze, not releasing it, as his finger looped over the
lace along the top of her corset and popped the first hook.
Then the next . . . and the next. His eyes narrowed as he
peeled it away from her. That was her only warning before
he drew down her loose shift and ran his tongue between
her breasts.

She grasped his shoulders and pulled him closer. With a
laugh, he found her lips again. All gentleness vanished from
his kiss. It demanded she give every bit of herself to this
pleasure. Stroking his bare back and letting her hands curve
down over his hips as he had caressed hers, she pulsed with
the accelerating need within her as he overpowered her
senses with his kisses.

He refused to be satisfied with her lips as he drew off her
blouse. He tasted her cheeks, her eyelids, the curve of her
jaw. His lips burnished her skin, setting it afire with longing.
Teasing her ear with the liquid heat of his tongue, he laughed
when she whispered his name again as she fought to keep
from being overwhelmed by this untamed passion. The
caress of his breath fanned the flames into a wildfire.

Her fingers splayed across his back when he slid the straps
of her shift down along her arm, and he probed beneath the
soft cotton over her breasts. The sensation of his mouth
against her was an exquisite delight. She wanted this craving,
but it would shatter her if it lasted a second longer.

Pushing his shirt aside, she dropped it to the floor atop
her discarded clothes. She swept her fingers along his broad
chest. His skin was becoming the inferno she could see in
his eyes. A hint of a smile curved his lips as he loosened
the button holding her skirt in place.

She laughed and pushed him away. When he regarded
her with astonishment, she held his shoulders to the pallet.

He groaned with the longing that also taunted her as she ran her tongue along her curves of his ear. She continued to explore each flavor of his delicious skin as he rid her of her skirt and petticoats.

He rolled her onto her back, then sat. His gaze swept over her as he unbuttoned one of her shoes with the same slow, fascinating caress as he had her corset.

She sat up so she could unhook the other. He laughed and pressed her back onto the pallet.

"I'm just trying to help," she whispered, barely able to recognize her own husky voice.

"I've been waiting for this, and I want to enjoy every moment."

"Of taking off my shoes?" She laughed as he pulled off her other shoe. "You have strange fantasies."

"Not so strange." His hands curved along the top of her stocking, and he slowly rolled it down her leg. Drawing it off her foot, he ran his hands up each side of her leg again.

She gasped with the craving that was becoming a hunger that must be sated when his hands slipped across her from one thigh to the other, then slowly rolled down the other stocking. He tossed it away, before sliding his hands back up her leg again.

She could not withstand much more of this without losing all of herself in the mindless bliss. When he had kicked away his boots and his own socks, she saw him reaching for the buttons on his denims. She playfully slapped his hand away and sat.

"I have fantasies of my own," she whispered as she put her hand on the topmost button.

"Do you?" His voice was as unsteady as hers, which thrilled her more.

"Yes."

"Do you want to share them with me?"

"I want to share more than my fantasies."

With a groan, he grasped her face and brought her mouth to his. She knew her fingers were fumbling on the buttons, but she did not pause as she undid his denims. Drawing them down and dropping them somewhere in the shadows, she smiled at him as she ran her hands up his strong leg. She did not stop when she reached the top. Stroking the silken skin that reacted to her very touch, she did not hurry to slide her hands away down his other leg. Her gaze absorbed the firm lines of his sculptured body

He reached for her as she began to let her fingers wander down his other leg. She paused and stared at him when they touched puckered skin that was broader than her palm and more than twice as long as her hand.

"Noah?" she whispered. "What happened?"

"Don't ask now, sweetheart."

"But you were hurt."

"Nothing hurts now but this longing to be part of you." His mouth took hers again. Creating a pattern of joy along her skin, he seemed determined to leave no part of her untouched.

Seized by the eager cadence of his breath, she moved with the tempo of a song created by two hearts and two bodies in perfect harmony. She gasped as the song became a crescendo when his fingers swept along her legs again to seek the fire within her. Touching him as intimately, she lost herself in the longing that flowed from her to him and back again in a wild rhapsody.

He drew her beneath him. His fingers brushed her hair back, framing her face, imprisoning her gaze within the passion blazing in his eyes. He brought them together, and the emptiness that had taunted her for so many years was filled with desperate desire. With his lips over hers, he dared her to reach for every delight waiting for them. She matched his motions and his need. She relinquished herself to the splendor that merged them into one perfect moment of ecstasy.

Emma stared up at the moonlight and smiled. When Noah shifted, she kept her head on his shoulder. He tipped her face up.

"I want to see that smile," he whispered.

"I shall wear it every time I remember this moment."

He kissed the spot on her neck where her pulse still pounded. "You shouldn't have to remember it too often."

"What?"

With a chuckle, he said, "This can't be the only memory you want to make with me, is it?"

She laughed too as her fingers stroked his chest. Her other hand ran along his leg. As they encountered the scarred skin, he drew his leg away and caught her hand in his, keeping her from touching him.

Looking up at his face, she saw his smile was gone. She leaned across him. "Noah, tell me, please."

"Some memories I prefer not to recall now."

"Don't you trust me with them?" She bit her lower lip to keep it from trembling.

"I trust you with everything I can, sweetheart." He framed her face and smiled. "I simply don't want to talk about bad memories when I want to create more splendid memories with you now."

She could not argue with that, for she did not want the joy to be tarnished either. Yet it had been. As soon as he held back this part of his past from her, she recalled how much she had not told him.

When he drew her into his arms and found her eager lips again, she expelled those thoughts from her head. The past was all around her, but tonight she wanted to think of only this man and the wondrous sensations they could share with each other while she forgot how short-lived this joy could be.

CHAPTER TWELVE

"Sean, stand still, so I can check that you washed behind your ears," Emma ordered as she inspected Sean from every angle.

Even though his cowlick refused to be lacquered down, his face was scrubbed. He wore a brown worsted coat with trousers to match. His shoes were well shined, and the bowtie at the throat of his neatly pressed white shirt was surprisingly straight. With his face already tanned from playing out-of-doors, he barely resembled the boy who had arrived in Haven with a sickly pallor and a bearing that suggested he was preparing himself for the next person who might do something to hurt him.

He wiggled away from her and put his hands over his ears. "No one's going to see behind my ears but you."

"Not if you don't let me cut your hair soon." She gave

him a playful slap on the shoulder. "If it gets much longer, I swear we'll have to braid it like Belinda's."

"Jenny likes it like this."

"Jenny Anderson?" she asked, trying not to smile. The Andersons ran the livery stable across the street from the store. She had wondered why their oldest girl, who was about a year older than Sean, had found so many excuses to come to the store in the past week. Somehow, Sean had always managed to be sweeping the porch when she arrived so the two of them could talk before Jenny did her shopping for her mother. "She is a very nice girl, Sean, but that is no excuse to let your hair grown down over your ears."

"I want to look like a slicker."

"Where did you learn such language?" She held up her hands. "No, don't tell me. I think I'd be better off not knowing the answer to that. Just watch what you say."

"I won't embarrass you, Emma, during the wedding." His face was abruptly sober.

She squeezed his shoulders and smiled. "And I'll try not to embarrass you either."

"You?"

"Of course." She drew on her best lace gloves. "When Jenny Anderson walks by, I could casually mention that I hadn't seen the back of your ears in more than a week."

"You wouldn't!"

Laughing, she said, "You're right. I wouldn't do that."

He grinned and curled the top of his ear forward. "See? All clean?"

Emma pretended to peer with concern at him. She would not tell him, but she was glad to see him come into the kitchen all dirty and laughing about how he had beat someone in a footrace or played hide-and-seek. Now that some of the other orphan train children were attending the village school, he was not as reluctant to attend each day. His chores were done more quickly, and Emma often had to call him in after dark to eat the supper that had grown cold on his plate.

A knock came on the door. Through the frosted glass, Emma could see three people on her porch.

Her smile broadened as she threw the door open for Noah, Belinda, and Gladys. She started to greet them, but could only stare. She had seen Noah dressed in his working clothes—cotton shirt, suspenders, vest, denims, and scuffed boots. The man standing before her now could have stepped out of an eastern fashion plate. Straight black trousers flowed down to his brightly polished boots. His black cutaway coat contrasted with the silver vest he wore over a flawlessly white shirt. The collar of his shirt, which reached nearly to his chin, was closed in front by a white tie that tilted slightly to the left—the only imperfection in his appearance. In his hand, he carried a black top hat edged with a band of silver.

This aristocratic man who looked as if his feet had never walked on anything but a sidewalk or through a fine garden unsettled her, for Noah wore these fine clothes with such ease. The questions she had tried to silence burst forth again, and she wondered why he spoke so seldom of his past. Was this elegance a part of his past?

Belinda peeked around him, smiling broadly. Her hair was pulled back in two braids beneath a hat decorated with silk roses to match the ones at the dropped waist of her dress. The full pink skirt was held out by crinolines and reached just below her knees. Pink-striped stockings and recently polished white shoes that buttoned up to her calves gave her an appearance as elegant as her father's.

"Look at the swells!" Sean whistled in appreciation, breaking her mesmerism with the sight before her.

She looked down at her gown. It was her very best, a silk only a shade deeper than the pink of Belinda's dress. Did fashionable ladies still wear cascades of ruffles down the back of their gowns below their bustles? And were the necklines still scooped so deeply that the sleeves were little more than a few layers of lace? She wanted to ask him, but her voice seemed to have vanished as she realized it was not her appearance that bothered her, but his.

This wondrously elegant man seemed so different from the one who had carried her in his arms across the floor of his new barn to make love with her in the moonlight. She loved that man who was not afraid to let her know how much he wanted her. He was plainspoken and kindhearted and so enticing that he made her breath falter each time she looked at him.

Noah's finger in the gray kid gloves reached beneath her chin and tilted her face up toward his. His smile and twinkling eyes were unchanged, and she was able to smile back at him.

"You look lovely," he said softly.

"Not as lovely as you."

He laughed. "I thought I'd do you proud today, Emma."

"You could do the fancy houses on Fifth Avenue proud in such clothes."

"No one would notice me if I walked down the avenue at your side. Today, you don't look like the sensible Miss Delancy of Delancy's General Store."

"She looks like a fairy-tale princess!" Belinda chirped. "Can I touch the ruffles on the back of your dress, Emma?"

Noah began, "Belinda, you shouldn't—"

"Of course, you can." Emma turned, listening to the lush sound of her gown's short train as it brushed the floor. "Just don't ask the same of any of the ladies at the wedding."

"Even if they look like fairy-tale princesses?" the little girl asked.

"Even if they do."

"Careful, Belinda," Noah said.

When she glanced over her shoulder, she saw his warm smile and the even more heated glow in his eyes that told her he wished *he* was the one touching her. She yearned to throw her arms around him and remind him that two weeks had passed since he shared that ecstasy with her in his barn.

"Tonight?" he mouthed, and she knew his thoughts matched hers.

She nodded, not knowing how he planned to get time for them alone when everyone in Haven would be celebrating the wedding with decorum and the party after with whiskey that would flow even faster during the shivaree at dark. Anticipation trickled along her like the ambling caress of his fingers, enthralling her.

Pulling her gaze from his, she looked down to see Belinda fingering the cascade of ruffles that dropped from the bow at Emma's waist. The little girl giggled with delight and ran her hand along the pink and silver embroidery that fell from the bow to curve around the front of her skirt in an soft drape.

"Just like what a fairy-tale princess would wear," Belinda whispered.

"Soon you shall have a dress like this of your own," Emma said, smiling down at the little girl.

"Don't rush her in growing up." Noah laughed.

She looked back at him, finding him less than an arm's length from her. A hint of a smile tipped his lips, and the now familiar sensation fluttered in her stomach. She closed her eyes to soothe her quivering as his breath brushed her hair. It would be so easy to lose herself again in that rapture. She could not. Not now.

He offered his arm. "Shall we go? Half the green is filled with wagons already." With another laugh, he said, "With everyone in the church, today would be the perfect day for a gang of bank robbers to ride through town."

"What?" she cried, freezing, her hand only inches from his arm.

His smile disappeared as his brows lowered. He took her hand and drew it down to his sleeve. "I was only jesting," he said. "You don't need to worry about your store with everyone about for celebrating the wedding."

"It was a discomfiting thing for you to say." She was aware that every eye was focused on her, and she tried to smile. Her expression seemed brittle, but it must have appeared less strained than it felt, because Noah's frown eased back into a lighthearted smile.

"How can you blame me for forgetting that you're a businesswoman with so much on your mind," Noah asked, "when you look like a—"

"A fairy-tale princess!" crowed Belinda and Sean at the same time.

Noah chuckled, but watched Emma, whose smile remained fragile. Why had she been so upset by such an offhand comment? He had only wanted to suggest that he and she could find a time to slip away when everyone's attention was on the bride and groom. Instead of teasing him back as he had expected, she had acted as if she faced some horror.

Her fingers were still trembling as he led her across the green with the children and Gladys in tow. He considered asking her what was wrong, but too many people greeted them and urged them to hurry into the white clapboard church. With each "good day," her fingers on his arm calmed a bit more. He was glad to see her smiling again when they walked up the steps to the church's front doors, which were both thrown open wide.

He smiled indulgently as she drew away to check that both Sean and Belinda were still looking their best. There was a gentleness about her that he saw only when she spoke with the children. She clearly loved having children near, and he wondered as he had so many times why she remained unmarried. Her eager touch when he had brought her to the new barn had dazzled him, so he knew she was not shy about expressing her yearnings. And he was very sure that he had not been the first to make love to her.

Who had been her lover before him?

He had pumped Gladys like a dry well, hoping she would have some gossip that could answer that question. If Emma had had a lover in Haven before now, she had been so circumspect about it that nobody even hinted at the decorous Miss Delancy having an affair. Keeping such a secret in this small town seemed impossible. If she had had a lover before coming to Haven . . . he fought not to frown as they walked into the church. She never spoke of her life before Haven. Not once had she said anything about it.

As he waited for the others to slip into one of the oak pews, he smiled. Today was not a day to dwell on the past. It was a day when two people were thinking of the future. He chuckled under his breath. *Three* people were thinking of the future.

"What's so funny?" asked Emma as he sat beside her on the red cushion that ran the length of the pew.

"I'm just in a good mood today." He rested his arm along the back of the pew, but did not curve his fingers around her shoulder. He was aware how many eyes would be watching them. There *had* been a wagonful of gossip since he had kissed Emma before he joined in the contest to raise the barn's walls.

"Me, too."

When her fingers slipped beneath his coat to settle clandestinely on his leg, he put his own over them. A single motion by those enticing fingers would be too much for his failing self-control. Pressing her back against the bright red cushion and kissing her with all the craving that had been whetted by two long weeks would create quite the scandal.

He lifted her hand to his lips and kissed it lightly through her lacy gloves. Her eyes glowed like the sunshine streaming through the stained glass windows marching along each side of the church. Curving her fingers over his, he turned reluctantly to see the wedding party come down the aisle.

Emma hushed Belinda as the little girl giggled in excitement when the obviously nervous groom and his best man came to stand by the simple altar. Glad that Noah did not release her hand, she smiled at Sally Young's sisters, who were serving as attendants. Their blue gowns had arrived at the store only a few days ago. Sally had insisted on store-bought gowns for her wedding, even though Mrs. Flexner could have made dresses just as pretty and for half the price.

Noticing the seamstress smiling proudly on the other side of the aisle, Emma looked more closely at the dresses. She grinned, for the garish flowers that had encircled the waists of the gowns and climbed up the bodices like overgrown weeds were gone. A single strip of golden lace now was the only decoration.

"What's so funny?" Noah whispered as she had to him.

"Mrs. Flexner." She quickly explained.

He muffled his laugh when everyone came to their feet as Sally Young appeared at the back of the church on her father's arm. The bride's dress remained unaltered, and it was bedecked with flowers that matched the ones edging her veil. Emma guessed those extra silk flowers had come from her sisters' gowns. Even the garish blossoms could not detract from the bride's loveliness. Sally usually wore dark clothes that accented her redheaded pallor. In her white gown with its bright flowers, she looked like—and Emma could think of no other description—a fairy-tale princess.

As they sat, Emma set Belinda on her lap and hushed the

little girl's excitement. Sean was staring, openmouthed, at the fancy clothes, and she knew he never had been to a wedding like this. He had never been to a church, except to sneak in to find shelter on a bitterly cold night, before he arrived in Haven.

More quickly than Emma wished, the ceremony was over, and the groom and bride were kissing for the first time as husband and wife. Belinda wiggled down off her lap and pushed to stand next to her father so she could watch the newest Mr. and Mrs. Smith walk back up the aisle.

With a laugh, Noah picked his daughter up and held her under one arm as if she were a bag of potatoes. She giggled and squirmed, but he paid her no attention as he offered his arm to Emma again. Emma took Sean's hand, and they walked out of the church together with Gladys following, dabbing at her teary eyes with a lacy handkerchief. That amused Emma, for Gladys had never met either Sally or Isaac Smith before the barn raising.

Once everyone had a chance to congratulate the newly-weds and kiss the bride, long tables were set up on the green with planks and sawhorses, just as they had been at Noah's farm. Food appeared out of every wagon.

"Sean, don't run about while everything is being brought out," Emma said. "I have to get the biscuits out of the warming oven."

"Go ahead." Gladys wiped a final tear from her cheek and smiled. "I'll watch him so he stays clean at least long enough to drop something on himself during the wedding feast."

With a laugh, Emma wove her way through the crowd that seemed to fill the green to overflowing. She saw bottles of whiskey surreptitiously being opened. The keg that had been delivered last night and stored in the livery where it could be kept cold with ice covered with hay was being rolled out. It would be set up beneath the trees. She would have to keep an eye on Sean to make sure he did not sample too much of the beer.

She felt oddly disconnected from the rest of Haven as she stepped up onto her porch. The voices diminished when she went into the house and to the kitchen. After pulling her apron over her head and tying it behind her, so there was no chance of getting anything on her silk gown, she opened the warming box of the oven. She used a pair of dishrags to protect her hands as she lifted out the trio of trays that held more than two dozen rolls each.

She was reaching for the fourth tray when hands caught her at the waist. Whirling, she smiled up at Noah.

"I thought I'd surprise you," he said.

"You can't surprise me, for I recognize your touch."

"Do you?" He ran his finger along the apron she had draped over her head. When it paused between the curves of her breasts, he murmured, "I'd like to become very much better acquainted with touching you."

She drew his mouth to hers, famished for his kisses. *This* was the feast she wanted today. His arms curved around her, drawing her tight to him. She wanted to be even closer.

He raised his mouth from hers. "We can't linger here. Gladys sent me to get you because everyone's about to drink a toast to the happy couple." He ran his tongue along her neck, and she quivered with the longing that refused to be quiescent. In a whisper, he said, "I know what would make this couple happy if we had an excuse to remain here a while longer."

"You could say you didn't find me right away." She ran her finger along his expressive brows.

He laughed. "And who would believe that?"

"I don't care what anyone else would believe. I care about taking any chance to be with you."

"You're a temptress, Emma Delancy." He reached behind her and undid her apron. Drawing the ties around, he let them fall at her sides. "Only such a vixen would think of sampling a bit of love in the middle of the day."

"The moonlight was just enough to make me want to see your face in the bright sunlight."

"When we are one?" he asked as he glided his hands up beneath her apron to curve along her breasts. His mouth captured hers, and she gripped his shoulders to keep her knees, which were as fluid as melting butter, from pulling her away from him.

From the parlor came Sean's voice. "Emma! Emma, Gladys says for you to hurry up."

"Hurry?" Noah asked quietly. "No, I won't hurry this, Emma. I want to go slow and relearn every bit of you. I want you to plead for release from this craving."

"I'm pleading now." She smiled as she sifted her fingers through his hair.

"Not enough, you aren't."

"Is that so?"

"I want you to plead not with your voice, but with your body."

When his fingers stroked her cheek, she gazed up into his ebony eyes, which revealed the desires she had not been able to silence within her. His lips grazed hers as lightly as he had caressed her face, but she was sure he had decorated her skin with liquid fire.

"Emma!" Sean's voice was insistent. He opened the kitchen door and peeked in. Grinning, he said, "You should leave the lovey-dovey to the bride and groom."

Noah kept his arm around Emma as he turned and said, "I didn't realize you were such an expert on courting, Sean."

"I know all about it." His thin chest puffed out in pride.

"I plan to kiss Jenny today." His eyes widened as he realized what he had said. "I mean . . ."

"You might want to save the kissing for another day," Emma said as she handed him a dish towel and motioned for him to pick up a tray of rolls. "Sometimes it is better to have such a special event be on a day that is special only for you. Why share it with this wedding?"

"Do you think I should wait until another day?"

"I think you'll be happier if you do."

As Sean nodded and went back out, balancing the tray as if he were carrying dynamite, Noah chuckled. He started to speak, but Emma held up her hand.

The front door closed, and she said, "All right. He won't hear you now."

"You have a real skill with kids."

"I'm learning as I go." She laughed. "Or maybe I'm thinking of how my mother said such things to me and my brother and sister."

"Brother and sister? Mother? You've never mentioned them before."

Emma wanted to curse her own carelessness. No one else, other than Noah Sawyer, had lured her into revealing what should stay hidden. She pasted on a smile and asked, "You didn't think I was hatched, did you?"

"Do they live around here?"

"No." She lifted her apron over her head and placed it on its peg by the door.

"That's too bad."

"I do miss them." She reached into the warming box for the last tray.

"No, I meant it was too bad for me."

"For you?"

He picked up two of the trays and grinned. "Think about

all the tales I might hear about you when you were a little girl.''

"Think about it all you want.'' She was able to smile back as she picked up the third tray and opened the door to the parlor.

"I'd rather think about you as a woman." He edged through the door, brushing up against her as he moved slowly past. He turned at an awkward angle and kissed her.

She reached out to balance the tray in his left hand. "Think of me as an *angry* woman if you send my cooking all over the floor.''

"Yes, ma'am.'' He gave her a wink before she walked past him to open the door to the porch.

Emma was not sure whether to be disappointed or relieved when he did not press up against her when he stepped out onto the porch. She was both, but she was glad he was being sensible in public. As they walked across the green, she introduced him to people who had not been able to attend the barn raising.

Noah set the trays on the table and looked around. "Where's Samuel Jennings? I thought he would be here today.''

"He doesn't like weddings,'' Alice said as she stirred up the mashed potatoes she had prepared.

"What makes you say that?''

"He never comes to any. He always has an excuse to avoid them.'' She hurried away.

"Don't listen to her, Noah.'' Emma chuckled. "Alice once was sweet on him, and she hasn't gotten over her irritation that he expressed no interest in marrying her.''

"But he isn't here.''

"Maybe one of the children isn't feeling well.'' She shook her head. "Three at once is quite a burden for a man all by himself.''

"One has been enough to keep me busy."

Emma did not have time to reply as shouts were called to get something to drink so the bride and groom could be toasted before the food was served. Someone handed her a mug of cider, and she raised it as shouts of congratulations rang through the afternoon. When Noah put his arm around her shoulders, she leaned her head against his shoulder and wished the joy of this afternoon could continue forever.

CHAPTER THIRTEEN

That time when she stood next to Noah during the toast was the last quiet moment Emma had with him that afternoon. As she watched Sean fill his plate, eagerly wanting to sample every new dish, she smiled at Gladys, who was trying to persuade Belinda that no one must touch the three-tiered wedding cake until the newlyweds had cut and eaten the first pieces. Emma led a parade of Sean, Belinda, and Gladys—who picked up the food falling off Belinda's plate—to find a place to sit on one of the blankets that had been spread across the grass for the women and children.

Looking across the green, Emma saw Noah talking with the other men. They were laughing and refilling their mugs with beer or with whatever was in the bottles that were being passed around. If she had not known better, she would have guessed he had been in Haven for years and years. The barn raising had allowed him to get to know the people of Haven and for them to know him. His hard work had gained their respect.

He turned, and she was caught by his gaze, even from across the green. When he smiled, she did, too. There was some invisible thread that connected them, and she did not want to let it unravel. Instead she wanted to wrap it around her like his arms.

Emma was aware of that link even when the children finished second helpings and ran off to play while the women began to talk about all the news from within the village and beyond. When the wedding cake was cut and served, with the youngest children vying for the pieces with the most icing, she sensed Noah watching her.

And why shouldn't he be? She was watching him. His easy good humor as he enjoyed a joke with the men, his smooth, graceful motions when he tossed horseshoes, the respect the other men offered him when the conversation turned to politics and the upcoming elections in the fall . . . she took note of all that and more. She wanted to discover every expression he wore and every movement he made so she could remember them when she was sitting alone in the evening after Sean had gone to sleep.

As the sun set, turning the river at the bottom of the hill a brilliant red, the guests returned to the tables to finish off the last of the food. Vulgar comments to the bride and groom warned her that the final event of the wedding, the shivaree, would soon be starting. She wanted Sean in the house before that rowdy, bawdy fun began. Other women were collecting their children, too, and taking them back to the wagons or to their homes in village.

"It's still early," Sean complained when Emma called to him to follow her back to the house.

When he yawned, she laughed. "All this sunshine and the good food have worn you out."

"Do you have weddings often in Haven?" he asked as she put her arm around his shoulders while they walked toward the house.

"Usually a couple of times a year."

"Only twice a year?" He frowned, then brightened. "Why don't you and Noah get hitched? He has been honey-fuggling you."

"Honeyfuggling?"

"Billing and cooing with you and kissing you and—"

She smiled. "I know what honeyfuggle means. I'm just surprised you do. That's not a New York City type of word. It's more of an Indiana word."

"I've heard it about town."

Although she wanted to ask what else he had heard, she did not ask, for her name was shouted. She turned and saw Reverend Faulkner waving madly to her.

"Wait here," she told Sean. "I shouldn't be long."

She went back to the center of the green where the minister was motioning to her to hurry. She wondered why he had such a head of steam up at the end of the day. Her steps slowed when she saw the unmarried women gathering near the bride.

"Reverend Faulkner," she began, "I need to take Sean back to the house before—"

"Not before the bouquet is tossed, Emma."

"That's for the young girls."

"It's for all the young ladies who have never been married."

Emma sighed. She usually had managed to be elsewhere when the bouquet was tossed. If she spoke the truth that she was no longer eligible for this silly ritual, she would ruin her life here in Haven. She had worked too hard to rebuild a life for herself here to let it get undermined simply because she hated this tradition.

She let the minister herd her to where a half dozen other women were waiting. Two of them could not be much more than fifteen, and they were giggling excitedly together as they whispered about which boy they would like to wed if they were lucky enough to catch the bouquet. Exchanging a glance with Alice, who looked no more pleased than Emma to be taking part in this, Emma stepped behind the young girls. Two of the bride's sisters came to stand with them.

"All set?" called the newest Mrs. Smith as she looked back over her shoulder.

"Go ahead!" cried one of the young girls.

"Throw it here, Sally!" shouted the other.

The bouquet soared into the twilight sky. The girls leaped forward. As they bumped into one another, Emma reached out to keep the smaller one from falling to the ground and ruining their pretty dresses. The bouquet struck the girl on the shoulder and dropped into Emma's hands.

"Oh, no!" she moaned.

"I'm glad it's you and not me," Alice said with a chuckle as cheers resounded around them.

"How about another try?" Emma suggested. "I don't think it bouncing off someone counts."

Alice wagged a finger at her. "You aren't going to escape that easily."

As if everyone had heard the teacher's hushed words, Emma was surrounded by the female guests, who congratulated her on catching the bouquet. Her face grew warm when she realized that the men were making jokes at Noah's expense.

Sean tugged on her arm, and she was grateful for the excuse to take him back to the house. He frowned at her as they reached the front steps.

"What's wrong?" she asked when she went into the house and lit a lamp.

"You said you wouldn't embarrass me." His nose wrinkled as he pointed at the bouquet. "And look what you did!"

"I didn't want to catch it. I was trying to catch Andrea Stewart before she could fall on her face."

"Just please don't do it again. It was embarrassing to have everyone talking about you getting married."

"Weren't you the one who just a few minutes ago was trying to persuade me to propose to Noah?"

"I was joking." He did not look at her.

"So were they."

He shook his head. "I'm not so sure. We're a family now, aren't we, Emma?"

"Yes, we are," she answered slowly, astounded where this conversation was headed. "If you want to be."

"I do want to be a family." A momentary grin brightened his face. "I have never had one. Except for my sister, Maeve."

Drawing him down to sit on the lowest step, she sat next to him. "Sean, I want us to be a family, too. When Maeve comes to Haven, she can be part of our family as well. You want that, don't you?"

"You know I do!"

She put her arm around his thin shoulders again. "And I want that, too. Families are made by welcoming other people into them, people we don't even know. Like babies and like you."

"And like a husband?"

"Maybe . . . someday."

He pondered that for a moment, then said, "I like Noah."

"I know."

"And you do, too."

"Yes." She smiled.

"So if you have to get married, I suppose he'd be a good choice."

She mussed his hair. "I don't need you matchmaking, too." When he giggled, she gave him a hug and stood. "I need to put these flowers in some water before they're completely wilted."

"If you get married, you won't have to try to catch the bride's flowers again, will you?"

"No, I won't have to do that again."

Again he thought for a few seconds. Standing, he said, "Then maybe you should get married so you don't embarrass me again."

She hugged him. "You can be sure I will try not to embarrass you ever again."

"So you're going to marry Noah?"

"I didn't say that."

He laughed again.

Patting his bottom, she said, "Now off to bed with you. Gladys should be bringing Belinda over here before the shivaree starts."

"What's a shivaree?" His eyes lit up. "There's more fun?"

"Not for the children. The adults are going to act silly one more time before they go home. It gets loud, so try to get to sleep before they start. That way, you can get a good night's sleep and be ready for the ball game I know you're planning to play tomorrow."

Rushing up the stairs, Sean careened around the corner and into his room.

Emma poured water from the bucket into a wide bowl and put the flowers in it. In the morning, she would untie the bouquet and find a vase that would hold the blossoms.

Shouts came from outside, and she went out to the porch. Torches had been lit, looking like giant fireflies on the green. When she heard the song that was being sung in drunken voices, she sat on the top step. The procession would be passing right in front of her. She would wait here until they reached her house.

When Gladys appeared out of the darkness carrying Belinda, who was already asleep, Emma smiled. "You can put Belinda in my bed, if you'd like."

"You don't have to stay here. Go ahead and have some fun. I'm too old for all this mischief." She chuckled. "I think I'll sit on the sofa and rest until it's time to go back to the farm."

Emma stood and opened the door for Gladys. "Make yourself a cup of tea, if you'd like."

Closing the door again, Emma went back to sit at the top of the steps. The torches were lurching toward the house. Shouts resonated through the thickening darkness.

Torches . . . shouts . . .

She gripped the edge of the step as the voices and the lighted brands tossed her back into the morass of her memories. There had been torches coming toward the house in Kansas, and she had heard the angry, drunken shouts through the walls. Those torches and the lynch mob had distracted the deputy guarding her long enough for her to slip out of the house and bolt away into the darkness. If they had gotten into the house while she was still there, they would not have been stopped from hanging her at the same gallows where Miles had been executed. They had considered him a criminal, but she had been seen as betraying everyone in town in order to get rich.

"Emma?"

A scream escaped from her lips before she could halt it. She clamped her hands over her mouth as she looked up at Noah, who was regarding her with astonishment.

"Are you all right?" he asked.

"You startled me."

"I thought you saw me coming up the walk. You were looking right at me."

She forced a smile. "The shivaree was making me think about other nights, and I was lost in my memories."

"May I?" He gestured toward the steps.

"Of course."

He sat next to her. He was as silent as she was while they watched the bride and groom being escorted past with catcalls and ribald jests. She thought of telling him that he did not have to remain here with her, but did not break the silence. As the parade continued out of town in the direction of the house Isaac Smith had been building since he asked Sally to be his wife, Noah stood and held out his hand.

"Do you want to join them?" she asked.

"No, but I thought I might see if there's some more beer in that last keg."

Emma laughed. "By the sounds of the guests, I'd doubt it."

"You may be right." He continued to hold out his hand to her. "Let's go and see how the river is faring."

"At this hour?"

"Why not? We watched it far later than this the night the creek rose."

Again she laughed. "We had a good reason then."

"Don't you think I might have a good reason tonight?"

She put her hand in his and let him bring her to her feet. There was an odd intensity in his voice, and she guessed he wanted to speak to her about something important when no other ears could listen. A throb of anticipation rippled through her. Maybe it was no more than he had found a place where they could be alone and rediscover rapture. As she imagined lying with him in a green bower, she had to fight to keep her feet from running.

The river's current had slowed to its normal spring speed, and Emma could see a few branches bouncing on the water. The moon was new, so only starlight glimmered in the river. Walking down the hill to the narrow shore that was edged with trees and wildflowers that had begun to bloom, she smiled when Noah swung their hands between them. She looked back up the hill and saw the town's buildings blocking out a portion of the sky. A few windows were lit with lamps, but most were dark. In the distance, she heard a roar of laughter, but here they could have been the only living beings in the world.

"Do you ever go across the river to Kentucky?" Noah asked without preamble.

"I have once or twice. The closest bridge to span the Ohio is nearly a day's ride south and west of here."

"A single strand of water keeps Indiana and Kentucky so separated. Sometimes, it's the simplest things that keep places and people apart."

She was uncertain how to answer, because she had no idea why he had asked her to come here to speak of this.

"But traditions keep us together, don't they?" he asked with a chuckle. "Weddings and graduations and funerals and births and all the other rituals of our lives. Traditions are important, you know."

"I know."

"We really shouldn't go against them," he said as they continued to walk through the soft darkness.

"Really?" She smiled up at him.

"It brings bad luck."

She gave an exaggerated shudder. "I think, after that flood, we've had enough bad luck to last a lifetime."

"I agree." He released her hand and stopped.

When she turned to face him, he dropped to one knee and clasped her hand between his. Her fingers trembled as she gazed down into his upturned face. Maybe he was just jesting with her. Maybe . . .

"Emma, will you marry me?" he asked quietly. "I've been thinking of asking you for some time now, but the time never seemed right." He smiled. "Too many children and other folks around. When you caught the bouquet, it seemed the time was perfect to ask you, because tradition deems you should be the next one married."

She drew her hand out of his. "This is a surprise."

"Why? I thought you understood after what we shared the night of the barn raising that I intended to ask you to marry me." He chuckled. "I would have asked you that night, but I seemed to have my mind—and my mouth—on other things."

"But it's still a surprise to be asked now, Noah."

He clasped her hands again. "So will you marry me?"

"I don't know."

His smile vanished as he stood. "Now I'm surprised. That isn't the answer I'd thought you'd give. I thought you'd say yes and feared you'd say no."

"But that answer is the truth." Now she was not being completely honest. She *did* want to marry him. She wanted it with all her heart. If she could be certain her past would never catch up with her, she would have thrown her arms around his shoulders as she told him that yes, oh, yes, she wanted to be his wife.

"Is it because of Belinda?"

"Belinda?" she gasped. "What does Belinda have to do with this?"

He shrugged. "I don't think she has anything to do with your reluctance, but I'm grasping at straws here, sweetheart. I know you love me."

"You do?"

Even in the starlight, she could see his eyes twinkling as

he caressed her face and said, "Yes, I do. What I don't know is why you won't marry me when you love me." He grasped her shoulders as his mouth found hers with ease through the darkness.

She clung to him as if she feared the river would overflow its banks and sweep her away from him. The dark and cold torrent of her past, more vicious and unforgiving than a flood, could tear them apart.

As his kiss deepened, she let her thoughts drift away on the waves of pleasure that surged over her. She ran her fingers up his strong chest, then beneath his coat to stroke his back as he pulled her even closer. Her breath was ragged when he lifted his lips away.

"Tell me," he said, "why you can kiss me like that and don't want to become my wife."

"Have you mentioned anything to Belinda about this?"

He frowned. "I thought you said she had nothing to do with your hesitation."

"She doesn't." She dampened her lips before saying, "But you should be sure she won't resent that you're asking someone to replace her mother."

"Belinda does not remember her mother."

"I didn't realize . . ."

"Her mother was killed in a fire." He closed his eyes. His breath sifted out of him in a long, slow sigh. "I was able to save only Belinda."

"The scars on your leg!"

"From that fire. If not for the need to take care of Belinda, who was little more than a newborn, I don't know how I would have survived the guilt and the grief of not being able to save the others in the house, too."

"Noah, I had no idea."

He seized her shoulders as his voice became urgent again. "Sweetheart, that's all in the past. I've come to terms with the guilt, and I've learned that the grief will be a part of me forever." His fingers tightened on her, and she saw strong emotions stiffening his face. "That's the past, Emma. I want to have a future here in Haven, and I want you to be part of that future."

"It isn't that simple."

"Why not?"

"I can't explain."

"Can't?" His hands dropped away from her shoulders. "Why not, Emma?"

"There are so many things to consider."

"If you're worried about Sean, I've already spoken with him, and he's given his blessing."

"Because he wants to attend another wedding and the party afterward."

"Whatever the reason, he's agreeable to this."

She nodded. "I know, for we spoke about this very subject just before he went off to bed tonight." Looking up at him, she whispered, "We spoke of families and how families are created."

Noah's smile returned. "So if he's willing, why aren't you?" His lips pressed against her neck, eliciting another quiver of longing from her. "And you are so willing, sweetheart."

"The store—"

His curse echoed across the water. "Emma, if you don't want to marry me, all you have to do is say so."

She closed her eyes and again imagined herself in his arms as she gave him a breathless yes to his proposal. "I can't say I don't want to marry you."

"But?"

"Please give me some time to consider your proposal."

"Time?" He jerked her back into his arms so fast that

she would have lost her footing if he had not pressed her to his chest.

His mouth on hers was not gentle, for his kiss revealed his unsated desire for her. He released her, and she wobbled. His hand beneath her elbow steadied her.

"I don't want to wait any longer to have you with me every night," he said. "Why do you want to waste time arguing about this when you must know I love you?"

"You love me?" she whispered, as her heartbeat thudded in her ears.

"Why else would I ask you to be my wife?"

Again she closed her eyes. The answer to his question burned in her mind, an answer that demanded she speak it because she wanted to be forthright with him. But how could she tell this honest man how her first husband had married her simply because she gave him respectability in their small town and the opportunity to rob nearby banks? Would he change his mind because she had been so stupid? She did not want to believe that, but she had seen those she had thought would be friends all her life turn their backs on her when they accepted as the truth the malicious tales about her.

Opening her eyes, she gazed up at him. He was not Miles Cooper. He was Noah Sawyer, a good and gentle man who had asked her to marry him because he *loved* her.

She loved him, too. She loved him with all her being, and she wanted to spend every night with him and every day and all the years they could have together.

Seven years had passed since she escaped the hangman's noose in Kansas. For seven years, she had lived here in Haven, where she had built a new life. Seven long years, and there had been no hint anyone was still in pursuit of her. Seven years during which she had visited Lewis Parker's sheriff's office in the courthouse regularly and had seen the wanted posters on his wall. Although she knew there had been one describing her, for she had seen it posted in St. Louis, she had never seen such a wanted poster in Haven.

Seven years of her life had been lost to that one horrible incident in her past. How much more was she going to sacrifice to her past? This love had come into her life when she had least expected it, and she would be a fool to toss it aside. Noah had said he had learned to put his past in the past. He could help her do the same while she reveled in his love.

Putting her hands up on either side of his face, she murmured, "Yes, Noah."

"Yes?" His eyes widened as if he could not believe what he had just heard. "Yes? You'll marry me?"

"Yes."

"I should ask you why you changed your mind, but I don't care." He kissed her lightly. "All I care is that you're going to be my wife."

As she welcomed his kiss, she hoped that was all she would care about from this point forward, too.

CHAPTER FOURTEEN

Sean was not the only who thought it was a shame for Emma to agree with Noah that their wedding should not be a grand one like the one just celebrated on the green. As soon as Alice Underhill heard how Emma and Noah planned simply to say their vows in front of Reverend Faulkner and two witnesses, the schoolteacher stormed into the store.

Emma smiled at her friend, but finished figuring out Mrs. Randolph's bill at the counter. When Alice continued to frown, Emma sighed. She had heard Reverend Faulkner greet her friend outside on the porch, and she knew Alice must be upset with the quiet wedding she had planned.

"Yes, Mrs. Randolph," Emma said automatically, for she had repeated the same words every day for the last two weeks, "it's too bad that you haven't heard back on your letter from Washington, D.C. It does take a while for mail to get from here to there and back."

"Has the mail been delivered today?" the old woman asked, tapping her fingers impatiently on the counter. She reached into a nearby jar and pulled out a handful of peppermints and set them on the counter. Mrs. Randolph only ate sweets when she was greatly perturbed.

"The mail came in this morning, and it's all sorted." She put her hand on the envelope in her apron pocket. The return address was the Children's Aid Society. Although she wanted to read it, she had not had a chance. It seemed as if everyone in Haven had schemed to keep her from reading it. Mornings when the mail arrived were always the busiest at the store. Usually that pleased Emma, but not today.

With a start, she realized she could not remember the last time she had received a personal letter. She had thought so often of sending a letter to her sister and brother, for she longed to know how they fared and how their lives had unfolded for the past seven years. Even more, she wanted to ask them one simple question: Did they believe she was guilty, as so many others had?

"Hmph! I'd think those men in Washington, DC, would know the importance of getting back to me speedily." Mrs. Randolph picked up her purchases and went out of the store, mumbling to herself.

Emma came around the counter. "Alice, will you watch to make sure Mrs. Randolph goes to her house and no farther?"

"Emma, we need to talk." Alice folded her arms in front of her black blouse, which was dusted with chalk from the schoolroom. "Right away."

Pulling out the letter from her pocket, Emma said, "I've been waiting all day to see if this the news we've been hoping for about Sean's sister. Please watch Mrs. Randolph while I put the pot on the stove and read my letter. Then we can enjoy a nice cup of tea.''

"Very well.'' Alice's frown did not lessen, but she went to the door to watch that the old lady went safely along the street.

Emma set the cast iron kettle on the stove and sat in the rocking chair in front of it. Her fingers trembled as she stared at the letter. Taking a deep breath, she opened it and read the single page.

My dear Miss Delancy,

We are in receipt of your letter requesting information about Maeve O'Dell. First of all, let me say that I am speaking on behalf of the whole Children's Aid Society when I write that we are so pleased to hear of how well Sean O'Dell has adjusted to his new life.

At this time, we have no information on his younger sister. We have workers in the area where Sean reported he had last seen his sister. They will continue to make inquiries about a six-year-old girl with that name, and this office will check with orphanages and other children's asylums here in the city, but you must understand how difficult it is to find a single child in such a populous area as New York City.

Please be assured and please assure Sean that we are making all efforts to find the child. We know it is not easy to be patient when you are so concerned for both Maeve and Sean O'Dell, but that is the only counsel I can offer at this point. I will be sure to contact you immediately if we find the child.

It was signed with Mr. Barrett's scrawling signature. With a sigh, Emma lowered the page to her lap. She must find a way to tell Sean without breaking his heart or destroying his hopes.

"Is it bad news, Emma?" asked Alice as she sat on the bench facing the rocking chair. "You look so sad."

Emma folded the letter. "In spite of my hopes for a quick miracle, the Children's Aid Society hasn't yet discovered the whereabouts of Sean's sister."

"I'm so sorry."

"We must continue to hope." She stuffed the letter into her pocket. Her fingers lingered over it as if she still dared to believe that if she reread the letter it would now contain the news that she had yearned to hear.

"Will you tell him?" Alice asked.

"Of course! Why would I keep this from him? She is his sister."

The schoolteacher pyramided her fingers before her face in a pensive pose, then said, "Maybe you shouldn't tell him just now. Sean is finally beginning to find friends beyond those who came with him to Haven on the train. He's concentrating on his reading and his ciphering, and he's proving to be a child with a rare intelligence."

"I'm glad to hear this, but what does it have to do with telling him the truth?"

"He's settling in here. He has found a home with you, and he's becoming comfortable with the folks here." She glanced toward the door. "Especially with Jenny Anderson, who has been helping him with his spelling."

"Sean has quite the case of puppy love for the girl." Emma smiled. "I think it's because she can hit a baseball as far as he can."

"So let him enjoy this time, Emma. Let him continue to hope."

"He asks me every day as soon as he comes in the door

if a letter has come from the Children's Aid Society. I can't lie to him.''

Alice sighed and shook her head. "I understand, but you must realize that such a blow may threaten to sever every root he has put down in Haven. Those roots are still very shallow.''

Coming to her feet, Emma poured two cups of tea and handed one to Alice. "I know that. I also know I must be truthful with him about this.''

"So you believe honesty is always the best policy?''

"Yes." She hoped her friend had not taken note of how Emma's voice squeaked on that single word. Honesty *was* the best policy, but not always possible.

"Then let me be honest with *you*, Emma Delancy.''

Emma's smile returned. She recognized Alice's tone. It was the one her friend always assumed when she believed Emma needed to heed an important lesson Alice was about to teach her. Sitting again in the rocker, she took a sip of her tea before saying, "Please do be honest with me, Alice Underhill.''

"You are making a huge mistake with your wedding plans. Why aren't you having a grand wedding like Sally and Isaac Smith had?''

Setting her cup on the table that held a checkerboard, she counted on her fingers. "First, we have to consider the time of year. It's time for planting. Folks can't afford to take another whole day off. Second, I decided this would be best, because Noah is a widower, as you know. This is a second wedding for him.''

"But not for you! A first-time bride's wedding day is supposed to be one she will remember all her life.''

"I will remember it." Her smile tasted hypocritical, but she was speaking the truth now. She never would forget the day she had been stupid enough to repeat her vows to love, honor, cherish, and obey Miles Cooper for the rest of her life. "Third, Alice, I don't want to put you through the ignominy of having to stand there and wait for the bouquet to come to you."

"Well, there is that." Alice smiled. "But you could throw it to someone else."

"It would come directly to you. I can guarantee that." Rocking in the chair, she said, "I saw how you and Barry Hahn were very cozy after the most recent Grange meeting."

Color rose up her friend's face. "He's a very nice man, and he's willing to wait to make his intentions known until after the school year and the end-of-the-year exercises come to a close."

"So you two have plans?"

"For a big wedding later this summer. Just as you should have."

Emma shook her head. "This sort of wedding is what Noah and I want. Will you stand up with me, Alice?"

"I thought you'd never get around to asking me!" She put down her cup and grasped Emma's hands. "I could not have endured not being there to see you married."

"Nor could I," came a deeper voice from the doorway.

Emma smiled at Noah as she came to her feet and met him as he walked across the store toward her. When he held out his hand, she put hers in it. She drew it back and shook off the sawdust that had been clinging to his palm.

"Sorry," he said with a smile. "I thought I'd knocked that all off before I came into town to find out if that new saw I had ordered was in."

"Not on today's train." She brushed more sawdust from his ruddy hair.

He ran a single finger along her cheek. "Then I guess I shall just have to keep calling here every day until it does arrive."

"And then you'll stop calling?"

"Don't bet on it."

She laughed as she turned to include Alice in the conversation. "I just asked Alice to be my maid of honor. You need to look for a best man, you know."

"Egad, I thought this was going to be simple." He rolled his eyes and smiled when Alice laughed.

"Two witnesses." She held up two fingers. "That's the way it's done."

"So I understand. Don't worry. I think I can convince Anderson to stand up with us. He can steal a few minutes away from the livery and smithy for the ceremony."

Alice exploded, "A few minutes? Noah Sawyer, this is an important day for Emma."

"And for me, too, I assume." He winked at Emma.

"But a wedding is the bride's day." Alice wagged a finger at him as if he were one of her mischievous students. "If you won't have a big wedding, then the very least you can do is allow us to give you a party at the next Grange meeting."

"And when is that?" he asked.

"When are you getting married?" Alice returned.

Emma laughed and slipped her arm through his, paying no attention to the sawdust that filtered onto her skirt. "You may as well accept the inevitable, Noah. Alice is determined that we have a wedding reception."

With a smile, he said, "We're planning to get married Saturday."

"It would be better on Friday." Alice chuckled. "That's the next Grange meeting."

"Do you mind," he asked, looking back to Emma, "getting married one night earlier, sweetheart?"

She shook her head, unable to speak as she gazed into his eyes, which blazed with his longing for her. She would have gladly married him the day after the Smith wedding, but he had asked for time to talk to Belinda and help the little girl deal with the changes about to come into her life. Belinda had been as thrilled as Sean to become one family.

"Then Friday it shall be." He smiled at Alice. "Will that do?"

"Admirably." She waved as she rushed to the door. "Excuse me. There is so very much to do."

"You would think she's the bride," Noah said as he locked his fingers behind Emma's waist.

She threw her arms around him. When his hands swept up her back to enfold her, she brought his mouth over hers. Dampening each tingling inch of her lips with the tip of his tongue, he smiled before he claimed her mouth. Craving surged over her, threatening to drown her in the depths of a savage sweetness.

He raised his mouth far enough from hers so he could whisper, "You're amazing, Emma Delancy."

"Amazing? Why do you say that?"

"Because you have an endearing way of letting others give you *your* way."

She laughed. "Have I been that obvious that I want to get married as soon as we can?"

"Only to anyone who sees you or speaks with you." He chuckled again. "I'm just glad you and I are on the same side in this battle to get us wed."

"I'll always be on your side, Noah."

"Unless you are on top."

Her cheeks grew fiery as she slapped his arm. "Such talk in my store!"

"Shall I save it for when we're alone in our bed?"

"Yes."

Her smile softened when his mouth caressed hers. At a

crackle from her pocket, she pulled back and drew out the letter.

"What is this?" Noah asked. "A love poem for your beloved husband-to-be?"

"No."

His face became as somber as her voice. She handed him the letter, and he quickly read it. When he cursed, she did not chide him for using such language in the store. She understood his frustration all too well.

"Alice suggests I say nothing about this to Sean right now," Emma said as she took the note from him.

"Dashing his hopes would be cruel."

"Letting them stay high when we might be asking him to believe in the impossible could be cruel, too."

"Noah!" shouted Sean as he ran into the store.

Emma shoved the letter into her pocket before Sean could see it. Listening while Sean chattered like a telegraph clicking at top speed, she kept her hand in her pocket. She looked at his animated face, and she knew telling him what Mr. Barrett had written would erase his grin. She would wait and hope another letter was already on its way to Haven with the glad tidings that Maeve O'Dell had been found.

She hoped this was the right decision, instead of just the easy one.

"I pronounce you man and wife," Reverend Faulkner said, his voice resonating through the empty church. He closed the book he held and smiled broadly. "You may kiss your bride, Noah."

"My wife," Noah murmured as he drew Emma into his arms. In the same dress she had worn to the Smiths' wedding, she was a glorious sight, but he could think only of how lovely she would look tonight when he leaned her back in the large bed he had finished painting late last night.

Her lips were soft and delicious, and he longed to savor them for much more than this quick kiss. He stroked her cheek as he gazed into her eyes, which revealed her thoughts matched his. Why had he let Alice Underhill persuade them to have a big party after the wedding? All he wanted now was to be alone with his enchanting bride, who had created such magic that he would forever be caught up in her spell.

"Patience, my dear husband," she whispered, "is a virtue."

" 'Tis a dangerous wife who can read her husband's thoughts with such ease."

" 'Tis a beguiling husband who puts such thoughts in his wife's head."

With a chuckle, he kissed her lightly again. A foolish move, for that only augmented the longing. As he shook the minister's hand, his leg was grabbed tightly. He bent down and scooped up Belinda, giving her a big kiss. With a giggle, she wriggled to get down.

Setting her on her feet, he smiled when she held her arms up to Emma. As Emma embraced the little girl, he turned to Sean, who was grinning so broadly that his thin face could barely hold his delight. Noah shook the hand that Sean held out to him. With a laugh, he pulled the boy into a hug. When Sean hugged him back, Noah looked over the boy's head to see Emma's happy smile.

Cheers resounded through the church, and Noah turned to see what must be half the village crowded at the back of the church. They were applauding and shouting out congratulations.

Noah laughed as he grasped Emma's hand just before their "guests" rushed forward to escort them out of the church and in a grand parade to the Grange Hall only two doors down. Wanting to make sure Belinda and Sean did not get left behind, he held out his other hand. He was surprised and more than a bit pleased when Sean grasped it and Belinda took Emma's hand. This was a good sign of a new beginning for all of them. They might not be a family yet, but they were well on their way—something he could not have imagined even a few months ago. He did not fool himself into thinking there would not be adjustments for all of them, including the decision of what to do when they had two houses, but those thoughts were not for tonight.

Even more people were gathered by the door to the Grange Hall, and he guessed many plows had been abandoned early in the fields around Haven. When he saw Emma's delighted smile, he whispered, "You shouldn't look so surprised, sweetheart. I'm not the only one in Haven who loves you."

"But you're the only one who loves me as you do."

He tapped her nose as if she were no older than Belinda. "I'm glad for that."

Emma was sure her heart would burst from all the joy in it. When she saw Lewis Parker coming out of his office in the courthouse, she waved to him.

He came over and kissed her on one cheek before shaking Noah's hand. "Congratulations to both of you. I'll be joining the party as soon as I get some messages that are waiting for me at the telegraph office."

"Don't be long," Emma said. "You always said you wanted to dance with me at my wedding. I wouldn't want you to miss that."

"Nor do I." He hurried along the street toward the telegraph office.

Emma laughed when Noah bowed deeply to usher her into the Grange Hall. Her laughter became a gasp of glee when she saw the decorations throughout the big, open room. Paper had been cut into dozens of different designs and hung from every picture on the walls. Looking across the room, she saw Alice smiling with pride, and Emma knew her friend must have had her students make these decorations.

"Do you like them?" Sean asked, confirming her guess as he added, "We've been working on them for a whole week, and no one told. We all kept the secret."

She hugged him. "I love them, and thank you for doing this for Noah and me."

"For Noah and you and Belinda and me and Gladys."

"Yes." She feared she would cry if she looked into his hopeful face a moment longer. How had this urchin become part of her life so quickly? She did not know, but she was grateful to whatever Providence had brought him to Haven.

"Look!" cried Belinda, tugging on Emma's dress and pointing along the tables that were burdened with food. "There's a cake with *four* tiers."

"One for each of us."

"Can I have the biggest one?"

With a laugh, Emma said, "I think it'd be for the best if we share."

Belinda tilted her head to one side and replied, "I don't want to get sick like Sean did."

"That's right."

The guests crowded into the hall, each one trying to talk louder than his neighbor in an attempt to be heard. The children were sent to fill their plates and find a spot to sit on the raised platform at the far end of the room. When Doc Bamburger pulled out his fiddle and began to play, several men rushed to get their makeshift musical instruments. A spoon and a washboard matched the three-quarter time of bare hands on a washtub.

Emma swung Belinda's hand in tempo with the music as she led the way to the platform where Sean was saving her a place on one side of him while Jenny Anderson sat on his other side. The little girl giggled when Emma began to sing the words to the tune they were playing.

"What's that song?" Belinda asked.

"It's a song we sing often here after Grange business is done."

"Will you teach it to me?"

"Of course."

"Tonight?"

Emma was sure her cheeks must be bright red as she said, "No, not tonight, but soon."

"Tonight she's going to teach it to me," Noah said when he took her hand.

He kissed her, and she longed to melt into this fantasy she had never believed would be hers. Her fingers in his hair shook with the power of the yearning she was trying to hold in check . . . for a few more hours.

Accepting congratulations from her friends, Emma was pleased to hear Gladys had made the cake for them in Reverend Faulkner's kitchen. She had been uncertain how the housekeeper felt about Noah bringing a wife into *her* house. All anxiety faded away when Gladys gave her a big hug.

"Make him happy, Miss Del—Mrs. Sawyer," Gladys said with tears in her eyes.

"I hope I can. I know he makes me happier than I've ever been."

"That's a good beginning."

Sean was thrilled to discover Gladys had put white icing over her delicious chocolate cake. Promising to have "just two small pieces, Emma," he took two plates that held servings which Emma would never have described as small. She knew he had learned his lesson, so she enjoyed her cake while sitting beside Noah.

"So much for our quiet wedding," he said with a chuckle.

"With a crowd this large, it may be easier to slip away without having to endure a shivaree."

He smiled. "Now there's a thought."

Emma had no chance to answer as Doc Bamburger began playing his fiddle again. This time, the other musicians did not join in, so the sweet sound of the melody filled the Grange Hall.

With a laugh, Noah grabbed Emma's hands and swirled her out to dance as the middle of the room was cleared. She heard Belinda and Sean cheer from the front of the hall, but she was caught anew by the desire in Noah's dark eyes. As her feet followed his smooth steps, all the music, even her own singing of the words to the old tune, faded beneath the frantic beat of her heart. She thought of how they would move together later tonight.

"This is a nice gathering," she whispered, "but . . ." She curved her fingers up over his collar to brush his nape.

"Didn't you tell me patience is a virtue?" Noah answered as lowly as his hand glided up her back, holding her closer than propriety allowed.

"Yes."

"But I see no patience in your eyes, sweetheart." He chuckled. "Some things are worth waiting for."

"Some things are difficult to wait for."

His mouth slanted across hers, and cheers filled the hall. When he stepped away from her too quickly, she was about to protest, then realized the music had stopped.

Emma had no chance to dance again with Noah. She was sure she had danced with every man in the hall by the time Doc Bamburger put down his fiddle and called for something to drink. As she started to look for Noah in the crowded room, she saw Alice and her beau standing in a corner as they gazed with love into each other's eyes.

Going to the table where she had left the bouquet of

wildflowers Sean had picked for her in the field behind the house, she picked it up and carried it to Alice. She placed it in her startled friend's hands and said, "For the next bride in Haven."

"You're supposed to throw the bouquet." Alice's eyes glowed with happiness.

"I told you I wanted *you* to have it."

Noah emerged from the press of guests to put his arm around Emma's shoulders. "You might as well accept the inevitable, Hahn," he said to Alice's bashful beau, who was turning a brighter red with each passing second. His voice softened as he said, "It's time to be heading home, sweetheart."

She nodded and bid her friends good night. Gathering up the children and Gladys, she laughed when she saw, in the lights from inside the Grange Hall, Noah's rickety buckboard had been adorned with more of the paper decorations. She helped the children into the back while Noah gave Gladys a hand in to sit between Sean and Belinda. Then Emma let him lead her around to the front of the wagon.

He lifted her up to the seat, his smile broadening as he stroked her side. Jumping up beside her, he picked up the reins. A few bawdy shouts came from the doorway of the Grange Hall, but they were quickly silenced as other men pointed to the children in the back.

With a wave, Noah turned the buckboard toward the road leading out to his farm. Emma nestled her head against his shoulder and looked up at the sky that was littered with stars and the widening moon. She had stopped believing in dreams coming true . . . until now. Her nightmares were behind her, and she would be happy again.

A small hand pulled on her skirt. Sitting straighter, Emma looked back to see Belinda being grasped and pulled back down to sit by Gladys who said, "Sorry she disturbed you. I'll keep a closer eye on her, Mrs. Sawyer."

Emma smiled when Noah chuckled at her new name. Leaning over the seat, she asked, "What do you want, Belinda?"

"You said you'd teach me that song soon."

"Not tonight is what she said," her father corrected.

"But she said soon. And isn't it soon by now?"

Putting her hand on Noah's arm to halt his reply, Emma said, "All right. I'll teach part of it to you, but you must wait to learn the other songs."

Belinda nodded so vigorously that her bonnet bounced to fall back onto her braids.

"You're spoiling her," Noah murmured.

"A child needs to be spoiled a bit sometimes."

"Just save some of this attention for your husband, Mrs. Sawyer."

"Are you jealous, Mr. Sawyer?"

She thought he would fire back a teasing retort, but he turned her to press her against him as he whispered, "I wish to jealously guard every moment we can spend together, and I don't want to share a single one with anyone else, not even the children."

"Soon," she said as quietly.

"That's hardly the answer I want."

"But you see how soon 'soon' came for Belinda." She kissed his cheek.

Emma looked back at the children as Noah laughed and drove them out onto the country road. He listened to her lyrical voice sing the words to the song the doctor had played earlier. He chuckled at the silly words and how the children tried to make their way through the first verse without missing any notes or words.

He gazed off into the night. This had been the right thing

to do. He was certain of that, but the familiar small nugget of uneasiness refused to be banished from his stomach. It was time to do as he had told Emma and leave the sorrow of the past in the past.

Looking away from the road that the horse could probably see better than he could, he admired the lovely woman sitting beside him. He had not guessed until he arrived in Haven and met Emma that he could be happy like this again. Yes, he had been happy to have Belinda safe with him after the fire, but she was a child. He had longed for the love of a woman who was everything he had dreamed of—alluring and gentle-hearted and intelligent and . . . alluring.

He laughed under his breath. How irresistible Emma was seemed to be the only thing he could think of tonight. She glanced at him, clearly curious at what he found amusing, but continued to sing with Belinda and Sean as the wagon turned onto the road to the barn. Noah smiled when Sean's voice cracked, but the boy continued gamely on.

When Noah saw a horse tied to the paddock fence that he had built last week, he stopped the buckboard. He jumped down from the seat and lifted Emma out.

"I don't know whose horse it is," she said before he could ask. "It's too dark to see the markings. Who would be out here *tonight?*"

He glanced toward the house and saw someone move on the porch. Whoever had ridden out here was waiting there for them. He considered telling Emma to stay here with the others, but told himself he was being silly. This probably was someone who had missed the wedding party and wanted to wish them well.

When he climbed up the steps to the porch, he saw a familiar face in the thin moonlight. He did not have a chance to speak before Emma said, "Oh, Lewis, we missed you at the Grange Hall. I looked for you so we could have our dance.''

"I was busy." His voice was oddly brusque, and Noah wondered if the man was chagrined that he had let his work get in the way of his friend's wedding.

Emma smiled. "There's some wedding cake left which we brought with us, and I'm sure Gladys can find us something to drink."

"Do you prefer coffee or tea, sheriff?" asked the housekeeper as she opened the door.

"Nothing for me," Lewis said. "I won't be staying long."

"What can we do for you?" Noah held the door open so the children could scurry in after Gladys. Motioning toward the rocker, he said, "Have a seat. I think I danced my feet off tonight, and I'm going to give them a rest."

Emma sat next to Noah on the swing at the side of the porch. As they rocked in unison, she put her hand in his. He smiled at her, then looked at the sheriff who was still standing.

Noah tensed, noting again how taut the man's shoulders were. "Is something wrong, Lewis?"

"I'm afraid so." He pulled a piece of paper out from under his coat. "Over the telegraph tonight, I received this warrant giving me the authority to make an arrest."

Emma gave a moan so soft Noah doubted any ears but his had heard it. Her fingers tightened painfully around his. Her voice broke as Sean's had when she began, "Lewis, you must let me—"

The sheriff paid her no attention as he said, "The warrant is for your arrest, Mr. Sawyer."

CHAPTER FIFTEEN

Emma stared at the sheriff. She must have heard him wrong. If he had said the warrant was for her arrest, she could have understood that her first marriage was returning to destroy her second one. But Noah . . .

She looked at Noah, but he was staring straight ahead, his face wiped clean of any emotion. Why wasn't he saying something?

She must! "Lewis," she asked, "would you repeat what you just said?"

The thin sheriff gave her a sorrowful glance, and his stern voice softened as he said, "I sure am sorry to be bringing this on your wedding day, Emma, but it was waiting at the telegraph office." He held up the page. "I sent a message back to make sure there hadn't been a mistake. There wasn't. I'm supposed to arrest Noah."

"Arrest Noah?" Emma jumped to her feet. "Why would anyone swear out a warrant on Noah?"

Noah put his hand on her arm as he stood more slowly. He took the page Lewis held out to him. His lips tightened as he read it.

"Noah, what is it?" she asked.

When he handed it to her, she ignored the fancy lettering at the top. She scanned the page and choked back a gasp. *Kidnapping!* He was to be arrested on a charge of kidnapping? This made no sense.

"Lewis, this must be a mistake," she said, her voice breaking as Noah plucked the warrant out of her numb fingers.

The sheriff sighed. "I didn't want to interrupt your wedding reception, so I figured it'd be just as easy to come out here to deliver this. I knew you'd be returning here after your wedding."

"It has to be a mistake," Emma said again. She gripped the porch pole to steady herself before she could be thrown back to the first time she had said those exact words to a lawman. She had been standing in the parlor of her comfortable house in Kansas. Then, her sister had been with her, so shocked by Miles's treachery that she could not speak.

Emma would not let Noah be tarred with someone else's wrongdoing as she had been. She would speak up! But why was he saying nothing in his defense? *Tell Lewis the truth*, she wanted to shout.

"Whether it's a mistake or not, it's official," replied Lewis. "Straight from Chicago."

"Chicago?" she whispered. Staring at Noah, who was still silent, she sat back on the swing before her legs gave out from beneath her.

She looked through the window at the furniture in the parlor and the dining room beyond. When she had asked about it, Noah had reacted as if she were attacking him . . . or accusing him of some heinous crime. She reached out and took his hand.

He flinched, and tears thickened in her eyes. She could not ask him how he could believe that she would turn against him when her lips still smoldered with the heat of his slow-burning kisses.

Then he put his other hand around hers and looked down at her. "I'm sorry, sweetheart. This isn't what I thought our wedding night would be like."

"Noah, why would anyone accuse you of kidnapping?" She faltered, then asked, "Who are you supposed to have kidnapped?"

"Belinda."

Emma pressed her hand over her heart that seemed to be trying to leap out of her chest. "Belinda? This is nonsense." Setting herself on her feet, she said, "Lewis, if this is some-one's idea of a shivaree, it isn't funny."

"No," the sheriff said, his eyes focused directly on Noah, "it isn't funny." His rigid pose eased as he looked at Emma. "I wish I could tell you that this was a jest on the newlyweds, but it isn't."

She whirled to Noah. "Tell him that it's a terrible mistake, that someone has mistaken you for someone else. How can you kidnap *Belinda?*"

"Emma, enough."

She bit her lip, recognizing the fury in his tightly restrained voice. So many questions needed to be answered, but she must not say anything that would create more trouble. That she had learned, as well, when the authorities came in search of Miles. Her own words of concern for her husband had condemned her even before he was found and lynched.

Noah folded the page and put it beneath his coat. "What's the next step in this process, sheriff?"

"Noah!" she cried, then clamped her lips closed.

Lewis shuffled his feet, abruptly looking as uneasy and uncertain as Sean had the day the sheriff had caught him with Noah's hammer and bag of nails. "My instructions are to keep you under guard until the authorities from Chicago can come to deal with you."

"Where? There isn't a jail in Haven."

"True." He grimaced, and Emma thought of the many times he had asked the town fathers to allow him to have a secure room at the back of the livery stable. "If you promise not to flee, Noah, I guess you can stay here tonight."

"I'm not running away. I'm going to fight this."

Lewis's face brightened, and Emma realized that her friend would have rather swum the length of the Ohio than bring this warrant here to Noah. "I'm glad to hear that."

"Do you know an attorney hereabouts?"

"I've heard that Samuel Jennings read the law before he decided to buy land outside of town and farm it."

Noah arched a brow. "I'd hoped to have someone with a bit more skill in the law to help me fight this. I have no doubts that the best lawyers money can buy will be sent here to make sure I hang."

When Emma moaned and pressed her face against Noah's chest, he put his arms around her. She pulled back with a choked gasp when she heard the crackle of paper beneath her ear. His thumb gently tilted her head back. She almost recoiled from the fury blazing in his eyes. What she had seen the night of the flood was only a hint of the rage he was trying to govern now.

The door opened, and Gladys and the children burst back out onto the porch.

Emma glanced at Noah as the children's joyful voices flowed around the porch, silencing the soft song of the peepers. His eyes were focused, as she had expected, right on Belinda.

"Sheriff," Gladys said, "as long as you're still here, you might as well join us for another toast to the newlyweds." She balanced the tray on the rail.

Sean took two glasses and Belinda one. With a grin, Sean held out one to the sheriff.

"I really am not thirsty," Lewis said as he took the glass.

"Nonsense!" Gladys laughed as Sean handed the other glass to Emma.

Her fingers trembled so hard she could barely hold it. Sean's smile faded, and she wished he was not so perceptive of the emotions around him. The skills that had served him well when he lived with just his little sister on the cruel streets could tell him too much tonight.

"Emma, is something wrong?" he asked, his voice quivering like her fingers.

She tried to make her answer cheerful. "I thought you two were off to sleep." Even Belinda stared at her when her strained voice broke, and she wished she had remained as mute as Noah.

"Noah," said Lewis as he set his untasted glass back on the tray, "it might be better if we discuss privately getting you a lawyer."

"Lawyer?" choked Gladys. She looked at the sheriff's face, then at Noah's. The tray teetered and fell off the railing with the crash of splintering glass as she reeled back in horror. Noah leaped forward and caught her before she could collapse.

Emma ran into the house and to the kitchen. She dipped the first cloth she could find into the water bucket on the table in the middle of the room. Whirling to go back to the porch, she was astonished to see Lewis standing in the doorway. She had not thought he would follow her instead of staying on the porch to watch his *prisoner*. She shuddered at the thought.

When he glanced over his shoulder, she realized he could see Noah through the dining room window. He looked back at her, but said nothing.

"Sean, take this to Noah," she said quietly when the boy skidded to a stop behind the sheriff. "Then take Belinda and go upstairs and get ready for bed. I'll be up to read you a story . . . sometime."

"Emma—"

"Go and help Gladys, then go to bed." She met his fearful eyes evenly. "Please, Sean."

He nodded and, taking the cloth, raced out the front door.

Lewis cleared his throat. He opened his mouth and then closed it.

"You might as well say what you want to say." She wiped her hands on her gown, not caring if the water stained the silk.

"I'm really sorry."

"I know that, Lewis."

"I had to deliver the warrant."

"I know that, too."

He faltered again before saying, "Emma, I trust you to remind him to do the right thing and stay here."

"Noah said he'd stay here. His word is still good, even though someone else clearly has perjured himself."

"But will *you* make sure he stays here?"

If the circumstances had not been so grim, she would have laughed at the very idea that she could halt Noah from doing whatever he wanted to do. His muscles had been honed by his work in his woodlot, and his will was just as strong.

"I'll make sure he doesn't leave Haven."

Lewis's head shot up. "Haven? That's a good idea, Emma.

In the morning, all of you need to move into your house. It's right in the center of town.''

"My house is much smaller—''

''But there are lots of folks in town who would be willing to share the duty of watching to make sure he doesn't jump the next train out of town.''

This time she could not halt her bitter laugh. ''Listen to you, Lewis Parker! You're making Noah into a vaudeville villain. We're talking about Noah Sawyer here. He won't run away from a fight, especially when he knows he hasn't done anything wrong.'' *As I did.* She must not say anything to make the situation more complicated.

Apparently no one had noticed in the darkness when the sheriff spoke of a warrant for someone's arrest how her face grew so cold that she knew all color had washed from it. She had had no doubts someone in Kansas had traced her here, determined she finally pay for a crime she had not been part of. In the split second before Lewis had continued, she had imagined being ripped away from the love she had discovered with Noah and Sean and Belinda. The idea that the warrant could be for Noah had not even entered her mind.

Emma took a steadying breath, then asked, ''What should we do now?''

''I'm going to stand guard on the house tonight.''

''Really, Lewis! Do you think that's necessary?'' When he regarded her with a stony expression, she relented and nodded. He was doing this as much to protect Noah as he was to guard him.

''You should move back into town at daylight. You need to persuade Noah that doing anything stupid now will mean his losing everything.''

''I don't think Noah Sawyer has ever done anything stupid in his life.''

He lowered his eyes. "Except—"

"Lewis, he couldn't kidnap his own daughter!"

The sheriff's strained face eased a bit. "That's true. I was so blasted upset when the order to arrest him came through and was confirmed that I didn't stop to think about the fact Belinda is his daughter." He frowned again. "Something isn't right about all this."

"That's what I have been trying to tell you."

"In the morning, I'll send a telegram to Chicago and start getting this cleared up."

"Thank you." She resisted the temptation to give him a big kiss on the cheek. Her gratitude would embarrass him.

"But until it is all cleared up, I must still keep him under guard."

"I understand, and so will he." Walking to the door, she patted Lewis's shoulder. "Don't worry. This will all work out." She wondered if he shared her amazement at how ridiculous this whole situation had become. She was comforting the very man who had arrested Noah.

He held the door for her, and she went out to see Noah helping Gladys to her feet.

When Emma looked around, Noah said, "Sean and Belinda have gone upstairs. Just as you told them to. Let me help Gladys to her room and then . . ." He looked at Lewis.

The sheriff clapped Noah on the arm before walking down the front steps. From the shadows of a nearby tree, he drew out a rifle. Coming back to the house, he sat on the steps.

Emma followed Noah and Gladys into the house. She started to close the door, but Noah shook his head. She understood what he did not say. There must be no hint that anything they said could not be heard by the sheriff.

"I can get to my room on my own, Mr. Sawyer," Gladys

said in little more than a wispy whisper. "You two need to talk."

"Thank you, Gladys."

"If I did anything to—"

He shook his head. "You know it isn't anything you did."

Emma's confusion must have been visible, because Gladys said, "You'd better talk to her right away, Mr. Sawyer."

Before Emma could ask a single question, Noah put his finger to her lips. *Not here*, he mouthed.

She fought not to look over her shoulder to see if Lewis was watching them. When Noah went to the door, she was surprised to hear him say, "If you need it, there's coffee in the kitchen. Help yourself."

"Th-thanks, Noah." Lewis turned back to look out over the fields that dropped down into the Ohio.

Noah came back to her and held out his hand. She put hers in it, and he smiled with relief. Did he think she would turn her back on him? She understood what he was going through better than anyone else in Haven, but she could not tell him that . . . not now.

As he led her up the stairs, she said nothing. He opened the first door on the right. When she was about to step through, he put out his arm.

"There are some traditions that shouldn't be ignored." He scooped her up into his arms and grinned. "The groom should carry his bride across the threshold of their bridal chamber." His smile dimmed as his deep sigh pressed against her. "We need all the good luck we can get right now."

Emma buried her face in his shoulder as he took her into the bedroom. When he set her down on the bed, he went back and turned the key in the door. Then, pausing, he unlocked it and opened it enough to give him a view of the stairs that were still brightly lit by the lamps on both floors.

She started to stand, but instead stared at the headboard of the bed. Their initials were carved into a twisting pattern of flowers and vines within a heart. Running her fingers along the "E," she slid them to the "N" that was on the far side of the much larger "S" in the center.

"This is beautiful," she whispered. "I had no idea you could do such wondrous work."

"I thought you'd like it."

She looked at where he still leaned on the wall beside the door. "*This* is the reason you wanted to delay the wedding, not Belinda."

"Guilty."

She closed her eyes to hold back her tears. "Noah, don't tease me now."

He crossed the space between the door and the bed in a pair of steps. Pulling her to her feet and into his arms, he held her as if he feared she would vanish. The paper rustled between them, and she stepped back again.

He drew it out and placed it on the chest of drawers. Then he turned and went to stand beside the door where he could have a good view of the stairs.

"Tell me, Noah," she said as she sat on the wide window-sill. A mistake, she discovered, because the empty bed was between them, a reminder of how this evening should have been spent. "Tell me why you didn't tell Lewis right away that you couldn't be guilty of kidnapping Belinda. You can't kidnap your own daughter."

He glanced toward the stairs, then back at her. "I'm not Belinda's father."

"What?" She had not guessed she could be any more shocked, but she was.

"I'm her uncle."

"But she thinks you are her father."

"Yes, she does, because no one has ever told her differently. Her mother was my brother's wife."

She swallowed roughly. "The woman in the photograph downstairs on the parlor mantel. Gladys said it was a picture of your sister."

"My sister-in-law. Martha married my brother Danny." He met her eyes without emotion as he said, "They both were killed in the great fire in Chicago five years ago."

"Noah, I—"

"Let me talk, Emma." A hint of desperation came into his voice. "Please."

She nodded, biting her lip.

"I told you how I was able to save Belinda, but I couldn't save anyone else."

She nodded again.

"I didn't tell you that the ones I couldn't save were my brother and his wife. The fire was swallowing their street with a wind shift by the time I arrived. I'd been trying to keep my furniture factory from burning to the ground, but it soon became clear it was lost. When I heard how widespread the fire was, I rushed to where my brother and his family lived. Danny tossed down the baby to me. We were set to catch him and Martha. Then something exploded in their house." He hung his head as his hands fisted at his sides. "And they were gone."

Tears overflowed her eyes, but she did not wipe them away. She went to him and drew him down to sit beside her on the floor. He put his arm around her, but kept looking over her head to make sure no one was coming up the stairs to hear what he was telling her. She put her hand over his left one and felt his fingers quiver.

With anger, she realized when he added, "If I'd not tried

244 *Jo Ann Ferguson*

to save that damned factory, I might have been able to save them.''

"You don't know that. They must have thought they were safe if they stayed in their house.''

He nodded. "Almost a dozen people died on that block alone. For a few minutes, I wasn't sure if we would escape the inferno.'' His gaze turned inward. "I'm no longer afraid of hell, because I have been there.''

She touched his leg, where the ropy scars remained as conspicuous reminders of his near death, but there were other unhealed wounds that festered within him where no one could see. "Why didn't you tell me? You could have trusted me with this.''

"I know I can trust you, sweetheart, but I didn't want to encumber you with this.''

"You are my husband. Your responsibilities are mine now.''

A swift smile crossed his lips. "You need to hear the rest before you accept that obligation so quickly. You may change your mind when you know the truth of why I'm not surprised to have that warrant finally chase me down.''

Her eyes widened. "You didn't tell Lewis that the warrant is mistaken because it isn't!''

"Now you understand.''

"But, Noah, you're her uncle. Her parents had been killed. Why shouldn't she live with you?''

"Because of the Gilson family.'' He leaned his head against the top of hers as he said, "I hope you never have to deal with anyone like them, sweetheart. They are little better than thieves. If anyone has an idea and mentions it in their hearing, they steal it and put it on the market before the fool who spoke of it can guess what is happening.''

"But Martha was a Gilson.''

"There's truth to the adage that every rule has an exception. She met Danny when she came to the factory to apologize for her brother stealing Danny's idea for a new line of furniture. Danny had been in his cups at a social gathering and had failed to notice Laird Gilson was there.''

Emma sat straighter and stared at him. ''Laird? Is he some sort of Scottish peer?''

He laughed without humor. ''He only fancies himself to be because his parents gave him that ludicrous name in an effort to inveigle themselves into favor with some British investor before Gilson was born. The whole family—except for Martha—has no scruples when it comes to making a profit to add more wealth to their ever expanding house along the shore of Lake Michigan.''

''I know the type of people you mean.'' How she wished she could be as honest with him about her own past! *That* burden remained her own.

''I'm sorry to hear that.''

She was surprised how easy it was to smile when she replied, ''Me, too.''

He drew his arm from around her and curved his hands around her face. His kiss was deep and tender and a promise that all they should be sharing on their wedding night was not lost. She leaned into the kiss, wanting it to last forever so they could remain in this rapture, think only of this perfect moment.

''No, Noah,'' she whispered when he lifted his mouth from hers. ''Just kiss me. Kiss me and kiss me until we're transported away from this muddle.''

''You have to know the whole truth, sweetheart.''

She opened her eyes to see his so close to hers. They were dim with a despair she had never seen on his face. She wanted to plead with him to be angry again. She could understand rage at being falsely accused. She could not comprehend this quiet acceptance that the time for the hardest battle was still ahead of them.

"Tell me, Noah." She dampened her lips as she whispered, "Tell me everything."

He rested his head on her lap, but where he could still see down the stairs. "I should have told you right from the beginning, but I was afraid you'd walk out of my life if you knew the truth."

"So you got me to marry you so I never can walk away from you." She ran her finger along his cheek, which was rough with whiskers. "An excellent plan, save for the fact that I'll always stand with you, no matter what." She tapped his lips. "Unless you don't want me to be standing."

He did not smile at her jest. Instead he stared up at the ceiling as he said, "I never thought Laird Gilson would have any interest in any child. He prefers to spend time with women of ill fame rather than with a lady who might be greedy enough to become his wife. Then he realized Belinda would inherit a share of the furniture factory we were already rebuilding."

"So he petitioned the court to have custody of Belinda?"

"Yes. From somewhere, he produced a woman he introduced to the court as his fiancée. I suspect she was one of his women of the night whom he'd gotten cleaned up to look like a lady."

She sighed. "A man who was about to be married would be believed by a judge to offer a better home for a child than a single man."

"Exactly the impression Gilson wanted to put into the judge's mind."

"Why didn't you find a fiancée of your own?"

"I guess I'm too blasted honest. I had hoped honesty would weigh in my favor, especially when Gilson's habits were introduced as evidence."

"But?"

"I didn't take into consideration that the judge would have more sympathy for the family who had lost a daughter than one who had lost a son. He ruled Belinda should go to the Gilsons, as if she could replace Martha."

Emma gasped, "That's absurd!"

"I agree. That's why I left orders on how to complete the factory with my other brother, Ron. I turned my share of the business over to him and, taking Belinda, left Chicago. So the warrant is not wrong. I *did* kidnap her, but it was to save her from Gilson and his family. The one thing I didn't think to do was change my name before Belinda was old enough to know her last name was Sawyer."

"You would have been found anyhow if this Gilson family wanted to find you." She shivered at the thought. *She* had changed her name to protect herself, and so far it had. When she told Noah the truth of her own secret, would he listen as she was to his?

"True, and they've found me. The success of the factory has enabled us to live wherever we wished, because Ron and I arranged for funds to be available around the country."

"Are you saying you own the factory that makes all the furniture you have downstairs?"

"Yes. I guess you should know, Mrs. Sawyer, that your husband comes from a very financially successful family." His lips tilted for a fleeting moment, then vanished. "It was time for Belinda to have a real home where she could spend time with other children and go to school. I thought Haven would be the perfect place." He sat and curved his hand along her cheek again. "Thank you for listening, Emma. It's time someone else knew the truth. It's a heavy burden to carry for all these years."

"Especially carrying it alone."

He shook his head. "Gladys knows the truth. She worked

for me at my furniture factory in Chicago before the fire. She has been faithfully traveling with us for the past five years until we settled here, where I thought no one would look for us. I wish I knew who had seen through my guise as a fairly incompetent farmer.''

''If someone in Haven had been suspicious, they . . . Oh, my!''

''What is it?''

''Mr. Atherton!''

''What?''

''You met him at the barn raising. He'd been around Haven for a week or so then, and he was always asking questions about people in town.''

''Including me?''

She barely could draw in a breath as she whispered, ''He was from Chicago. He said he was a friend of the Smiths, but I never saw him with them.''

He stood and slammed his fist against the door. ''Probably a Pinkerton man.''

''But who had alerted him to come here to search for you after all this time?''

''Emma?'' came a soft voice from the other side of the door before Noah could answer the unanswerable.

Standing, Emma opened the door wider to see Belinda standing on the other side. The little girl cuddled up against Emma and murmured, ''Sean said you were going to tell us a story. How much longer are you going to be talking with Papa?''

She fought not to wince as she heard Belinda's innocent question.

''I don't know how much longer I can stay awake,'' Belinda continued.

''Belinda . . .'' She put her hand on Noah's arm. ''I did

tell Sean I'd tell them a story if they came upstairs and got ready for bed."

"Go ahead. We aren't going to solve this tonight." He rubbed the back of his neck as he pulled off his dress collar. Tossing it atop the warrant on his dresser, he said, "I think I'll start gathering my thoughts so I can see if Jennings is interested in helping sort this out."

Emma hesitated, then said, "Belinda, go and get in bed. I'll be right there."

"Promise?"

"Yes." She gave the little girl a slight shove and smiled when Belinda skipped along the hall. Turning back to Noah, she said, "I thought you wanted someone with more skill with the law than a man who gave it up to become a farmer."

"Right now, I need all the allies I can round up."

She put her arms around him. "You have me."

"You don't know how much that means now, sweetheart," he whispered.

Looking up at him, she knew she should be honest with him now, when he was sure to understand. She wished she did know how it was to have even one person who believed in her profession of innocence. She needed to share her own tale with him and have him believe she had not played any part in Miles's crimes.

"Now *I* am a married man," he continued, "and the judge has to take into consideration the fact that I have a wife who will help me raise Belinda. After the excellent job you've done with Sean in such a short time, no one will doubt you would be a good mother to her."

"I hope the judge recognizes that."

Her hopes shriveled into despair when he replied, "If he does not, there are dozens of folks in Haven who will gladly testify how much you've done for this community and to any aspect of your character."

She somehow continued to smile. What Noah had said was true . . . as far as it went. She must be honest with him. The time had come to trust someone with the story of what had happened in Kansas. She must trust this man she had trusted with her heart.

"Noah, I need to tell you about—"

His mouth claimed hers, silencing her. Although she wanted to give herself to the pleasure and to him, she turned her head away enough to say, "I need to tell you—"

"Just tell me that you love me, sweetheart. That is all I want to hear now."

"Noah—"

This time when his lips captured hers, he did not let her escape. Nor did she wish to. She wanted this ecstasy, even if it was only for this one night. She would make him listen to her in the morning. For tonight, all she wanted was this.

CHAPTER SIXTEEN

Noah had never thought he would be so grateful everyone around Haven was busy with planting. The street, as the sun rose to shine into the Ohio, was empty except for him and Lewis Parker, who was walking silently beside him.

He knew this moment of quiet would soon be gone. Coming back to the village before dawn, because he and Emma had wanted to protect the children from the bombardment of questions that was sure to hit them as soon as they were seen, he had tried to persuade Emma not to open the store today. He reminded her Belinda and Sean were still waiting for their bedtime story, and that spending the day with the children might be for the best.

"I need to be in the store today," she had replied as she brushed her hair. "If I don't, the rumors will become even more outrageous. Maybe I can put the brakes to a few."

He had put his hands on her shoulders and drawn her

back against him. In the looking glass, he could see his face bore lines of sleeplessness and anxiety . . . as Emma's did. He had not planned to sleep much last night with his new wife in his bed. She had not said anything, but he knew her fear for him and Belinda had tainted her happiness last night. As well as his. Each time she tried to turn the discussion to anything serious, he had silenced her with kisses until she surrendered to their desire once more.

"I'm a lucky man," he whispered. He kissed her nape as she lifted her hair off it to twist it into a chignon.

"Lucky?" Her hair fell back over his fingers, then flowed along his arm as turned to face him. "Noah, usually I enjoy a good joke, but not *today!*"

"I wasn't joking." As his hands cupped her face, he smiled. "I'm lucky you didn't walk out on me last night."

"I love you. I wouldn't leave someone I love to handle this calamity alone."

He frowned when she looked hastily away. He recognized her expression. He had seen it far too often during the night, and it had been on her face when he had asked her to marry him. Yes, he recognized the expression, but he had no idea why she was wearing it now, other than something was unsettling her. Not just Gilson, but something she did not want to share with him.

His thumbs under her chin tipped her face back toward his. "And that is why I'm lucky, sweetheart."

She had flung her arms around him and thrilled him with her kisses. He might have changed his mind about getting to the telegraph office as soon as it opened and made love to her again in her bed if she had not drawn away. In her eyes, he had seen the craving that plagued him, but she had known, as he did, that they might have a very short time to prevent Gilson from taking the next step in his abominable scheme.

Looking back along the street, Noah saw someone climbing the steps to the store's porch. Reverend Faulkner, if he was not mistaken. He sighed. Maybe the minister would be able to offer Emma some hope.

Noah had none. When he had taken Belinda and left Chicago, he knew what the cost of the precipitous action could be. He had been willing to risk it . . . then. Belinda had meant no more to him then than the sole legacy his brother had left. Even more importantly—then—Noah had been determined that no Gilson would ever possess a splinter of the Sawyer family's business. In the years since, the company had become secondary, for he had come to love the little girl who considered him her father. And she was his daughter now, too.

Gilson would not have her.

Throwing open the door of the telegraph office, Noah saw no one was inside. He looked back at the sheriff, who leaned against one wall of the train station. As Lewis drew out a bag of chewing tobacco and stuffed some into one cheek, Noah knew Emma had been right when she told him the sheriff took his job seriously.

Seriously enough to hang Noah? That was a question he was not in a hurry to get an answer for. What he was in a hurry for was to send this telegram.

"Kenny!" he shouted.

The back door opened, and the telegraph operator peered out, one hand holding his unbuttoned trousers closed. Frowning, Kenny asked, "What is it? I heard you in the outhouse."

"I need to send a telegraph. It's an emergency."

Kenny buttoned up his trousers as he came into the office. "An emergency? What sort of an emergency?"

"You'll hear." Waiting for the young man to take his seat behind the low wall, Noah clasped his hands behind him as he paced the two steps in either direction across the small room. "Ready?" he asked, pausing.

"Go ahead, Noah," Kenny said, his finger just above the key that would send the message.

"This is to go to Chicago."

"To Montgomery Ward & Company, right?"

He shook his head. "That's Emma's business. This is my business today. Send the message to Ronald Sawyer, Lincoln Park, Chicago, Illinois." He took a deep breath, then said, "Gilson found us. Been arrested."

"Arrested?" Kenny gasped, even as he continued to send the message.

Noah did not pause. "Send lawyer. Need to keep Belinda out of Gilson's hands." He smiled as he added, "Got married yesterday. Sign it with my name."

"What in the blazes is going on?" the telegraph operator asked as he sent the end of the message. "Who got arrested?"

"Me."

"You? You're joshing me."

"I'm afraid not." Noah continued to smile as he hooked a thumb over his shoulder. "Just ask Sheriff Parker."

Kenny's eyes grew wide, but before he could ask another question, the telegraph began clicking. He grabbed a piece of paper and began to write furiously.

Noah walked out of the telegraph office. When he saw that the sheriff was asleep, tobacco juice dripping along his chin, he considered leaving the man there to rest. That might give the wrong impression, and he needed every good impression he could get right now.

Shaking the sheriff awake, he said, "I'm heading back to Emma's house, Lewis. Why don't you go and get some sleep?"

Lewis stumbled to his feet. Spitting out the tobacco, he

mumbled, "Can't. Not until I get someone to watch over you."

"Alice Underhill is right across the street. She can watch to make sure I keep my promise to stay around Haven until this gets all straightened out."

"Alice?" His eyes grew as round as Kenny's had. "She's a woman!"

"So I've noticed." Noah chuckled, but put his arm under the sheriff's to help guide the man up the street. "I'll send Sean to her house to get her, and you can sleep on the sofa in Emma's parlor."

"I need to do my duty." The sheriff's exhausted voice was slurred and his steps so unsteady that anyone watching them would think Noah was helping a drunken Lewis Parker up the street.

Noah did not slow as he passed the store. Emma would send for him if she needed him. Tonight, he would hold her and let himself lose all his anxiety in the depths of her sweet passion once more. If not for her love . . . he sighed. He did not want to think of that. Her love was the one thing that Gilson could not poison, and Noah would make sure his enemy never would.

"It's all a horrible mistake." Emma was sure she had repeated those words a thousand times by the time she got ready to close the store that Saturday afternoon.

As soon as people had seen that Delancy's General Store was open for business, they had poured through the door like a freshet. Somehow, with a speed astonishing even for gossip in Haven, the story of Noah being arrested on his wedding night reached every ear in town. Now the day was over, and she could close the store and go home and learn if Noah had heard back from his surviving brother in Chicago.

She sneezed as she swept the back corner of the store. This had become Sean's job, but she had told him to take the day to play with Belinda in the yard behind the house. He had given her a baffled frown when she asked him not to go out on the green today. For as long as she could, she wanted to protect the children from the horror hovering over them like a malignant shadow.

Sweeping the dust and dirt—much more than usual, because of the many people who had come in and out today—toward the front door, Emma paused when a man walked across the porch and through the door. He was dressed with an elegance that was completely out of place in Haven. She froze and stared when she realized she had seen such a fancy outfit before—twice before. Noah had worn such clothes to the Smiths' wedding and to their own yesterday.

This man's suit was dark brown, almost the very shade of his hair and the thick mustache that seemed to explode from beneath his nose to cover both his upper and lower lips. When he walked toward her, she saw he also held in his gloved hand a cane with a carved ivory handle and what appeared to be a gold tip. Every inch of him announced he was very rich and wanted everyone to know that.

She said nothing as he glanced around the store, the hint of a condescending smile curving along the outer edges of his mustache. Usually she would have bristled like a frightened woodchuck if someone had looked down their overly long nose at her store, but some sense—the same sort of survival instinct that had guided her to Haven—warned her to wait and see what this dandy wanted.

"I would like to speak with Mr. Delancy," the man said without the courtesy of a "good afternoon."

She would be more polite. "Good afternoon, sir. There is no *Mister* Delancy. I run the store."

"Is it Miss or Mrs. Delancy?"

She did not hesitate as she answered, "Folks around here just call me Emma."

"How very informal of you! I guess that's one of the interesting parts of life in the country."

"I guess so." She kept her broom between them. She did not like the way this man eyed her up and down as if she were just another piece of the merchandise for sale.

A nagging suspicion in the back of her mind grew louder. The fancy clothes, the even fancier carriage she could see parked in front of the store with a driver waiting patiently, the man's arrogant expectation that she would welcome his salacious stare. . .she prayed she was wrong.

"How may I help you, sir?" she asked when he continued to ogle her. "I trust it won't take long. I don't want to seem inhospitable, but I'm ready to close the store."

"I will not keep you long ... *Emma*." His smile was warm, but his eyes remained calculating. "I have a single— and hopefully simple—request."

Now she really wanted to stiffen with fury at his tone, which suggested anything more complicated than the most elementary task might be beyond her country bumpkin comprehension. She could not keep her irritation from chilling her voice as she asked, "What request?"

"Can you give me directions to Noah Sawyer's farm?"

She did not react, for she had expected this very question. "Of course, mister . . ."

"Gilson. Laird Gilson." He bowed slightly toward her as if they stood in a ballroom instead of her store.

Even though she had already guessed this *must* be the man who wanted to ruin Belinda's life as Miles had ruined hers, she could not halt the icy river of disgust racing down her back. She wanted to take her broom and bat him over the head with it while she demanded how he could try to destroy a little girl's happiness simply to get a share of a successful furniture factory.

As he straightened, he said, "A man who used to live in Haven suggested I should stop here to get directions."

"A man who used to live in Haven?"

"Mr. Baker."

She had not anticipated *this*. When she bought the store, she had endured Mr. Baker's odd ways and his whining about being penniless. Then he had left Haven. Somehow, he must have met Laird Gilson and revealed that Noah and Belinda were here. But how? She could not understand how this had happened.

"Emma?" asked Gilson. "I'd like those directions now."

She clasped the broom tightly as she said in the most pleasant tone she could manage, "Ah, Mr. Gilson, giving you those directions is very simple. Noah Sawyer's farm is outside Haven. Take the road past the school and keep going until you get to a ruined bridge. Then turn away from the river and follow the creek until you come to another bridge. Cross that and drive back down to the road that would have connected across the ruined bridge. His farm is not far from there."

"That sounds like a roundabout trip."

"It's the quickest way since the bridge was washed away earlier this spring." She must continue to be honest with him, because he had to trust her directions. If he asked anyone else in Haven, they would direct him to her house.

He tipped his hat to her again. "Thank you, Emma."

"Good afternoon, Mr. Gilson."

Instead of leaving, he stepped forward and plucked one of her hands off the broom. He bent over it and pressed his mouth to it. She yanked it away, putting it behind her to wipe the moisture on her skirt.

"I've heard how shy country misses are," he said with a smile.

"We simply know to mind our manners."

He laughed, but the sound was as cold as the shiver that ran its frigid finger down her back again. "Clever as well as pretty, I see. Would you join me at the Haven Hotel for dinner this evening, Emma?"

"The hotel has no public dining room."

"I know."

It was so tempting to think of slapping his face to wipe that superior smile off it. Instead she said coolly, "I believe you have mistaken my store for another sort of business establishment, Mr. Gilson." She walked past him and put her hand on the door. "Good afternoon."

He tugged on the top of one glove, cleared his throat, and nodded toward her as he left her store. Her hope that she had persuaded him to treat her properly vanished when he turned and said, "I trust we shall speak again, Emma, soon. Very soon."

She did not answer. Closing the door, she quickly locked it. Her name was called, and she whirled with a gasp.

Noah put his hands out to steady her. "Calm down, sweetheart."

"*He* was just here." She pulled him back away from the door. "Don't let him see you."

"Gilson?"

"Yes! How did you know?"

His smile was even icier than Gilson's. "I saw the carriage come into town. I came through the barn and the storage room and got here just in time to hear you tell him to get out and to see his lecherous looks at you. Are you all right?"

"As long as I don't have to talk to him alone again. He makes me feel as if a whole mound of ants are creeping across my skin."

"Gilson does seem to have that effect on many women who aren't interested in his money." He took her hand. "Let's get back to the house. Poor Lewis is going to think I have tried to give him the slip."

"Lewis?"

"He's still napping on your sofa." He chuckled. "He refused to let Alice Underhill be my guard because she's a woman, so he watched over me until he fell sound asleep about four hours ago." He glanced out the window. "What did Gilson want?"

"Directions to your farm. He's on his way out to there now. That gives us some time to find out how and why Mr. Baker contacted him."

"Baker?" He looked toward the stairwell door.

"That's what he said." She released his hand and threw open the door to the dim stairwell. Gathering up her skirts, she climbed the stairs that twisted up to another door at the top.

She opened it. Her nose wrinkled as she smelled something that had gone bad. She would have to find it and get rid of it before the odor seeped down into the store. She opened both windows at the front of the main room.

Papers crunched under feet as she went to peer into the other room, a bedroom which reeked even more than the main room. Holding her breath, she sprinted across the room and pushed up the window. Fresh air burst in, and she went back out into the front room.

"What a mess!" Noah said. He kicked yellowed newspapers aside.

"I had no idea he lived like this."

"A single spark, and this could have burned your store to the ground."

She nodded. "I will get it cleaned up . . . after."

"A good idea."

"If—" She gave a soft cry as the breeze slammed the door shut.

Noah chuckled as he brushed her lips with his. "Don't be so jumpy, sweetheart. You need every bit of your wits about you now Gilson has arrived." He reached to open the stairwell door. "What's this?"

Emma stepped over the scattered papers as he ripped down one that had been nailed to the door. When he swore under his breath, then more loudly, she took the page he held out to her. She choked as she read the faded page that had the words *Wanted* in huge letters across the top. Beneath those letters were a description that fit Noah perfectly and described Belinda as she must have been when she was a baby. A reward of a thousand dollars was offered for information leading to the arrest of Noah and the return of Belinda to her uncle.

"Where did he get this?" Noah growled. He balled it up and threw it at the far wall.

She looked out the window toward the courthouse. "The only place he could have gotten that would have been from Lewis. I know Lewis doesn't hold onto all the wanted posters that come to Haven. He concentrates on the ones issued in Cincinnati and Louisville."

"Because he doesn't expect any other criminals to come to Haven."

"Yes," she whispered as her throat threatened to close and leave her to gag on her own lies.

"Are the rest of these pages wanted posters?" He bent to pick up another.

She grasped his hand, halting him. When he frowned at her, she said, "I need to tell you something, Noah. Something very important." She forced a swallow past the lump in her throat. "Something I should have told you before."

Closing her eyes as she tried to gather her waning courage, she said, "Or last night."

"What is it?" He caught her hands in his. When they trembled against his rough palms, he asked, "What did Gilson say to you?"

"It isn't Gilson. It's—" The breeze shifted, and the odor of decaying food struck her like a blow. "Let's talk about this downstairs."

"A good idea. We need to decide what we're going to do now that Gilson has come to Haven."

Emma was so tempted to let him change the subject to that important topic, but she could not remain silent. If one of these pages had contained a description of her, Mr. Baker might have revealed that to Gilson also. She hurried down the stairs even more swiftly than she had gone up them, not wanting Noah to see her fear that if there was a five-year-old wanted poster for him in that debris, could there be one only a couple of years older which described Emma?

Shadows darkened the corners of the store—of *her* haven. Noah's hand on her elbow steered her to the rocking chair. When she sat, he pulled another chair closer. Something she had said or done must have revealed to him that she was not willing to share what she had to say with anyone other than him.

A fist pounded on the front door. She looked toward the door to see Lewis's face pressed to it. With a glance at Noah, she rose and went to the door. She unlocked it and stepped back as he burst into the store.

"Noah, you told me that you wouldn't sneak away!" he shouted. "I thought I could trust you, but I turn my back for a minute—"

"For four hours," Noah said coming to his feet and walking toward the sheriff. "If I'd been planning to take

Belinda and leave town, don't you think I would have done it as soon as you fell asleep on Emma's sofa?''

"You should have wakened me if you were leaving the house.''

"I should have." He sighed as he put his arm around Emma's waist. Smiling down at her, he said, "I saw Laird Gilson's carriage out in front of the store, and I didn't want to wait even the time it would have taken to wake you. I didn't want Emma to have to face him by herself, but she'd dealt with him by the time I got here.''

"Gilson?" Lewis's brow rutted with concentration. "The man who had the warrant sworn out for your arrest?''

"I think he hoped to get here to see me dragged away in chains.''

"Noah!" she moaned. "Don't even jest about such things.''

"I have to, sweetheart." He tipped her face toward him and kissed her gently. "Joking at Gilson's expense is the only way to keep me from hunting him down and choking him with my bare hands." His smile returned as he said, "I trust you didn't hear that, Lewis.''

"Not a word." The sheriff took a deep breath and released it with a long sigh. "I hope you can fight this, Noah." He brightened. "Why don't you and I go to see Judge Purchase?''

"He's the local judge," Emma explained, wondering why she had not thought of this herself. It might be as simple as she never felt comfortable around Judge Owen Purchase. The judge was a genial man, but she could not forget that, if he knew the truth, he would be the one to send her back to Kansas to hang. "He sometimes rides a circuit, but he has been overseeing cases in Haven all winter.''

"Do you think he'll see me?" Noah asked.

"We can call on him, and then you'll know." Lewis's

grin became even broader. "He'll have to hear the case here first because you were arrested in Indiana instead of Illinois."

"True." Noah's smile did not dim as he added, "I know you wanted to talk to me, Emma, but can it wait?"

"I guess it must."

He kissed her again so swiftly that she did not have a chance to put her arms around him before he had released her and was walking out of the store with Lewis. Closing the door behind them, she locked it again. She needed to tell Noah about why she was in Haven, but she could not in Lewis's hearing.

Tonight . . . tonight when they were alone, she would tell him.

"Emma!"

She whirled as she heard Sean's distressed voice. She did not want to think what else might be wrong now.

The door from the storage room struck the wall as it was shoved open. Sean ran into the store. Before she could chide him for being so thoughtless, she saw the paper he was holding in his hand. It was the letter from the Children's Aid Society.

"Where did you get that?" she asked.

"It fell out of your apron pocket when I was hanging your apron back up in the kitchen." His voice broke as he cried, "Why didn't you tell me that they'd looked for Maeve and couldn't find her? Why did you hide it where you thought I wouldn't ever see it?"

"Sean, I will explain. Just not now. I have to—"

He threw the page on the table. "You told me you would let me know when you got an answer back from them. You promised me you would."

"I know I did, but—"

"You lied to me."

"I didn't want to upset you when there was no real news. They—"

"Can't find Maeve!"

"I know." She started to put her arms around him to offer him the comfort she needed so desperately.

He flung out his hands, knocking her arms away. The epithet he snarled at her shocked her motionless. Grabbing the letter, he raced out of the store. The storage room door slammed as viciously as it had opened.

She started to follow to calm him, then paused. What could she say to him? That she had gone against her better judgment in protecting him? That she had been urged to keep this secret until she had good news for Sean?

This she could not blame on Noah. It had been her choice. What had she said all day at the store? That this was just a horrible mistake.

It was, and this horrible mistake was one she had made all on her own.

CHAPTER SEVENTEEN

Noah came into Emma's bedroom, which was much smaller than his at the farm. And lacier, he noted with a smile, something many of her friends would find unexpected about the competent storekeeper. Even through the shadows of the unlit room, he could see lace dripping from the white curtains and along the pillowcases that leaned up against the simple headboard.

He undid his collar and placed it on her dresser. He turned back to the bed and touched the wooden headboard. With a sigh, he recalled her delight with the bed he had made especially for them. When he had imagined sweeping her up into his arms and bringing her up here to her bed, it had not been because he could not return to his own home without Lewis Parker trailing after him like Emma's dog, who followed her cats endlessly about the yard.

Cursing Gilson would do no good now. The man was

here and was determined to do whatever he could to discredit Noah and take Belinda away forever. Gilson must have some trick prepared, for he would not have come to Haven, where Noah was sure to have garnered allies, unless he was ready to discredit him completely. Or was it as simple as Gilson could not resist watching gallows built for Noah?

No, he did not want to think of the future tonight. Tonight, he wanted to lose himself in the love Emma offered him. He turned as the door opened. The light from the lamp in the hallway glowed like the morning sun on Emma's golden hair.

"Noah?" she asked quietly. "Are you in here?"

Instead of answering, he tugged her into the room and up against him. Kicking the door closed, he did not need light to know how her eyes brightened at his touch. That memory was followed by one of the sight of them closing as she offered her lips to him. The familiar sensation of need flowed through him whenever her face came into his mind, and he knew it was more than her lips that he wanted.

"Sweetheart," he murmured, "you've enchanted me with your magic. Now I'm going to spin you a spell of mine."

She ran her fingers along his unyielding chest where his shirt had fallen open, but said, "Noah, we need to talk. I must tell you—"

"Later. For now, I want to hold you and be within you."

"Noah . . ." Her voice faded as he pressed his mouth to the base of her neck. She quivered and slid her hands up along his chest to dip over his shoulders.

He leaned her back on the bed where a wide swath of moonlight streamed like a cool river. Shadows danced as the tree beyond her window moved in the breeze. When she held her hand up to him, he let her draw him down over her soft curves, which soon would be against his mouth.

He released her hand and snatched the pins from her hair,

which dropped onto the coverlet to add a golden warmth to
the moonlight. Gently he brought her mouth to his. His
tongue traced her lips, savoring each inch. When she moaned
and clutched his arm, heat riveted every muscle and burned
deep within him. He ached to discover how fiercely it burned
inside her.

When he teased her lips apart to taste again the silken
slickness, her gasp burst into his mouth. He rolled onto his
back, bringing her to lie atop him. His hand against her back
kept those beguiling curves against him.

"My beautiful wife," he whispered before she pressed
her mouth to his.

She gave him no time to say anything else, silencing him
again and again as he had her by the door. She finished
unbuttoning his shirt and hooked a finger under each sus-
pender holding it in place. When he teased the half circle
of her ear with his tongue as she was lowering his suspenders
along his arms, she paused to bring his mouth back to hers.
Her eager breath fanned the fire within him into an inferno.

He drew back her gown to find even more of the lace
that surrounded them. When she pushed him away and knelt
to pull off her dress, he chuckled.

"Don't stop there, sweetheart," he said as he sat back
against the pillows and folded his arms in front of him. He
relished the sight of her bare skin luminous in the moon's
cool radiance.

"You want me to undress myself?"

"I want to *watch* you undress."

With a smile that was brighter than the moonlight's, she
shook her hair back and ran her fingers along the lace at the
top of her shift and down to the top hook on her corset. He
held his breath as he watched her fingers—as he became
her fingers, stroking that silken skin and gliding down over
her alluring breasts—unhook it slowly. Had he been mad

to allow her to undress herself? She seemed intent on tormenting him with such slow, deliberate motions.

She tossed her corset aside and ran her hands up her sides. When he reached out to do the same, she slapped his fingers away.

"You said you wanted to watch." She slipped one finger under the left strap of her shift and, lowering it, smiled. "So watch."

"You're a devilish woman."

"And I plan to bedevil you tonight." She dropped the right strap off her shoulder.

He laughed when she sat back and began to undo one shoe. When she dropped it to the floor, he murmured, "You're going to have Lewis running up here to see what's going on."

"I suspect he knows."

He was amazed when she balanced one foot on his shoulder. Her eyes glittered with longing as she rolled down her stocking. She slid her foot down his chest to rest on his leg as she put her other heel on his opposite shoulder. His breath pumped in tempo with her fingers drawing down her stocking along her lithe leg. Again her foot glided along him in a teasing caress. As she laughed and rose to her knees to lower her stockings over the side of the bed, he wondered how much longer he could resist this temptress. She drew one arm out of her shift, then the other. Holding it to her breasts with one hand, she lifted the hem.

He knew he could endure no more of this taunting pleasure when she drew it up along her. Grasping her, he tore the shift from her hands and threw it away along with the shreds of his self-control. Her delighted laugh vanished beneath his mouth as he pulled her into his arms and beneath him.

Kicking off his boots, he tasted the downy skin between

her breasts. His tongue inched along her as he reached to undo his trousers.

"No," she whispered, "I want to see you undress."

"Next time, sweetheart. A man can prevail against such temptation only so long."

She laughed with joy. Each breath brushed against his naked skin. Within seconds, his clothes were tossed aside as well. He leaned over her, and she moaned as her naked legs entwined with his.

As if he had never touched her before, he kissed her while his fingers moved along her, creating the scintillating fire that scorched him. Lingering on the gentle upsweep of her breast and then stroking the curve of her hip, his fingers wandered across the softest skin along the inner length of her leg. She writhed against him, and his mouth covered her gasping lips.

When he probed deep within her, she whispered, "Please."

"Please what?" he whispered against her ear. In her most intimate depths, she quivered, and his yearning threatened to escape his tight control.

"Don't wait any longer. Please."

His breath caught on the jagged edge of indescribable pleasure at the very second he joined them together. Hearing her gasp, he brought her lips back to his as they moved in the undeniable rhythms of love. A voice whispered endearments, but he was not sure if it was hers or his or simply the fused symphony of their hearts. The melody wove around and through him, escalating into a rhapsody. Then, as he heard her give herself to the ecstasy, everything exploded into a wanton abandonment of all his senses but the pleasure he wanted to share only with her.

Again and again . . . and again.

* * *

*They were coming. She could hear their voices—
shouting, angry, lusting for vengeance. The familiar
voices with such an unfamiliar fury.*

*She whirled. Escape. She must escape, or they would
make her pay for the crime that was not hers. She had
to leave.*

Now . . . before it was too late.

*The shooting at the bank was over, but the questions
would now begin. And she had no answers. At least,
none anyone would believe.*

*How could she have been so stupid? That question
had been on everyone's lips as soon as last week's
grim events became known. No one would listen to
her. Even if a few people did, no one else would believe
them. After all, how could she have been so stupid?*

*She had believed Miles when he said work was
going well, that all their dreams would come true,
that soon he would have enough money to take her
on that honeymoon to St. Louis she had dreamed of
when she found she loved him.*

And she had believed he loved her.

*Everything had been lies. There had been no work,
and she had nothing left but nightmares.*

*Tears burned in the back of her throat, but she
refused to let them fall. Had Miles ever loved her, or
had that been just another lie?*

*She had been a fool. Never again would she be such
a fool.*

*Picking up the small carpetbag she had packed
clandestinely, she looked around. Only the fire on the
hearth lit the room. Yet she could see the quilt lying
across the back of the battered settee, the tarnished
candlesticks on the mantel, and the rag rug covering*

*the uneven floor. She would never see any of these
things again.*

*A fist struck the front door, followed by a shout of,
"Open the door!"*

*She took one step toward the back door, then
another, hoping no shadow would reveal where she
stood. Her breath snagged on the fear halting her
heart.*

*"This is the sheriff. Open up, or we'll take down
the door."*

*Time and hope and all her dreams had run out. She
turned and pulled the quilt off the settee. Throwing
its dark side over her shoulders, she fled through the
kitchen and out into the night, far from the men milling
around the front porch.*

She had to leave.

Now . . . because it was too late.

Behind her, she heard, "She has to know."

"How could she not know?" another voice asked.

"Only a fool wouldn't have known."

*At that voice, which should not be here in Fort
Pixton, Kansas, she stopped with her hand on the
doorknob. Turning, she saw a man standing in the
door to the parlor. His hands were hidden behind his
back. Not Miles, but Noah. No one in Fort Pixton
would understand, but she had thought Noah would.*

"Only a fool wouldn't have known," he repeated.

*"Then I was a fool." Her own voice was steady,
even as her heart thumped with both yearning and the
fear he would walk away from her forever. "I was
young, and he was charming. He charmed people in
the bank, and he charmed me. If I had been wiser
then, I might have seen through his pretense."*

"Only a fool wouldn't have known." He drew his

*hands from behind his back. In them was a noose.
Walking to her, he slipped it over her head. It dropped
to rest on her shoulders. He reached to tighten it but—*

Emma woke with a start. The bedclothes were tightly
wrapped around her legs, just as the noose had been about
her throat. Sitting, she touched her neck, fearful she would
find the thick rope around it even when she was awake.

Dawnlight was seeping between the heavy curtains drawn
over the window. She untangled the bedding and rose. As
she rested her hand on the footboard, she stared at the pillow
that was as indented where Noah had been lying. Where
was he?

Pulling back the curtains, she saw a motion in the thinning
darkness. Someone was in the paddock between the house
and the barn in back of the store. Not someone. It was Noah.
What was he doing out there at this hour?

A furious knock sounded downstairs, and her dog began
barking. Throwing her wrapper over her nightgown, Emma
raced down the stairs before the noise could wake Gladys
and the children. Her cap almost bounced off her head, but
she grabbed it and settled it back on her hair. Who was
calling at this hour? She glanced at the parlor. Lewis was
not sitting on the sofa. Maybe he had sent someone else to
watch Noah.

She threw open the door and choked back a gasp of horror
as she locked eyes with Laird Gilson. His hand against the
door halted her from closing it. When she released the knob
to go for Noah, he grasped her wrist before she could take
a single step.

He came into the house and shut the door behind him.
Slowly his gaze ran along her. She tugged the collar of her
wrapper closer to her chin, but it did no good. His brazen
appraisal seemed to strip away every defense she had.

"Emma." Gilson shook his head like a disappointed father chastising a child. "What a disappointment to discover such a lovely woman has a twisted mind and cruelly sent me on a useless goose chase that took half the night! What am I going to do with you, Emma?"

"You're going to take your hand off me right now! Then you're going to leave." She tried to twist her arm out of his hold. When his fingers dug into the sensitive bones in her wrist, she winced.

"And if I don't? Will you call to your *husband* for help?" His feigned smile became a fearsome scowl. "Will you, *Mrs. Sawyer*?"

From the kitchen door, Noah said, "She doesn't need to call for me. I'm right here." He tried not to let his eyes linger on the relief lighting Emma's face. If he did, he might not be able to keep his fist from driving into Gilson's bulbous nose.

He focused his eyes on his enemy. A superior smile tipped Gilson's bushy mustache, which he must have grown to hide the scar on his upper lip. He had been attacked by a servant in his own household. Rumor suggested Gilson had been trying to force the servant's sister into his bed. There never had been any confirmation, because both the servant and his sister were not seen again in Chicago. More gossip hinted Gilson's men had killed them both. Noah was not sure if any of it was true, but Gilson was quite capable of ordering such atrocities.

Coolly, Noah added, "I see your manners haven't improved."

Gilson shoved Emma away. She cradled her wrist in her other hand, and Noah's rage threatened to blind him.

"Did you think I wouldn't find you?" Gilson asked.

"It took you long enough." He laughed tersely. "If Baker

hadn't come running to you to get the reward you were offering, you still wouldn't have found me.''

"And, of course, I had *Mrs.* Sawyer's help.''

Emma cried, "I'd never help you take Belinda away from Noah!''

"But you were much more honest with Atherton when he was visiting this backwater town.''

Noah replied, "If she was honest with your spy, that's only because Emma is pleasant to everyone who comes into her store. So tell me, Gilson, why are you bursting in on us instead of letting the authorities handle this?''

With a snort of derision, Gilson said, "Because I want to see you get what you've got coming to you.'' His tone changed into the beguiling one Noah knew he had used to fool so many people, much to their detriment. "I must say you've developed a good eye in women, Sawyer.''

Stepping between Emma and the lechery in Gilson's eyes, Noah said, "You have come to gloat that you found me, and you have. So get out of here.''

"Don't get huffy, Sawyer.'' He drew a folded paper from beneath his black coat and shook it open. "I've come to get what is mine.''

"There's nothing of yours here!'' gasped Emma.

He grinned at her again and chuckled. "It's a good thing you are his wife and not mine. No wife of mine would dare to speak back so to any man. Sawyer, you should teach your wife a woman's place.''

"She knows what it is. Her place is one of respect in Haven, where many folks depend on her for getting the supplies they need to keep their livelihoods going.'' Noah did not look at Emma. He needed to watch Gilson closely, for he was not sure what the greedy coward would do. He knew Emma must be bristling with fury at Gilson's condescending words.

Seeing he could not irritate Noah with words, Gilson ordered, "Give me the child, and I'll arrange for the charges to be dismissed."

"How kind of you! Only someone stupid would make any sort of bargain with you."

"You can accept my offer, or you can face the consequences."

"Noah," Emma whispered, "you can't let him take her!"

"She's mine by order of the law," Gilson argued. "Don't intrude into this argument with your female lack of logic."

"Haven is her home now," Emma argued. "She believes Noah is her father."

Gilson's eyes swept along her again. "And you aim to be her mother? It's too bad, pretty thing, that you hitched yourself to Sawyer. I will need someone to look after the kid, and I could tumble you without too much trouble."

Noah caught Emma's hand as she raised it to strike the smile from Gilson's face. Maybe he should have let her hit Gilson, because the very touch of her soft skin against his palm urged him to toss Gilson out onto the street so Noah could warm Emma's soft lips as he had last night. Was he as witless as Gilson believed him to be? He had to keep his mind on saving Belinda from this covetous cur.

"This isn't the way, Emma," he said quietly.

"That's right." Gilson chuckled. "Listen to your husband. He knows when he's beat. Be a good girl and get the kid."

"No."

At Noah's terse answer, Gilson took a threatening step forward. When Noah did not move either to defend himself or to halt him, Gilson hesitated. The lack of resistance obviously perplexed him. "Get her and bring her to me right now, Sawyer."

"No."

Emma put her hand on Noah's arm as Gilson glowered at them in frustrated rage. Her fingers trembled, but Noah was as unmoving as the rocks in the foundation of the house.

In an unruffled voice, Noah ordered, "The children are still asleep. I won't have them disturbed now or taken from this house until this matter is dealt with."

"This matter *has* been dealt with. The court decided five years ago that I should raise her."

A double blur rushed down the stairs and toward them. Noah caught Butch by the collar before the dog could jump on Gilson. He tried to nab Sean, but the boy eluded him.

"Leave them alone!" Sean shouted. "Your business ain't with them."

"Who's this boy?" Gilson's nose wrinkled with disgust. "Do you let women and children fight all your battles now, Sawyer?"

Emma stepped forward and put her arm around Sean. He twisted away. She glanced toward Noah, then said, "Sean, please come and sit in the parlor while—"

"You deal with this double-dealin' skunk dressed up like a fancy gent?"

Noah laughed as Gilson's face turned an unhealthy shade of red. "I don't think I've ever heard a better description of him than that, Sean."

"Ever heard?" Sean repeated, frowning. "How do you know about any of Dickie's boys?"

"Dickie's boys?"

Sean looked at Emma, then lowered his voice. "You said not to speak of Dickie and his boys in front of a lady."

Noah nodded, understanding what the boy thought was happening here. He set his hand on Sean's shoulder. "This isn't one of Dickie's bully boys from New York City, although Gilson is probably well acquainted with their like in the interior of every low brothel in Chicago."

"Chicago?" Sean scowled at Gilson. "If he's not one of Dickie's boys, then who is he? He shouldn't be speaking to you like that."

Emma took Sean's arm and drew him toward the parlor. She sat him in the rocker as she asked in little more than a whisper, "Is Belinda awake, too?"

"Yes, but I told her to stay upstairs with the door closed. I didn't want her to get into the middle of this. Dickie's boys can play rough."

"Good. She'll listen to you. Please stay here. This is between Noah and that horrible man."

"What does he want?" Sean pressed.

"Wait here. I'll explain after he leaves." She ruffled his hair, which was mussed from sleep. "I promise I'll explain, Sean, and I won't ever break another promise I make to you."

He nodded, his eyes growing round when Gilson cursed viciously.

Emma went back into the hallway. Quietly, she said, "Mr. Gilson, this is my house, and I've asked you already to leave."

"I'm not leaving without Belinda," he snarled as he rounded on her.

"I won't have her ripped away from her family until this matter is settled once and for all."

"*You?* You have nothing to do with this, Emma."

She heard Noah growl something at Gilson's use of her given name, but she kept her eyes on Gilson. "On the contrary, I have much to do with this. As Noah's wife, I'm part of his family and Belinda's family. In addition, as I've told you, this is *my* house. Belinda is *my* guest, and I shall not have her removed from here against her"—she gave him a smile as arrogant as his—"or my will."

He laughed. "You have as good luck with women as you

have had in court, Sawyer. Do you want me to shut her up for you? Yapping women need to be taught a lesson or two.''

''There's no need to silence her when she is speaking the truth. This is Emma's house, and she has asked you to take your leave.'' Noah walked to stand beside her. He put his arm around her as he continued, ''If you'll go now, there will be no need to send for the sheriff.''

''Sheriff? No hick sheriff is going to stop me from getting that child.''

As if on cue, the door to the porch opened, and Lewis stepped inside, carrying a cup of coffee. ''Good morning.'' His smile faded when he looked at Gilson. ''After our conversation a few minutes ago, I didn't expect to see *you* here, sir.''

''Tell Sawyer he should hand the child over to me right now.''

Lewis shook his head. ''I can't.''

''What do you mean you can't?'' Gilson slapped the paper against his hand. ''I have the court's decision right here. It says I have legal custody of Belinda Sawyer and am trustee for her inheritance.''

''I know what it says, but Judge Purchase told me yesterday Belinda is to stay here, where I can keep an eye on her as well as Noah.''

''You're lying!''

Lewis's smile became chilled. ''If you want to wake up Judge Purchase this early on a Sunday morning, I can give you directions to his house. *You* can ask him if I'm lying about following his orders. I'm not going to bother him before he's had his first two cups of coffee.''

Gilson squared his shoulders as he shoved the page back beneath his coat. ''There's no reason to disturb the judge now. Tomorrow is soon enough.'' He scowled at Noah. ''If you weren't a complete fool, Sawyer, you would know this is a battle you can't win." He patted the breast of his coat where he had placed the paper. "I have all the proof I need right here. Once the judge sees this order, he'll give me Belinda and send you to hang for kidnapping her five years ago."

"Good morning, Mr. Gilson," Emma said coldly.

"*You* are welcome to call any time you wish, my dear Emma, once you're no longer married to Sawyer. Or before. Room 5 at the Haven Hotel. I'd be very happy to comfort your widow, Sawyer."

"Good morning, Mr. Gilson," she repeated.

He winked at her before swaggering out of the front door. She slammed the door shut and locked it, then closed her eyes. Leaning her hands against the frosted glass in the door, she fought to hold back the tears of anger that burned in her eyes. Anger and fear.

When fingers settled on her sleeve, she turned to Sean, whose lower lip was trembling. His face was as pale as it had been when he became sick from eating too much of Gladys's cake.

"He said he's going to take Belinda," he whispered.

She squatted in front of him, pulling her gaze from his frightened eyes long enough to watch Noah hold the kitchen door aside for Lewis. As the sheriff entered, Noah looked back at her and offered her a bolstering smile.

"Emma?" whispered Sean.

Looking back at the boy, she took his hands. "He said that, but it doesn't mean it will happen."

"He said he has some kind of proof."

"He has some papers from a court in Chicago, and Judge Purchase will have to review them. If there's a way, the judge might dismiss them as useless and ask Mr. Gilson for other information."

"How can that man take Belinda away? She and Noah belong together. They are family." Tears filled his eyes. "They are *my* family."

She gathered him into her arms and held him while he cried. He had lost one sister to the maze of New York City. He had quickly come to consider Belinda another sister to ease his grief at losing Maeve, and he feared he would have her taken away too.

"What's wrong with Sean?" came Belinda's voice from the stairs. "Did he fall down and get hurt?"

Emma stiffened. Unlike Sean, Belinda had never been without her family. Would the little girl be able to understand the horror the rest of them shared? Quietly, Emma began, "Sean—"

He pulled away and, wiping away his tears, said in a raspy whisper, "I won't say anything to her. I don't want to scare her. I know how scared Maeve was when she thought we wouldn't be together."

Emma hugged him again. His longing for a family was so simple and pure . . . and honest. As she released him to let him run up the stairs to Belinda, she came to her feet. They were giggling by the time she climbed the stairs to go up and change.

She could not wait any longer to be honest with Noah. She must make him listen to her . . . before it was too late.

Emma stood as she heard the front door open. She had been sitting here, petting Queenie, who offered her a comforting purr, for more than an hour while Noah and Lewis went to talk again to the judge. When she saw Noah's victorious smile as he let Lewis enter before him, she wanted to cheer and she wanted to cry. This was only the first, so very minor skirmish with the biggest battles still ahead of them. They might have won this one, but she feared what would happen to Belinda—and to all of them—if the little girl had to go with Gilson back to Chicago.

Noah grasped her at the waist and swung her around. As Butch barked wildly, he set her back onto her feet and kissed her. She gripped his shirt, wanting to stay within his arms, where she had been honest with him from the first.

But he released her as he said, "Judge Purchase agreed that having Belinda stay here with you to watch over her, sweetheart, was the best choice for now. He trusts you to do what's right for her."

"I'm glad." She tried to hush the dog, but Butch was too excited.

"I'll take him out back," Lewis said. "C'mon, Butch. Time for you to run around with the puppy and chase some squirrels."

"Thank you," Emma replied.

Her uneasiness must have shown on her face because the sheriff said, "I think I'll take a few minutes to enjoy the sun. It's going to be a warm day."

Emma did not wait for Lewis to go into the kitchen before she said, "Noah, we need to talk."

"Yes, we do." He put his arm around her shoulders and went with her into the parlor. When she closed the pocket doors, he said, "I never noticed those."

"I don't use them often, but we need to speak. Privately."

He chuckled. "I can think of a few other ways to enjoy this privacy!"

"Noah, don't!" She edged away from his hands that were reaching out to enfold her to him.

"Don't?"

"I have been trying to tell you something important for days. You must let me tell you." She sat on the sofa and motioned for him to take the rocking chair next to it.

Puzzlement dimmed his eyes, but he sat in the chair. "I'm listening, sweetheart," he said, folding her fingers between his again.

"Really listen, Noah. Don't try to seduce me with your kisses when I must tell you this."

"You drive a hard bargain." He flashed her an enticing grin that tempted her to throw aside her resolve to be honest with him and just surrender to passion once more. "You have my word. I won't try to seduce you . . . now."

Emma submerged the shiver of delight at his suggestion. She hoped he would still feel the same after what she had to tell him. "You know that I came here to Haven about seven years ago."

"Yes."

"I came here from Kansas."

"Did you?" Impatience was creeping into his voice, and she knew he could not figure out why she was discussing this when he wanted to devise a plan to halt Gilson's scheme.

"I thought I'd be able to build a new life here."

That got his attention. He scowled. "A *new* life? What was wrong with your old life?"

Knowing she must withhold none of the story from him, she looked directly into his eyes as she told him what she had hoped no one in Haven would ever hear. She did not play down her mistakes or how she had been foolish to believe Miles Cooper and let him draw her into his web of lies and crime. When she finished the tale with how she had fled in the middle of the night, she waited for Noah to say something. Instead he stared at her, as he had in the nightmare when he lifted the noose around her neck.

She quickly added, "*This* is why I hesitated when you asked me to marry you. I didn't want to tell you about the past I had to create for myself to replace what I left behind in Kansas."

"You were married to a bank robber?" he asked in not much more than a strained whisper.

"Yes, but I didn't know he was a bank robber when I married him. Noah, you must believe that."

"You were married to a bank robber?" he repeated as if he had not heard her. He released her hands and stood. He walked away as if he could not bear to look at her now that he knew the truth.

"I didn't know he was a bank robber when I married him. You must believe me, Noah. I was a silly girl who believed he really loved me."

"As I believed you loved me."

She jumped to her feet. "I do love you, Noah."

"Maybe you do. Maybe you don't. I don't know what to think about anything about you any longer. I thought I knew you, Emma."

"You do. I am the woman you married. The woman who runs Delancy's General Store and . . ." Her voice broke. "The woman who loves you. The woman who left Kansas is as dead as the man who betrayed her."

"Betrayed? He might have betrayed you, but you've betrayed me."

"*Might* have betrayed me? Are you suggesting I was Miles's accomplice, as everyone else believed?" She fought to keep from dissolving into tears. She had dared to hope Noah would listen and accept the truth . . . unlike everyone else. Instead he was accepting the accusations . . . like everyone else. "Noah, I told you I didn't know a thing about—"

He faced her. "I do know if Gilson doesn't know of this, he will soon. He has a week before the hearing begins. His network of spies are most efficient, as you have seen—both the Pinkerton men he hires and those he can buy with his offers of rewards.'' He scowled at the pocket doors. ''He'll set them to work to unearth every fact about you.''

''I know that. That's why I knew I couldn't delay telling you the truth any longer.''

''So you wouldn't have been honest with me otherwise?''

Hurt by his sharp question, she fired back, ''Would you have told me the truth about Belinda otherwise?''

''I'd planned to be honest with you when I asked you to marry me, but you were so blasted stubborn about agreeing to accept my proposal that everything else went out of my head.''

''How convenient for you to say that now!''

''But it's the truth.'' He closed the distance between them, but she stepped back, bumping into the sofa. The volatile fury in his eyes was now aimed at her, as she had hoped it would never be. ''Emma, even you must admit that saying I was my brother's daughter's father instead of her uncle is a small lie in comparison with what you've been hiding.''

''I tried to tell you the night we were married and last night, but you halted me with your kisses.''

Emma was unsure if he had heard her, because he turned on his heel and walked to look out the front window. She saw his gaze shift toward the courthouse beyond the village green. Wanting to reach through his shock and hurt, she went to him. She slipped between him and the window. She put her hands on his arms. He did not shake them off, but continued to frown in silence.

''Noah, please listen to me. I know this is a horrifying story. I don't know how I'd judge anyone else if I learned of it happening to them.'' She tightened her grip on his arms. ''But I was—I *am* innocent.''

''Then why did you run away?''

''I told you. They were set to lynch me, as they had Miles. How could I prove I was innocent if I was dead?''

"But you didn't try to prove your innocence. You ran."

"You make it sound as if I'd made the decision lightly.
I tried for several days to get someone to listen to my pleas
for justice. They could think only of their rage and need for
vengeance. Hanging Miles wasn't enough. Would hanging
me have been enough? Or would they have gone after my
family, too? I couldn't stay and put them through that hell."

"So you ran."

Tears bubbled out of her eyes as she whispered, "I gave
up my family and everything I had known to come here and
use the money my grandfather had left me to buy the store."
Her chin rose as she saw the suspicion in his eyes that she
had not believed she would ever see there. "No matter what
anyone might think, I didn't buy my store with any of the
money Miles stole. I never even knew where he hid it."

"So your name isn't Delancy?"

"No, it was Emma Stephenson before I married Miles."
She hesitated, then said, "Delancy was my mother's mother's maiden name. I used it when I moved here because I
thought maybe one day Leatrice and Howard—"

"Who?"

"My sister and brother. I thought that maybe one day
they would try to find me and ask me to come back to Fort
Pixton." She bit her lower lip as another pair of tears flowed
down her face. "For seven years, I hoped they would contact
me, but they never have."

He reached up to wipe away one of her tears, then, with
a curse, walked away again. "What a disaster! I'd thought
I might get a better hearing from a judge if I had a wife.
So what did I find myself? A wife who is accused of being
an accessory to a bank robber's crimes! I might as well hand
Belinda over to Gilson now and put my head in the noose."

"Noah, you can't give up. You must fight him."

"Instead of running away as you did?"

She flinched at his barbed words. "You have people who will heed you. I didn't. It's not the same. You must stay and fight Gilson."

"I intend to, but one of my best weapons against him is now a liability."

"Best weapon?" She took one step toward him, then paused, shaking her head. "Is that why you married me, Noah? To help you in your battle to keep Belinda?"

He stared at her without speaking. Then he opened the pocket doors. She winced when she heard the porch door slam shut behind him.

Closing her eyes, she dammed the tears within them. "Miles Cooper, are you watching in hell now? Have you had your final laugh at my expense, or will this torment go on as it ruins the rest of my life?"

CHAPTER EIGHTEEN

Emma took Belinda's hand and Sean's as they stood at the end of the church service. When Noah took Belinda's other hand, Emma struggled to keep her smile in place. Nothing must suggest they were not the happy family they had been even a few hours ago.

When Noah returned just as Gladys was putting breakfast on the table, he had said nothing to any of them. Gladys had chatted throughout the meal as if nothing seemed amiss, and Belinda had giggled with the housekeeper about something the two dogs had done. Sean was quiet and barely touched his eggs and bacon. Emma understood, because she was not hungry either.

Noah had been equally silent when they walked across the green with the sheriff in tow to attend church. Even during the service, he had not said anything, not even singing with the rest of the congregation. She knew he was deep in thought, but she could not guess what he thinking. She hesitated to ask. He might not tell her. Or he might, and her hopes that they could rebuild the trust between them would be decimated.

How could he think *she* had changed her heart simply because he had? Or had he changed his heart? Had he ever really loved her, or was she just a way to help him keep Belinda?

As she watched him tip his hat to Mrs. Parker, she wondered if she had let Noah bamboozle her exactly as Miles had. She had promised herself she would never let another man delude her and her heart. She had kept that promise until her heart refused to listen any longer to sense. That rebellion had begun the moment Noah had first come into her life.

"Awful," Mrs. Parker was saying as she stood directly behind Emma in the aisle. She edged in front of Emma and stopped, paying no attention to the frowns of those who were waiting to walk out of church. "Just awful to hear someone is trying to spread these horrible lies about Noah and that sweet child."

"It is awful, isn't it?" Emma replied, although she wanted to remind the sheriff's mother how often she had repeated gossip that was untrue.

"I hear that rude man is staying at the hotel."

"Yes." She glanced to where Noah and the children were now halfway to the church door.

"What was Mrs. Riley thinking to allow him to take a room there?"

"It's her business. She can't turn away folks simply because she doesn't like them."

"I hope he doesn't try to speak to me." Mrs. Parker put one hand on her waist and shook her other hand to emphasize her words as she added, "I fear I could not be polite to such a despicable man."

"Yes, I can understand how difficult that would be." She saw Reverend Faulkner was talking to Sean as if today were no different from any other Sunday. Pushing past Mrs. Parker, she said over her shoulder, "Excuse me, Mrs. Parker."

"Well!" she heard the older woman exclaim, but Emma did not turn to apologize. Circumventing any more questions would be wise, because Emma did not want to do anything to jeopardize the already precarious situation.

She realized she had been worrying needlessly. The rest of the townsfolk seemed eager to avoid her. Although she guessed it was because, for once, they did not know what to say to her, she never had felt so alone. Not even when she had left Kansas and traveled to the Mississippi and up the river to the Ohio and then followed the Ohio to this small town whose name offered what she was seeking. Then, when she had fled, she had known she had no other choice but hanging. Now she had so many choices, but all of them urged her to return to her husband's arms.

"Good morning, Emma," Reverend Faulkner said as she reached the church's door. "How are you faring today?"

"As well as can be expected." She wished she could tell this man she trusted every bit of the truth. Maybe he would have some counsel to ease the chasm that had opened this morning between her and Noah.

"Hold on to your faith that it will all work out."

"I'm trying to."

"Noah seems to be holding up very well under these difficult circumstances."

She followed his gaze to where Noah had paused as Kenny ran up to him. The telegraph operator handed him a slip of paper, and Noah opened it. The message must have been short, because he folded it quickly and put it beneath his coat, nodding his thanks to Kenny. Belinda still had her hand in his, and Sean . . .

Emma smiled through her sadness. Sean was standing on the other side of the green and talking with Jenny Anderson. The sight of the two friends was comforting, because not everything had fallen apart since she had said her vows with Noah and their lives had been thrown into a jumble.

"If you need me," Reverend Faulkner said, taking her hands in his warm ones, "don't hesitate to send for me."

"Thank you." She had meant few words as sincerely in her life.

Emma hurried down the steps, again noting that everyone seemed to be busy with other conversations as she approached. Yet, she felt their curious glances on her back when she passed.

Noah held out his arm to her as she reached them. She gazed into his dark eyes while she put her hand on it. How could she ask him to forgive her? He already knew she had not meant this to unfold as it had. She was unsure how she could ask him to forgive her for falling in love with him.

"Did you get good news about a lawyer?" she asked softly.

"Lawyer?"

"I saw Kenny deliver a message to you. I assumed you have sent to Chicago for legal help."

"This isn't the place to speak of such things."

His tone was so cold that she recoiled. His voice had been this icy the day he had accused Sean of stealing from his buckboard. He had forgiven Sean, but the rage tightening his face suggested he could not forgive her, too. His fingers over hers on his arm kept her from running to the house, where she could hide from him and everyone while she let her tears fall.

When a hand tugged on her skirt, Emma looked down at Belinda. The little girl was holding a bunch of dandelions.

"For me?" Emma asked as she bent to run a finger over the flowers.

"Aren't they pretty?" She shoved the blossoms into Emma's hand.

She nearly dropped the dandelions, which had been picked so near the yellow petals there were barely any stems remaining beneath the flowers. "Very pretty."

"Can we put them in a vase?"

"Maybe a glass would be better, because then you could look at them more easily." She did not want to tell Belinda that the flowers, with their short stems, would fall out of the vase or sink into the water.

"A glass would be better," Belinda said with a grin at Noah.

"Emma knows all about these things," he replied. "You can trust her."

Was there a thaw in his voice? Emma did not dare to press, for his tone might be only because they stood on the green where the other villagers seemed reluctant to leave. Her anger threatened to burst forth.

"Let's go home." When Belinda regarded her with dismay, Emma knew her cheerful voice had been too artificial. She gave up all attempt to pretend nothing was wrong as she added, "We want to get these pretty flowers in water right away."

Belinda giggled and began to skip across the green. Right past where Gilson was coming out of the hotel, Emma realized. Would he try to snatch the little girl in front of all these witnesses?

Noah tightened his hand over hers before she could give chase. "Wait," he murmured.

"For what?"

"For that."

She relaxed when she saw Sean race to catch up with Belinda. Grasping her hand, he twirled her about, leading her away from where Gilson had paused at the bottom of the stairs on the narrow front porch of the hotel. Gilson was staring at Belinda, frowning. Belinda's giggles filled the shockingly silent green as Sean shouted a challenge for her to try to beat him back to the house.

Gilson walked along the main street in the direction of the river. Emma wished he would go to the railroad station and buy a ticket for the next train north.

"Let's go," Noah said in a hushed voice. "We need to get those flowers in water."

She saw he was smiling, and she tried to do the same as she went with him toward her house. When Lewis fell in behind them like a well-trained soldier, she heard the buzz of whispers. The rest of the churchgoers began to scatter away from the green.

"The show is over," Emma said, not hiding her frustration.

"Show?"

"Noah, don't be obtuse."

"Again?"

She fisted her hand on his arm. "This isn't the place, as you reminded me, to speak of such things."

"Point well taken." Again his voice eased from its frigid fury. "So what show are you talking about?"

"The confrontation between you and Gilson. Right here on the green in front of them."

"Do you think they'd prefer a duel with pistols at ten paces or just fisticuffs?"

"Which would you prefer?" she asked, knowing that she was moving the conversation into perilous territory. She feared she had little more to lose.

"Neither. I'll meet Gilson in court and trounce him legally."

"I'm not speaking of him now."

Noah stopped on the steps to the house's front porch. As Butch bounded out, followed by Belinda's puppy, he moved aside while they chased some hapless squirrel toward a tree in Alice Underhill's yard. "You're speaking about you and me, aren't you? Why?"

"You're shutting me out, Noah. I know you believe you have no reason to trust me now, but you must. I'm your most ardent ally. I'd do anything to help you keep Belinda."

"I know." He sighed and put one foot on the lowest step. He halted and, turning, pulled her into his arms. "I know you'd do anything to help us."

She pressed her face to his chest, not caring if everyone within a dozen miles of Haven was watching. "I wondered if you'd ever hold me again."

"What?" He tilted her face back. "Why would you think that?"

"After I told you about what happened in Kansas, you walked out and slammed the door. Then you said nothing all morning." She felt the most peculiar yearning to laugh as she asked, "What was I supposed to think? You are so angry."

"My anger isn't focused on you."

"It seems to be."

He ran his finger along her cheek. "I have to admit I was upset that you had never told me about ... about what happened seven years ago, but I've spent this morning trying to decide how to defeat Gilson in court." His gaze became a gentle caress. "Sweetheart, I was so lost in my thoughts I didn't notice your distress."

"I thought you were so furious with me that you couldn't forgive me."

"Sweetheart, you have to trust me more. I wouldn't shut you out if I was angry." A hint of smile tugged at his lips. "I would let you know."

"Instead of saying nothing?"

"I forget that you don't know I become very focused on solving a problem and fail to notice most of everything else until I have a solution." He paused as he heard Belinda laughing inside the house. "I'm so used to Belinda and Gladys knowing that I never considered you'd think I was furious with you."

"You have every right to be." She sighed. "I'm sorry I have complicated matters."

"I agree. You have." He caressed her cheek. "But you have nothing to be sorry for. If my past hadn't intruded, you would never have needed to worry about what happened to you causing problems."

"Don't worry that he can find out more than I have told you, because there's nothing else."

"He *will* introduce your past at the hearing."

"If he has found out the truth."

"I suspect he has or will by the time the hearing begins a week from tomorrow." He pulled out of his pocket the piece of paper Kenny had given him. "This is a listing of all the messages your buddy Atherton telegraphed during his brief stay in Haven."

"Kenny gave you his messages?" she asked, astounded. The telegraph operator guarded the confidentiality of incoming and outgoing messages as zealously as she had her past.

"No, just where he sent them. Most of them are to Chicago, but there are several to Kansas."

"Noah, I'm so sorry."

He put the page away and tipped her face up to his again. "I told you once that the past is the past, and we have to learn to deal with it. I learned to handle the grief in mine. Now we have to figure out a way to put yours to rest."

"I was doing well with that until you came to town." This time, she did not resist laughing.

"Make me a promise."

"Of course."

"Promise me you'll let me handle this. I have some ideas of how to halt Gilson."

"Tell me what I can do to help."

"Watch over the children, stay away from Gilson, and put up with my silences through this."

"I will."

"Promise me, sweetheart. You'll stay away from Gilson and will watch over the children."

"I promise."

As he kissed her, she wondered how long she could go on pretending as if she believed they could defeat Gilson when he had the law on his side. How much longer could she act as if she feared only for Belinda? She knew the answer. They would pretend as long as they must, for otherwise she would have to admit how much she feared her second husband would meet his end in a noose, as her first had.

Noah reread the message he had written at the table in the bedroom where Emma had delighted him last night with her sensual touch. Here he could work without the chance of Belinda coming in. She was eager to test her new reading skills on everything. Although she might not understand these words, he must keep her from asking Emma or Sean or Gladys to explain one of the words or phrases when Gilson might overhear.

The message was not a short one, but Noah had to make

himself very clear. These telegrams he had been sending
were costing far more than a small fortune. The next one
needed to go to his brother so Ron could arrange to have
more funds sent to Haven. He was not asking for more than
a few hundred dollars. He doubted if he would need more.
Gilson's plan could not have included bankrupting the factory, because Gilson wanted to control Belinda's one-third
share of it and reap the profits of the Sawyer family's toil.

Setting the message aside, he picked up the one that had
been delivered to him while they ate lunch. His face, which
he could see in the mirror above the table, became pensive
as he reread it. He understood why Gladys had insisted he
should read it, for it was signed by Gilson.

He tilted the paper to see it better. *This* message was
unquestionably clear. Gilson wanted to meet with him to
discuss a compromise which would benefit both of them.

His lips tightened. It was as he had expected from the
beginning. Gilson had no interest in Belinda. All he wanted
was to be paid off the amount of her inheritance from her
father. Noah knew that, by this time, Gilson knew what the
exact value of Belinda's share of the business was and would
want every penny that he could obtain quickly. Gilson could
not afford to go to court, where public sentiment might
easily turn against him. Noah would gladly pay him, but
this would not be Gilson's only demand. Gilson would not
be satisfied until he had control of the business *and* Belinda.

Noah folded the note and put it in an inner pocket of his
coat so Emma would not see it. By Jiggs! He had not guessed
he was hurting her this morning. He *had* been furious with
her when he had stormed out of the parlor, but one look in
the direction of the hotel where Gilson was staying had been
enough to cool that anger. Emma could not be blamed for
a mistake she had made when she fell in love with the wrong
man.

That pinch of jealousy returned. He did not like to think of that worthless crook holding Emma and kissing her and making love with her. But she could change her past no more than Noah could change his. What mattered was now. She had promised him to keep a watch on the children so he could concentrate on finding a way to stop Gilson.

Picking up the messages he needed telegraphed, he walked down the stairs. He smiled when he saw Gladys by the door. Standing guard? He would not add to her distress by teasing her now.

She turned and regarded him with red-ringed eyes. Dabbing at one, then the other with the hem of her apron, she said, "Forgive me, Mr. Sawyer."

"For what? For caring so much about Belinda?"

"And you. If that man has his way, you will—"

He held up his hands. "Let's not talk about that. Belinda is the only one who should be on our minds."

"I'm worried about both of you, and so is Mrs. Sawyer. She took all the rope in the store and hid it beneath the hay in the barn."

"Did she?" Noah chuckled. "However, that's not the only rope in town."

"If I know Mrs. Sawyer, by the time that court is called to order next week, there won't be a length of rope found in this town long enough to go around your neck." She shuddered and looked away.

"It still may be possible to stop Gilson."

Gladys's head snapped up, her eyes filling with hope. "Thank heavens, but how?"

"How else? By giving Gilson what he has wanted from the beginning. Money."

"That's what I figured." She reached beneath her apron and pulled out a handful of money. "I have nearly fifty dollars here. Take it."

"You've been saving to buy a ticket to visit your brother in Buffalo."

"Take it, Noah." She held out the money. " 'Tis two lives we must save."

Although Noah wanted to refuse the generous offer, he took the money. It might take days for his brother to get money to him. He needed to pay for these telegrams *today.* Quietly he said, "Thank you, Gladys. I'll repay you as soon as I can."

"Just keep Belinda away from that man!"

"I shall!" He added nothing else as he went out the door and along the street toward the telegraph office.

The sunlight was glorious, and birds sang as they flitted from tree to tree. He could hear children's excited voices as they played some game. Someone was singing the first hymn that had been played in church this morning. Everything was exactly as it should be, and all wrong.

A gunshot echoed through the bucolic afternoon. Birds scrambled with strident squawks up into the air, and the singing and children grew silent. He froze, then realized the sound had come from behind the livery stable. Anderson must be shooting at the rats which got into his feed. He had been complaining about that at the Smiths' wedding.

Continuing along the street as the birds settled back into the trees, Noah opened the door to the telegraph office. Kenny came to his feet and held out his hand. Without a word, he began tapping the messages into the wire that followed the train tracks north.

"All sent," Kenny said as he handed the pages back to Noah. When Noah nodded, but did not move, the telegraph operator asked, "Anything else?"

"I need to wait for an answer to that first one you sent."

"Sometimes it takes a few hours to get a message delivered."

"Someone should be waiting for this one. Either we'll get an answer fast, or there won't be any answer." Noah stared at the telegraph, willing it to begin tapping.

It did, and he leaned forward as if he could pull the very words out of the air.

Kenny frowned. "This isn't the answer you're waiting for, Noah. It's from New York City." The telegraph ceased, and the telegraph operator began tapping on it.

"What is it?" Noah asked.

"I didn't get any of the message. Something must be going on along the lines. I'm telling them to resend the message." He lifted his finger away from the key and watched the telegraph, waiting with patience.

Noah pushed away from the low wall. As the minutes ticked by on the large, round clock on the wall and the telegraph remained silent, he began to fear, for the first time, that there was no way to save any of them from what could happen next week at the hearing.

"Will you play hide-and-seek with me, Emma?" Belinda asked as she followed Emma down the stairs.

"I'm busy gathering the laundry for tomorrow." She looked over the pile of bedding so she did not bump into the little girl and send them both tumbling down the stairs. "Why don't you play with Sean?"

"He isn't here."

Emma tossed the bedding into a pile on the hall floor. Taking Belinda's hand, she asked, "Are you sure? He told me he was going to stay here and play with you all afternoon."

"He isn't here."

She frowned. Sean had promised her he would stay by Belinda's side and watch over her while Emma and Gladys did the chores that needed to be done this afternoon. If Gilson or anyone else Sean did not know came into the yard, Sean was supposed to alert her right away.

Had she expected too much of the boy? No, for he had *offered* to play with Belinda and keep the little girl from suspecting anything was wrong. When Emma had hesitated, he reminded her he had taken care of his little sister for the past three years until he was caught trying to steal some food and was taken to the Children's Aid Society. *Carted off* had been his exact words, which still seethed with his anger that no one had heeded his pleas to let him go so he could take care of his sister.

From the corner of her eyes, Emma saw Gladys at the top of the stairs, but she continued to look at Belinda. "Do you know where Sean went?"

"He told me to come inside and ask you to play with me."

"Yes, but did he say where he was going?"

Belinda nodded, her eyes growing large as she realized both Emma and Gladys were listening eagerly to every word she said.

"Where did he say he was going, Belinda?" Emma asked.

"He told me not to tell you."

"You must."

"I promised." Her lower lip began to tremble. "It's wrong to break a promise."

Emma squatted in front of the little girl. "I know it's wrong to break a promise, Belinda. I wouldn't ask you to do so if I wasn't worried that something bad might happen to Sean."

"What bad could happen to him?"

She tried to come up with an example that would not reveal to the little girl why they all were so edgy. She could not when her mind was so filled with frightful thoughts. "Belinda, please tell me."

"Are you afraid something bad is going to happen to *me?*"

When Gladys gave a soft moan as she came down the stairs, Emma wanted to urge the housekeeper to be silent. She could not, for she must answer Belinda's question. Taking a deep breath, she said, "There is a very bad man who has come to Haven."

"Very bad?"

"Very bad."

"Will he hurt me or Sean?"

She shook her head. "You're safe as long as you stay close to the house and one of us. Sean will be safe if he stays here, too, until the bad man goes away again."

"I want the bad man to go away now."

"So do I, Belinda." She glanced at Gladys, then asked, "Belinda, where's Sean? As long as that bad man is in Haven, it is all right to tell me even though you promised Sean you would not."

Belinda did not speak for a long minute, then whispered, "He said he was going to pay a call on someone named Dickie and his boys."

Emma gasped in horror. One of Dickie's boys was what Sean had called Gilson when he had feared the man was someone out of Sean's past. Although neither Sean nor Noah had explained exactly what Dickie's boys might do if they had come to Haven, she knew they were trouble. Just as Gilson was.

"Dickie?" asked Gladys. "Who's that?"

Coming to her feet, Emma said, "I know whom he's talking about." She reached for her bonnet on the peg hanging by the door. How could Sean be so foolish? His attempt at heroics could be dangerous, for Gilson would not hesitate to hurt the boy. "Gladys, stay here with Belinda."

"Where are you going?"

"To save Sean from his own foolishness." *If I am in time*, she added silently. She did not want to think what would happen if she was too late.

CHAPTER NINETEEN

Emma held her breath as she paused in the silent corridor of the town's hotel. She had managed to sneak in while Mrs. Riley was busy in her kitchen. Now she stood before the door with the brass number five set at eye level.

She had never been on the upper floors of this hotel. In the time since she had traveled from Kansas, she had forgotten about the odors that stayed in a boarding house long after the residents had moved on. Odors of sweat and burned food and smoke from trains and dust from dry roads. Dusk clung to the far end of the hall, which overlooked the green, as if something horrible lurked there. Nothing could be worse than what she might face in the room on the other side of this door.

A strange disoriented sensation surrounded her. Emma Delancy—no, Stephenson. Emma Stephenson Sawyer could not be standing in this hallway. Emma Stephenson Sawyer was not the person about to sneak into the hotel room of the man who wanted to see her husband hang. It was someone else treading this imprudent path.

What if Sean had not come here? If she was mistaken, she could be about to make matters worse. But if she was right, the boy needed to be brought to his senses before he did something in a naïve effort to protect the family he had gained here in Haven.

She strained to hear any sound that would tell her what was happening in the room. Nothing. She put her ear against the wood. The door swung open. She waited for the length of a single heartbeat. When no one called out or came to the door to see why it had opened on its own, she edged forward and peeked into the room beyond the iron bed that was set in the middle of the narrow space.

Her nose wrinkled. Smoke hung in the air, coiling near the open window. Seeing ashes in the bowl set beside the ewer on the washtable, she gasped when she recognized the writing on one piece of paper that had not been completely burned. This was the page Gilson had said proved he had a right to take Belinda with him.

"Oh, Sean," she whispered, "how could you be so foolish?"

She looked out the open window. As she had guessed, a tree stretched out a thick branch toward the hotel. It was just the right strength to hold a nimble boy. He must have come in this way and slipped out the same way.

She must go, too. And she could not climb down the tree. Her dress was too close-fitting to allow her to do what she would have managed with ease when she had been Sean's age. She turned—and pressed her hands over her mouth as she stared at Laird Gilson.

"This is, indeed, a surprise," he said, entering the room and closing the door. "I'd thought you would at least wait for Sawyer's body to be cut down from the gallows before you paid me a call.''

''I'm not paying you a call, Mr. Gilson. I came here looking for . . .'' She realized it was useless to lie. ''I came here looking for Sean.''

''Sean?''

''The young boy you met at my house this morning.''

He smiled. ''I guess that excuse is as good as any.'' His smile disappeared when he sniffed. Pushing past her, he cursed as he saw the ashes in the bowl. He swept the bowl off the table and cursed as it struck the floor and shattered.

Emma rushed to the door. She was not going to stay here to see what this volatile, violent man might do next. Her hand was caught in a viselike grip before she could turn the doorknob. Spun about, she was shoved up against the door. Her eyes blurred when her head struck the thick door.

''You know burning that paper was stupid, don't you?'' Gilson growled. ''That was not the only copy of that court order.''

''Where are the others?'' shouted a young voice from behind him.

''Sean!'' she cried as the boy jumped out of the cupboard. Its door crashed against the wall. She had not guessed he would hide from her in there. As Gilson whirled to face the boy, she gasped, ''Sean, you . . .''

Her voice dried up as she stared at the pistol Sean held with the cool confidence. It was aimed at Gilson, whose face lost all color.

''You don't treat a lady like that,'' Sean growled, as his thumb reached to draw back the hammer. ''And you aren't going to take Belinda away.''

Somehow, Emma squeaked, ''Put the gun down, Sean. This isn't the way to solve this.''

''Dickie's boys—''

"This isn't the way to solve this in *Haven*. We aren't Dickie's boys." Her voice grew stronger as she added, "Sean, put the gun down, and we'll go home. Let Sheriff Parker and Judge Purchase do what they can to protect Belinda."

Sean looked from her to Gilson. His thumb lowered away from the hammer, but he held the pistol steady. "Not until he gives the rest of his proof to me. Then it'll all be gone, and he won't be able to take Belinda away."

"You little bastard," Gilson snarled. "You should be sent to hang beside Sawyer."

"Hang? Noah?" Sean choked, horror filling his eyes. "What're you talking about?"

Gilson took one step toward the boy. "You heard me. Sawyer's going to hang for kidnapping the girl, and you'll hang beside him for arson."

"Arson?"

"For attempting to set this hotel on fire."

"Emma!" Sean was abruptly a frightened child, even though he still held the pistol pointed at Gilson.

"Don't listen to him." She moved toward Sean, but Gilson pushed her back. Knowing this was not the time to confront Gilson for his lack of manners, she said, "Listen to me, Sean. He's lying to you. You shouldn't have come here, but no one will believe you tried to burn anything other than that single page in order to protect Belinda."

Gilson laughed. "Are you so sure of that, Emma? Do you think a woman who sneaks into a man's hotel room will be believed by any jury of decent people?"

"You're twisting the truth of everything that has happened." She looked past him and held out her hand. "Sean, let's go." When she tried again to edge around Gilson, he swung his arm, shoving her back against the hall door so hard her ears rang.

"Don't hit her!" shouted Sean.

Gilson rounded on him. The gun fired just as Gilson struck the boy across the face. The bullet hit the ceiling, and Emma covered her head with her arms as she threw herself toward where Sean was lying, motionless, on the floor beside the bed.

"Sean!" She put her hand against his cheek, then pulled it back when she saw the imprint of Gilson's fingers on his face. Rage filled her. It blinded her to everything but the gun lying on the floor by Sean's outstretched hand.

She reached for it. The gun was snatched out of her hand so fiercely that her palm burned. When Gilson pointed it at Sean, she shifted so she was between the gun and the boy.

Gilson laughed. "Do you think I would hesitate to shoot *you*, Emma? You've presented me with a dilemma. Would it be more enjoyable to shoot you now and watch Sawyer mourn your death, or would I prefer to see him go to the gallows knowing you're still alive and—"

"About to be preyed on by you?" She shook her head. "If you think I'd be willing to let you hurt us more, you're even a greater idiot than I have heard."

His smile vanished. "You are going to regret that sass. When—"

A fist pounded on the door. Mrs. Riley called out, "Open up! Now!"

Grabbing her arm, Gilson jerked Emma to her feet. His hand clamped over her mouth before she could do more than gasp. He pushed her next to the door hinges, so when the door opened, she would not be seen. She did not move, because he kept the pistol pointed at Sean. Gilson did not have to speak his threat. She understood it. A single word to alert Mrs. Riley, and Sean would die.

Mrs. Riley pounded on the door again.

"Coming, Mrs. Riley," Gilson said, his voice now so carefree that Emma wanted to scream out in despair.

When he opened the door, his thumb on the gun, which he must be keeping out of Mrs. Riley's view, shifted to the hammer. Emma pressed back against the wall.

"Good afternoon, Mrs. Riley," he said.

Mrs. Riley's voice trembled. "I heard a gun fire."

"So did I. I had just opened the window to try and see who it might be when you arrived." He chuckled, and Emma clenched her fingers into fists. "It sounded as if it came from out behind the hotel," Gilson said as he smiled at Mrs. Riley. "Nearly scared me out of my skin."

"It sounded like it came from up here."

"You might ask the sheriff to check the crest of the hill behind the hotel."

Emma could hear Mrs. Riley's uncertainty as she said, "I'll do that, Mr. Gilson." Emma understood all too well. If Mrs. Riley falsely accused one of her guests of firing a gun in her hotel, the word might spread, and no one would stay here. She closed her eyes in defeat when Mrs. Riley added, "I'm glad to hear you're all right, Mr. Gilson."

"I'm fine." He closed the door and turned to face Emma with a lecherous smile. Twisting the lock on the door, he said, "I'm doing very, very fine."

Pushing past him, she dipped a cloth into the bowl and she wrung it out. She bent to press it against the reddening spot on Sean's face. Her arm was seized, and she was pulled to her feet again.

"Are you so beastly," she cried, "that you won't let me tend to the child you struck so viciously?"

"Hush, my dear. We wouldn't want Mrs. Riley to come back, would we?"

"I'd be glad to have her come back."

"Would you?" He aimed the gun at the prone boy as he

had before. Smiling at her, he asked, "Would you, really, Emma?"

"Shoot him, and you'll be sent to hang."

"Instead of Sawyer?" He laughed. "The boy tried to shoot me. A plea of self-defense would save my neck and stretch his."

She prayed for the right words to end this, so she could tend to Sean and take him back home, but none came. He threw all her words back at her. When Gilson set his foot on the iron footboard, he grinned.

"I'm honored, Emma, that you decided to call." He put out the hand holding the gun toward her face, but she moved away as far as she could when he held her arm. "Come now, my dear. Fancy talk is what you want to hear, isn't it?"

She kept her chin high. "What I want, Mr. Gilson, is to take Sean home."

"Is he your son?" He laughed. "Is Sawyer collecting a whole household of children that he didn't father? Maybe he can't."

Instead of answering his insulting questions, she said, "Be honest, Mr. Gilson. You don't want to be burdened with Belinda. She's much better off here."

"With a kidnapper?"

"With her uncle."

Sean groaned.

"Let me help him!" she cried.

"If I do, what will you do for me in return?"

She yanked her arm out of his grip. "You're disgusting."

"And you're a beautiful woman who should have someone better than Sawyer."

"You obviously don't want to be reasonable." She stared at the door, yearning for nothing more than to escape. Then she realized that was not true. She did want something more.

She longed to protect Sean and Belinda and Noah. Just as Sean did. That desperate need had led them to this.

Emma bent toward Sean, but froze again when Gilson jabbed the pistol between her and the boy. Straightening, she asked, "What do you want me to do before you'll let me tend to him? Plead on bended knee?"

"A bit of perjury would be a good place to start."

"I can promise you I'll say whatever you want the judge to hear, but we both know that's a promise I won't keep."

"That's quite true." He ran the pistol's barrel along her arm. "So why don't you help me even things out a bit?"

"What do you mean?"

As he leaned toward her, she almost gagged on the odor of whiskey. Was the liquor making him act so crazy? Judge Purchase would not take kindly to hearing of how Gilson was acting. Gilson should know that.

He chuckled and said, as if she had spoken her thoughts aloud, "No one's going to know what happened here but you and me, Emma, my dear."

"And Sean."

"He won't wake up in time to know." He pushed on the bed. "It's good that this doesn't squeak. I don't want to wake the boy before we're done."

She was going to be ill. She pressed her hands to her stomach as Gilson set his foot on the floor and moved toward her. She backed away. Until she could get Sean, she could not leave. Gilson knew that, too, as he edged to her left to keep himself between her and the boy.

He laughed as she bumped into the wall. Ripping her bonnet from her head, he tossed it aside.

"Mr. Gilson, don't do this," she whispered. She tried to turn her face away, but he caught her cheeks and forced her to look at him. He squashed her against the wall while the odor of what he had been drinking swelled over her, threatening to sicken her.

"Please me, Emma, my girl, and I'll take you with me instead of the kid."

Her reaction was pure instinct. Flinging out her fist, she struck him in the chin. He reeled back. She pushed past him and ran to where Sean was lying. Bending, she slipped her arms beneath him. She started to straighten, then faltered. He was even heavier than she remembered.

Gilson's hand on her arm swung her to face him. She gasped as Sean rolled away from her, still senseless. She fell to sit on the floor with a thump that resonated through her.

Cursing, he pulled her to her feet and propelled her toward the bed. His hand clamped over her mouth as he forced her down onto it. She kicked at him. He swore and pinned her beneath him.

"Stop!" Her scream was muffled against his hand.

He laughed as he lifted her skirts. "I doubt if I'll be stopping for a long time, my dear Emma. Not until you're as docile as a kitten."

She ripped his hand off her mouth and spat at him. He clamped his mouth over hers as he pressed her to the bed. Her flailing legs tangled in her skirts and petticoats. When she reached up to claw at his face, he caught her hands and pinned her wrists to the bed with a single hand. He undid the top button on her blouse and then the next and the next as she struggled to escape.

He was too strong. He had her hands. All she had were her feet. Desperately, she fought to free them from her skirt. No. It was taking too long, for he was pushing her blouse aside as his hand curved up along her breast. Ignoring her nausea at his touch, she jerked her knee upward. His screech rang through her head, but his grip on her loosened.

Arching her back, she rolled toward the edge of the bed. He did not release her. They crashed to the floor. She pushed against him, then kicked his shin. He yelped, but slapped her as savagely as he had Sean.

She moaned as she crumpled to the floor, the salty flavor of blood thick in her mouth. She moaned again when he ran his fingers along her leg where her dress was bunched under her. His leg clamped hers to the floor.

"That's right," he murmured. "Make it fun."

"You won't think it is fun if you don't get off her, Gilson." Lewis Parker poked Gilson's shoulder blades with a rifle as he ordered, "Get up!"

Before Gilson could move, he was hauled away from her. Noah held him by the collar. He glanced at Lewis, then drove his fist into Gilson's stomach, knocking him back against the wall. Gilson took a step toward him, then froze as Lewis aimed the gun at him.

"He has a pistol," Emma whispered, her jaw aching more with each word.

"If you do, Gilson," Lewis said with a calm Emma had to admire, "you'd better put it on the bed right now. Nice and easy."

As Gilson cursed and obeyed the sheriff's orders, Noah knelt beside Emma, gathering her to him. He tried to control his rage. As she began to rebutton her blouse, he bit back his curses.

"Sean," she whispered. "We need to help Sean."

"Where is he?" Noah asked.

"On the other side of the bed."

"Wait here."

Noah could not silence his oaths when he saw the boy sprawled on the floor. Lifting him carefully, he turned to lock eyes with Gilson, who had not moved. Did his enemy realize that the only thing keeping Noah from ridding the world of his miserable hide was the fact that he did not want Emma to witness it?

When Gladys had burst into the telegraph office with Belinda in tow, Noah had been horrified to learn Emma had gone to stop Sean from trying to destroy the proof that Gilson had legal custody of his sister's daughter. Fury at her foolishness had mixed with fear for her at Gilson's hands. Before he could call Lewis into the telegraph office, Mrs. Riley had rushed up to the sheriff with her concerns. He and Lewis had left the women, Belinda, and the telegraph operator to stare after them as they raced to the hotel, hoping they would not be too late. Getting a key from the box in Mrs. Riley's private rooms, they had come up the stairs and into the room to see Gilson strike Emma.

He gritted his teeth as he placed Sean on the wrinkled covers of the bed that revealed what had happened. He brushed plaster dust from the boy's face. He looked up and saw the hole in the ceiling.

"Mrs. Riley was right to send for you, Lewis," he said as he reached down to help Emma to her feet. "It must be against the law to fire off a gun in a hotel."

Gilson sneered, "If it is, then the kid should be arrested. He tried to shoot me. She witnessed that."

"He didn't fire the gun!" Emma cried. "It went off by mistake when you hit him."

"Hush, Emma," Noah replied. "Let Lewis handle this, as I told you he would."

She did not lower her eyes. "Noah—" She rushed to Sean when the little boy moaned and opened his eyes. "No, don't move yet," she said, sitting and cradling him against her.

Gilson laughed. "Are you too scared to face me alone, Sawyer? First you send that harlot you call your wife. Then you bring the law to accuse me of a crime I didn't commit."

"Maybe you didn't fire the gun, but rape is a crime in this state."

"Rape?" He laughed again. "She was willing."

"Is that why you beat her?"

"She likes it rough. Maybe you should try it."

Again Noah had to restrain his longing to reach for Gilson's throat and throttle every bit of life from him.

Before he could reply, Lewis said, "Noah doesn't take the law here in Haven lightly, Gilson. He respects it, as you're going to learn to do." He poked at the man with his rifle again. "C'mon. We're going to go and see Judge Purchase."

"If this is how you hope to be rid of me, Sawyer," Gilson snarled, "let me tell—"

"Let me tell *you*," interrupted Noah, "that the only reason I brought Sheriff Parker is because I didn't trust myself not to flay the skin from you."

"Let's go," Lewis said. Pausing in the door, he smiled coldly. "Emma, Noah's still under arrest, so you'll make sure he gets back to your house, won't you?"

"Yes." She looked up at Noah, but quickly away when he frowned at her.

Picking up Sean again, Noah said, "You heard the sheriff. Let's get out of here."

No one stopped them as they went to Emma's quiet house, but Noah did not fool himself into thinking that the peace would remain long. Mrs. Riley jumped to her feet as they walked up onto the porch. Cooing at Sean, she stared at Emma, who assured the innkeeper she was not hurt. Mrs. Riley mumbled something and rushed back to her hotel.

When Gladys put her apron over her mouth to hold in her soft cry of dismay while she followed them into the house, Noah said, "Send for the doctor."

"Is she—"

"Sean needs to be checked." He started up the stairs, then asked, "Where's Belinda?"

"Taking a nap."

"Take him to my room," Emma said, "and I'll get some cool water to put on his bruises."

"Mrs. Sawyer," Gladys replied, "you need to be tending to yourself, too."

When Emma put her hand to her reddened cheek, Noah saw her wince, but she said, "I'll be fine. Sean was hit much harder."

He recognized her stubborn tone, and Gladys must have, too, because she hurried out the door to get the doctor. He carried Sean up the stairs and placed him on the bed. Stepping back, he watched as Emma came into the room with a bowl and some cloths. She set them on her dresser before she drew off the boy's shoes and settled an extra blanket over him.

"Emma," Sean whispered as she wrung out a cloth and put it on his scarlet cheek, "I'm so sorry. I shouldn't have gone to—"

"We'll talk about it later." She glanced at Noah and again did not meet his eyes for more than a second. "You need to rest now. How do you feel?"

"My head aches." Tears ran down his face, and he did not wipe them away. "I should have shot him."

"Don't say that," she said softly.

"He can't take Belinda away now, can he?"

"We'll talk about that later." She stiffened when the sound of the door opening came up the stairs.

"Wait here with him," Noah said as he went out into the hallway to greet Doc Bamburger, who was so round that his bright red vest gave him the appearance of a well-fed robin with gold-rimmed glasses perched on its beak.

When the doctor went into the bedroom and closed the

door behind him, Noah walked down the stairs. How much more could go wrong today? He had been a fool when he had thought not receiving an answer back to his desperate telegram would be the worst thing that could happen.

Someone knocked on the door as he was walking into the parlor. He turned, but Gladys motioned for him to stay where he was. Pulling the curtains in the windows that overlooked the porch, he sat. He was grateful to hear Gladys tell whoever was calling that no one could come to the door now and that the caller should return tomorrow. He lost count of the number of times she answered the door and repeated those words before the doctor came down the stairs.

Standing, Noah motioned for him to come into the parlor. Doc Bamburger set his black bag on the closest table and said, "I believe Emma keeps some brandy in the kitchen. I'll be right back."

The doctor was as good as his word, because he returned just as another knock came at the door. Pouring a generous serving into a glass, he handed it to Noah.

"Drink it. Doctor's orders." His smile was fleeting.

"How are they?"

"Sit down and drink up. The best prescription anyone has ever come up with." The doctor sat on the sofa, which creaked a protest beneath his hefty weight. "Sit down, Noah. There's nothing you can do for either of them just now."

"Will they be all right?"

Doc Bamburger pushed his glasses up his narrow nose. "The boy was hit very hard. The blow may have been concussive. I've told Emma to keep him quiet for a week and keep putting cold cloths on his bruises when he complains of pain. A couple of his teeth are loose, but I suspect they'll tighten themselves back into place."

"And Emma?"

"Her cheek may bruise, too." He hesitated, then said, "She refused to let me examine her otherwise."

"That isn't a surprise, but he didn't have time to do more than strike her once."

"He? What happened?"

Noah explained, leaving out the fact that Sean had taken a gun with him to Gilson's hotel room.

The doctor's face became as gray as Emma's. He poured more brandy into another glass and downed it in a single gulp. Then he heaved himself to his feet. Opening his bag, he drew out some packets and put them on the table.

"If she swoons, you can mix this with some water and give it to her," Doc Bamburger said.

"Swoon? Emma?" Noah shook his head as he came to his feet. "I can't imagine her doing that."

"You might be surprised. She's a woman, and women are fragile."

"If you'd seen her fighting him off, you wouldn't use the word fragile to describe her."

Quietly, from behind him, Emma said, "I didn't have much choice." As the doctor's face reddened, she went on, "Thank you for coming so quickly. I'll make sure someone is always with Sean until he's more himself."

"By tomorrow, you probably will find him eager to get back to playing with his friends." The doctor chuckled. "It isn't every day a boy gets to be such a hero."

Emma glanced at him, but Noah said nothing as she bid the doctor a good day and saw him to the door. She closed the door so hastily behind the round man, Noah was not surprised to hear another knock. He frowned when he heard an echo from the kitchen. Someone was at the back door.

Going into the kitchen, he was astounded to see that it looked and smelled like a normal day. Chicken soup bubbled on the stove, and a loaf of bread was partially cut on the table. He opened the back door to see Alice Underhill's strained face. He was about to explain that they were not receiving guests when Emma called to Alice to come in.

"She's here to help watch over Sean," Emma said, acting as if she had not noticed Alice's shock when her friend saw the swelling on her face. "He's upstairs in my room. If you'll sit with him, Gladys can watch over Belinda and—" More knocking came from the front door. "And answer the door."

Alice reached out toward her. "Emma—"

"Thank you for coming to sit with Sean," she replied. "Noah, I know you and I need to talk." She turned on her heel and went into the parlor.

"Who hit her so hard?" Alice shuddered as she stared after Emma in dismay. "Gladys asked me to come over to help with Sean, but she didn't say Emma had been hurt, too. What happened?"

"She was protecting Sean." He did not repeat the tale again. Alice soon would hear of it all, anyhow. He patted Alice's shoulder, then followed Emma into the parlor. Closing the pocket doors, he pretended not to see Gladys's consternation.

"I believe this is yours," Emma said, handing him the glass that Doc Bamburger had filled with brandy.

"Thank you."

"You're welcome."

Was this what she wanted? For them to act like strangers again?

"You have every right to be angry with me," Emma said as she sat on the sofa. Her voice was as calm as if she were discussing the cost of a bag of flour.

He could not silence the fury bubbling up in him when he saw the vivid mark of Gilson's hand on her cheek as she glanced toward the front windows when yet another knock came at the front door. Sitting in the rocking chair, he said, "You promised me you'd let me handle this and that you'd stay away from Gilson."

"I promised you, as well, that I'd guard the children." Her voice still had no emotion. "I know I shouldn't have gone after him, but I thought I could stop Sean before he did something stupid."

"And instead you did something stupid."

"Stupid?" She gasped, her eyes widening with amazement. "I saved his life. Gilson would have killed him if I hadn't been there to divert him."

"Divert him?" He stood, unable to sit when his head was filled with the image of his enemy pressing Emma to the floor and lifting her skirt to reveal her slender legs. The resentment that had battered him each time he thought of her first husband was nothing compared with this jealous rage. He wished he could reach into his mind and tear out the memory of Gilson's fingers on her. "Is a diversion what you call rape?"

Her composure cracked further as she whispered, "Don't say that."

"Why not? That was what he was attempting." He shook his head. "Emma, when are you going to stop being so blasted foolish?"

"You keep calling me foolish, but was it foolish to try to save a child who depends on me?" She rose slowly. "Would you have stood by and done nothing if Belinda had been in such a perilous situation?"

"Belinda wouldn't have gone to the hotel with a gun." He cursed and took a drink of the brandy. It burned through him, but could not scorch away his fury. "Where did he get that?"

"From Jenny Anderson. The pistol belongs to her father. Sean told me he asked to borrow it when they were talking after church. He'd do anything he can to keep this family together.'' She laughed with a bitterness he had never heard in her voice before. "But we aren't a family, are we? Not a real one. You're outraged at me for trying to save Sean because now you believe I've further compromised your attempts to keep Belinda.''

"You shouldn't have gone after him as you did.''

"So I should have stayed here and let Gilson kill him?''

"You can't be sure that would have happened.''

"No, I can't be. Maybe I made matters worse going after him or maybe he'd be dead now if I'd remained here, afraid to do anything.'' She closed her eyes, and when they opened again, they were filled with jeweled tears. "I thought you were different, Noah, but you aren't any different, are you? You married me to get what you wanted, letting me think that you loved me.''

"Don't be silly!''

"How many more times are you going to call me foolish and stupid and silly? The only thing I've done that was foolish and stupid and silly was believe that you love me.'' She threw open the pocket doors and said, "But a promise is a promise, Noah. I'll do what I can to help you keep Belinda from having to go with that horrible man.''

"Emma—''

"Don't say anything you don't mean.'' She faced him, her tears now clinging to her eyelashes. "I'll do as I promised, Noah. I'll play your game that you really love me, and everyone outside this house will believe we are the happy family you need to persuade the judge to let you keep Belinda. Don't worry. No one will suspect anything otherwise from me. Miles taught me how to live a lie.''

He put down the glass and crossed the foyer to grasp her by the shoulders before she could go up the stairs. "Emma, wait.''

She stiffened beneath his fingers as she asked, ''And if I don't, will you treat me as he did?''

He was not sure if she meant Gilson or her first husband. He lifted his hands away from her. When she went up the stairs, he heard a soft sob. Not from her, but from Gladys, who had been watching from beside the door. He knew he should say something to his housekeeper.

But what? He had known, from the moment he took the baby and left Chicago five years ago, that saving Belinda from Gilson would demand a great toll. He just had not guessed the greatest sacrifice would be Emma's love.

CHAPTER TWENTY

They were coming. She could hear their voices—
shouting, angry, lusting for vengeance. The familiar
voices with such an unfamiliar fury.

She whirled. Escape. She must escape, or they would
make her pay for the crime that was not hers. She had
to leave.

Now . . . before it was too late.

The shooting at the bank was over, but the questions
would now begin. And she had no answers. At least,
none anyone would believe.

How could she have been so stupid? That question
had been on everyone's lips as soon as last week's
grim events became known. No one would listen to
her. Even if a few people did, no one else would believe
them. After all, how could she have been so stupid?

She had believed Miles when he said work was going well, that all their dreams would come true, that soon he would have enough money to take her on that honeymoon to St. Louis she had dreamed of when she found she loved him.

And she had believed he loved her.

Everything had been lies. There had been no work, and she had nothing left but nightmares.

Tears burned in the back of her throat, but she refused to let them fall. Had Miles ever loved her, or had that been just another lie?

She had been a fool. Never again would she be such a fool.

Picking up the small carpetbag she had packed clandestinely, she looked around. Only the fire on the hearth lit the room. Yet she could see the quilt lying across the back of the battered settee, the tarnished candlesticks on the mantel, and the rag rug covering the uneven floor. She would never see any of these things again.

A fist struck the front door followed by a shout of, "Open the door!"

She took one step toward the back door, then another, hoping no shadow would reveal where she stood. Her breath snagged on the fear halting her heart.

"This is the sheriff. Open up, or we'll take down the door."

Time and hope and all her dreams had run out. She turned and pulled the quilt off the settee. Throwing its dark side over her shoulders, she fled through the kitchen and out into the night, far from the men milling around the front porch.

She had to leave.

Now . . . because it was too late.

Behind her, she heard, "She has to know."

"How could she not know?" another voice asked.

"Only a fool wouldn't have known."

At that voice, which should not be here in Fort Pixton, Kansas, she stopped with her hand on the door knob. Turning, she saw a man standing in the door to the parlor. His hands were hidden behind his back. Not Miles, but Noah. No one in Fort Pixton would understand, but she had thought Noah would.

"Only a fool wouldn't have known," he repeated.

"Then I was a fool." Her own voice was steady, even as her heart thumped with both yearning and fear that he would walk away from her forever. "I was young, and he was charming. He charmed people in the bank, and he charmed me. If I had been wiser then, I might have seen through his pretense."

"Only a fool wouldn't have known." He drew his hands from behind his back. In them was a noose. Walking to her, he slipped it over her head. It dropped to rest on her shoulders. He reached to tighten it, but she caught his hands.

"I must be a fool," she whispered as she lifted the noose from over her head, "for I fell in love with you." Letting the rope fall to the ground, she put her hand up to touch his cheek. "And I cannot fall out of love with you."

"Do you want to fall out of love with me?"

"No!"

The cry in her dream rang through Emma's head as she opened her eyes and stared out into the gray light of morning. The same nightmare had haunted her every night for the past week. During the day, another nightmare had stalked

her. She had thought so many times of what she would say
to Noah if she could have even a minute alone with him.
Between sitting with Sean and trying to keep him entertained
with stories and drawing so he remained quiet and her work
at the store, where she had refused to answer any questions
her neighbors posed about what had left her face with such
a bruise, she had seen Noah so seldom he might as well
have been living out at his farm.

Last night, his younger brother, a pleasant man who was
trying his best not to appear out of place in Haven, and Mr.
Evans, an attorney from Chicago, had arrived. Noah had
spent the evening talking with them behind the closed parlor
doors. She would not have been turned away if she had
knocked, but she had not.

Rolling to her other side, she saw Noah's side of the bed
was undisturbed . . . again. She sat and leaned her forehead
in her hands. It had been her suggestion, after all, that they
simply *pretend* to be a happy family. She should not fault
him for agreeing, especially when that plan could gain him
the very thing he wanted—custody of Belinda.

Emma got dressed, making certain that her hair, for once,
would remain in its chignon. Then she went to help Gladys
with the children. Even Belinda seemed to understand the
importance of the hearing, for she was unusually subdued.
When he wobbled as he came down the stairs, Emma did
not ask Sean if he would rather stay home. She knew how
much he wanted to be there.

She smoothed the pointed hem of her short gray coat over
her skirt. Its sedate navy piping around the collar matched
what was sewn along the hems of her sleeves and skirt. At
her throat, she had closed the collar with a round pin decorated with garnets. She set her gray silk bonnet on her hair
and turned as she heard the door from the kitchen open.

Noah's brother, Ronald, was so tall his head brushed the

top of the doorway. His hair was a brighter red than Noah's, and his black suit was unquestionably more elegant. His expression was grim. Behind him came Mr. Evans, who was as short as Lewis Parker. A pince-nez sat on his nose, bobbing with each step.

Emma noticed them in the moment before Noah walked toward her. In the fine suit he had worn when he stood in front of Reverend Faulkner with her, he caused her heart to quiver. She longed to press her face to his chest as his arms came up to enfold her. She hurried to tie the ribbons on her bonnet before the very sight of him disintegrated the serenity she had carefully constructed during the past week.

"Ready?" Noah asked.

"Yes." She arranged on her lips the smile she had practiced all week. Taking Sean's hand, she felt her smile slip when Belinda grabbed her other hand and then reached for Noah's.

Over the children's heads, Noah's gaze held hers for only a moment. He led them out onto the porch and down the street toward the courthouse. The road was lined with wagons and horses tied beneath the trees on the green. Her neighbors stood in front of every house they passed. Most of them fell into line behind, creating a bizarre and oddly silent parade toward the courthouse.

Noah lifted Belinda into one arm and put his other one around Emma's shoulders as they climbed the steps to the courthouse door. She did not relax against his strength, for if she let her poise falter even a moment, she might fall utterly apart.

As they entered the short hall that led in one direction to the town offices and in the other to the courtroom, her steps slowed. Laird Gilson waited by the single door that opened into the courtroom. She heard Sean mutter something under his breath, but said nothing as Noah herded her past his enemy.

Gilson started to speak. The man beside him hissed him to silence, and Emma guessed the rail-thin man was Gilson's attorney. Rail-thin? A better description would be serpent-thin.

The courtroom was so crowded that every seat on the four benches was full. More spectators were pressed against the walls.

Emma did not look to the left or right as she walked with Noah to a table in front of where Judge Purchase would be sitting. The jury box was empty, for the judge would make his decision on Belinda's future alone.

When Noah drew out a chair at the table, Emma sat and took Belinda onto her lap. Sean went with Gladys and Noah's brother to where a spot was being cleared on one of the benches for them. Noah glanced back toward the door.

"Who are you looking for?" Emma asked quietly.

"It won't matter if they don't get here in time." He looked from his pocket watch to the door.

"I think everyone in town is already here."

"Yes." He sat beside her. "I can take Belinda, if you wish."

"It might be better," Mr. Evans interrupted as he set a stack of papers and a thick book on the table, "if Mrs. Sawyer continued to hold her. That gives the judge the impression that she's a true mother to Belinda."

In spite of herself, Emma flinched. When Belinda asked her what was wrong, Emma gave her a teasing answer that set the little girl to giggling. She saw Noah look back at the door again and again.

"Do you want to send Gladys or your brother to check?" she asked.

"No. That won't do any good, because they won't know whom to look for."

"Who?"

He cursed quietly but vehemently when he looked over his shoulder again.

Emma shifted and saw a man coming through the door. At first, she had thought Noah's reaction was at Gilson's arrival. Then she realized she did not recognize this slight man who was wearing clothes that looked as if he had been sleeping in them for the past month.

"Who is that?" she asked.

He scowled. "A reporter from one of the Chicago newspapers. I recognize him. He always is after the most lurid stories he can find in order to sell more copies of his newspaper."

Emma's next question went unasked when a door behind the judge's bench opened, and Judge Purchase entered. Rising, she stared at him. In his somber black robes, he barely resembled the jovial man who often came into the store just to talk and catch up on the news in Haven. His light brown hair was smoothed back, and he walked with a dignity that contrasted with the bounce that usually lightened his steps.

Motioning for them all to sit as he took his place, he looked about the courtroom. One brow arched, but he said nothing about the size of the crowd of spectators as he picked up a single piece of paper. Emma's arms tightened around Belinda as she recognized the bold handwriting through the paper. He held another copy of the order granting Gilson custody.

Judge Purchase lowered the page to the top of the table where he sat. "This appears to be in order."

Mr. Evans came to his feet. "As you can see, your honor, that decision was made five years ago. There have been some changes in the circumstances of both Mr. Sawyer and

Mr. Gilson since then. They have a bearing on this custody decision.''

"Is that so?'' He folded his hands on the page. "Then we shall proceed. Mr. Evans, I would like to hear why you have brought a petition to have me send this back to a court in Illinois to be overturned.''

Only an occasional cough or rustle was heard in the courtroom as Mr. Evans outlined how Belinda had come to know Noah as her father. The little girl glanced with curiosity at Emma, but said nothing when Emma put her finger to her lips. There was more rustling and a few whispers when Mr. Evans mentioned how Gilson had been unable to pay his debts in recent months and seemed to owe money to unsavory people in businesses no one would deem lawful.

"During this time, your honor," Mr. Evans concluded, "Mr. Sawyer has provided an excellent home for Miss Sawyer. He has recently married.''

"I'm quite aware of that," Judge Purchase said before looking at Emma. "Mrs. Sawyer?''

"Yes, your honor?''

He motioned to a seat beside his table. Unsure why she was being asked to testify first, she handed Belinda to Noah and rose. She went forward and vowed to tell the truth in her testimony. She had to repeat the words so Judge Purchase could hear them, because the incoming train blasted its whistle just as she spoke. Sitting, she ignored the temptation to rock her feet like a scared and anxious child.

"Mrs. Sawyer," the judge began with a kindly smile, "I believe we've known each other for nearly eight years now.''

"It is closer to seven, your honor. I bought the store here in Haven in the summer of 1869.''

"Ah, you're right. Will you be willing to answer a few questions?''

"Of course. I don't want Belinda to have to go with that man!"

Gilson's lawyer jumped up. "Your honor, she's slandering my client."

"She's speaking her opinion, Mr. Jacobs," the judge said. "You may sit down and listen while she answers my questions."

Grumbling, the lawyer complied.

Judge Purchase turned to her and said, "Tell me about what you've observed of Miss Sawyer's relationship with Mr. Sawyer."

"Noah—Mr. Sawyer—loves her very much, and Belinda loves him just as much. Shortly after I first met him, he brought a wounded puppy all the way from his farm for me to tend to in the middle of the night because he feared the puppy would die and Belinda would be heartbroken."

"So he coddles her?"

"No more than any father would." She looked to where Noah held Belinda. His face had not lost the intensity of the past week, but, for the first time in that time, she met his eyes steadily. Her breath caught as the powerful emotions within them surged all around her.

Could she trust them to be real? Could she trust herself to decide? Astonishment rushed through her as she realized it was not Noah she had been afraid of trusting, but herself. Trust in him had been easy, for she had seen how Belinda loved him and how Gladys respected him. Even when he had accused Sean of being a thief, he had been willing—however reluctantly—to listen to her. It had been when he asked her to listen to her heart and open it fully to him that she had let distrust and fear consume her again.

He was not Miles Cooper. He was Noah Sawyer, a strong-willed man who allowed no compromises for himself . . . or anyone around him. When she had turned away from him, too scared to trust that he was being honest with her, he had tried to reason with her. She had not listened to him as she had insisted he must listen to her. Only then had he turned away from her.

"Mrs. Sawyer?" Judge Purchase's voice drew her attention back to him.

"I'm sorry," she said.

"I asked if you had ever seen any example of Mr. Sawyer being unsuitable as a parent to Miss Sawyer."

"Never! He—"

Mr. Jacobs leaped to his feet again. "Your honor, are you really going to believe the testimony of a woman who was married to a bank robber?"

She closed her eyes as she heard the sharp intake of breaths all around the courtroom. Even though she had known this was coming, she had not found a way to prepare herself for the moment when everyone in Haven learned of her past.

"A bank robber?" asked Judge Purchase. "Are you sure you are speaking of *this* young lady?"

Mr. Jacobs held up a yellowed strip of newspaper. "This is the front page of the *Fort Pixton Gazette*, your honor. From Fort Pixton, Kansas. If I may ask the court's indulgence to allow me to read the first few lines . . ."

"Go ahead." The judge looked at her, and she knew he was waiting for her to protest. How could she?

" 'Last night,' " Mr. Jacobs intoned, emoting as if he were on stage instead of in a courtroom, " 'the sheriff and his deputies discovered, after dispersing the crowd outside the house, that Mrs. Miles Cooper had escaped from custody before her trial on charges of being an accomplice to her husband's many robberies of banks in this county. Emma Cooper is being sought throughout Kansas. A description of her has been sent to sheriffs in this state and in Missouri. Anyone who sees a blonde woman with green eyes and who is nineteen years old should contact their local authorities at once." He looked up. "I can read more if you would like, your honor."

"What makes you believe this Mrs. Cooper has anything to do with Mrs. Sawyer? Emma is not an uncommon name."

"You need only ask her yourself, your honor. She is under oath."

Mr. Evans came to his feet. "Your honor, Mrs. Sawyer isn't on trial here."

"That's true," Judge Purchase replied, "but the question has been raised. It's impossible to rule in this case without confirming or denying this information."

Noah stood. "Your honor, there must be another way to deal with Belinda's custody without besmirching Emma's name. She's respected by one and all in Haven. If she—"

"I'll answer the question," Emma said quietly.

"Emma!" He came around the table. "Think what you're about to do."

"I've thought about it. I've thought about it for seven long years."

"Mr. Sawyer," Judge Purchase said, "you and your attorney should be seated. You, too, Mr. Jacobs. Mrs. Sawyer is willing to answer this question, and it behooves us to give her the opportunity." His voice grew gentle and a bit sad as he turned to her and said, "You may say as little or as much as you wish, Emma. Your husband's attorney is correct. You are not on trial here."

"But she'll be soon in Kansas," chortled Gilson.

The judge pounded his gavel against the table. "Mr. Jacobs, you will instruct Mr. Gilson to be silent unless addressed from the bench, or I'll have him removed."

"Yes, your honor," Mr. Jacobs said before bending to whisper something in Gilson's ear. Both men grinned.

"Emma?" the judge asked.

She smiled as she saw Belinda clamber back up into Noah's lap when he sat again behind the table. Over Belinda's head, he met her gaze. All she had to do was open her heart and let him into the places she had thought she would keep closed and safe forever. She did not want safety any longer. She wanted to become part of life again, not just existing but living with those she loved . . . those who loved her. She did not need a haven, other than the one in his arms.

Her voice did not tremble as she said, "I'm the woman written about in that article."

Gasps sounded around the room, but everyone became silent, not wanting to miss what else she might say.

"I was married to Miles Cooper," she continued. "I didn't know of his crimes until he was caught. However, it was assumed that I must have known, because I was his wife. He was hanged by a mob the night before his trial. Then the mob came in search of me. I slipped out of the house where I was being imprisoned while my guards were trying to halt the lynch mob. Then I ran. As far and as fast as I could, hoping my past would never catch up with me. It has." She took a steadying breath. "Noah knew nothing of this when he married me. Why would he have married me if he had? He'd have known he jeopardized Belinda's future if he married a woman who was wanted as an accomplice to bank robbery in Kansas. So don't condemn him. My past has nothing to do with his ability to be Belinda's guardian . . . her father."

Mr. Jacobs rose again. "We appreciate Mrs. Sawyer being so forthcoming, your honor, but we disagree with her assessment of Mr. Sawyer's capability to be Miss Sawyer's guardian. He made a huge mistake in judgment in marrying this woman. If he didn't know of her involvement in those crimes when he married her, he mostly certainly did afterward. You saw him. He wasn't surprised by our questions, simply upset that she would answer them. He should have taken Miss Sawyer out of Mrs. Sawyer's care the moment he discovered the truth.''

Emma feared her heart had stopped beating. She had not thought the truth would do more damage. ''Your honor, you can't let my mistakes become Noah's.''

''You have put me in a very difficult situation, Mrs. Sawyer,'' Judge Purchase said.

Her shoulders sagged as he addressed her so formally once more. Everything was lost. She could tell by his regretful tone. He had been looking for a way—any way—to help her and Noah.

''I fear I have no choice under these circumstances,'' the judge said, ''but to—''

''Wait!'' called a voice from the back of the courtroom. ''Before you make your judgment, your honor, you may want to see this.''

With a cry as she saw a man and a woman she had feared she would never see again, Emma jumped to her feet. ''Leatrice! Howard!''

Her sister and brother pushed their way through the crowd toward the bench as Judge Purchase hit his gavel on the table and called out, ''Let them through, or I shall clear this courtroom of all spectators. Mrs. Sawyer, please sit down. The same for the rest of you.'' He frowned and asked, ''Who are you two?''

Emma bit her lip as her brother gave her a quick smile before replying, ''Your honor, I am Howard Stephenson. This is Leatrice Bridges. We are Emma Cooper's brother and sister.''

''Yes, I see the resemblance, but I need proof of that.''

Howard handed the judge a page. ''You'll see that is an

affidavit signed and witnessed by Judge Michaels. He said you know him."

"Yes, we read law together in St. Louis." Scanning it, he said, "I'll take his word that you are Mrs. Sawyer's brother and sister. You said you had something to show me."

Howard drew out several more pages and placed them on the table. "You will see, your honor, that not only has our sister been declared innocent of any crimes, but the bank president has signed this letter of apology for his false accusations. All are in agreement that Emma had nothing to do with Miles Cooper's crimes."

"So I see." Judge Purchase put the pages onto the table and squared his shoulders. "This puts everything in a completely different light."

Mr. Jacobs jumped up. "But, your honor, Mrs. Sawyer fled without waiting for justice. Someone who runs away at the first hint of trouble isn't a good guardian for the child."

"Would you have remained to be lynched, Mr. Jacobs?" returned the judge. "Avoiding that seems to me to be a sign of great intelligence and good judgment."

"I still argue Mr. Sawyer should have come forward about this as soon as he knew of it."

Judge Purchase asked quietly, "Did you ever believe your wife was guilty of these crimes, Mr. Sawyer?"

Noah held Belinda as he stood. "No. I admit I was shocked when Emma told me the truth and hurt that she hadn't been willing to share this with me before she did, but I never believed she was guilty. How could anyone who has seen how she deals so fairly and honestly at her store believe she had been part of a scheme to rob banks?"

The judge hit his gavel on the table. "I've heard enough. Sit down, Mr. Jacobs, while I give you my judgment." He

waited until the room was silent before saying, "In light of
what I've heard here and what I heard when Mr. Gilson was
brought before me last Sunday, I judge there is enough
evidence to send this custody order back to Illinois to be
reheard. In the meantime, I believe it would do great damage
to Miss Sawyer to have her in anyone's custody but Mrs.
Sawyer's until the custody can be reheard. So, until that
time, temporary custody of Miss Belinda Sawyer is with
Mrs. Noah Sawyer."

Cheers came from every direction but the table where
Gilson and his attorney sat. They stood and tried to walk
out as the spectators rushed forward.

Emma stood and said, "Thank you so much, Judge Purchase."

"You didn't make it easy for me." He smiled at her sister
and brother. "Thank heavens you got here when you did."

"The train was late coming into Haven," her brother
said.

"*You* were the ones Noah was looking for?" Emma
looked toward the table where Noah had sat, but she could
not see him through the crowd gathered around it.

Leatrice began to weep as she flung her arms around
Emma. Howard put his arms around both of them. Hoping
that this was not a dream that had come to banish the seven-
year-old nightmare, Emma clung to them.

"How did you know where to find me?" she asked.

Handing a handkerchief to Leatrice, who was sobbing
loudly, Howard said, "We didn't find you. Noah Sawyer
found us." He looked past her. "We're more grateful than
you know, Mr. Sawyer."

Emma whirled to discover Noah behind her. "You did
that for me after all the horrible things I said?" she asked.

"Actually I started looking for them *before* you said all

those things." He grinned. "But what you said was not entirely untrue."

Her happiness foundered. "You married me because—"

"I thought you'd make a good mother for Belinda. I told you that."

"Yes, you did." How could her heart be joyous and sad at the same time?

He put Belinda on the chair where Emma had been sitting. "And I married you because I love you, Emma. I know you have no reason to believe another man you think has been using you for his own ends, but, if you believe nothing else in your life, believe that I love you." He framed her face with his broad hands. Tilting her face up toward his, he whispered, "I don't think either of us can deny that what we share is love, Emma."

"I do love you."

"If you think I am saying this only because of Belinda, you're wrong. I know it will help in the custody battle still ahead that Belinda has a father *and* a mother, but that isn't the real reason I asked you to marry me. I could have found other ways to defeat Gilson. If I wanted to hurt you, Emma, that could be the way, but I don't want you hurt ever again. I accused Sean of being a thief, but you were the one who stole my heart with the gleam of your green eyes and your impish smile. I love you, sweetheart."

"And I love you. More than I ever thought I could love any man."

"Really? No doubts this time?"

"Really. No doubts." She laughed. "But I'm going to need you to keep convincing me of that, Noah, for the rest of our lives."

"Something I will be glad to do, sweetheart." He bent to kiss her.

Before he could, Sean rushed up with a squeal to hug

Emma, then Noah. Belinda jumped down from the chair, giggled, and threw her arms around Emma.

Over their heads, Noah cupped her chin and said, "Let's go home, sweetheart. We'll celebrate with everyone and then we'll celebrate alone."

Smiling, she took Belinda's hand and Noah's. He grabbed Sean's and led the way out of the courtroom.

"Noah! Noah!" Kenny pushed his way toward them. "The message from New York City finally came through."

Noah took it and read it quickly. Handing it to Emma, he smiled. She read the few words and, for the first time since she had left Kansas, surrendered to tears. Even when the others asked her what was wrong, she could not speak. She put her arms around Noah and wept for all the times she had given up on ever finding happiness. As Noah's lips found hers, she feared her heart would burst with happiness.

"Are you going to be able to stop crying long enough to share the good news with everyone?" he asked quietly.

She shook her head, then nodded with a laugh as he kept his arm around her when she looked at the children staring at her in amazement. Her family. Excitement glowed on their faces as she gave the slip of paper to Sean to read.

All the rough times were not behind them, she knew, but she never would have to fight her battles alone ever again. The good tidings and the trouble would be shared. As she looked up at Noah, she drew his mouth to hers and lost herself in the exquisite joy that had been hers for longer than she had trusted herself to believe.

EPILOGUE

Through the warm rain, the train pulled into the Haven, Indiana, station with a cloud of steam and a ringing bell. The conductor jumped down from the third car back. Turning, he held out his hand to help a woman and a child down the steep stairs to the platform. The woman thanked him as she adjusted her stylish bonnet and looked in both directions along the seemingly empty platform.

A door from the station burst open, and another child raced out. He paused, then turned and motioned to a little girl. Grabbing her hand, he almost pulled her off her feet as she tried to keep up with his longer legs. He did not let her hand go as he threw his other arm around the child who had stepped off the train.

As the three of them twirled about in a merry dance and collapsed into a giggling pile, the woman smiled at the wide-eyed conductor and stepped around them. She walked toward

the station and held her hand out to another woman who
was watching the children with a happy smile.

"I am Miss Black," she said. "You must be Mrs.
Sawyer."

"Yes, I am." Emma took the woman's hand and shook
it. She knew she should introduce the woman to Noah, but
she could not pull her gaze from the jumble of children on
the damp platform. This week had brought the news that
Gilson was abandoning his claim for custody of Belinda
because he could not afford to have his crimes made public
in Chicago and all charges against Noah had been dropped
and the tidings that this train was finally on its way. Once
she had not believed she could be blessed with so much
happiness, a family and a husband who loved her. This week
she was being twice blessed.

Sean untangled himself from the pile and led both children
back to where Emma and Noah stood. He grinned widely,
although he was crying at the same time, and said, "This
is Emma, and that is Noah. Emma is my mother now, and
Noah is my father." He sniffed, wiped his nose on his sleeve,
and then said, "Emma, this is my sister." He smiled at
Belinda before correcting himself. "My *other* sister,
Maeve."

Squatting in front of the little girl, Emma put one hand
over the fingers Noah settled on her shoulder as she said,
"Welcome to Haven, Maeve."

"Haven?" the little girl asked, uncertain.

Emma blinked back her own tears. From the moment
Kenny had come to the courtroom with the telegram that
the Children's Aid Society had found Sean's little sister,
they had been waiting eagerly for Maeve's arrival. Now, at
last, the little girl was here.

Emma held out her hand to Maeve. When Sean grinned
and picked up Maeve's hand and put it on Emma's palm,

he also grabbed Belinda's hand, setting it atop the younger girl's. Noah put his hand under hers as Sean put his over Belinda's.

"We're a family," he announced. "Forever and ever."

Emma looked up at Noah and knew it would soon be time to tell the children that Maeve would not be the last one to become a part of their family. When he smiled, she wondered how she could ever have believed she understood what love truly was before she met this man who was the father of the child growing within her.

Smiling at the little girl, who regarded her with the beginnings of a bashful smile, Emma whispered, "Welcome to Haven, Maeve." She looked up at Noah and added, "Welcome home."

This is a preview of the
next book in this series

Everyone needs a haven . . .

Rachel Browning has brought a little girl off the orphan train to the River's Haven Community, a utopia near the village of Haven. The child, nicknamed Kitty Cat, is the way, Rachel believes, to ease her heart's loneliness. Kitty Cat's visit to a steamboat being repaired in Haven brings Wyatt Colton into Rachel's life. This rogue is trouble from the first, and, as he upsets her quiet life, Rachel has to decide if she is willing to risk falling in love when the cost could be losing everything.

Look for *Moonlight on Water* in July 2002

Author's Note

The orphan trains took children from the congested eastern cities to homes in the country for more than fifty years. At first the children were "placed out"—the term used by the Children's Aid Society—in nearby New England states. As the country expanded, so did the scope of the program, and the children, both individuals and whole families of children, were sent to many Midwestern states. The program was an overall success, with most of the children settling into their new lives and with many going on to become leaders in their adopted communities.

Montgomery Ward & Company's relationship with Grangers and the many Grange Halls that still exist in farming communities was a forerunner to the many catalogs that come to our mailboxes each year. With the growth of the railroads, the company could ship to almost any corner of the Midwest and then beyond.

I like hearing from my readers. You can contact me by email at: jaferg@erols.com or by mail at: Jo Ann Ferguson, P.O. Box 575, Rehoboth, MA 02769. Check out my web site at: www.joannferguson.com

Happy Reading!

COMING IN APRIL 2002 FROM
ZEBRA BALLAD ROMANCES

__WITH HIS RING: The Brides of Bath
by Cheryl Bolen   0-8217-7248-1 $5.99US/$7.99CAN

Glee Pembroke had always been secretly in love with her brother's best friend, Gregory Blakenship. So when she learned that he must marry by his twenty-fifth birthday or lose his inheritance, she boldly proposed a marriage of convenience, while planning to win his love.

__THE NEXT BEST BRIDE: Once Upon a Wedding
by Kelly McClymer   0-8217-7252-X $5.99US/$7.99CAN

To Helena Fenster, the only thing worse than her twin sister marrying the man she loves, is having to tell him that his fiancée has jilted him. Rand Mallon's reaction is quite surprising—he's prepared to marry Helena in her sister's place. Yet how can she marry the man she adores when it's obvious that, for him at least, one woman is as good as another?

__NIGHT AFTER NIGHT: The Happily Ever After Co.
by Kate Donovan   0-8217-7273-2 $5.99US/$7.99CAN

Maggie Gleason never wants to marry. So when she hires a matchmaker, it's to find a teaching job, not a husband. Scenic Shasta Falls, California turns out to be the perfect match for an independent woman determined to start a whole new life. The boarding house where she lives even has a magnificent library . . . if she can get past the mysterious recluse in the room next door.

__LOVER'S KNOT: Dublin Dreams
by Cindy Harris   0-8217-7072-1 $5.99US/$7.99CAN

Dolly Baltmore, Millicent Hyde, and Rose Sinclair had conquered their past heartaches to discover that love was more than possible—it was irresistible. Lady Claire Killgarren isn't so sure, but with help from her newly happy friends, and a very special man, she's about to find that she'll give anything to be caught in a lover's knot . . . for all time.

Call toll free **1-888-345-BOOK** to order by phone or use this coupon to order by mail. *ALL BOOKS AVAILABLE APRIL 01, 2002*

Name _____

Address _____

City _____ State _____ Zip _____

Please send me the books that I have checked above.

I am enclosing	$ _____
Plus postage and handling*	$ _____
Sales tax (in NY and TN)	$ _____
Total amount enclosed	$ _____

*Add $2.50 for the first book and $.50 for each additional book. Send check or money order (no cash or CODs) to: **Kensington Publishing Corp., Dept. C.O., 850 Third Avenue, New York, NY 10022**

Prices and numbers subject to change without notice. Valid only in the U.S. All orders subject to availability. **NO ADVANCE ORDERS.**

Visit our website at **www.kensingtonbooks.com.**

DO YOU HAVE THE
HOHL COLLECTION?

__Another Spring $6.99US/$8.99CAN
  0-8217-7155-8

__Compromises $6.99US/$8.99CAN
  0-8217-7154-X

__Ever After $6.99US/$8.99CAN
  0-8217-7203-1

__Something Special $5.99US/$7.50CAN
  0-8217-6725-9

__Maybe Tomorrow $6.99US/$7.99CAN
  0-8217-7349-6

__My Own $6.99US/$8.99CAN
  0-8217-6640-6

__Never Say Never $5.99US/$7.99CAN
  0-8217-6379-2

__Silver Thunder $6.99US/$8.99CAN
  0-8217-7201-5

Call toll free **1-888-345-BOOK** to order by phone or use this coupon
to order by mail. ALL BOOKS AVAILABLE DECEMBER 1, 2000.
Name_____
Address_____
City_____ State _____ Zip _____
Please send me the books that I have checked above.
I am enclosing $_____
Plus postage and handling* $_____
Sales tax (in New York and Tennessee) $_____
Total amount enclosed $_____
*Add $2.50 for the first book and $.50 for each additional book. Send check
or money order (no cash or CODs) to:
Kensington Publishing Corp., 850 Third Avenue, New York, NY 10022
Prices and numbers subject to change without notice. Valid only in the
All orders subject to availability. **NO ADVANCE ORDERS.**
Visit out our website at **www.kensingtonbooks.com.**

Discover the Magic of
Romance With
Kat Martin

__The Secret
0-8217-6798-4   **$6.99US/$8.99CAN**

Kat Rollins moved to Montana looking to change her life, not find another man like Chance McLain, with a sexy smile and empty heart. Chance can't ignore the desire he feels for her—or the suspicion that somebody wants her to leave Lost Peak . . .

__Dream
0-8217-6568-X   **$6.99US/$8.99CAN**

Genny Austin is convinced that her nightmares are visions of another life she lived long ago. Jack Brennan is having nightmares, too, but his are real. In the shadows of dreams lurks a terrible truth, and only by unlocking the past will Genny be free to love at last . . .

__Silent Rose
0-8217-6281-8   **$6.99US/$8.50CAN**

When best-selling author Devon James checks into a bed-and-breakfast in Connecticut, she only hopes to put the spark back into her relationship with her fiancé. But what she experiences at the Stafford Inn changes her life forever . . .

Call toll free **1-888-345-BOOK** to order by phone or use this coupon to order by mail.

Name_____

Address_____

City _____ State_____ Zip_____

Please send me the books I have checked above.

I am enclosing $_____

Plus postage and handling* $_____

Sales tax (in New York and Tennessee only) $_____

Total amount enclosed $_____

*Add $2.50 for the first book and $.50 for each additional book.

Send check or money order (no cash or CODs) to: **Kensington Publishing Corp., Dept. C.O., 850 Third Avenue, New York, NY 10022**

Prices and numbers subject to change without notice. All orders subject to availability. Visit our website at **www.kensingtonbooks.com**.

Put a Little Romance in Your Life With

Betina Krahn

__**Hidden Fire** 0-8217-5793-8	$5.99US/$7.50CAN
__**Love's Brazen Fire** 0-8217-5691-5	$5.99US/$7.50CAN
__**Passion's Ransom** 0-8217-5130-1	$5.99US/$6.99CAN
__**Passion's Treasure** 0-8217-6039-4	$5.99US/$7.50CAN